M

WITH

D0832482

Fiction Hunt.A
Hunt, Angela Elwell,
She always wore red /

MAY 0 2 2008

Praise for *D*

". . . a lighthearted read
—Sandra

"*Doesn't She Look* that A nt is ne of
the most versatile at ved
—BJ Hoff, author of the Mountain Song Legacy series,
the American Anthem series, and the Emerald Ballad series

"Not only did this story entertain and pull me into the lives of a family in the midst of a huge season of testing and trial—it also challenged me spiritually and twisted my heart."
—Novel Reviews

". . . a top-notch inspirational plot that maintains a lighthearted touch."
—*Library Journal*

"Angela writes with humor, tenderness, and creates such emotional tension that I had to remind myself to take a breath! I can't wait to see where Angela takes her Fairlawn series—*Doesn't She Look Natural?* is highly recommended."
—CBD reader

"*Doesn't She Look Natural?* is an entertaining and thoughtful read and a promising beginning to a new series."
—Faithful Reader

She Always Wore Red

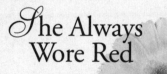

She Always Wore Red

Angela Hunt

EVANSTON PUBLIC LIBRARY
1703 ORRINGTON AVENUE
EVANSTON, ILLINOIS 60201

TYNDALE HOUSE PUBLISHERS, INC.
CAROL STREAM, ILLINOIS

Visit Tyndale's exciting Web site at www.tyndale.com

Visit Angela Hunt's Web site at www.angelahuntbooks.com

TYNDALE and Tyndale's quill logo are registered trademarks of Tyndale House Publishers, Inc.

She Always Wore Red

Copyright © 2008 by Angela Elwell Hunt. All rights reserved.

Cover photo by Dan Farrell. Copyright © 2008 by Tyndale House Publishers, Inc. All rights reserved.

Designed by Beth Sparkman

The words *Red Hat Society* and any associated typed drawing are registered trademarks of Red Hat Society, Inc., Fullerton, California, in connection with association services promoting the interests of women and various merchandise. Red Hat Society, Inc., has not published, produced, sponsored, certified, or approved this book or any portion thereof.

Scripture quotations are taken from the *Holy Bible*, New Living Translation, copyright © 1996, 2004. Used by permission of Tyndale House Publishers, Inc., Carol Stream, Illinois 60188. All rights reserved.

This novel is a work of fiction. Names, characters, places, and incidents either are the product of the author's imagination or are used fictitiously. Any resemblance to actual events, locales, organizations, or persons living or dead is entirely coincidental and beyond the intent of either the author or the publisher.

Library of Congress Cataloging-in-Publication Data

Hunt, Angela Elwell, date.
    She always wore red / Angela Hunt.
       p. cm. — (Fairlawn)
    ISBN-13: 978-1-4143-1170-8 (sc : alk. paper)
    ISBN-10: 1-4143-1170-2 (sc : alk. paper)
    1. Divorced mothers—Fiction. 2. Female friendship—Fiction. 3. Funeral homes—Fiction.
I. Title.
    PS3558.U46747S53 2008
    813'.54—dc22   2007046704

Printed in the United States of America

14   13   12   11   10   09   08
 7   6   5   4   3   2   1

For Jane O.

When we warm to others
In whom we see ourselves,
We may be startled to discover
Otherness.

—Darien Haynes,
"Impromptu"

➤ ❮

*T*he nameless cadaver on the cover of my anatomy textbook—a middle-aged man who is no longer black, white, or brown—would be counted among the orange in a census of the embalmed.

Someone should have adjusted the tint before they juiced him.

I flip the book open and study the color photographs of the cadaver's aortic arch and brachiocephalic veins, then close my eyes and try to commit the multisyllable words to memory. Here I am, near the end of my first semester of mortuary school, and I'm still having trouble keeping my veins and arteries straight.

Behind me, an irate mother in the carpool line is honking, though we have a good three minutes before kindergarten dismissal. She probably has to pick up her child and get back to work before the end of her lunch hour. While I sympathize with her impatience, I wish she'd lay off the horn so I can concentrate.

I open one eye and examine the book propped on my steering wheel. The right internal jugular branches off the right and left brachiocephalic veins, which lie outside the brachiocephalic trunk. *Brachiocephalic* sounds like some kind of dinosaur. Bugs would like that word.

I turn the book sideways, but the photograph on the page looks nothing like a prehistoric animal. In fact, I find it hard to believe that anything like this jumble of tunnels and tubes exists in my body, but skin covers myriad mysteries.

I snap the book shut as the bell at Round Lake Elementary trills through the warm afternoon. The kindergarten classes troop out into the sunshine, their hands filled with lunch boxes and construction paper cutouts. The tired teachers stride to the curb and peer into various vehicles, then motion the appropriate children forward.

My spirits lift when my red-haired cherub catches my eye and waves. Bradley "Bugs" Graham waits until his teacher calls his name and skips toward me.

"Hey, Mom." He climbs into the backseat of the van as his teacher holds the door.

"Hey yourself, kiddo." I check to make sure he's snapped his seat belt before smiling my thanks at his teacher. "Did you have a good morning?"

"Yep." He leans forward to peek into the front seat. "Do we hafta go home, or can we stop to get a snack?"

My thoughts veer toward the to-do list riding shotgun in the front passenger seat. I still have to run to the grocery store, swing by the dry cleaner's to pick up Gerald's funeral suit, and stop to see if the bookstore has found a used copy of *Introduction to Infectious Diseases*, Second Edition. Textbooks are usually pricey, but medical textbooks ought to come with fixed-rate mortgages. Still, I need to find that book if I'm going to complete my online course by the end of the semester.

"I'll pull into a drive-through," I tell Bugs, knowing he won't mind. "You want McDonald's?"

He nods, so I point the van toward Highway 441.

"Mr. Gerald make any pickups today?" Bugs asks.

I ease onto the highway, amazed at how easily my children have accepted the ongoing work of the funeral home. "None today."

"See this?"

I glance in the rearview mirror and see Bugs waving his construction paper creation. "Yes."

"It's a stegosaurus. Can I give it to Gerald?"

"I think he'd like that." I force a smile as an unexpected wave of grief rises within me. Like a troublesome relative who doesn't realize she's worn out her welcome, sorrow often catches me by surprise. Gerald, the elderly embalmer at Fairlawn, has become a surrogate father for my sons. Thomas, my ex-husband and my children's father, has been gone for months, but in some ways he's never been closer. He lies in the Pine Forest Cemetery, less than two miles from our house, so we can't help but think of him every time we drive by.

I get Bugs a vanilla ice cream cone at the McDonald's drive-through, and then we run to the grocery store and the dry cleaner. I'll call the bookstore later. No sense in going there when a simple phone call will suffice.

Finally we turn into the long driveway that leads to the Fairlawn Funeral Home.

Gerald has poured a new concrete pad next to the garage, and as I park on it, Bugs notices that the call car is gone. "Uh-oh." He looks at me. "Somebody bit the dust."

I press my lips together. A couple of months ago I would have mumbled something about the old station wagon maybe needing a wash, but now I know there's no reason to shield my children from the truth—we are in the death care industry. The squeamishness I felt when we first arrived vanished the day I walked into the prep room and gloved up to help Gerald lay out my ex-husband.

"Come in the house," I tell my son. "I'll pour you a glass of milk."

_R_andolph Harris crosses his leg at the knee and runs his fingers along the trouser leg to reinforce the pleat.

The private detective across the desk swivels his chair toward the wall and brings the phone closer to his mouth, employing body language intended to remind his guest that he is not part of the telephone conversation.

Randolph folds his hands and struggles to be patient. He set this appointment for one, canceling two patients in order to drive to this shabby strip mall and meet with Dexter Duggan. He expects a modicum of professionalism in return, but no secretary greeted him at the door, nor did the sandy-haired detective invite him into the inner office until five minutes after the appointed time. When the phone rang at six after, Randolph expected Duggan to ignore the call, but instead the man picked up and launched into a whispered conversation.

Randolph heaves an indiscreet sigh and looks around the office. A laminated map of North Carolina hangs above the desk, with pushpins marking the cities of Raleigh, Charlotte, and Asheville. A bookcase against the paneled wall holds rows of phone books, city names printed on the spines above logos of walking fingers. The second shelf holds camera equipment—several old Nikons, long lenses with capped ends, a battered leather bag, a stainless steel canister with a black lid.

A couple of framed photographs balance on the lowest shelf, crowded by a pair of mud-caked boots, a Durham Bulls baseball cap, and a smudged panama hat. He focuses on the photographs: a smiling boy, probably six or seven, and a bikini-clad woman standing next to a ski boat.

Oh yes, Dexter Duggan is a class act.

Randolph will stand and walk out if Mr. Duggan doesn't end his call by one fifteen. The hands on the clock behind the desk shift, trimming Randolph's wait to three minutes.

Content now that he's decided to waste no more than a quarter hour on this appointment, Randolph studies the detective. Duggan's jeans and flannel shirt would be more appropriate for a hunter than the owner of a detective agency, but perhaps the fellow has been spying on someone from a pickup. The cramped office suggests that the Duggan Detective Agency is a one-man operation, though someone must be employed to answer the phones. Then again, perhaps a detective can get by with voice mail, call forwarding, and a cell phone. After all, a private snoop doesn't have to deal with insurance companies, physician referrals, and clients who are mentally unbalanced.

Randolph smiles when the clock advances to 1:13. Duggan is nodding now, submitting to whatever is being stipulated on the phone. Is he talking to an unhappy client? No, this has to be a wife or a girlfriend. For Duggan to take the call in the middle of a meeting with a prospective client, whoever's on the line must wield considerable influence in the man's life.

The minute hand moves again. In sixty seconds Randolph will leave and find another private detective. The Charlotte yellow pages list twenty-eight independent investigators; any one of the other twenty-seven is bound to have better manners than Dexter Duggan.

Randolph lifts his chin and watches the second hand sweep around the clock's face. He'll be on his way in—

"Sorry." Duggan drops the receiver onto the phone, then leans forward and folds his arms on the desk. "I've got a woman checking out a suspected industrial theft in Gastonia, and I've been expecting her call." The way Duggan hunches in his chair like a scolded puppy contradicts his story, but calling attention to his prevarication will not strengthen the client-detective bond.

Randolph straightens in his seat. "I'm assuming my case will receive the same care and attention . . . should we come to an agreement."

"Of course." Mr. Duggan flashes a boyish grin. "What brings you to my office, Mr. Harris? Asset investigation? Suspected infidelity?"

"It's *Doctor* Harris. I'm a psychiatrist in private practice." Randolph clears his throat. "I'm here because my daughter, McLane Harris, is missing. I'd like you to find her."

Duggan lifts a brow. "I don't search for children until the police have exhausted their resources."

"This is not a criminal matter, nor is my daughter a kidnap victim. She's twenty-four and quite independent. She left home two and a half months ago, and I haven't heard from her. I'm beginning to worry."

Duggan's gaze darts to Randolph's bare ring finger. "Could she be living with your ex-wife?"

"My wife died several months ago."

"Oh. Sorry." The man doesn't miss a beat. "Have you spoken to the police? You know, to rule out foul play?"

Randolph folds his hands. "I see no need to involve the authorities when it's quite clear my daughter purposely left home. She packed suitcases and took most of her belongings."

Duggan takes off his reading glasses and deliberately cleans the lenses with his shirttail. "A twenty-four-year-old woman has every right to leave home. She may not want to be found. If you contact her, she may be upset."

"I'm her father," Randolph drawls, his voice heavy with irritation. "Why should she be upset?"

"I'm just saying. Not everybody wants to be found. If she's done nothing illegal and she's not in danger, she may take offense at your snooping into her business. Some people are better if you leave 'em alone awhile; they come around once they have time to think."

Randolph forces himself to take a deep breath and temper his frustration. "I didn't say she wasn't in danger, but she could be. She's being inappropriately influenced by a man who does not have her best interests at heart."

"Are we talking scam artist, pimp, or bad boyfriend?"

Randolph tamps down another spike of irritation. This man deals with human garbage every day. He can't be blamed for assuming the worst. "Listen," he says, resting his hand on his knee, "my situation is serious, but it's not what you're thinking. My daughter is involved with a man; she imagines herself in love with him. It's impossible, of course, and marriage would be unthinkable, but I'm sure they've either eloped or they're living together somewhere. The man is a marine, so he shouldn't be hard to locate."

Duggan pulls a legal pad from beneath a stack of magazines and picks up a pencil. "Does your daughter have credit cards?"

"She has two Visa accounts. I'm a cosigner on both. She took the maximum cash advance on both cards the day before she left. I don't think she'll be using them again."

"Stuck you with the bill, did she?"

"I don't care about the money. I care about my daughter, and I want her home before this man ruins her life."

Duggan makes a note, then taps his pencil on the tablet. "Does she have a cell phone?"

"She left it on the nightstand. She's no fool. She knows I know that number. I would imagine she's bought a new phone."

"Did she take her car?"

"Yes. A 2006 Altima, dark green, North Carolina plates. I can get you the tag number."

"Have you reported the car stolen?"

Randolph shakes his head. "How could she steal what's rightfully hers? I'm not reporting her to the police."

"Fine. So tell me about the boyfriend."

"She's known him only a few months. He's older than she is. They met at some club she frequented with her college friends. I never met him."

"She never brought him home?"

"I wouldn't allow him in the house."

"Why not?"

Randolph stiffens at the question. "Is that germane?"

The detective blinks. "Beg pardon?"

"I fail to see why my reasons should apply to this conversation."

Duggan shrugs. "I'm curious, is all. Your daughter meets a young man, but you won't let her bring him home. She's twenty-four and in love, but you won't support her. Anybody would want to know what you have against this guy."

Randolph grits his teeth. "You don't understand."

"If you don't explain, I never will."

In the office next door, someone flushes a toilet. The sound of swirling water and humming pipes fills the office as Randolph leans forward. "Look here, Mr. Duggan—I raised my daughter to be a God-fearing Christian woman. Some kids come out of college with crazy ideas but not McLane. She maintained a sterling character and impeccable reputation until she met *him*."

Duggan leans back and sets his tablet on his knee. "So what he'd do? Besides sweeping your daughter off her feet."

"He met her in bars, for one thing, and McLane wasn't the sort to hang out in such places. One night, worried about her, I found her car and waited in the parking lot until she came out. That's where I saw him—and that's when I decided she would never bring that man to my house."

A mischievous grin tugs at the detective's mouth. "Drunk, was he?"

"I don't know, but he had his hands all over her. Completely inappropriate."

Duggan nods and makes another note on his tablet. "You know this man's name?"

"Jeff—Jeffrey, I suppose—Jeffrey Larson of the Marine Corps. Second Marine Division, my daughter says."

Duggan scribbles on the tablet. "Has this Larson gone AWOL?"

"I wouldn't know. I've made no inquiries about the man, nor do I intend to. He's not my concern."

A thoughtful look enters Duggan's eyes. "What will you do if I find them together?"

Randolph grips the armrest of his chair. "Have you a daughter, Mr. Duggan?"

The detective snorts. "I can barely hang on to a wife."

"Well, a father has certain expectations for his daughter, and Jeffrey Larson is not what I expected for McLane. She graduated from college with honors and was well on her way to becoming a doctor before she met this man. Jeff Larson, on the other hand, apparently joined the marines because he has no higher ambitions than to blow things up and kill people."

Duggan makes a strangled sound deep in his throat, then looks up. "Well. Uncle Sam likes to know where his soldiers are, so it shouldn't be hard to find this guy. Let's hope your daughter is with him."

"You're missing the point—I'd like her to be as far away from him as possible." Randolph retrieves his wallet from an inner suit pocket and slides a picture from the plastic sleeve. "This is McLane." His throat tightens as he studies the girl smiling up at him. "The photo is fairly recent; I snapped it on her birthday in March. Two days before her mother passed away."

The detective hesitates. "Had your wife been sick? Perhaps your daughter took off because she was tired or depressed—"

"Shana's death was an accident. She was driving home after dark, misjudged a turn, lost control, and hit a pylon." Randolph's throat clogs with emotion.

But Duggan seems not to notice as he reaches for the photo. "Could your daughter's disappearance have anything to do with your wife's death?"

"What do you mean?"

Duggan studies the picture. "Sometimes people like to mourn in private, sorta process the change in their lives. Maybe she couldn't do that with you around."

"McLane was upset about her mother's accident; we all were. But she accepted it. No, her disappearance has more to do with Jeff Larson than with her mother's passing."

"What makes you so sure?"

"Because the weekend before, she asked if Jeff could come to the house for dinner. I refused."

"How'd she react?"

Randolph smiles. "Did she storm around and throw things? McLane and I do not have altercations. She was more sad than angry, I think— and I believe that's when she decided to leave."

Duggan squints at the map on the wall behind him. "Do you think they went to the marine base at Jacksonville?"

"I have no idea."

"Does your daughter have friends near Camp Lejeune? Someone who might let her sleep on the couch for a few days?"

"She has college friends. None of them were in the military." He takes a flash drive from his pocket and slides it across the desk. "She took her laptop with her, but I copied her address book from the desktop computer in the library."

Duggan's eyes narrow. "Were you able to read her e-mails? You might find—"

"She erased every message or transferred them to her laptop. But she didn't erase the address book."

Duggan takes the flash drive. "I doubt this information will help us, Doc. Apparently your daughter's a smart girl. She gave her departure a great deal of thought."

"But you'll take the case, correct? And you'll call me if you find her." He fishes a business card from his wallet and flips it across the desk.

The detective scans the card. "No home number?"

"It's unlisted."

Duggan flips the card back. "Might be nice for me to have it."

Randolph takes a pen from his pocket and writes his home number on the card. "Anything else you need?"

"Just a deposit. My rate is $100 an hour, plus expenses for travel or long distance calls. Five hundred ought to get us started."

Randolph reaches for his checkbook. "How long do you think it'll take to find McLane?"

The detective grins. "Not long. People run as much as ever these days, but it's getting harder and harder to hide."

3

The phone is ringing as Bugs and I enter the house. My son drops his backpack and lunch box and then scoots up the stairs. I nearly trip over Skeeter, our Jack Russell terrier, who is spinning over the foyer tiles in a frenzied welcome dance.

At least a half dozen holiday catalogs slide from my arms as I run into the office to catch the phone. There's an answering machine on the business line, but Clay, my thirteen-year-old, an eighth grader at Mt. Dora Middle School, isn't home, and someone might call the Fairlawn number if something's happened to him.

"Hello?"

I hear a startled gasp, followed by "Is this the funeral home?"

I draw a deep breath and realize that I've answered in a completely unprofessional manner. "This is Fairlawn. May I help you?"

"Russell Solan calling," the man says. "I need to speak to someone about arranging a funeral."

He keeps talking, but I'm distracted by the sound of frantic barking from upstairs. Bugs must be up to something. Skeeter doesn't bark like that unless he's terribly distressed or wildly excited.

I pick up the pencil on the end table and grab the message pad. "Excuse me, sir. May I have your number? Our director, Mr. Huffman, is not available, but I can have him give you a call the moment he comes in."

"Please." A note of urgency lines the man's voice. "I don't think my pal is going to last much longer."

"I'm so sorry."

Mr. Solan gives me his number, and I jot it on the notepad. Then I step into the foyer and bend to pick up all the things Bugs and I have dropped—the catalogs, Bugs's backpack and lunch box. My anatomy book lies open and upside-down by the front door, reminding me of veins and arteries and brachio whatchamacallits.

Whatever made me think I could go back to school? For thirty-nine years, the neurons in my brain have been filing information away, and now I'm pretty sure the drawers are either full or stuck. I'm not sure there's room for more than a dozen new fifty-cent words.

I reach for a couple of bills that litter the first stair step like autumn leaves. After adding them to the stack in my arms, I go upstairs and drop my load on the kitchen table. Bugs is sitting in his favorite chair, a cookie in his hand and an angelic smile on his face.

I narrow my eyes at the cookie. "Did you have to climb on a chair to reach the cookie jar?"

His blue eyes widen in pretend innocence. "Skeeter helped me."

I glance at the dog whose head barely reaches my knees. "Really? And how would Skeeter help if you slipped and fell?"

"He'd bark something fierce until someone came."

I shake my head as I open the fridge and grab the milk. "I heard him barking, and I think he was tattling on you. Don't stand on the chairs, Bugs. It's not safe. You can either wait for me to come upstairs and reach things for you, or you can . . ."

"What?"

"You can grow. It'll happen sooner than you think."

I pour him a glass of milk. As he dunks his cookie into the cold liquid, I unzip his backpack.

"What do we have here?" I sort through his papers, trying to focus even though my thoughts keep drifting toward the material I need to study and the dinner I ought to be planning. I pull out a picture of several stick figures wearing black rectangle pants and black triangle hats. "Are these Pilgrims?"

"Native Americans," Bugs informs me, "in Pilgrim clothes. I thought they'd get cold without 'em."

"Thoughtful of you." I take out another creation, a construction paper band adorned with strips of white, yellow, and red. "Is this an Indian headdress?"

"A skirt for the Native American girls. See?" He points to the picture, where an aloof stick figure is wearing something that looks more like a comb than a grass skirt.

"That's good." I check the bottom of his bag and am relieved to find no notes from his teacher. This child, at least, seems to be doing well at his new school. I'm not so sure about Clay. . . .

I dump Bugs's sandwich crusts into the trash, throw away his empty juice carton, and notice a candy wrapper in the lunch box. I didn't pack any candy this morning. I hold up the wrinkled pink paper and read the label. "You had Laffy Taffy?"

Bugs grins. "Tommy had leftover Halloween candy. Mrs. Greerson said it was okay as long as he shared with everyone."

How nice—a teacher who believes in equal opportunity tooth decay.

"Fine. But when you've finished your cookie, I want you to brush your teeth. If you get cavities, you won't feel so laffy, Taffy."

Bugs giggles, then dips his cookie again and nibbles with determined slowness. At this rate, it'll be dinnertime before he finishes, but that's okay. As long as he's occupied, I might be able to squeeze a few more veins and arteries into my crowded brain.

I slide into the chair at the head of the table and open my anatomy book. I am trying to memorize the location where the brachial artery divides into the radial and ulnar arteries—the cubital fossa, or forearm—when the front door opens and slams.

Clay rushes up the stairs, but instead of coming toward the kitchen, he turns down the opposite hallway, stomps into his bedroom, and slams the door.

Bugs and I look at each other, each of us undoubtedly wondering the same thing: what is wrong with Clay?

15

❀❀ ❀❀ ❀❀

Clay lifts his head as his mother opens the door and stands in the doorway. "Hey," she says, her voice soft. "You doin' okay?"

He lowers his gaze to the Nintendo in his hand. "Don't I look okay?"

She stares at him, her lips thinning. "Want a snack?"

"Not hungry."

She hesitates, probably expecting him to say something else, but he's not in the mood for talking. Finally she closes the door.

Clay waits for the sound of her steps moving down the hall; then he throws the video game onto the bed.

Why can't things be the way they were this summer?

He stands and looks out his window toward Brett's house. Brett has gone back to California to be with his dad, leaving Clay with a big bunch of nothing.

Mom keeps promising that he'll make new friends, but he's been going to that stupid new school for three months and everyone still acts like he's invisible. The other kids have been friends practically since kindergarten, and they all know he lives in the funeral home. Brett thought the funeral home was cool in a freaky sort of way, but the kids at Mt. Dora Middle act like Clay might give them AIDS or something.

A group of skater kids hangs around outside the school every morning, skateboards in hand, but they didn't even glance at Clay the day he carried his skateboard to school. He tried riding his board home that day, but when he rolled over a rock on the sidewalk, the board went flying up and nearly knocked him out. He came home with a headache and went to bed, barely waking up in time for supper. Mom had her nose in a book and didn't even notice the bruise under his bangs.

Sometimes he feels invisible even at home.

He looks at the wooden shelf Gerald hung by the window. Two old Little League trophies stand there, along with a brand-new Madden cartridge, still in shrink-wrap. The game is the last gift his father gave him, and though it wasn't the best gift in the world (since Clay already had the game and could beat it blindfolded), still . . . it was the last thing.

He pulls his baseball glove from the shelf and wriggles his fingers into it, then drops into the chair at his desk. The glove smells of leather and sweat and summer, scents that remind him of his dad.

His eyes drift toward the window. The cemetery lies just down the road. He never thought he'd ever step into a graveyard, but he's visited the place a lot in the past few months. It's quiet and kinda nice. Dad is there, along with the old man who died and gave them this house. If Mom's uncle hadn't died, they wouldn't be here, and if they weren't here, Dad wouldn't be dead. They'd probably still be in Virginia.

Mom and Dad split up in Virginia, and Clay and his mom and brother had to live at Grandma's house. Things weren't so great in Virginia, either, so maybe it's stupid to miss the old days.

But he misses Brett, who'd been a friend.

It'd be nice to make another friend in this town . . . someone who would treat him like a person and not like an alien.

🜲 🜲 🜲

"Lydia's fine, Mom, and I'm sure she'd want me to send her love." I shift the phone from one ear to the other as Clay comes out of his room and heads toward the kitchen. I try to catch his attention, but he's still in a funk and won't look up. "Oh yeah, Clay's doing great. Growing like a weed."

For the last half hour, I've been sprawled on the sofa as Mom filled my ear with all the latest news about her Red Hatter chapter. Her stories are hilarious, but I need to get off the phone and find something to prepare for dinner. I was hoping Clay would ask about supper and give me an excuse to hang up, but he's unusually uncooperative these days.

"Mom . . ." I pause as I hear the front door open and close. "I have to go. Someone's here."

I click the disconnect key as Lydia's voice floats up the staircase. "Anyone home?"

"Come on up." I stand and move to the top of the stairs. "We're all here."

"Am I interrupting?"

"Only in a good way."

I drop the phone back into its charger and enter the kitchen.

Lydia follows me and gapes at the textbooks and papers spread over the table. "Good grief, Jen. What are you trying to do, set some kind of learning record?"

"I'm trying to squeeze eighteen months of study into twelve." I open the fridge and pull out a pitcher of lemonade. "Want some?"

"No, thanks."

I grab a glass from the cupboard. "I'm doing okay in school—at least I *think* I am. My Intro to Funeral Services class was an intensive, so that's done. Intro to Infectious Diseases is an online course I can work on at my own pace, so anatomy is the only class I have to worry about from week to week. It's tough, though, and there are only two tests. I passed the midterm, but I could still flunk the final."

Lydia sits in the chair closest to the doorway and grins at Clay, who's behind me popping the top on a can of soda. "Hi, Clay." She pats his arm as he trudges out of the kitchen; then she lowers her voice. "How's your big guy doing at the middle school?"

With a lopsided smile, I pour lemonade. "I think he's okay. The school hasn't called about any problems, and he hasn't come home with a black eye. But he never talks about friends . . . and I worry that he hasn't found any."

Lydia props her chin in her hand. "I remember those days. Kids aren't the most communicative at that age. Getting a decent conversation out of Brett used to be as hard as pulling chicken's teeth."

I sink into a chair at the table. "So when do they start talking again?"

"When they want you to let them drive." She crosses her tanned arms, but her smile fades as she studies me. "I hate to say this, girlfriend, but you look awful. What are those Samsonites doing under your eyes?"

I give her a wan smile. "Ha-ha. I've been getting up early to study;

that's all. And I've had a couple of late nights. You know how it is at a funeral home—the phone rings at all hours."

"You know what? You need to take some time for yourself. You need to do something just for you."

I shake my head. "I'm not the day spa type. Besides, I don't have time."

"I'm not talking about a day spa. I came over to offer an invitation, but I have a feeling you're going to say no."

Despite the pressures weighing on me, Lydia's piqued my curiosity. "An invitation to what?"

"My book club."

I can't stop a burst of laughter. "You're kidding, right? The thought of reading another book—"

"Maybe you should say yes," she says, leaning toward me. "If you don't make time for some fun, you're going to drive yourself crazy. All work and no play makes Jen a dull neighbor, and I'm not used to dull neighbors."

"B-but," I stutter, "I'd have to read a *book*."

"You catch on quick."

"Since when do I have time to read for fun?" I drop my hand on a stack of syllabi: Human Anatomy, Funeral Services Careers, and Infectious Diseases 101. "See these? Before Christmas I have to complete every assignment and memorize the material. Then I have to keep studying it because the State of Florida is going to quiz me on everything before they give me a license."

Lydia nods, as patient as a teacher with a slow student. "That's why I think you'd like the book club—no tests. Since I figured you might not have a lot of time for reading, I picked a book I've seen in your bookcase. I'll bet you've already read it."

I'm still not convinced, but since she thought about me when she made her selection . . . "What book?"

"*Five Miles South of Peculiar.*"

I close my eyes as a memory comes whipping back. "Young girl with a mother who prays and gets miracles?"

"That's the one."

"They go looking for the older sister and—"

"Stop!" Lydia claps her hands over her ears. "Don't spoil the ending. I haven't finished it yet."

I blow out a breath. "I did read that one—and enjoyed it."

Her dark eyes dance. "So now you have no excuse not to come to our first meeting. It's Thursday night, seven o'clock, at my house. Come hungry, because I'm making a positively decadent dessert."

I take a deep breath and slowly exhale. The last thing I need is another appointment in my schedule, but Lydia's been a good neighbor . . . and maybe she's right. I've been studying until my brain hurts and living in a household of males. I can't remember the last time I sat around and talked to people who hadn't been molded by a Y chromosome.

I glance at the calendar by the sink. "Thursday night? I'll try."

"Don't try; just come. I'll be looking for you."

4

Three hundred dollars to the gas company? Joella gapes at the bill, then glances at her checkbook. She can pay it, but the amount is ridiculous. Three hundred dollars to heat a house for one person? And this is only November. Next month's bill will be higher, and January's even worse.

She sets her checkbook aside and picks up the small calendar she keeps on the desk. Jen says she is always welcome at Fairlawn, and it might be a good idea to spend part of the winter in Florida. The weather is certainly better, and the Red Hatters of Mt. Dora would fill her days with activity. Plus, it'd be nice to visit with Jen and the boys.

After circling the date of Thanksgiving, she flips the page to see when Christmas falls this year—on a Monday. She could go down the week before. As long as things go smoothly, she might stay through January. Then again, why rush to come back? Some of her friends go to Florida right after Thanksgiving and don't come home until Easter. She could become an official snowbird.

She smiles and laces her fingers together as she glances around her living room. She could lower the thermostat, leave the keys with a neighbor, and cancel her newspapers. She'd save money, enjoy the Florida weather, and spend time with her family. Add to those benefits the pleasure of not having to shovel snow and scrape ice off the windshield . . .

What is she waiting for?

She reaches for the phone, ready to call Fairlawn again, then relaxes her hand. Jen sounded a bit tired when she said good-bye, so this may not be the best time to call. Her schoolwork can't be easy, and it's nearly dinnertime. She's bound to be busy.

But she'll be excited to hear that Joella is coming for the winter. What woman wouldn't welcome a pair of helping hands, especially during the holidays?

※※ ※※ ※※

"Veins drain." I say the words aloud to remind myself of the rhyme. "We inject fluids through the arteries because they have thicker walls. We *drain* through the *veins.*"

No one is listening, which is probably a good thing. It's closing in on dinnertime, and my family has assured me that sandwiches and mortuary talk don't mix.

I open my anatomy book again and study the map of the human circulatory system. I know the final exam will major on arteries and veins, so I'm concentrating on this chapter. The veins at the base of the neck are of particular importance to morticians, and I stare at a diagram of the divisions of the brachial plexus until I'm almost certain I could sketch it in my sleep.

The crunch of a car moving over our gravel driveway interrupts my concentration.

I walk to the kitchen window and peer out. Our call car is not clean and shiny from the car wash, which means Bugs was right; somebody bit the dust. Gerald must have taken the call after he dropped Bugs at school this morning.

With mixed emotions I watch the old station wagon crawl up the drive. I'm grateful that business has picked up since the brief hiatus Gerald took when my great-uncle had to enter a nursing home. Business means income, and income means we can afford to eat.

I'm not as frantic about our finances as I was six months ago, but we do need steady work. Fairlawn was an unexpected inheritance, but the house required a lot of expensive repairs. Thomas's death last summer resulted in a bequest for Clay and Bugs, but I've put those funds into savings accounts I won't touch until they're ready for college.

So I'm grateful that most of the people in Mt. Dora are again thinking of Fairlawn instead of taking their funeral needs to mortuaries in Eustis or Tavares. Still . . . a body in the prep room means I'll spend several hours over the next couple of days assisting Gerald. I don't mind the work—in fact, I've begun to find it fascinating—but between taking care of the house, my sons, and my schoolwork, how am I supposed to find time to arrange a funeral and embalm a body?

I glance at the refrigerator door, where I've posted my schedule and to-do list. Tomorrow I'm supposed to take Skeeter to the vet for a checkup, I have class from nine to twelve, and I have to pick up Bugs at kindergarten. I'll hurry home because Gerald will want to get started on our new arrival as soon as possible. At some point the family will arrive for the intake interview, and I will have to question them about the funeral service.

I lose sight of the call car as Gerald pulls into the garage. He's been so kind, allowing me time to get over my skittishness, then gently guiding me through every step of the process. I've gained a new appreciation for the old system of apprenticeship.

I pick up my half-empty glass of lemonade and gulp down the remaining swallows, fortifying myself for the chemical smell that will soon invade the prep room.

I'd better go help.

When Gerald comes through the back door to the prep room, it's not formaldehyde I smell but fried chicken. He may have a body in the call car, but he has dinner in his arms. I could kiss the old man.

"I figured you'd had a busy day," he says, dropping a pair of bags onto a prep table, "so I stopped by KFC on my way home from the pickup."

For the merest second my old squeamishness rebels against the thought of eating food that has ridden with a corpse, but common sense prevails. After all, the body has been sealed like a Ziploc.

"I don't know how to thank you." I reach for one of the bags and inhale the warm aroma. "Oh, that smells heavenly. Did you get mashed potatoes and gravy?"

"And biscuits." Gerald sets a smaller bag on the table and pushes it toward me. "I even got corn on the cob, though I wasn't sure the boys would eat it."

"They'll eat anything," I promise, embracing the bags. "And I'll eat anything I didn't have to fix myself. Thanks for being so thoughtful. Do you need help with the body?"

He turns toward the door. "She's on a gurney and she's not heavy."

"By the way, who did you pick up?" I hold my breath, afraid he'll say a name I'll recognize.

"Waldine Loveman," he says.

I breathe a sigh of relief when the name is unfamiliar.

Gerald's eyes soften with memory as he rubs a hand across his face. "Waldine's another one of our prearranged contracts. She and her husband moved to Eustis a couple of years back, so I'm thinking this service might be a little smaller than usual. Her husband passed last year, and the neighbors told me that Waldine hasn't been sociable in months. Rarely ventured out of the house."

My scalp tingles at the thought of what might lie ahead of us. The hardest preparations involve bodies that have gone undiscovered for several days. Decomposition begins rapidly, particularly in Florida's warm climate, and I'm not sure I'm ready to handle a case of advanced deterioration.

Gerald must have seen my expression because he pauses in the doorway. "Waldine's neighbor called me," he explains, a sympathetic smile creasing his face. "Waldine spoke to her last night, but when she didn't pick up her paper this morning, the neighbor went over to check on her. Found Waldine in her easy chair with the TV clicker in her hand."

I press my lips together and stifle an urge to laugh. I don't know what I'll be doing when the Lord calls me home, but I hope I'm not watching something like *Desperate Housewives*.

"So, any idea when we'll hold the funeral? Maybe Thursday?"

"You free that day?"

I nod. "I can be. Anytime after I pick up Bugs would work."

Gerald braces a hand on the doorframe and turns toward the garage. "Maybe one or one thirty, then. That'll give the senior saints at Grace Methodist time to come over after their Thursday luncheon. That's where Waldine went to church when she lived in town."

I leave him to handle the body while I carry the food upstairs. Because Mt. Dora is a small town and death is big news, most of our funerals are packed—a couple have been standing room only. But since Waldine Loveman has been away a few years, maybe we can use the smaller west chapel and have a nice, quiet service.

After the pace of my hectic day, nice and quiet sounds as good as a hot dinner I didn't have to cook.

5

I don't care what Lydia says—power walking at 6 a.m. is not good for the soul.

I pull my sneakered foot behind me and groan as my quadriceps—which, I have recently learned, is not one muscle, but four: the vastus lateralis, vastus medialis, vastus intermedius, and the rectus femoris—stretch.

"That's right," Lydia calls from the other side of her car. "Elongate those quads, because we're getting in a *good* walk today."

Honestly, the woman's enthusiasm for sweat is downright embarrassing.

I pull my other foot behind me, jiggle my sneaker up and down a couple of times, and make a couple of *oofing* sounds. "Ready."

Lydia jogs in place for a second, grinning like a jack-o'-lantern, then tilts her head toward the road. "Let's go."

We set off. She's chosen a part of town that's new to me, though I've driven down this road several times. We parked at the middle school Clay attends, and we're heading west on Lincoln Avenue at a breath-stealing pace. Once we pass the school complex, we turn right into a residential area where the houses are flanked by spreading live oaks that look at least a hundred years old.

"Pretty," I say, gasping. "All the trees."

"Uh-huh." Lydia doesn't waste her breath when we're power walking.

We keep on, our elbows working like pistons, and I nod at a couple who are stepping out of their house and walking to their cars. Two houses later, I nod at another man who pauses to look at us; then I glance at my watch. No wonder we're seeing so many people—it's prime drive-to-work time.

"Hey," I say, glancing at Lydia out of the corner of my eye, "have you noticed something about this neighborhood?"

"Whaddya mean?"

"These people are all black."

She lifts one shoulder in a shrug. "This is East Town."

I'm not sure, but I think she has quickened her pace—either that, or I'm slowing down. I lengthen my stride to keep up with her. "What's East Town?"

She stops, bending forward with her hands on her knees. As she draws in deep breaths, she looks up at me through sweaty bangs. "Way back when things were segregated, most African-Americans lived here. There's actually quite a bit of history—East Town had the first pool in central Florida that would permit blacks, and their school was famous for its quality education."

I bend forward, too, as all four of my quadriceps muscles begin to complain. "It seems strange today, though—seeing a neighborhood this segregated."

Lydia straightens and presses her hands to the small of her back. "I don't know. People cling to what they know. I don't think African-Americans stay here because they're racist. I think most families stay here because it's home."

"I didn't say they were racist." Even the word makes me uncomfortable. "I don't think racism's that big a problem anymore. It's hard to believe black people actually had to attend separate schools—"

"And ride at the back of the bus?" Lydia arches a brow. "All of that may be over, but you'd be surprised how people cling to old attitudes. I remember bringing home a black friend from school once. My mom was polite to her, but after my friend left, Mom went into the kitchen, picked up the glass my friend had been drinking from, and threw it into the trash."

I blink, struggling to believe what I've just heard.

"Oh yeah," Lydia says, bending forward again, "racism is still around, but it's gone underground. People of different races get along fine at work and in public, but watch them in their homes. That's when they'll surprise you."

I gape at her, and I'm still gaping when an old woman with white hair steps out of the house where we've stopped. She stands on her porch, eyes narrowed, arms folded, and watches us . . . as if we're up to no good.

Lydia draws a deep breath, gives the woman a cheery wave, and looks at me. "We'd better get moving."

We turn and power walk back to the car.

ⓧ ⓧ ⓧ

After receiving Skeeter's good health report from the vet, going to my Tuesday morning class, and picking up Bugs, I walk down to the prep room and pull on latex gloves, a rubber apron, and a mask. When he sees that I'm ready, Gerald wheels Waldine Loveman out of the cooler, and I help him transfer the body bag to our preparation table.

After Gerald unzips the bag, I see that Waldine is still wearing her housecoat and nightgown. Gerald stands back as I cut the garments away and set them aside. I can't help but notice that Waldine's nightgown has been washed so many times the thin cotton is nearly transparent in places. Her housecoat, a simple number with snaps up the front, is whispery soft. No wonder she liked to wear it while she watched TV.

As I survey our latest client, I feel myself mentally shift gears. It's hard to explain to someone who isn't involved in the field, but once the clothing is gone, the body on the table becomes simply that—a body. This sort of detachment is probably what allows morticians to perform their work without suffering from emotional overload, but I know one thing for sure: the embalmer's job is to halt decomposition to the point that the family will be able to hold a viewing and a funeral without being repulsed by the sights, smells, and sounds of a decaying corpse.

Six months ago, I would have shrunk from the sight of a dead client; now I study the body with clinical interest. My pulse quickens, and from out of nowhere I remember that I used to enjoy dissection days in high school biology. Frogs and worms fascinated me. Something about the way the organs fit together perfectly reminds me that God knows what he's doing . . . even when I don't.

With a detached eye, I glance at the clipboard that traveled with this patient, and then I check the body. Waldine Loveman is a well-nourished Caucasian female who apparently died of natural causes at age eighty-six. Her skin is remarkably free of scars. I've seen everything from appendectomy to cesarean scars on our last few clients.

"Go ahead." Gerald nods and ties on his mask. "You know what to do."

I do, but only from watching Gerald, so my fingers tremble as I pick up a sharp pair of scissors and place the point of a blade at a spot in the hollow of the neck. I press downward until the blade cuts the skin. Then I make a small incision and slowly slice my way through the adipose layer beneath the epidermis. I set the scissors aside as Gerald offers an arterial hook.

"Good job," he says. "Now reach in and catch the jugular."

"Are you sure you don't want to do this?"

"We learn best by doing, missy. I'm here and I won't let you make a mistake."

I draw a deep breath and thank the Lord that I'm not a surgeon with a *living* patient. I shouldn't be nervous. At this point, it's almost impossible for me to make a blunder Gerald couldn't rectify. Still, I don't want to mess up. Though I didn't know her, I want to treat Waldine Loveman with respect.

With gloved fingers I slip the hooked end of the arterial hook into the incision. As I probe the area, I superimpose an image from my anatomy book onto the body's pale flesh. The internal jugular vein and the common carotid run alongside each other, parallel to the trachea. The jugular lies closest to the skin, right . . . there.

I lift the bluish vein out of the incision, startled, as always, by its surprising size.

"Excellent." Smiling his approval, Gerald presses on the skin, then threads two pieces of string under the vein and ties them in a loose knot. "Now, go for the carotid."

Again, I take the arterial hook and go fishing. The hard object to the right is undoubtedly the trachea, so the carotid artery lies just to the left.

My hook retrieves a smooth, pale tube.

"That's right." Gerald threads another pair of strings under this artery, ties them, and hands me the scissors. "Now make the T-incision."

I gulp and bend over the body. I wince as I slice a T into the artery and the vein; then I step back so Gerald can take a look. My left hand is open and extended, and I'm startled when he snaps a piece of chrome tubing into my gloved hand. Like I'm some kind of surgeon?

"Always wanted to do that," he says, the corners of his eyes crinkling above his mask. "Fit it into the arterial opening, please. Remember—point the head toward the heart."

I try to squeeze the head of the metal tube into the first T-incision, but I must have made the cuts too small. I hesitate, wondering if I should make the opening bigger, but Gerald clears his throat.

I lift my hands and step to the side, watching in wonder as he seats the tube with the smallest twist of his hand.

"Takes practice," he says, handing me the other tube. "You do the drain tube."

"We drain through the veins."

"You've got it."

The drain tube is easier, or maybe this time I'm more relaxed. When both devices are in place, I tie the loose strings around the metal tubes to prevent them from slipping during the pumping process.

"You're becoming a pro," Gerald says, smiling. "How are your nerves?"

I feel as jittery as ever, but my kneecaps no longer engage in instantaneous jiggling the moment I approach the prep table. I must be getting used to this. I reach for a bottle of arterial fluid. "I think I'm okay."

As Gerald fills the tank of our embalming machine at the sink, I uncap four bottles of formalin—a mixture of formaldehyde, lanolin, tint, and deodorant. Once the Porti-Boy tank has filled to the correct level with water, I add the arterial fluid and wait for the liquids to mix. When the solution is a uniform pale pink, I connect the end of the Porti-Boy's hose to the metal tube we've inserted into our client's carotid artery.

Gerald checks the pressure dial and flips the power switch. With a series of steady clicks, the pump injects arterial fluid into the carotid. Within a matter of minutes the incoming liquid pushes black blood through the tube connected to the jugular. The liquid flows out of the body and onto the table; then it travels along the table gutter, into the sink, and down the drain.

I lean against the counter and watch, amazed again at the efficiency of the human body. I've learned that the human circulatory system is a long circular highway with hundreds of smaller side streets. Unless blocked or broken, all the avenues lead back to the heart. The embalmer creates a detour, forcing a preservative into the body's highway system even as he pushes dead blood into the public sewers.

I pick up a spray attachment near the sink, ready to break up any clots that might clog the drain, but my attention is diverted by a knock on the prep room door.

"Mom?"

I stiffen. My children have gotten used to the idea of living in a funeral home, but they've never witnessed an embalming. I don't think I want them to.

Gerald jerks his chin toward the door. "Go see what the boy wants. I'll keep an eye on this."

I pull down my mask and move to the door, opening it a couple of inches.

Clay stands in the hallway, his face set in its usual expression of boredom.

"What is it?"

"Some guy's out here with a load of flowers. Says they're for some service you're having tonight."

I groan and rub my forehead. Deborah Whiting, a former Mt. Dora resident, passed away and will be buried in Delaware, but her family wanted to have a memorial service in the town where she spent so many of her younger years.

"Have him put the flowers in the west chapel," I tell Clay. "I'll come out to position them in a few minutes."

I close the door and turn back to our client, but Gerald waves me forward. "Nothing's going to happen here for a while," he says, keeping an eye on the blood flow. "Go on out and see to the chapel. I'll join you in about an hour."

I snap off my gloves and prepare to shift gears again, leaving the role of clinical embalmer to slip into the guise of interior decorator.

I'm a little distracted as I walk down the hallway that leads to the foyer, so I'm startled when the front door swings open and I am nearly run over by an aggressive wreath on a three-legged stand. Some overly imaginative florist has glued a plastic princess phone onto the circular foam support and tied a banner around the arrangement of tinted carnations and gladioli. *Heaven called,* it says in glittery letters, *and Debbie answered.*

Well, no wonder. If heaven called me on a princess phone, I'd probably keel over, too.

I try not to wince as I greet the deliveryman carrying the monstrous arrangement. "Hi. That's, um . . ."

"Awful, ain't it?" The man lowers his burden and plants his hands on his hips. "Where do you want it?"

I'm tempted to tell him to stick it in the garage, but someone tonight will be looking for this atrocity.

Wordlessly, I point to the west chapel.

6

&'m checking Clay's algebra homework at the kitchen table when
the foyer clock strikes the hour of seven and nags me about something.

A funeral? No. We buried Waldine Loveman this afternoon, and
we've had no intakes since.

A class? No . . . I was feeling relaxed about whatever this was, and I
wouldn't feel that way about class.

"The book club." I drop Clay's homework. "This looks okay, Son.
Anything else you want me to check?"

Without a word he shakes his head and picks up his paper, then
stands and slouches toward his room.

If Lydia weren't a good friend, I'd forget about the book club meeting. I can think of ten reasons to stay home and only one reason to
go—I promised Lydia I'd try to come. Maybe I can slip out early.

"Gerald?" I push myself up from the table and call toward his
room. "I've got a book club meeting at Lydia's house. Can you make
sure the boys are in bed on time? And—"

Gerald steps out of his room and smiles. "I don't mind making
their lunches. You go on and have a good time. Don't worry about
rushing home."

We've lived in the same house only five months, but sometimes
I think the man can read my mind. "Thanks." I give my anatomy

textbook a distracted glance before grabbing my copy of *Five Miles South of Peculiar* from the bookcase and heading for the stairs.

We live less than fifty yards from Lydia's house, and the night is cool, but perspiration has soaked the hair at my temples by the time I stride up her sidewalk. Her front windows glow with warm light, and I can hear the sound of laughter and light voices.

My spirit lifts. Maybe Lydia is right—all work and no play does make a dull neighbor.

A hand-painted sign on the door says Come On In!, so I step into the foyer and see that Lydia has arranged a circle of folding chairs in her living room. They're empty, though, because all her guests are in the kitchen.

I drop my book onto a chair and make my way toward the others.

Lydia stands at the island in the center of her kitchen, a coffeepot in one hand and a mug in the other. "Jen!" she cries, her face lighting. "The coffee is crème brûlée. Want some?"

"I'd love a cup." I glance around the circle of women, only a few of whom I recognize.

"Y'all go around and introduce yourselves," Lydia commands as she pours the coffee. "I'd do it, but my mind goes blank when I'm put on the spot."

I know how she feels. The woman next to Lydia tells me her name, followed by the next woman, and the next. Their names pour through my brain like water through a sieve, but I smile and try to imprint their faces on my memory. Next week I may be in Albertsons and run into one of these ladies. If I can place the face, I can rely on the old trick millions of Southerners use every day: I'll call her "sugar" or "sweetie" and pretend to remember who she is. That trick has come in handy during the last few weeks.

But my favorite social convention by far is the technique Southern women employ to insult their neighbors. They'll utter a barb, insert a "bless her heart" in the middle of it, and get away with outright slander, even at a funeral.

The last woman in the circle, McLane Larson, is pretty with auburn hair. Something about her strikes me as familiar, but when

Lydia mentions that she's a newcomer to town, I dismiss the feeling as déjà vu.

"I found McLane wandering Baker Street with a dazed look on her face," Lydia says, "so I invited her for a cup of coffee and learned that she'd just moved into the Biddle House."

One of the other women lifts a brow. "I thought Ryan Evans lived in the Biddle House apartment."

"The Hatters have remodeled," Lydia explains, "and there are now *two* apartments in the house. Ryan rents one and McLane has the other."

I give McLane a smile. "So, how do you like living in a house owned by our chapter of the Red Hat Society?"

She laughs and stirs cream into her coffee. "I love it. The ladies are very protective . . . and interested. And the house is really quiet at night. Ryan doesn't make a peep, and the ladies hardly ever stay late. One of them told me they don't like to drive after sunset."

"My mother's the same way." My mouth curves at the thought of Mom, safe at home in Virginia. "She says she has trouble with depth perception when it's dark."

Lydia holds up a plate of cookies. "I know I promised a decadent dessert, but these homemade oatmeal raisin cookies are as good as it gets tonight."

"Honey, these cookies are *good*," a redhead across the room says, holding up a half-eaten morsel as proof. "My mother-in-law tried to make this recipe the other day, but that woman, bless her heart, can't cook to save her life."

Lydia grabs a cookie herself. "Who wants to take one into the living room? If we don't get started on the book discussion, we'll be yakking all night."

I have a feeling Lydia is trying to keep things moving on my account—she knows how hard it is for me to get away, and she probably suspects that I have a lot of reading to do before bed. But I'm feeling relaxed and glad to be out of the house. I sip the fragrant coffee and smile at McLane, no longer caring if I make it home early.

We file into the front room, where most of the women sit in folding

chairs, graciously leaving the formless purple sofa for Lydia and the strag-
glers. I sit in the middle of the sofa, on the gap between the two velvet-
draped cushions, with McLane on my right and Lydia at my left.

Lydia sets her copy of *Five Miles South of Peculiar* on the coffee
table, then passes out three-by-five cards. I'm not sure what we're
supposed to do next, but if she wants me to write down my favorite
recipe, she's out of luck. I can barely remember my name these days.

"You're probably wondering what those are for," Lydia says, pulling
an assortment of pens and markers from her pocket. "It's simple. I've
been in groups where some ladies are swayed by others, so before we
discuss anything, I want you to evaluate the book and jot your rating
on your card. One star means you hated it. Five stars means you think
it's the best thing since spray-on tans. We'll go around and explain our
ratings before we jump into the discussion questions."

I grin as she offers me a pen. She has a point—peer pressure is
powerful. I've seen people who dislike a particular casket grow silent
when a more opinionated family member walks into the display room.
Lydia's approach will allow us to enjoy everyone's unadulterated opinion before we begin to dissect the novel.

I hesitate as I consider my rating. The book was wonderful, the
writing sheer poetry, but the author lost my interest whenever he
launched into the poetic story within a story, so I draw four disjointed
stars on my note card. I follow Lydia's example and turn it facedown
on my lap.

I glance at McLane, who has also drawn four stars. "Looks like we
have the same taste," I whisper.

"Everybody finished?" Lydia looks around the circle, then nods to
the woman sitting across from her. "Sharon, why don't you start by
telling us what you rated the story."

And so the discussion begins. One by one we share our opinions
about the writing, the subject, and the theme; one by one we reveal a
little about ourselves through the mirror of the novel.

I learn that Sharon likes happy endings and Myrna likes history,
especially about the Civil War. Becky likes the writing but thinks the
characters, bless their hearts, are a little stiff. Julie likes the book but

would have preferred to see it as a movie because she's a visual learner. Nicole thinks the mother a tad unrealistic, and McLane wishes the novel had more romance.

I peek at her left hand—no diamond but a simple gold wedding band.

"Of all the books I've read this year, nothing has come close to *Cold Mountain*," she says. "Those characters communicated through letters, just like my husband and I do—if you count e-mail as letters, that is. And the impending realities of war . . . well, ever since Jeff left for Iraq, the dangers of war are never far from my mind."

I stare at Lydia—did she know about this?—while several of the women murmur in sympathy.

"We got married two weeks before he had to ship out," McLane says, a blush coloring her cheekbones as she looks around the circle. "We knew the risks, but we decided we wanted to be married no matter what. We had a short honeymoon at Disney World; then Jeff went back to the base to get ready to go overseas. I didn't have anyplace else to go, so I came here."

"Whatever for?" The question slips out before I can stop it, but McLane doesn't seem to mind my nosiness. Nor, thank heaven, do the other women notice how surprised I am that anyone would choose to live in a town this small.

She shrugs. "Mt. Dora looked like a nice place. Plus, I heard I could probably find a job in one of the downtown shops. I'll be getting a check from Jeff, of course, but we need to start saving up . . . you know, to buy a house and start a family."

Lydia smiles at me in pleased surprise. Just the other day we were talking about how most young women these days want everything *but* a husband and family. McLane is special.

Her husband must be special, too. Though I have mixed feelings about the war, I am in awe of those who are willing to place their lives on the line in armed conflict. Every woman in this circle is surely hoping that this young woman's husband comes home safely. We haven't heard much good news from Iraq lately, and none of us thinks the conflict will be ending soon.

But the war is a touchy subject, so when Lydia gives me a pointed look, I understand what she's silently urging.

"I loved the book," I say, flashing my note card. "I don't think it's my favorite of all time, so I gave it four stars instead of five. But I did like it a lot . . . even though the ending made me cry."

Lydia grins and picks up her card. In her eyes I read a message of thanks for keeping us from a divisive topic.

※ ※ ※

Randolph turns the key in the lock, then steps into a thick silence broken only by the warning beep of the alarm system. He closes and locks the heavy door behind him and punches the code into the keypad.

The roar of quiet fills his ears. A few months ago, he would have been greeted by the sound of clattering dishes in the kitchen and the dull bass thump of whatever music McLane was playing upstairs. Now even that sound has vanished.

No Shana, no McLane. No family, not anymore.

He tosses his keys onto the foyer table and enters the den, where his computer sleeps in hibernation mode. He touches the mouse to nudge the machine to life and checks his in-box. No reminders from his office, no word from his daughter. Even the spammers seem to be avoiding him.

He pulls a copy of the *New York Times* from under his arm and drops it onto the corner of the desk, then settles into his chair and leans back until his field of vision fills with the delicate lace pattern of the ceiling. What is a man in the prime of his life supposed to do when his family disappears? He is fifty-five, too young to say farewell to a beloved wife and daughter. He had planned to work until sixty-five in order to pay off the mortgage and support McLane through graduate school, but his daughter has abandoned her plans for higher education, and Shana's insurance policy took care of the mortgage balance.

Why is he working at all?

The question is purely rhetorical; he works to fill his days. Without his patients he would have no reason to get out of bed.

Yet another responsibility drives him as well. He picks up the phone and dials the number he's memorized. The detective doesn't answer, but a husky female voice informs Randolph that he's reached the office of Dexter Duggan, licensed private investigator. "Detective Duggan is in the field, but if you'll leave your name and number . . ."

Randolph clears his throat. "Mr. Duggan, this is Dr. Harris. Just thought I'd check to see if you've made any progress on finding my daughter. I'll be at my home number for the rest of the evening. I'd appreciate a return call."

He drops the phone back into its cradle and folds his hands over his belt line, vaguely aware that his stomach feels as hollow as a drum. He worked through lunch today, which also might account for the faint throbbing in his temples.

"You need to eat, darling." Amazing how Shana's voice still plays in his head. Sometimes he can close his eyes and almost convince himself that she's just left the room, a trail of the light floral perfume she favored lingering. It would be easy to sit here, lost in the memories of his dead wife, so easy to pretend the accident had never happened.

But he knows the dangers of denial. He will not indulge in unhealthy fantasies.

He stands and crosses the foyer, then moves through the dining room and into the kitchen. The polished granite counters gleam in the overhead lights while stainless steel appliances stand at attention between yards of spotless countertop.

He opens the freezer, where a stack of dinners waits on a shelf. He takes the top box, rips it open, and pulls on his reading glasses to scan the instructions: five minutes, full power. Easy enough.

He slides the dish inside the microwave and punches in the time. While the oven hums, he leans against the counter behind him and drops into the well of memory.

"Dad, I'd like to bring a friend home for dinner tomorrow."

"Really? Who would that be?"

"Jeff Larson. I met him outside Chico's."

"You met him at that bar?"

"*It's not a bar. It's a restaurant that happens to have a bar in it. And Jeff's nice. He's a marine. I think you'd like him.*"

"*I'd rather have a quiet dinner, just the two of us.*"

"*Please. I like Jeff, and I'd like him to meet you.*"

"*Not this time, McLane. It's too soon.*"

"*Dad . . . it's been months. Mom wouldn't want us to mourn forever.*"

"*She wouldn't want you to give up your dreams, either. Stick to your schoolwork. Stay with your dreams.*"

If he said yes that night, would McLane have tired of Jeff Larson? She had lost interest in so many young men, none of whom were nearly as smart or as ambitious as the bright star they thought they could hold in their arms.

But he said no, and she defied him. She kept seeing the boy, and then she ran away with him. . . .

The phone rings. Randolph pushes his glasses back to his nose to study the cordless unit on the counter. Caller ID reveals the name of his answering service, so he picks up the phone. "Dr. Harris."

He registers a twinge of disappointment when the operator tells him a patient has called. One of his obsessive-compulsive cases needs a refill of Anafranil, yet she's overdue for an evaluation. "Tell her I will squeeze her in tomorrow morning," he says, "but I can't call in a script without seeing her. She won't be thrilled to hear that, but it's the best I can do."

He hangs up as the microwave begins to beep. His dinner is ready and life must go on.

He lifts the steaming dish out of the oven, slides it onto a tray, and fills a glass with ice cubes. After grabbing a bottle of water from the fridge, he carries his tray to the bedroom, where he settles on the tall bed, sets the tray on his lap, and clicks the television remote.

Some of his colleagues might think he has the perfect life—a lovely home, a successful practice, an adult daughter who has left the nest without requiring frequent infusions of cash. While his friends and acquaintances have been sympathetic about his wife's passing, he knows a few of them would be thrilled to be fifty-five and single again.

But nineteen years ago Randolph gave his heart to Shana Reyes and her daughter, and he's not the sort to take it back.

Lydia gives me a satisfied smile as she pours the last of the coffee down the drain. "I thought you had to rush home."

I sink to a barstool at her kitchen counter. "I ought to be studying, but you were right—it does feel good to take a break."

"I thought you'd enjoy a night out." Lydia sets the coffee decanter in the dishwasher, then gathers the coffee mugs scattered over the kitchen island. "So . . . what'd you think of our little book club?"

"I enjoyed it. I liked those women; they were sharp. Why haven't I seen them around town?"

"Most of them work, so you won't find them downtown during the week. And none of them are old enough for the Hatter crowd—" she grins—"so I doubt your mother brought any of them around when she was here."

"McLane is practically a baby. How sad to be so young and alone. Why isn't she with her family?"

Lydia opens the dishwasher. "I wondered about that, too. I asked about her family right after we met, and she mentioned that her mother had recently passed away. She didn't volunteer anything else, and I didn't want to pry."

I flip through my mental files for recent obituaries and come up with no obvious connections to McLane. "I'm thinking she's not from around here . . . at least not from Lake County."

"I know." Lydia stops loading the dishwasher long enough to crinkle her nose. "Her accent was really thick. What do you think? Georgia?"

I shake my head. "More like the Carolinas. We lived near Fort Bragg when I was in high school. After we left, it took me a year to stop pronouncing *pine* and *pane* in the same way." I slide a couple of used spoons over the counter. "Has that poor girl come up with any leads on a job?"

"None that I know of. She's a college graduate, so she could probably handle almost anything, and she mentioned that she's done some graduate work. I don't think she's in school now, though."

"She's bright. She'll find something." I reach for a couple of crumpled napkins, then wad them into a compact ball and toss them into Lydia's trash can. "I can't figure out why she'd come to Mt. Dora. If I were young and newly married, this is the last place on earth I'd choose to live."

"Mt. Dora's not that bad."

"No, no, of course not." I give Lydia an apologetic smile. "I love it, but I had a reason to settle here. Why did she come?"

"Because it's a charming town with friendly people?"

"She could find that almost anywhere."

"Because . . . we're famous for our hospitality and antiques?"

"You think a girl like that is into *antiques?*"

"Well, who knows?" Lydia closes the dishwasher with a well-aimed back kick and tosses her dish towel over her shoulder. "She must have her reasons. I'm just glad she came tonight. I know she's glad *you* came."

I run my hand over the countertop, then hesitate. "Why would she be glad I came?"

"She wanted to meet you. I thought I mentioned that."

"You didn't. Why would she want to meet me?"

Lydia shrugs. "Maybe she's thinking about applying for a job at Fairlawn."

"Doing what? We're barely bringing in enough to pay Gerald's wages."

"I don't know." Lydia heaves an exasperated sigh. "Maybe someone mentioned that you used to be in politics, and she wants to pick your brain. Maybe she knows someone from where you used to live in Virginia."

I'm trying Lydia's patience, but I can't let it go. "Still . . . don't you think that's odd? I'm not famous or anything."

"All the Hatters know you, and they adore your mother. Or maybe Ryan mentioned you."

That's probably it. When Ryan Evans is not tightening the perms of Red Hatters or straightening the locks of the younger set at his salon, he's doing the hair and makeup of our casketed clients.

Lydia snaps her fingers. "I'll bet she saw that article the *Daily Commercial* did on you last month. Face it. You're a local celebrity."

I roll my eyes. "That article wouldn't attract anybody. If anything, it'd make people *not* want to meet me."

"Being the only female funeral director in three counties is big news around here," she says, grinning. "Maybe McLane saw it and wants to follow in your footsteps."

I blow my bangs off my forehead. Lydia is making fun of me now, and she's probably right—I'm turning a molehill into a mountain. So what if McLane wanted to meet me? The Hatters probably mentioned me, and she was eager to connect a familiar name to a face.

"Hey, thanks for inviting me tonight," I say, sliding off my stool. "I had a good time."

"Want to take some cookies to the boys?"

"They'd love 'em. But not too many or I'll end up eating them, and I can't afford the extra calories."

Lydia pops four oatmeal raisin cookies into a sandwich bag and zips the seal.

"Thanks again," I tell her, scooping up the cookie bag on my way toward the door. "But I still think it's weird that anyone would want to meet me."

"Good grief, let it go." Lydia rests one hip against the doorframe as she waves me off. "Don't you have enough to worry about?"

She's right, of course. From time to time, bless my heart, I find myself worrying too much.

7

$\mathcal{I}$'m trotting down the staircase, intent on remembering everything I need at the grocery store, when I nearly run into an elderly man in the foyer. His eyes are red-rimmed and serious, his face lined with care. A few months ago I would have smiled and moved past him, focused on my to-do list, but now the saving grace of second thought holds me in place.

I am no longer Jennifer Graham, political powerhouse. I am the owner of the Fairlawn Funeral Home, and this occasion requires that I wear my gracious hostess cap. Especially if this man is a potential customer.

I look up and offer a subdued smile. "May I help you, sir?"

"I'm Russell Solan," he says, removing a battered felt hat. "I called for an appointment to speak to someone about making arrangements for—"

"Mr. Solan." I bring my hand to my forehead as the name registers. "I'm sorry. Did you make that appointment for this morning?"

"No, ma'am. I was waiting for Buddy to . . . well, I didn't feel the time was right. But he's not doing so well today, so I figured I'd better get down here while I can still get away. My wife is with him now."

I place my hand on the old man's arm. "Mr. Huffman would be happy to talk to you about making your arrangements. But he had to go out on a call, and I don't think he'll be back for at least an hour. I'd love to talk to you, but I have an errand to run. Would it be possible for you to come back this afternoon?"

I know I'm begging, and begging is unprofessional, but Mr. Solan looks like he might be nice enough to understand. He hesitates, inching his fingers along the brim of the hat, and finally nods. "I suppose I could come back tomorrow, but I don't think Buddy has much longer. I was hoping to take care of everything before he passes."

"That's an excellent idea." I gently take his arm and guide him toward the front door. "I know that families are relieved of a great burden when funeral arrangements are made before the hour of passing. When that time comes, you want to be able to reflect on your memories and not be distracted by details."

He walks with me across the front porch and down the stairs. "It's killing me," he says, his voice tight. "The suffering. Buddy's been my best friend for so long I can't imagine what I'll do without him. Seems like only last month we were in New York, riding around Central Park in that limo. . . ."

I check my watch—I have less than an hour to buy a week's groceries. I give Mr. Solan a sympathetic nod. "I know it's hard. If you stop in tomorrow, Mr. Huffman should be here. If he's occupied, I'll make sure I'm available. We'll help you take care of all the details."

"Even on Saturday?"

"Even on Saturday. We're here when you need us."

Given the circumstances, anyone else might have stopped to debate that point, but Mr. Solan is of no mind to argue. I give the man's arm a final squeeze, then fish my keys from my purse and head toward the minivan.

The old man continues to talk, his words rumbling over the sidewalk as I get into the driver's seat. "Oh, Buddy, Buddy. I never thought you'd be the one to go first."

I glance at him, wondering if he's talking to me, but his eyes are on the sidewalk, his hands busy with his hat.

Now he's talking to himself . . . or maybe to the Lord. "It'd be easier if he'd just go to sleep." The November wind blows his words right toward me. "If he cries through another night, I might have to put him out of his misery."

I close the van door but hesitate before sliding my key into the ignition. Did I hear that right?

❧ ❧ ❧

Randolph tells his receptionist to hold his next patient and put the caller through.

A moment later he leans back and tents his fingers as Dexter Duggan's rough voice tumbles through the speakerphone. "Just checking in, Doc. Haven't found your girl, but the marine is serving in Iraq. Baghdad, as a matter of fact."

"What do you mean, he's in Iraq?" Randolph's gaze freezes on the graceful outline of a Grecian statue spotlighted in his bookcase. "Where's my daughter?"

"That's why I'm calling—that's one bright girl you've got there, Dr. Harris."

Randolph sighs and turns toward the window, waiting for an explanation.

"The marine was easy enough to trace—Corporal Jeffrey Larson, Squadron twenty-nine, deployed on the twenty-third of September from the New River Air Station in Jacksonville, North Carolina. The man has an exemplary record, a couple of commendations, and a wife."

Randolph feels a burst of heat ignite from someplace beneath his ribs. "The man was married while seeing my daughter?"

"His spouse is listed as McLane Larson. Her contact address is a post office box in Jacksonville."

The words slam into Randolph's brain with the force of a blow. Married? Impossible. She couldn't have married that boy; she wouldn't have. Her mother would faint at the possibility of such a match.

McLane was delusional, not herself. She acted in some sort of temporary insanity. Perhaps she was still in the grip of grief. Perhaps she thought marrying that boy would strike some sort of cosmic blow against the injustice that had taken her mother.

Randolph struggles against his roiling emotions and forces himself to speak in a calm voice. "Is she still in the state?"

"Not a safe assumption. That PO box is one of those confidential setups—that's why I said your daughter was bright. Mail to the PO box gets forwarded, and those records are sealed. I'd need a court order to get that information."

"So . . . you've hit a dead end."

"Not necessarily."

Randolph closes his eyes and waits to hear the detective's next idea. Dexter Duggan has proven more resourceful than he would have guessed. If he continues to be resourceful, Randolph may regret hiring this man.

"I've covered all the obvious angles," the detective drawls, "so what I need to investigate now are the things that aren't so obvious. Your daughter's smart, but she's no expert at evasion—ordinary people never are. She's left a trail, and it's probably obvious. But I need to know where to start looking."

"And how do you propose to do that?"

"You need to give me a head start. You know your daughter, so you tell me. If she were going to lie low while her hubby is overseas, where would she go?"

Her hubby. Randolph grimaces at the sound of those words, then pushes them from his mind. He'll find McLane and get her into therapy. The marriage can be annulled; the matter will be easy to handle with the boy overseas. McLane will come home, get help, and enroll in nursing school. A mind like hers shouldn't go to waste.

He draws a deep breath. "I've already given you her address book. You'll find her friends listed there."

"I've spoken to several of them, and they either haven't seen her or aren't talking. So what I want to know—what I'll find most helpful— are the things you *don't* want to tell me. What was going on in your daughter's life that you don't want anyone else to know?"

The question snaps like a whip, making Randolph flinch. "I have nothing to hide."

"Come on. Everybody has secrets, even doctors and their daughters.

Sure, your girl might have run away because she wanted to marry this man. But she could have married him and come home, couldn't she? So is there any other reason—anything at all—that might cause her to run away?"

This is the part he's been dreading. Randolph shifts his weight and crosses his legs, grateful that the detective can't see him. "It's probably irrelevant."

"Tell me anyway."

Randolph rubs his jaw. "This isn't common knowledge, but McLane was five when I married her mother. I adopted her, and from that moment I've thought of her as mine. She saw me as her father, too, and we were a close-knit family. I didn't think she even remembered those early days until her birthday this past year."

Duggan clears his throat. "What happened?"

"Shana didn't ask my opinion, probably because she knew I'd object, but she took McLane out for a special lunch and told her the complete story of her conception. She reminded McLane that I wasn't her biological father . . . and she confessed that McLane resulted from an affair with a married man."

Duggan makes a growling sound. "Doesn't sound like much of a birthday present."

"That wasn't the gift. Shana wanted McLane to know that she has a sister. The louse who fathered her had a daughter, so McLane has a half sister."

"Now we're getting somewhere." Duggan's voice simmers with approval. "Do you know the sister's name?"

Randolph exhales a sharp breath. "Unfortunately, that's all McLane could talk about until the day her mother died—then she seemed to put it out of her mind. The woman's name is Jennifer Norris."

8

$\mathcal{A}$fter picking up my infectious disease textbook on Friday afternoon, I open the door to Daniel Sladen's office and nearly bump into McLane Larson on her way out.

"Oh!" I smile and move out of the way as a flush brightens her face. "Didn't mean to plow you over."

She tilts her head and looks at me as if she wants to say something, but before she can speak, Daniel calls out, "Jen! Come on in."

McLane ducks and murmurs a soft good-bye.

I watch her step onto the street before turning to Daniel, who's standing behind his secretary's desk. He handles estate law, so I can't figure out why McLane would be here unless . . .

I point toward her retreating figure. "Did she inherit something from one of your clients?"

For an instant his face goes blank; then he grins. "Ms. Larson? She was applying for a job."

"Oh." I smile at the secretary and blush when I realize that I'm snooping. "It's really none of my business, is it?"

Mara Potter, a red-haired woman whose teeth have been whitened to the point of luminescence, waves away my disclaimer. "Honey, in a town this small, everything is everybody's business. Isn't McLane the sweetest thing? I was real taken with her."

I give Daniel a noncommittal smile. "I don't know her well, but she seems nice enough. And her husband's stationed in Iraq, if that makes any difference."

"Should it?"

"Well, if you want to support the troops . . ."

"I do, as a matter of fact, but that has nothing to do with why I hired her. She's quick and she types ninety words a minute. She starts next week, just in time for Mrs. Potter to go see her grandkids in Kentucky."

My smile broadens as I study the man who inadvertently brought me and my family to Mt. Dora. When he called with the news that I'd inherited Fairlawn, I never imagined that I could become friends with a lawyer. "You're a good man, Daniel Sladen."

"That's what I keep telling people, but the lawyer thing gets in the way." He hands a sheet of paper to Mrs. Potter, then cocks a brow in my direction. "What brings you downtown?"

I grip the strap of my purse and glance at the clock. "I was wondering if you wanted to grab a quick lunch. Gerald is picking up Bugs today, so I have a few minutes before I have to head home."

"I'm sorry, but I've got a client coming in to review some trust documents. I think he's received some bad news from his doctor, and he's getting his affairs in order."

I frown. "That reminds me. Do you know Russell Solan?"

"Of course."

"And Buddy?"

Daniel laughs. "All native Mt. Dorans know Buddy. He was quite the celebrity about ten years ago. He and Russell flew to New York and appeared on the *Late Show with David Letterman.*"

I'm about to ask how they merited that honor, but the door opens and an elderly man enters. He is stooped and walks with a shuffling step, but his eyes are blue and bright when he looks up at Daniel. "You ready for me?" he asks, his voice hoarse.

I don't know who this fellow is, but he's not Russell Solan. I step back, twiddle my fingers in a wave, and point to the door.

Daniel nods and greets his client.

I leave the office and stand for a moment in the sun. The wind is brisk today, cool and blessedly dry. The live oaks along the sidewalk will keep their leaves until new growth pushes them off in the spring, but the maple tree across the street has lost nearly all its leaves.

I resign myself to going home early and walk toward the minivan, but my steps slow as I approach the curb. McLane sits on a green bench in front of the pharmacy, her eyes wide and staring at nothing. One hand is pressed to her stomach, and her complexion is slightly green.

A few feet away, I stop and wait for her to notice me. When she doesn't respond, I wave my hand in front of her face. "McLane? Are you awake?"

She blinks wetness from her eyes and gives me a distracted glance. "Jennifer. Hi."

"You look . . . exhausted." I swallow hard, afraid to voice the first thought that leaps into my mind. "Have you heard bad news . . . about your husband?"

Her coppery hair gleams as she shakes her head. "I got an e-mail from Jeff last night. He's fine."

I sink onto the bench. "You feeling okay?"

She lifts one shoulder in a halfhearted shrug. "A little queasy, but I'm good. It's not the flu or anything."

"You getting along okay at the Biddle House?"

"Everything's great. The ladies are wonderful."

"Well, then . . ." I glance around, wondering whether I should be on my way or keep probing. I hardly know McLane, so she may not want me to ask her a zillion questions. But she's upset. Anyone could see that. I settle back against the bench and pretend that I intended to join her. "I'm glad I ran into you. Daniel tells me you'll soon be working for him."

"Yes. He seems like a nice man."

"He is." I study her, hoping my words will make some kind of impression, but she's still wearing that just-been-hypnotized look. Nothing to do, then, but be blunt. "You look upset," I say, bending to peer into her eyes. "Are you *sure* you're okay?"

The direct approach seems to shake her out of her daze, and for the first time, she looks directly at me. She takes her cell phone from her pocket. "I got a call."

"From . . . the military?"

"From my doctor."

I frown. What could be wrong? Surely she's too young to have a serious medical problem. "Who's your doctor?"

"Mullgrew, I think. Or Mulligan. I stopped by the office this morning but had to leave to keep my appointment at Mr. Sladen's firm. So they called with my results."

I don't recognize the doctor's name, so this information is useless. "Results for . . . ?"

"I'm pregnant." Her eyes crinkle at the corners, but her mouth dissolves into a tremulous line. "I didn't mean to be pregnant. Jeff and I wanted to wait. But you know what they say."

"Um . . . about the best-laid plans of mice and men?"

"About no birth control being 100 percent effective." Without warning, she lowers her face into her hands and erupts into noisy tears.

I stare, horrified. Then I do what almost any woman would do— I put my arm around her trembling shoulders and whisper that she should calm down and everything will be all right.

While I'm making empty promises, I search my memory for something—anything—that might help. McLane ought to be with her family, but Lydia said her mother passed away. But what about her father? And her husband must have parents somewhere.

Unless she doesn't get along with his folks. Not all young brides are accepted by their mothers-in-law, and the fact that McLane came to Mt. Dora instead of moving near her husband's family reveals a lot.

I let her cry and nod quietly at a couple of passersby who give us curious glances.

When McLane's sobs have slowed, I reach into my purse for a packet of tissues. "I have some free time," I say, offering her the tissues, "and you could probably use something to eat. Let me treat you to a nice bowl of soup. There's a great little restaurant right down the street."

She sniffs and pulls a tissue from the cellophane wrapper. "I don't want to hold you up. I'm sure you have things to do."

I do, but something tells me this situation is more important than anything on my to-do list. "Honestly, you won't be keeping me from anything. As a matter of fact, I was hoping Daniel would be free for lunch, but here you are instead. That's probably a God-thing."

She blinks and the corner of her mouth lifts in a half smile. "You think God has something to do with this?"

I laugh, realizing there's no way she could know what I've learned in the last few months. "Honey, God has something to do with everything, whether we're willing to admit it or not. So, what do you say? Let's have a light lunch and celebrate your good news."

Her chin quivers, but she nods as she returns the packet of tissues. "I think I'd like that."

❈ ❈ ❈

I touch the rim of my sweating soft drink glass to McLane's. "To you and your baby. May you have a safe and healthy pregnancy, and may your baby look just like you."

She chokes on a chuckle, then pats her chest to calm the remnants of a cough.

I sip my drink and glance around the nearly empty restaurant. "I'm not that funny. Nobody gets choked up at my jokes, not even at home."

"It's just that . . . well, never mind." She takes a deep breath and stares at her steaming bowl of chicken soup. "This smells good."

"I'm sure it is—the food in this place is great. You're going to be great, too. I remember pregnancy as the one time—well, the two times—in my life when I ate all I wanted and didn't care if my clothes got snug."

"That does sound nice." She picks up her spoon and stirs the soup.

I slice into my salad, which consists mostly of iceberg lettuce, toma-toes, and boiled eggs. To save on calories, I asked the waitress to skip the dressing, so this dieter's delight is about as appetizing as grass and cardboard. For a second, I'm jealous of the girl across the table. "Your dad—does he live in North Carolina?"

She looks up, her eyes distracted, and smiles. "Did I mention that the other night?"

"It was a hunch. I recognized your accent. I lived in North Carolina once. My father served in the army, so we were stationed at Fort Bragg for a while. I spent my sophomore and junior years at Terry Sanford High School."

McLane snorts softly. "I've heard of that school. Some of my college friends graduated from Terry Sanford."

"I'm surprised the place is still standing. You're so young—"

"Twenty-four's not so young, is it?"

I lift my hand, conceding her point. "What is it they say? Old is always ten years older than me, and young is at least ten years younger. But you're right. Twenty-four isn't so young. I got married at twenty-two. I was twenty-seven, though, when I had Clay, my oldest."

"I'll be twenty-five when this baby's born." She whispers this, as if she can't quite believe it. "Jeff will be twenty-six."

"And when's the baby due?"

She closes her eyes. "June 12, the nurse said. In the summer."

I let out a long, low whistle. "If I were you, I'd plan to have that baby in the Carolinas, where it's cooler. Last summer was our first in Florida. The boys and I sweated like mules for four months."

McLane bends over her soup and avoids my gaze. "I'll cope."

I take a bite of my salad, wondering if I've said something to offend her. Does she think I was implying she wasn't welcome here? Or that she couldn't stand the heat? "I'm sorry to rattle on," I say, cutting another slice of lettuce. "You may want to have the baby near your husband's home. When does his tour end?"

She shakes her head. "No one knows. Things are uncertain over there."

"Um . . . does Jeff want to make a career out of the military?"

"He can do other things." McLane looks at me with defensiveness in her eyes. "Jeff wants to be a teacher when his tour is up. He'd be a good one, too. You should see him with kids—that's what first

attracted me to him. I was walking by and I saw him on a basketball
court, playing with a bunch of kids. He was laughing and cutting up
with them, but then I saw him step between a couple of teenagers who
were in each others' faces and about to fight. He's no coward."

Not sure what has set her off, I lower my voice. "I'm sure he's not.
A coward wouldn't volunteer for Iraq."

As she stares into her soup bowl, she exhales. "Anyway, when I saw
all those kids around Jeff, I knew he was a good guy. Because kids
know. A person who's all wrapped up in himself usually doesn't have
time for kids, you know?"

I take another bite of my salad as her comment strikes home.
Thomas hardly had time for children, even our own. He could play
the part of dutiful father when the situation demanded it, but he
rarely spent time with Bugs or Clay.

"My ex-husband," I confess, "used to think that quality time with
the kids meant sitting at the kitchen counter with his BlackBerry
while the boys ate their dinner. He didn't have a clue where kids were
concerned."

"Does he see your kids much now?"

"They see him . . . in Pine Forest Cemetery." I swallow hard and
shake my head. "Sorry. That sounded awful. Thomas passed away in
July. The divorce was rough, but his death was rough in a different
way. Especially on my boys."

McLane stirs her soup again. "You have a hard time with death . . .
yet you run the funeral home."

I laugh. "It's the last job on earth I ever thought I'd enjoy, but I'm
beginning to think the profession suits me. The medical aspect is fascinating, but the real work comes before and after the funeral. We deal
with the dead, sure, but we deal just as much with the survivors. And
no two situations are alike."

"I was thinking about coming to see you. At the home."

My internal antennae perk up. "At Fairlawn?"

"I was wondering what I'd do if . . . you know, if something happened to Jeff. I don't want to think about it, but my mom died in
March, and I know how hard it was for Dad to deal with the funeral.

Some part of me keeps insisting that it's better to be prepared than to be caught by surprise and have to make hasty decisions."

"That's military thinking," I assure her. "My father drilled that 'hurry up and wait' mind-set into me. My family was early to every event we attended, and we always brought extra food and supplies." I tilt my head as memory softens my voice. "My dad wasn't perfect, but he was always prepared."

A clear spark of interest lights McLane's eyes. "Do you miss him?"

"My dad or my husband?"

She blushes. "Your dad."

I've learned a lot about my father since he's been gone, but McLane doesn't need to know the sordid details. "Dad's been gone six years. Time eases the sense of loss." I spear a chunk of lettuce and wonder at her question. I don't remember mentioning that my dad passed away, but I suppose I did speak of him in the past tense.

I really should turn this conversation in a more hopeful direction. "Now that you know you're pregnant—" I smile across the table— "will you go back to North Carolina? It'd be nice to have family around during those months when you're as big as a bus. Being pregnant isn't the hardest thing in the world, but it's not the easiest, either."

"I'm an only child, so Dad is all that's left of my family."

"Surely Jeff has relatives in the area."

"Not really. He was raised in Virginia by an aunt who has eight kids of her own. In a way, the Marine Corps has become his family."

"Your father, then. You'll probably want his help."

"Dad doesn't know that I'm pregnant . . . and he's not happy with me right now."

I crack a smile. "Not calling home often enough?"

"I wish it were that simple. But don't worry about me, because I'm not alone down here. I came to Mt. Dora because I have a sister in town."

"Really." I drop my hands to my lap and sigh in honest relief. "Is it anyone I know?"

"Actually," McLane says, lifting her gaze, "it's you."

"Hey." Clay turns as Toby Talbott, one of Mt. Dora Middle School's gruesome threesome, slings his backpack over his shoulder and steps away from the lockers.

Clay glances around, almost certain Toby is talking to someone else, but there's no one else in the hall. He looks at Toby. "You talkin' to me?"

"You're Clay, right?"

"Yeah."

"So did you finish your algebra homework in study hall?"

Clay lifts his chin. He and Toby are in the same study hall, so Toby had to have seen Clay working. After all, Clay certainly saw Toby messing around. He and Tyler Henton sat in the back of the room and spent the entire hour launching spitballs at the girls in the front row.

The girls didn't seem to mind, though. Tyler Henton—dark-haired, dark-eyed, and tall—always makes the girls giggle, not complain.

"Yeah, I finished my homework."

"Cool. Can I see it? I'll give it back to you Monday morning."

Clay wets his lips and looks at the sheet of notebook paper sticking out of his algebra book. His mom will probably ask to see it tonight, but he could always do the problems again. In fact, he ought to, because Toby Talbott isn't his friend and probably can't be trusted. Still . . . he's talking to Clay, and that's got to count for something.

Clay slides the assignment from the book and hands it to Toby. The problems are scrawled in Clay's handwriting, but there's no name at the top of the page.

"Sweet." Toby shoves the paper into his backpack, then hoists the bag over his shoulder. "You heading out?"

"Yeah."

"Let's go."

Clay closes his locker and follows Toby out of the corridor and into the sunlight. Tyler Henton and Percy Walker, a thin, chocolate-skinned eighth grader with glasses and short hair, are waiting on the sidewalk, grinning at the bus kids as they stomp aboard the big yellow boxes.

"See you later, suckers!" Tyler calls, swinging his arms like some kind of hip-hop king.

Clay stands still as Percy strafes him with a curious look.

"This is Clay," Toby says, slipping a hand into the pocket of his baggy jeans. "He's cool. He's in study hall, remember?"

"Oh yeah." Toby crosses his arms. "Where do you live, dude?"

Clay points down Lincoln Avenue. "Off Heim Road, just past the railroad tracks."

"Come on, then."

Clay holds his breath as they set out, Tyler and Toby leading, he and Percy following. As they move away from the school, he glances at Toby and wonders why the guy decided to get friendly all of a sudden. Was it just because he needed someone's algebra homework, or did these guys really want to be Clay's friend?

Everyone at school knows about the gruesome threesome. They hang together nearly all the time; rumor has it that they've been tight since first grade. Tyler, the tallest and darkest, has the sort of looks that make girls turn and stare. Toby is more ordinary, like Clay, and Percy is quiet and smart.

Since school started in August, the gruesome threesome has report-edly been the force behind a false fire alarm during homeroom, the blackout in the school cafeteria (and the resulting food fight), and the library computer that kept flashing pictures of Britney Spears that sent the librarians scurrying to pull the plug. Everyone knows the threesome has the brains, brawn, and bravery to pull such stunts off, but so far, no one has been able to prove they did anything.

So they walk the halls of Mt. Dora Middle like conquering heroes . . . and now they are walking with Clay.

He stubs the toe of his sneaker against the sidewalk, just to be sure he isn't dreaming.

"Hey." Tyler turns around, as cool walking backward as he is walking forward. "Percy, about the catacombs—you serious about checking them out?"

"Serious as a snakebite." Percy sniffs, then rubs his nose with his palm. "It's a local legend, but no one wants to talk about it. I think we should expose everything."

"That'd be wicked cool." Tyler cracks his knuckles. "How about tomorrow? Wanna go then?"

Tyler looks at Clay as if Clay is supposed to come, too. But come to what?

Clay forces a laugh. "What are you guys talking about?"

Toby stops on the sidewalk, widens his eyes, and waves his hands like some kind of bogeyman. "Don't tell me you haven't heard the legend of the haunted catacombs."

Clay hasn't, but he isn't about to let on. He laughs and sticks his hands in his pockets. "Of course I've heard of them. They're some kind of graveyard, right?"

"Close," Percy says, frowning at Toby. "I hear there's a crypt down there, but the catacombs aren't haunted. Everything is supposed to be exactly as people left it. Except now everything's dusty."

"What people?" Clay asks.

Tyler jerks his chin at Percy. "Fill in the new guy, will ya?"

"The catacombs," Percy says, shifting his backpack from one shoulder to the other, "is the largest private bomb shelter ever built in the United States. It's buried somewhere around here, probably under an orange grove or something. A bunch of rich families pooled their resources and built it during the Cold War. They swore everyone to secrecy and even stocked a room with guns—you know, in case they had to shoot people who tried to get in without paying."

"Get out." Clay grins at Tyler, convinced he's about to be punked. "What is this, something like a snipe hunt? You planning to take me out in some grove and leave me there?"

"We're not kidding." Percy's eyes darken with seriousness. "My mom says it really happened. She read a thing about it, an article."

Clay stares at Percy. "You'd swear that's true?"

"I can prove it." Percy rubs his nose again. "I'll google the catacombs tonight and print out some pages from the newspaper. The catacombs are somewhere in Mt. Dora, and I think we can find 'em."

"Why hasn't anyone else found them?"

"Oh, they've tried," Toby says. "But they're not us."

"We could find 'em." Tyler grins, then spins on his heel and strikes out again. "Nobody cares about the place but us. We could find it and keep it to ourselves for a while. We could go through all the secret stuff—"

"There's gotta be a Geiger counter," Percy says. "And food, drugs, supplies—"

"And guns," Toby adds. "Don't forget. They had guns and ammunition."

Clay looks down as they walk on. He wouldn't mind exploring a secret bomb shelter, but Toby has to be wrong about the guns.

Doesn't he?

※ ※ ※

I stare at McLane, unable to trust my ears. "Excuse me?"

She lowers her hands to her lap. "I'm sorry to spring it on you, but it's true. I've checked all kinds of records, and I know Mom wouldn't lie to me, not about this. You're my sister. My half sister."

I reach for the edge of the table as the room begins to spin. "That can't be right. I'm an only child."

"I know. You didn't know about me . . . and I can't blame our father for not telling you."

Her words fall like rocks into still water, launching a series of ripples that brush up against the raw places of my heart. Until a few months ago, I considered my father a paragon of virtue. Then Mom told me a few secrets of her own, and I began to see cracks in the sterling facade. I have a feeling I'm about to see more than a crack.

"Maybe—" I turn in my seat so I can brace my back against the wall—"you should start at the beginning."

McLane takes a deep breath and looks up, her gaze barely skimming my face before she lowers her eyes to her stagnant soup bowl. "I knew none of this until this spring, when my mother finally told me the truth. She figured I deserved to know my history."

"Deserved." I repeat the word in a flat voice. What did I do to deserve having my world rocked like this?

"When your father was stationed at Fort Bragg," McLane continues, "he and my mother . . . well, I'm sure you get the picture. I was born in March 1982. I think that's about the time your family was transferred to Virginia. Your father—*our* father—went to work at the Pentagon, right?"

She's speaking English and I understand the words, yet they make no sense. My mother has admitted that Dad was unfaithful at several points in their marriage, but she didn't mention a child. I'm sure she would have . . .

Unless she doesn't know.

I bring my hand to my mouth as my appetite vanishes. "My mother . . . she never said a word."

McLane's brow wrinkles, and something moves in her eyes. "I don't think she knew. My mom said she went out with your father because he told her he was divorced. Later she found out he wasn't, but then he said he was going to leave his wife. She trusted him because by that time she thought she might be pregnant, but when she told him, he wanted her to get an abortion. She refused, so he broke off their relationship and requested a transfer. He got promoted, and my mom got . . . me."

I cross my arms and pointedly look away. "That's illogical. Dad would have gotten into trouble for something like that."

"Only if she reported him. She didn't. She loved him, you see." McLane runs her fingertip over the edge of her napkin as a blush floods her neck. "I've never even seen a picture of our father. Mom got rid of every trace of him when she married my dad."

"Your dad—the man who still lives in North Carolina."

She nods. "He adopted me after he married Mom. I was five when they got married, and I really don't remember him not being around. I might never have known the truth if Mom hadn't told me. I'm glad she told me before she died or . . ." She shrugs. "Well, I don't think Dad would have ever said anything. He's old-fashioned about things like that." Her eyes brim with tears as she stares out the window. "He's old-fashioned about a lot of things."

I know I ought to ask questions to test this unbelievable story, but all I can do is grasp at dangling threads. "Your mom died . . . this past spring? What happened?"

She exhales softly. "Depends on who you ask. Dad insists it was an accident; he won't even consider another possibility. But I know my mom, and I also know she'd just been diagnosed with cervical cancer. I think she ran her car into that bridge on purpose. Dad disagrees, but psychiatrists always think they understand other people better than anyone else. Besides, he wasn't there when Mom told me about Nolan Norris."

I cringe when she says my father's name, and if words were objects, I would snatch his name from her mouth. He was *my* father; I was his only daughter, so how can she be telling the truth? I feel . . . violated. As if someone has ripped my father's face out of my favorite family photos and laid claim to my personal past.

"How do you know this?" My tone is no longer friendly. "How do you know she didn't sleep with someone else and blame my father for her pregnancy?"

McLane's voice softens, but her expression remains resolute. "Looking at you, it's like looking in a mirror. Besides, my mother wasn't the type to sleep around. I saw something in her eyes that day. In giving me the truth about my father, I think she was tying up loose ends. I think she was telling me good-bye."

I cover my mouth with my hand, overcome with feelings and thoughts I can't begin to express. This young woman has experienced enough heartbreak in the last few months to devastate most people, but so have I.

I don't want another heartache. I don't want to know that I have another relative. I don't want to be bound to more tragedy even by heartstrings. I don't need more grief in my life, and I don't need a sister.

A herd of emotions charges toward me, but the one leading the pack is anger. How *could* my father put me in this position? Four months ago I learned he was unfaithful, and now I've learned he was also dishonorable. What sort of man cheats on his wife and abandons a pregnant woman? And how could he tell her to get an abortion? My father used to go to church with us every Sunday. I thought he believed that human life is precious and created in the image of God.

Who *was* my father?

Abruptly, I push away from the table. "I have to go." I fumble for my purse, then yank a ten from my wallet and drop it by my plate. "Sorry to eat and run, but Clay will be coming home soon. I ought to be there."

The excuse is as weak as pale tea, but McLane seems to understand. Her hand crosses the table, trespassing into my space, and catches my fingers. "I know this is crazy, but I didn't know any better way to tell you. Despite the shock of it all, I was glad to learn about you. You're the reason I came to Mt. Dora . . . and you're the sister I always wanted."

I can't look at her face. Instead I stare at her hands, at her long fingers, which are amazingly like mine. Anyone walking by might assume we were sisters because we have the same hands, the same pale arms, the same pointed chins and wide foreheads.

But this woman acquired those features dishonestly.

I stand up so forcefully that my chair nearly topples backward. "Congratulations on the baby," I whisper, finally daring to meet her eyes which, unlike mine, are brown. "I'm sorry, but I need some time . . . to think about this."

"I understand. Really, I do."

I bite my lip and shove the money toward her. "That should cover everything. I have to go home."

I can't go home, not like this. McLane's news has left me tongue-tied, short of breath, and red-faced. Though anyone else might glance at me and assume I was having a hot flash, Clay, Bugs, and Gerald would know I've been rattled to the core.

Uncertain of where to go, I drive down familiar streets until I'm halfway home. Instead of heading to Fairlawn, however, I follow McDonald Street until it dead ends at Pine Forest Cemetery.

I put the van in park and stare at the gate in the white picket fence. Beyond the gate, in neat rows, lie dozens of rectangular brass markers, each adorned with a name and a linked pair of dates. Nothing else. Nothing to tell a curious passerby what sort of person lies beneath the thick green sod.

My father lies at rest in Arlington National Cemetery, his grave marked by a plaque and a simple white cross. None of the tourists who visit that site will know that one of the brave soldiers buried there was an unfaithful cad.

I drape my arms over the steering wheel and lower my head. Why do the dead get to go to their eternal rest without cleaning up the mess they've left behind? My father is responsible for more of a muddle than either Mother or I realized, and now I have to break the news to the rest of the family.

How do I tell Mother that my father has another daughter? I know Mom wanted more than one child, but she never conceived again. Yet McLane wears a face like mine, she has my hands, and she's not my mother's daughter.

After Mom told me that Dad was an expert lothario, all my memories of Dad and his pretty secretaries took on a new and sinister significance. I thought of the many nights he was away "training" in some secret location. I remember Mother being tense and upset on those occasions, but I always assumed she was worried about his safety.

She *was* worried . . . but not about his being injured in a training exercise. My mother worried that Dad would find someone else and never come home again.

This news will send Mother to bed with a migraine.

And my boys—how in the world do I explain that girl to my children? *Sorry for the late notice, kids, but because your grandfather had a little problem with lust, this lady is your aunt.*

Clay will be confused, but he's savvy enough to realize that his grandmother, who has no children but me, was Grandpa's only wife. If McLane were older than me, Clay might assume Grandpa had a wife before he married my mother, but I don't see how Clay can look at that girl's youthful face and come up with any explanation but the truth.

And the truth, as they say, sometimes hurts.

Bugs may accept that my father had a daughter I didn't know about, but one day he'll wonder how that could happen. Then he'll saunter into my room and want to know why I expect him to exercise self-control when his grandfather, the much-acclaimed general, obviously did not.

A crow flaps into a sprawling live oak near the gate, drawing my attention. He studies me with brilliant black eyes, then tips his head back in some sort of chortling avian laugh.

Smart-aleck bird.

I fail to see any humor in this situation. I thought my family was finished with calamity. I hoped we might have a few months, even years, of smooth sailing, but life has just dropped me on another land mine.

With an elbow propped in my open window, I lift my gaze past the tree and study the cloudless blue sky. *Father, you didn't do this; did you?*

Like a voice on the wind, my own words come back to mock me: *Honey, God has something to do with everything, whether we're willing to admit it or not.*

I snort softly and tuck my head back inside the van. What a mess I am—willing to preach to McLane about God's sovereignty, yet unwilling to accept it myself. The girl will be sorry she ever came to me for advice, but I told her the truth.

Like a sister should.

✦✦✦ ✦✦✦ ✦✦✦

McLane locks her car door, then tosses the end of her wrap over her shoulder and makes her way toward the Biddle House. The private walkway is whiter than the city sidewalk, bleached by years of sun and rain. Several corners are crumbling, with pebbles beginning to show beneath the concrete casing.

She shivers beneath her light wool mantle. The sun is still shining, but there's a bite in the wind that brushes her face and tugs at the flowing fronds of the palm in the corner of the lot.

She glances around and wonders how many of the Hatters are still inside. Hard to tell, since several of them don't drive and either are dropped off or walk from their nearby homes.

Maybe she can slip inside without attracting attention. She loves the old ladies, but she'd rather not talk to them now. She doesn't want to talk to anyone in this condition.

McLane steps onto the small porch, tries the door, and finds it unlocked. She winces as the heavy door slams behind her, then ducks and hurries toward the steps. None of the Hatters are near the foyer, so she might make it up to her apartment without any of them noticing her watery eyes.

She kicks off her pumps and ascends the wooden staircase without making a sound. She turns on the landing and glances at the final rise. The coast is clear.

She's nearly to her door when a male voice says, "McLane! How goes the job search?"

She sniffs, wipes a trace of wetness from her cheek, and turns.

Ryan Evans, the other tenant, stands in his doorway, a potted geranium in his gloved hands.

She gives him the brightest smile she can muster. "Oh! I found a job."

"Really? Where?"

"Um, the law firm right down the street."

Ryan props the geranium on his hip and pulls off his gardening gloves. "Lawson, Bridges, and Sladen? That the one?"

She nods.

"Good. They're nice folks."

"They seem to be."

"Well, girl, you seem to be doing okay." He squints at her and frowns. "Maybe I spoke too soon—you look upset."

McLane presses her lips together in an effort to appear determined, but the gesture only makes her chin quiver. "I'm okay. It's just . . ."

"You can tell me." In one smooth motion, Ryan sets the geranium on the floor and sweeps toward her. "I don't gossip and the biddies are all downstairs."

Under his sympathetic gaze, the tears she has been holding in break forth in a noisy deluge. In the midst of her streaming sorrow, she leans against the wall and manages to blubber a few syllables that vaguely resemble words. "It's . . . it's Jen-Jennifer. I've up-upset her something aw-awful."

"Jennifer Graham?" Ryan makes a face as he taps his chin with his index finger. "Don't you worry about a thing. Whatever happened, Jen's not the type to hold a grudge."

"You know her that . . . that well?"

"Honey, I *work* for her. She was a little stiff when she first came to town, but she's warmed right up."

McLane sniffs again. "*Stiff*—that's a good word to describe how she looked when she left me."

"Well, she's from up north, bless her heart. It's going to take her a while to loosen up."

"Oh." McLane attempts a small smile. "Okay. You know her better than I do."

Ryan holds up a pair of crossed fingers. "Jen and I are like this. Fairlawn is always open to me because I do hair and makeup whenever they have a client. I was afraid they wouldn't need me once Jen took over, but I guess they appreciate my artistry."

McLane tries to smile, but her lips only wobble uncertainly.

Ryan shakes his head. "Come on, honey. It can't be that bad."

"Yes, it can."

"What kind of fight did you and Jen have?"

"It wasn't a fight, exactly." Her eyes well up again. "It's something else, and I've made it worse because . . . I'm pregnant."

Ryan steps back, mouth agape. "Why, that's amazingly great! Have you told your husband? Have you told the biddies?"

"I haven't had a chance. I just heard the news when I saw Jen."

Ryan's smile fades into a frown. "You and Jen didn't argue over the baby, did you? Because that makes no sense."

"The baby has nothing to do with Jen and me, and I'm sure you're right about things blowing over. I'll send Jeff my news right away."

"He'll be thrilled." Ryan squeezes her arm. "And the Hatters are going to have kittens when you tell them the news. Your baby will have a dozen grannies, so get ready for a boatload of booties!"

Though dazed and exhausted, somehow McLane manages to laugh. "I hope you're right."

10

"It's been so distressing, so distressing." Russell Solan rubs at a red spot on his wrist and refuses to meet Gerald's eye. "Buddy is failing so fast. He gets weaker every day, and it's ripping my heart out."

Russell showed up at Fairlawn's front door a few minutes after nine. Jennifer, still in her robe, sent Gerald down to take care of him, so Gerald ushered the old man into the south chapel and offered him a cup of coffee. Russell didn't want coffee; he wanted to make arrangements for Buddy. Gerald handed the client the standard intake form and several brochures, then left him alone while he went upstairs and downed a cup of java.

Now Gerald sits in a wing chair, resting his elbows on his knees. In the gentlest voice he can manage, he presses Russell for more information. "What does the doctor say? How long does Buddy have?"

Russell rolls his eyes toward the ceiling. "What do doctors know? They tell me he could slip away at any time, or he could snap out of it and bounce back to his old self. Not that he's a young pup, you know—he's up in years, and we all know it."

Gerald laughs softly. "I do understand. Seems like I feel a new ache every day."

Russell stops rubbing his wrist long enough to meet Gerald's gaze. "I'd like to think they're right about the rebounding, but I look in Buddy's eyes and know that we've reached the end. He's been trying to find a way to tell me good-bye—" He stops when a shrill ring cuts into the conversation. Lifting a finger, Russell takes a cell phone from his pocket. "Hello?"

Gerald leans back in his chair to give his client some privacy. He's seen Russell Solan around town, but they've never been formally introduced. He's also heard people talk about Russell and Buddy, but Gerald can't remember ever seeing Russell's brother. The man must be an invalid, maybe a shut-in of some kind. If he's older than Russell, it makes sense that he'd be confined at home, because Russell looks like he's as old as the Sphinx.

Russell clicks off the phone, then turns sorrowful eyes on Gerald. "My wife's with Buddy now because I could never forgive myself if he died all alone. So if we can hurry and get this settled, I can go back home and sit with him."

"I see." Gerald pulls a laminated sheet from his notebook and slides it across the coffee table. "For prearranged funerals we usually order caskets, but if a sudden need arises, you can choose a resting vessel from our display room. These—" he motions to the page—"are standard models in wood and metal."

When Russell doesn't respond, Gerald straightens and folds his hands. "If I had some idea of your budget, I might be able to guide you in your decision. Does Buddy have an insurance policy to cover burial expenses?"

Russell looks up, confusion in his eyes. "I never heard of such a thing."

"Never heard of—well, then." Gerald forces a smile. "No insurance, no problem. There's, um, the standard Social Security death benefit to the surviving spouse. Was Buddy married?"

Russell sits back in his chair, a frown puckering the skin between his eyes into deep ridges. "I don't know if you'd call it that, exactly."

Gerald averts his eyes, realizing that he's ventured into unconventional territory. Since he doesn't know Russell or Buddy, maybe he'd better let the client explain the situation. "Mr. Solan," he says, lightly tapping the casket brochures on the table, "why don't you tell me how I can help you."

Russell dabs at his nose with his handkerchief. "Well, I reckon I'll need one of those things, and I'll spare no expense." He draws the laminated page closer and frowns at the images. "I'm not sure these are the right size."

Gerald presses his hands together. "We can order caskets of varying sizes, but you'd be surprised how simple it is to adjust the fit. How big is Buddy?"

Like a spring-fed well, Russell's eyes fill with water again. "Weighs close to three hundred pounds. A big boy."

Gerald draws a deep breath and remembers the time he had to purchase a piano crate to bury another man of considerable girth. "Is he of average height?"

After Russell blows his nose, he flexes his right hand in midair, as if he's measuring a child. His hand stops just below his chin. "This ain't workin'. You got a tape measure?"

Gerald stands and moves into the office, where he takes a tape measure from a drawer. He returns and hands it to his client, then watches, mystified, as Russell stands up, extends the tape, and lowers the edge to the floor, measuring the distance between the floor and his hip. "I'd say Buddy's about thirty-four inches at the shoulder."

Gerald brings his hand to his mouth and coughs. Russell has just described a human bowling ball. It's possible, of course, that Buddy is a genetic anomaly, but it's more likely that Russell is off his medication. "Mr. Solan," he says, sitting down, "what sort of person is your brother?"

Russell sinks to the sofa. "Who said he was my brother?"

Gerald points to the intake form. "You did. Right here, under client's name, you wrote Buddy Solan."

"That's what the vet always writes on his pill jars."

"Excuse me?"

"He's a mastiff, Mr. Huffman. The king of dogs."

"A . . . dog."

Russell nods. "Buddy's been with me thirteen years, which is a ripe old age for one of the big guys. Maybe you haven't heard, but he put this town on the map about ten years ago. He's a celebrity, so when he goes, I want a full-course funeral, the sort of service Buddy deserves."

Gerald rubs his chin. How does he tell a grieving man that what he wants is simply not possible? "Most people cremate their pets these days. We don't have a crematorium at Fairlawn, but there's one in Apopka, with a real nice pet cemetery."

"But I don't want Buddy buried in Apopka; he's a local dog. He's lived in Mt. Dora longer than you. This is his *home*."

Gerald draws a deep breath and considers the flash of fire in Russell's eye. Obviously this is not a time for negotiation. A man under duress is not at his most reasonable. He gathers up the materials on the coffee table. "Tell you what—I'll do some checking around and see what we can do for you. If Buddy expires, give me a call right away. I promise we won't leave you hanging."

Russell extends both hands, his eyes red-rimmed and grateful. "Thank you, Mr. Huffman."

"Call me Gerald. And know that I once loved a dog, too."

❧❧❧ ❧❧❧ ❧❧❧

"Yes, Mom, things are fine." I tilt the telephone away from my mouth, half-afraid my mother will sense the dread in my expression. "The boys are good, Gerald is great, and I'm making progress with my schoolwork. How are you and the Hatters getting along?"

My mother loves to talk about the activities of her Red Hat chapter, but she also loves to know what's going on in my life.

"What's wrong?" she asks. "You don't sound like yourself."

Her maternal instincts are razor sharp, so even though we're separated by 844 miles, I can feel her boring into my brain. I close my eyes, and my mind fills with the image of my mother as a cockroach in pink curlers, antennae waving toward the phone.

"Who would you like me to sound like?"

She ignores my pitiful attempt to redirect the conversation. "Are you sick? Have you been taking vitamins?"

"I'm fine. I'm just a little tired; that's all."

"You should take the boys to a movie or something. Get out of that stuffy old house."

"Maybe." I shift into a more comfortable position on the sofa, knowing I may be here awhile. Mom usually checks in on Saturday, and we often talk for more than an hour.

"So," she says over the rattle of dishes in the background, "what's new in Mt. Metropolis?"

"Very funny." I glance down the hall to be sure Clay's bedroom door is closed. "I think Clay might have finally made a few friends. I saw him walking home with some boys yesterday."

"Nice boys?"

"How should I know? He didn't bring them home."

"Well, it's about time those kids welcomed him."

"You know how it is—kids are really into cliques at that age."

"Clay will do fine. And how's my baby Bugs?"

"He's good." I glance into the kitchen, where Bugs is pounding restorative clay and helping Gerald make a nose. I don't know whether the nose is for practice or for a prospective client, and I don't want to ask.

"How are the ladies getting on at the Biddle House?"

"Funny you should bring that up," I say, easing into a topic I can't avoid forever. "The Biddle House has a new tenant."

"Who?" I can almost see the antennae waving again.

"A young woman from North Carolina. Her husband's a marine in Iraq."

"What unit is he with?" My mother, the military wife, *would* want to know every detail.

"I'm not sure."

"I can't believe you didn't ask. My Hatter chapter is sending care packages to men in the Marine Air Control Group. Who knows, we might be sending things to this girl's husband."

"Maybe." I clear my throat. "Anyway, McLane seems to be finding her way around town." *She certainly found her way to me.*

"What kind of name is McLane?"

"I don't know, Mom; it's a name. Are you going to let me tell this story?"

"Ex-*cuuuuse* me. Carry on."

"Thanks." I draw a deep breath, then smile at Bugs, who is holding up a nose the size of my fist. If he makes one any bigger, I can send it to Mount Rushmore. "I met McLane at Lydia's book club—"

"Since when does Lydia have a book club?"

"Mom."

"Sorry."

"Anyway, I saw her at Daniel's office yesterday—he's hired her to be his receptionist."

"How are you and Daniel getting along?"

I lift my gaze to the ceiling and count to three. A conversation with my mother can be as exhausting as a heated battle of Ping-Pong.

"You and Daniel must be getting along fine," she says, sighing. "Or you wouldn't have gone to his office. So you saw this girl there?"

"Right. Then I saw her outside, and she looked positively shell-shocked. I found out why—she's pregnant."

Mother whistles. "And how long has her husband been overseas?"

"Not long." I hurry to allay my mother's suspicions. "They're newly-weds, and apparently they weren't planning on having a baby so soon. McLane was pretty shaken up by the news."

"She'll be okay. I'm sure her family will step in and help her out."

"That's just it—she's pretty much by herself down here. Her mother passed away a few months ago, and apparently she and her dad don't get along. So she's all alone."

"I wouldn't say that. She has you, doesn't she?"

For an instant I am speechless with surprise. I'm almost convinced Mother has somehow insinuated herself into the curves and recesses of my brain, absorbing all the facts I'm not ready to accept . . . or share.

"I know you," Mom continues, "and you have to remember how hard it was when we had to move every time your father was reas-signed. You understand, so you're the perfect person to help this young military wife."

"I don't know," I say. "Things are pretty hectic around here. I've got the boys to look after and school. Plus, I've been helping Gerald with every client. He's letting me do more and more—"

"Everybody has twenty-four hours in a day," Mom insists. "How hard would it be to call that girl and see if she needs anything? Take her to lunch every couple of weeks. Invite her to your church. It's not like anyone expects you to *adopt* the woman."

"No." I look toward the window, where the late morning sun is gilding the stained glass diamond in Fairlawn's turret. "No one's asking that." *Yet.*

"Then help her out. It's the Christian thing to do."

"Mom . . ." I close my eyes and lie back on the sofa, inching closer to the truth. "McLane—this girl—told me a really sad story about her family. Unfortunately, she was the product of an affair between her mother and a married man. When her mother refused to have an abortion, the man abandoned them and moved away."

Some women might have a change of heart after hearing that news but not my mother. "That girl is not responsible for what her gutless father did," she says, indignation rippling through her voice. "I'm surprised at you, Jen, for thinking she could be blamed for that."

"I didn't blame her for anything."

"That's what you were implying. Otherwise, why bring it up?"

Why, indeed? I sigh into the phone. "Maybe you're right. Maybe I should help her out."

"You'll be glad you did. You know what the Lord said—when you do it for one of the least of these my brothers and sisters, you are doing it for me."

"Yeah, I know." Guilt lands like a heavy arm across my shoulders.

"Now," Mom says, getting down to business, "let's talk about Thanksgiving. When do you want me to fly in—Tuesday or Wednesday? I won't be able to stay long because I have to be back for our church's Christmas kickoff the next weekend."

The long arm of guilt gives my shoulders a squeeze. Thanksgiving is coming . . . and McLane will be alone on the holiday. Without family, without her husband.

And she'll be thinking of me.

"Jen?" Mom's voice is sharper now. "You still there?"

"I'm here. I was thinking . . . maybe I should invite McLane to dinner."

"That'd be nice, hon. You'll set a good example for the boys, too."

I almost snort into the phone. Bringing my mom and McLane together might be a good example of what happens when gunpowder and fire get too close.

But if Mom is only going to pop in and out, I might not have to tell her about McLane's connection to our family. Mother is too much of a lady to publicly mention the unfortunate circumstances of McLane's conception, so I might be able to entertain my mother and my guest at the same dinner without divulging the entire truth . . .

As long as Mom leaves town in a hurry.

"Doesn't matter," I tell her. "Come whenever you can."

❄❄ ❄❄ ❄❄

Before my Saturday—and my noble intentions—can slip away, I drive to Baker Street, park at the curb, and walk over the narrow sidewalk that leads to the Biddle House. Three separate buzzers have been installed by the front door, and they're all labeled.

My finger has barely left the button marked "M. Larson" when the door opens and Ruby Masters, one of Mt. Dora's most effusive Hatters and a friend of Mother's, pulls me into the foyer. "Jennifer Graham, what are you doing out on the stoop? Come on in and have a seat in the parlor."

"Thanks, but I came to see McLane."

"And it'll take her ten minutes to come down all those steps. Take a look around. We've done a lot since your mother went back to Virginia."

Mom spent less than two months with these Hatters, but apparently she made a lasting impression. As Ruby leads me into the front room, I have to admit the ladies have done a fabulous job with the house. The old wallpaper has been replaced with a golden paint that reminds me of Tuscany, and the antique furniture has given way to a sofa that feels as supple as soft butter.

"This is a lovely room." I clasp my hands and can't help noticing that a fire blazes in the fireplace even though it's seventy degrees out-side. "So . . . cozy."

"The kitchen is spectacular. Mitch Wilkerson—you remember him, don't you? Ginger Sue's son?"

I nod, wincing at the memory of how much I paid Mitch Wilker-son to install a new back porch at Fairlawn.

"Mitch ripped out all the old cabinets and put in new. There's a new granite countertop and new appliances."

I'm delivered from enduring the complete tour when McLane appears in the parlor doorway. Her eyes widen when she sees me, so I ask Ruby to excuse me and rush over to meet her.

"Jennifer?" McLane asks. "*You* rang for me?"

"I did." I keep my voice low. "I wanted to apologize for leaving so abruptly yesterday."

"That's okay. I—"

"It wasn't okay." I reach out and take her hand. "Yes, your news was a lot to absorb, and I could never have imagined anything like your story. But now that I know who you are, I . . . I don't want you to spend Thanksgiving alone. I want you to join my family at Fairlawn."

She gives me a slow smile, then bites her lower lip in an expression I recognize as one of my own. "Are you sure about this? I don't want to pressure you."

"I wouldn't be here if I weren't sure. You're my half sister. I'm not sure exactly what that means, but I suppose I should find out."

McLane gives me a teary smile and opens her arms.

I hesitantly step forward and pat her on the back as she clings to me like a shadow.

A moment later, I hear clucks of approval from Ruby Masters and two other Hatters who have crept in from the kitchen.

"You're *sisters*?" Ruby says, a glint of wonder in her eyes. "Imagine that!"

I stifle a groan as McLane releases me and we turn to face the Hat-ters. I had hoped to keep this new relationship secret for a while, but now that the Hatters know . . .

I might as well take out an ad in the paper.

I am less than a mile from Fairlawn when the enormity of what I've done hits me so hard I slam on the brakes and slide to a stop beside a pair of boys on bicycles. Fortunately, I'm the only vehicle on the road.

The kids gape at me as if they're afraid I'm going to scold them for something, so I wave them on and wait until they're at least twenty yards down the street before I ease the van back into motion.

I am such a fool. I have invited McLane to Thanksgiving dinner where my highly intuitive mother will be joining us. I embraced her and called her my half sister in front of three Red Hatters who know Mom . . . and who will be thrilled to hear she's in town. They'll call or come by the house before the turkey gets cold.

Was I momentarily *insane* when I thought I could manage Mom and McLane at the same dinner table?

I turn into the driveway, my ears filling with the pop and crackle of the gravel beneath the van's tires. Just a few months ago, Mom told me that she cried at Dad's funeral not out of loss but out of relief. Her days of worrying about him are over now, but I'll bring all those feelings back if I tell her why McLane Larson came to Mt. Dora.

So why not let her come down and enjoy Thanksgiving in blissful ignorance? Why should I discuss the past when I know McLane's story will hurt her?

McLane would remain quiet, I'm sure. But there are at least three Hatters who know our secret. And while I'm not certain about this, I think one of the Hatter bylaws has something to do with never divulging a confidence to one person when you can share it with two.

I could unplug the phones on Thanksgiving Day and maybe hang a Closed sign on the front door. I could book Mom's flight home on Thursday night and say that I want her to be well rested for her church's big Christmas kickoff. Maybe I could start a rumor that everyone at Fairlawn has come down with a highly communicable disease. Are people still frightened by typhoid?

I put the van in park at the end of the drive and close my eyes. I'm not sure this is a righteous prayer, but I ask God to show me how to conceal McLane's past from Mom forever.

My foot hasn't hit the ground before I realize I can't hide the truth. Not from Mom, not from my family. They deserve to know about our connection, and they need to hear the story from me.

A warm and beefy aroma drifts down the stairs when I open the front door. "I don't care what that is," I call, heading up the staircase. "If it's dinner, I'll eat it."

Gerald grins at me as I walk into the kitchen. The boys are setting the table, and Gerald has heated a family-size tray of Salisbury steaks and whipped up a bowl of mashed potatoes. A basket contains something covered with a red and white dish towel. When I peek inside, I discover that he's baked a can of refrigerated crescent rolls.

Gerald's cooking isn't like my mother's, but packaged entrees and refrigerator rolls are better than pizza five times a week.

"I was beginning to wonder if I should send out a search party," Gerald says, glancing at the clock. "I was afraid you'd had car trouble or something."

"Nothing like that." I drop my purse on top of the dishwasher and look around. "Anything I can do?"

Gerald smiles at Bugs. "We've got everything under control."

Grateful for anything I don't have to cook, I pull out the chair at the foot of the table while Gerald sits at the head. Clay hands me a glass of iced tea and sets cups of milk in front of his place and Bugs's.

When we have all taken our seats, Gerald bows his head and thanks the Lord for the day and the meal.

After we chime in with amens, three pairs of arms reach for food.

"Hey!" Bugs grimaces when Clay snags the bread basket first. "Don't be such a grabber."

"Look who's talking." Clay smirks as he takes two rolls from the basket, then slides it toward his brother.

I know I ought to reprimand him for his smarmy attitude, but I have more pressing matters on my mind.

Gerald spears a slice of steak lurking beneath the gelatinous gravy and sets it next to one of Clay's rolls. "Be sure to spoon out some of that juice over your potatoes. It'll liven 'em right up."

I help Bugs get a piece of steak, too, and cut it into small pieces. "What'd you guys do while I was out?"

Bugs stabs a bite of meat and pops it into his mouth before saying, "Miss Lydia has a gerbil at her house."

"Don't talk with your mouth full. A gerbil? Did you walk down to see it?"

Bugs makes a point of swallowing. "It's gonna have babies. We get to see 'em."

"Oh my." I give Gerald a look. Are he and Lydia trying to teach my innocent one about biological reproduction?

Gerald shakes his head, wordlessly telling me not to be concerned.

I'm not sure I understand what happened this afternoon, but I'll ask for details after dinner. I turn to Clay. "What did you do today? By the way, did you get that solo you wanted in the school choir?"

He sinks lower in his chair. "I didn't try out."

"Why not? You have a good voice."

He lifts his hand, blocking my view of his eyes. "Can we just forget about it?"

I'm bewildered, but Bugs provides an answer: "He sings like a girl!"

Clay scowls.

Bugs lifts his chin and begins to howl like a crazed soprano, a high-pitched assault that brings Skeeter trotting into the kitchen. The dog sits next to me and lifts his ears.

I'm pretty sure Clay is kicking Bugs under the table when I begin to cut my own sad slice of steak. "That's enough, boys. Clay, you shouldn't be ashamed of your talent. Your father always said his singing improved after his voice changed. Yours will change soon, and you'll be comfortable with it in no time. Isn't that right, Gerald?"

"Right. Now you boys eat up and take another piece of steak, or Skeeter's belly's going to bust from too many leftovers tonight."

I pause as three heads bend over three plates. They're intent on eating, so maybe this is a good time. I lower my fork so I can concentrate on their reactions. "You know what? The other day I made a new friend."

No reaction, unless Bugs's snatch of another crescent roll counts for something.

"This lady and I started talking, and we learned that we're related. We're half sisters."

The boys are still focused on their food, but Gerald lifts his head, his attention trained on me. "A half sister?"

"Yes," I say, using the same voice I'd employ to report on the weather. "McLane Larson. She's new in town, so I don't know if you've met her. But you will. I'm going to invite her to dinner sometime."

Bugs stabs a huge bite of meat, then holds his fork upside down and eyes me over the tips of the tines. "Does this mean I have a new grandma?"

"No, honey, you only have one grandma because your dad's mother has passed away. McLane is . . . well, she'd be your aunt."

Clay crinkles his nose. "Is she a half aunt?"

"I'm not sure there is such a thing."

"If she's a half," Bugs says, "does that mean she's short?"

"She's not short. She's of average height."

"So do I have to call her Aunt Mc—what's her name again?" Clay asks.

"McLane. And you don't *have* to call her that, but I think she'd like it if you did. Anyway, I'd like to get to know her better. Maybe you would, too."

I watch Clay and search for signs of comprehension. He's become an enigma to me lately; he keeps his feelings so tightly wrapped that I worry about him exploding. Sometimes he rides his bike down to the cemetery and talks to his father. I've driven by and seen him sitting cross-legged at the edge of the grave, one hand supporting his head while he gestures with the other. At those times I'd give my right arm to be able to hear what he's saying.

"Did you go out today?" I ask, watching Clay. "Did you ride your bike very far?"

He shrugs. "I went riding, yeah."

"To the cemetery?"

"Just around. I was looking for some friends. Didn't find 'em."

I nod, inwardly relieved. *Friends*—what a lovely word. I'm so glad Clay has made some, even if he couldn't find them today. "Speaking of friends, I'd like McLane to join us for Thanksgiving. What do you all think of the idea?"

Bugs grins. "Okay."

Clay runs his roll along a smear of gravy. "I don't care."

Gerald looks at me with something like sympathy in his eyes. "Isn't life surprising?" he says, his words heavy with meaning. "Sometimes things are not at all what they seem."

⚜ ⚜ ⚜

Curled in the center of my bed, I study photos featuring reproductive organs of a desiccated female cadaver. The uterus, I learn, lies on the bladder, so when the bladder is empty the uterine body is anteflexed, but when the bladder is distended the uterus may become retroflexed.

I'm not quite sure what those terms mean, but both conditions sound painful. I highlight the unfamiliar words, then write *define?* in the margin. I'm about to turn the page, but my eye lingers on a picture of the uterus.

At this moment, that girl at the Biddle House has a baby growing in her uterus . . . my niece or nephew. The child sheltered within her young body shares my DNA, my heritage, part of my past. Now that McLane and I have met, we may well share a future.

Her son or daughter will be the closest thing I have to another child of my own. With Thomas gone and me approaching forty, I'm not likely to have another baby.

The thought brings tears to my eyes, and for a moment I'm genuinely jealous of my half sister: so young, so pretty, so pregnant with possibility. The world is opening before her while I stand on the back slope, breathless and tired.

But that's crazy. God has a purpose for everything, and he's probably brought us together so I can help her. I have experience she might need. I grew up as a military brat. I'm a mother and, in a sense, a widow. My small store of wisdom has been hard-won, but McLane is going to need it.

Because she's my sister.

The realization crashes into me like a runaway toddler. I have a sister. A girl who came from miles away to know me. A young woman who risked a new start in a strange town because she wanted to be near *me*.

As a kid, I wanted a sister so badly that I begged Mom to buy me the biggest doll she could find. She finally found this ungainly doll I named Donna, and Donna and I went everywhere together. Mom made play clothes for me and matching outfits for Donna, and one day I cried because I'd outgrown my Donna dress, but she hadn't outgrown hers.

I don't need a Donna doll anymore. I have a living, flesh-and-blood sister. And a niece or nephew on the way.

When a surge of excitement warms my blood, I tip my head back and laugh. If Jeffrey Larson—I have a brother-in-law!—is detained overseas, by this time next year I'll be diapering a baby and telling Bugs and Clay to be quiet so Aunt McLane can sing a lullaby. . . .

I hug my pillow as my eyes fill with nostalgic tears. I will never have daughters, and my children's infant days are long gone. But I may yet know the pleasure of carrying a baby up the Fairlawn staircase.

Though McLane and I don't share the same memories, dozens of studies have demonstrated that genetics accounts for remarkable similarities between siblings raised apart. McLane and I share DNA, and that's a powerful link.

I have a sister. A charming young woman who has my father's eyes. Though my hair is dark brown, Bugs has red hair, and like McLane, he got it from my father.

I have a sister who came to Mt. Dora not because the town was charming or picturesque or ripe with employment opportunities. She came to Mt. Dora to be near me.

I am touched . . . because God has finally sent me a sister. So I am going to do all I can to care for McLane and her unborn baby.

I'm startled when Bugs shuffles into my room. In a sleepy voice, he asks if I've seen Skeeter.

I push my anatomy book aside. "Hey, kiddo. I thought you were asleep."

"Not without Skeeter."

"Well, have you checked the west chapel? Sometimes he likes to nap in there."

Bugs walks closer and squints at me. "You crying, Mom?"

Lately we've all been sensitive to the sight of tears. Thomas has been gone four months, but thoughts of him still hover at the edges of our minds.

But tonight I'm not crying over Thomas.

"I'm okay, sweetie." I dash the wetness from my lashes and hold out my arms for a hug.

Bugs steps into my arms and slips his hands around my neck; then he leans back to peer into my eyes. "You sure you're okay?"

I laugh. How many times has he heard that question from me? I run my fingertip over the soft curve of his cheek. "You know what? I was sitting here thinking about babies, and I realized I'm probably never going to have another one. That made me a little sad."

"Why would you need another baby?"

"I don't *need* one. But babies are nice because they grow up into fine boys like you."

Bugs tilts his head. "But you already have me."

"I know. And I'm so glad I do." I give him another hug, feel the response from his sturdy arms, and send him off to search for the dog. While I listen to the shush-shush of his footed pajamas on the wooden floor, I lower my head and weep in a simple overflow of emotion.

Maybe it's hormones.

11

Gerald missed church this morning. Pauline Danvers, an elderly lady who lived on Overlook Drive, passed away in the night and now lies downstairs in our preparation room. Gerald stayed at Fairlawn to begin the embalming.

After church and a quick lunch at Burger King, I leave the boys at home with Gerald and make plans to drive to the Biddle House.

Before leaving, I check to see if Gerald needs my help, but all he asks is that I make a note on the calendar—Mrs. Danvers's funeral will be held Tuesday afternoon at two.

"Promises to be one of our smaller affairs," Gerald calls as I move toward the office. "Though Pauline was once one of the most respected women in town, I think most of her kin have died off or moved away. She didn't get out much in her latter years, except to go to church. At St. Marks, they said you could set your watch by her."

The thought of a sparsely attended funeral is always a little sad, but I'm pleased we're picking up business from some of the town's blue bloods.

A welcome chill lies in the breeze that strikes my cheek as I drive toward the center of town. Florida's winter, I've discovered, is unbelievably consistent—sunshine, sunshine, and more sunshine, with only the occasional shower or cold snap to break the monotony.

Because I have two drawers stuffed with wool sweaters, I'm hoping for at least a few days of atypical weather.

I lock the van and glance around before heading toward the Biddle House. This is a quiet street, a couple of blocks away from the storefronts that draw tourists year-round. Most of the houses are white stucco with painted shutters. Several have striped awnings that shade wide front porches, relics of a time when neighbors visited after supper and called out to passersby.

I slide my hands into my pockets and wait for an approaching BMW to pass. As I give the driver a go-ahead smile, I notice a silver Lexus parked kitty-corner to the Biddle House. A car on the street is no big deal, but there's a man inside, a man who's just sitting, the brim of his ball cap dipping as if he's nodding to music while one hand thumps the back of the empty passenger seat. Is he waiting for someone? Maybe he's come to pick up one of the Hatters who stopped by the house for lunch.

I squint at the Lexus and spot the Hertz sticker near the license plate. The car is a rental, which means the guy's either driving a loaner or he's not from around here.

An inner alarm clangs, and I have to suppress a laugh. I must be feeling at home in Mt. Dora because already I'm as nosy as the folks who've lived here fifty years.

When the BMW has coasted by, I cross the street. Halfway up the sidewalk, I glance over my shoulder and see that the stranger has gotten out of the rented Lexus. He's walking toward a parked Altima with North Carolina plates.

That has to be McLane's car.

What in the world?

I flinch when the front door slams. Ryan Evans is coming toward me, a book under his arm. "You weren't coming to see me, were you?"

"Sorry, not this time."

"Good, 'cause I'm on my way to a singles meeting at church. Hey, you could come too, you know."

"Thanks, but I have plans." I smile, then discreetly point over my shoulder. "Do you know that man? the guy looking at McLane's car?"

Ryan shifts his gaze toward the road. "What man?"

I turn. The stranger is gone; the silver Lexus has pulled away. It's at the end of the street, turning right at the stop sign.

"That man in the Lexus," I say, no longer bothering to keep quiet. "Do you recognize him?"

Ryan's eyes narrow as he studies the vehicle in the distance. "Nice wheels."

"The guy was sitting there when I drove up; then he got out to look into McLane's car. He was peeking in the windows. Doesn't that seem odd?"

Ryan shrugs. "Maybe he thought her car belonged to someone else and realized his mistake."

"Or maybe he planted a car bomb under the bumper."

Ryan stares at me as if I've suddenly grown a second head. "You're kidding, right?"

"Sorry. Been watching too much *CSI*." I step toward the house. "You seen McLane today?"

He smiles. "She's in her apartment and bored stiff. She'll be thrilled to see you."

※ ※ ※

Clay leans his bike against an oak tree and watches as the other boys chain their rides to a pedestrian crossing sign. Toby has linked his chain through his and Tyler's back wheels, leaving Percy to fend for himself.

"Hey!" Percy bumps Toby's bike with his front tire. "What about me?"

Toby grins. "No room, man. Work something out with Clay."

Percy glances at Clay, who shrugs. He doesn't carry a lock and chain because nobody in their right mind would want to steal his old bike.

"Sorry." He gives Percy a quick smile. "But how long is this gonna take? I'll stay out here and keep an eye on things if you want."

Percy looks at Toby and Tyler, who are already walking toward the candy store. "Aw, man. They're not waiting."

Clay straddles his seat and crosses his arms. "I'm not even sure they're gonna ask."

He didn't find Tyler, Toby, and Percy when he went riding yesterday, but he ran into them today. They were coming down Heim Road, which was practically his street.

Were they looking for him?

The possibility thrilled Clay, but when he saw them, he simply braked and acted like he'd been waiting for them all along.

They still wanted to look for the catacombs, Toby explained, but they had no idea where to start searching. Tyler thought the old man who ran the candy store might have an idea where the bunker was buried. After all, the guy was rich and as old as Adam. He was bound to have been one of the people who bought a share in the catacombs.

So they pedaled to the shopping district. Tyler and Toby charged in to ask the old guy about the catacombs, but Clay had a feeling they weren't going to get the information they wanted.

"Why should that man tell them anything?" he asks Percy, nodding toward the candy store. "I mean, if nobody talks about this place, why is this old guy going to spill his guts just because Tyler asks? If Tyler has the guts to ask."

Percy pushes at the bridge of his glasses and studies the tall windows at the front of the shop. "Oh, Tyler has guts. And he gets away with a lot. I don't know why, but he does."

"Does he know this store owner?"

"I don't think it matters." Percy sniffs and rubs his nose. "Man, my allergies are driving me crazy."

"What are you allergic to?"

"Everything." Percy takes a tissue from his pocket and blows his nose. "Mom says it's too bad we live in Florida. The pollen blows all year long."

"Can't you, like, take medicine or something?"

Percy snorts. "I do."

They wait. Clay squints and tries to peer into the glass, but the glare of the late afternoon sun makes it hard to see past the candy-covered shelves in the window. He can barely make out the figures of people inside the store, and the man behind the counter looks like a shadow.

Clay tilts his head back and gazes up into a tree. A squirrel crouches on a branch above him, its black eyes bright. It runs forward a step, clings to the side of the branch with all four paws, then sits upright and scolds Clay in a rough voice.

He turns as the quiet afternoon erupts into a burst of jangling and yelling. The door of the candy shop opens, setting off the bells hanging above the entrance. The owner holds the door, his face reddening as he shouts. "When will you kids learn this is not a game? Get out and stay out! Don't come back unless you want to buy something!"

Clay feels the corner of his mouth twist in a small smile. *So . . . Tyler Henton doesn't always get what he wants. Good to know.*

Percy sprints over to Tyler and Toby. "Did he tell you anything? give you any kind of clue?"

Tyler smiles as Toby bends to unlock the bicycle chain. Once Toby stands, Tyler grabs his bike with one hand and digs into his pocket with the other. "He didn't tell us anything, but I wouldn't say the trip was a complete waste." He opens his hand, revealing half a dozen wrapped candies. He drops a couple into Toby's outstretched palm, tosses a few to Percy, and looks at Clay. "Want some?"

Clay glances at the stolen candy before meeting Tyler's dark eyes. "No thanks."

"Come on." Tyler takes a step in Clay's direction. "Whassa matter? Don't you like sour drops?"

Clay lifts his bike off the tree. "I'm not hungry," he says, bracing his feet on the pedals. "But I'll race you to the railroad tracks." He sets off, not knowing if the others will follow. For a moment he hears nothing but the rush of wind in his ears.

Then he's trailed by laughter and the sound of challenging voices. The guys are still with him.

✺ ✺ ✺

Though Mt. Dora is famous for its downtown shopping, I rarely venture into the touristy areas. Today, however, I enjoy walking with McLane into cluttered antique stores, gift shops, and boutiques.

As we exclaim over lovely old furniture and unique gift ideas, I discover that my sister and I share the same tastes. We both like pottery and dislike Victorian furniture. We adore lace and abhor art deco. We love the impressionists and think Andy Warhol was overrated.

I'm amazed, though, when McLane figures a discounted price without using a calculator. "Wait." I turn to her, puzzled. "That sign said to take 14 percent off."

"So?"

"So you can figure 14 percent in your head?"

"Can't you?" She walks away, probably with numbers waltzing on the backs of her eyelids.

I stare at her in bewilderment. No, I can't figure 14 percent in my head. I can barely subtract 10 percent from a number without pen and paper. I can punch buttons on a calculator, but numbers and I have never been on a first-name basis. Apparently McLane inherited a mathematics gene from her mother.

In the Village Antique Mall, I pause before a display arranged on an old hope chest. A crocheted baby blanket is draped over the chest's worn interior, and in the center of the blanket is a gorgeous vintage christening gown, complete with bonnet. Most old gowns are fragile or yellowed with age, but this one is pristine and still soft enough for a baby's tender skin.

"Look at this." I lift the christening outfit from the blanket and hold it up, shaking out the long lace along the hem. "Isn't this the most beautiful thing?"

McLane's eyes soften. "I used to think all babies were baptized in gowns like that, so one day I asked Mom where my outfit was. She said she didn't have it."

I finger the delicate tucks at the neckline. "Did you grow up in a church that doesn't baptize infants?"

"I grew up in a Methodist church, and yes, they baptized babies. But our minister didn't believe in—how'd Mom put it?—'advertising babies born in difficult circumstances.' At my baptism, the pastor met Mom in his office, poured a cup of water over my head, and said a quick prayer. That was it." She gazes at the christening gown with a wistful expression. "I didn't really understand that story until this past summer. Now I know what the pastor meant—he didn't want the church to see an illegitimate child."

McLane turns away, a look of sadness on her face, and in that moment I know what I have to do. My church doesn't baptize infants, but since McLane's does, I'm going to make sure she and her baby don't feel slighted.

I hold up the gown again and check for flaws or stains, but it's perfect. The number on the price tag nearly stops my heartbeat, but how often do you have the opportunity to provide your new sister with her baby's first gift?

While McLane browses through a selection of old books, I carry the christening gown and bonnet to the cashier. The woman behind the desk takes her time swiping my credit card and congratulating me on my good taste, so she's wrapping the outfit in tissue paper when McLane wanders up to the front of the store.

She sees the gown and lifts a brow. "You decided to get it?"

"It's for you. For your baby."

Her lips part; then she shakes her head. "It's too much. And it's too early. I'm barely pregnant."

"No one is ever *barely* pregnant, and it's never too soon to prepare for your baby."

The woman hands me my parcel, and I give it to McLane. "This isn't very ceremonial, but may you, your baby, and your grandbabies enjoy this."

She hugs me right in front of the storekeeper and the uniformed deputy who's stepped in to enjoy a bit of shade. When I release McLane, she wipes tears from her cheeks and clutches the tissue-wrapped bundle as if it's the most precious thing in the world.

So I invite her to the house for supper.

❧ ❧ ❧

I drop McLane at the Biddle House to freshen up; then I grab my cell phone and call Gerald. "Red alert," I tell him as I sit at the curb on Baker Street. "I've invited McLane for dinner and I've nothing planned. I don't even know where to put her at the kitchen table."

I can almost see Gerald scratching his head. "Can't we just pull up another chair?"

"I don't want to crowd her at her first dinner with us! Surely someone has needed a dining room in that house before now. What did Uncle Ned do when he had guests?"

"We never . . . well, okay, I know what to do. Don't worry, missy. Just come on home. The boys and I will take care of the table."

"But what do we *eat*? If we don't have anything decent in the fridge, I'll need to stop by the grocery store—"

"We have a chicken," Gerald says, his voice matter-of-fact. "Ned's wife used to do this thing with a fryer. . . . It'll be fine. Let me get everything ready."

I'm not sure what he intends to do with the poor fowl in our freezer, and I don't have much faith in his planning. But Fairlawn's only a five-minute drive from downtown, and I could stop at Albertsons to pick up some fresh flowers. . . .

And maybe an entrée. And a salad and dessert.

Thirty minutes later, I'm driving home with a rose bouquet, a cheesecake, and a fresh head of lettuce. A pan of frozen lasagna is riding shotgun in the passenger seat, and I'm thanking heaven for Stouffer's. If I can toss a decent salad together from the odds and ends in my refrigerator, McLane won't think the cooking gene on my mother's side of the family is completely recessive.

When I bring the groceries through the doorway, I find all three of my guys in the west chapel. A large table occupies the center of the room, and it's been covered with one of my linen tablecloths. Bugs moves chairs toward the table while Clay sets my good dishes on place mats.

"Well." I give Gerald a grateful smile and drop my groceries into a chair. "I wouldn't have thought of eating in here."

"It's an all-purpose space," he says, gesturing toward the folding chairs he's stacked in a corner and hidden behind a potted plant.

I bite my lower lip and glance around. The usual rows of chairs have disappeared, but something else has changed—the long, narrow table that usually supports the casket is also missing. "Where's the, um . . . ?"

His grin widens. "We're eating on it."

"We're eating on the *casket* table?"

He lifts a corner of the tablecloth, exposing a scarred sheet of plywood. "I had this out in the garage. Figured if we put it on the casket table and covered it, no one would be the wiser."

"Great idea, huh, Mom?"

I sigh and look at Bugs, who is beaming at Gerald's brilliance. Clay is scowling, probably because I voiced my skepticism. Bottom line: I wanted a dining room table and they provided one. Why am I complaining?

I swallow hard and thread my fingers through the loops on the grocery bags. "Okay, then. I picked up a frozen lasagna just in case you didn't have time to cook. If I get it into the oven—"

"We're all squared away, so you can put the lasagna in the freezer."

"But what—?"

"Trust me. You'll be proud."

I tighten my grip on the grocery bags. "I don't like surprises. This dinner is important to me, so please tell me what you have in mind."

Gerald gives Clay a she-doesn't-trust-us look and crosses his arms. "You boil a chicken. Pull the meat from the bones. Boil rice. Set out bowls of pineapple chunks, grated cheese, chow mein noodles, some steamed broccoli, and slivered almonds. Warm up some chicken broth. Give your guests a plate and some chopsticks and let them pile it on as they please."

I have to admit, the idea sounds simple . . . and good. "You have all that stuff in the pantry?"

"And the chicken's on the stove." He nods at the roses blooming at the top of my grocery bag. "Better get those in water."

Surprised that the men have risen to the task so capably, I climb the stairs. After checking the simmering chicken, I'm bending to reach for a vase when the phone rings—the family phone, not the business line.

When I see the caller ID, I stifle a groan and pick up the receiver.

"Hey, Mom." I tuck the phone under my chin and move to the sink so I can fill the vase. "Are you freezing up there in Virginia?"

"Nearly," she answers. "Did I call in the middle of something?"

"I'm getting dinner ready. What's up?"

"I thought I should plan my flight reservations for Christmas. When do you want me to come?"

I wince as a thorn pricks my thumb. "Well . . . what were you thinking?"

"I've cleared my calendar, so I could come for the entire month. I might even stay a couple of weeks into January . . . unless you think that would wear out my welcome."

I close my eyes, grateful that Mom can't see my expression. Introducing Mom and McLane at Thanksgiving will be tough enough. I had hoped I could limit the time those two spend together, but how am I supposed to do that if Mom lives with us for six weeks?

12

wake at 5 a.m., disturbed by a vague pain I can't quite place. As I stroke my jaw, realization sinks in—my jaw hurts. My *teeth* hurt and maybe even my tongue. My entire mouth is in such agony that pain has awakened me long before sunrise. What is wrong with me?

I sit up and frown into the darkness. The night light in the hallway throws shadows throughout my bedroom, enabling me to see well enough to tiptoe into the bathroom. I flip on the lights and rummage for aspirin in the medicine cabinet. Tylenol, Aleve, Excedrin—what do you take for a *mouth*ache?

Finally I swallow a Motrin and head back to bed. Moonlight streams through the lace-covered window, so I curl up in a silver rectangle and try to sleep. But it's five o'clock, which is close to six, and six is almost six-thirty, which is when I need to get up. So I roll onto my back, fold my hands, and stare at the ceiling.

Maybe I should relish this bit of uninterrupted quiet time. The TV isn't blaring, the kids aren't calling for my attention, and no one is going to knock on the front door to inquire about caskets. The phone might ring with news of a death, but there's no escaping that reality when you live in a funeral home.

Five minutes later, I am tucked into the wing chair that occupies a corner of my room. A reading lamp hovers over my shoulder, but

I don't turn it on—bright light would feel intrusive. My anatomy book sits on my lap, but I don't open the cover.

I want to feel the silence. I want to enjoy the peace of quiet darkness, the calm that comes from knowing that my loved ones are safe in sleep.

I want to revisit a happy memory and enjoy it again.

Our first family dinner with McLane went better than I'd hoped. She charmed the boys by talking directly to them and asking questions about their interests. Bugs adored her, and even Clay perked up and joined the conversation when she asked if he had a favorite Nintendo game.

Gerald—whose potluck chicken dinner turned out to be a hit— doted on McLane, declaring that she reminded him of his daughter. Because he doesn't talk much about his family, I spent most of the night studying McLane and trying to figure out why she reminded Gerald of his daughter and I didn't. McLane and I look alike, we have the same tastes, and except for that math thing, you could almost say we were formed of the same mold. It must be the age. Gerald hasn't seen his daughter in a while, so maybe she was McLane's age when they were together last. Surely there's no other reason.

The phone rings, dredging up a lingering uneasiness at the marrow of my bones. At Fairlawn, a call before sunrise always means someone has died. Is it someone I know?

I lower one foot to the floor, about to grab the phone, but it stops ringing. Gerald, who has been answering nighttime calls for years, will talk to the caller and pick up the body despite the early hour. Some calls—those from the coroner and the hospital—can wait until morning because those facilities have coolers in which to refrigerate the bodies. When someone dies at home, Gerald hates to wait. Because decomposition begins only moments after a person takes their last breath, waiting makes the embalming more difficult.

I rub my jaw and manage a grim smile. I've learned that death is not an instantaneous matter; cells die one by one in orderly sequences. The process of dying goes on for hours before the body releases its last signs of life, but eventually death's invasion is complete. Six months ago, those thoughts would have turned my stomach, but now they are simple science.

So, Gerald will soon be heading out in his call car while I sit and wait. Why am I awake? Though the pain in my jaw has subsided to a dull ache, I stare at the dark window and wonder if God has awakened me to pray. For what? For whom? My boys are safe in bed, but is someone I love in trouble?

I close my eyes and listen for the still, small voice that occasionally whispers to my heart, but even the Spirit is quiet this morning. So I pray for the people I love, beginning with Clay and Bugs, then mentioning Gerald. As my circle of concern expands, I pray for Mother, McLane, the new baby, and Jeff in Iraq.

I'm not particularly prone to mystical experiences, but as I pray for the baby, I can almost see that tender soul, shining like a lamp from within McLane's thickening womb. The sight is awe-inspiring, and before I know it, tears are trickling down my cheeks. I can't wait to welcome this beautiful new creation from God.

I swipe tears from my face, grateful that the boys aren't awake to disturb this special time. I look toward the eastern horizon, where the darkness has thinned, and thank God for loving this baby, who is approaching as steadily as the rising sun.

That child will soon be with us . . . and so will my mother. And it'd be wrong of me to hide one from the other. I know I have to tell Mom about McLane, and I know it will hurt. But, given time, my mother's love for my father might persuade her to love this baby. After all, the baby will be a part of Dad, just as McLane is.

Maybe I haven't given Mom enough credit. She's the one who urged me to reach out to McLane in the first place. Not because of who McLane's parents were, but because I'm a Christian and I'm supposed to love people.

Mom's a Christian, too.

Though I have been expecting it, I flinch when I hear the sound of a car engine roaring through the stillness. A moment later, Gerald's station wagon pulls out of the garage and heads toward the heart of town.

I watch until the car is only two red dots gleaming against gray velvet. Nice of him to take this early morning call. As his apprentice, I volunteered to share the burden of early morning pickups, but Gerald said he didn't have to get two boys ready for school every weekday morning. The man made a good point.

I run my hand along my jaw and realize that the pain has eased. Still, I should probably visit a dentist. Since our arrival in Mt. Dora, I haven't had a lot of time for personal maintenance.

I should call, though, in case the teeth are the first things to go.

⚇ ⚇ ⚇

By the time I shower, dress, and go downstairs, the call car has returned. The exterior door to the prep room is standing open, and when I step onto the back porch, I see Gerald pulling the gurney out of the back of the old station wagon.

I shiver in the early morning chill. "You need me?"

"I wouldn't turn down a helping hand."

I help him lower the gurney to the pavement; then we lift and lock it at waist height. I nod at the white plastic body bag. "Who is this?"

He glances at the clipboard. "Joanne Jones. Picked her up at the hospital."

"The hospital called this early?"

"They were running out of space."

I blow out a breath as we wheel the gurney up the ramp and into our prep room. The clipboard, I notice, doesn't give much information other than the name, date of death, and name of nearest kin.

I'm startled when Gerald unzips the bag. Most of the bodies I've seen have come to us clothed in a hospital gown, but this woman hasn't been granted that consideration. The Y-incision of an autopsy mars the gray-blue flesh from chin to pubic bone and shoulder to shoulder, and someone—maybe the medical examiner?—has closed the incision with dark running stitches.

I reach for the edge of the preparation table as my knees go weak.

Gerald scans my face. "You haven't seen an autopsied case before?"

I shake my head. "Sorry. It was just . . . unexpected."

Gerald makes a quiet sound of sympathy while he tenderly runs his hand over Joanne Jones's forehead. "Her family will be in later this morning. You think you can handle the intake by yourself?"

I stare at the torso, in which the main veins and arteries have been severed by a scalpel. How are we supposed to pump embalming solution through a body in which the delivery vessels have been cut? "Gerald . . ."

"Autopsied cases are different," he explains, his voice calm and steady. "They require special handling. That's why we have to charge extra. So if you can counsel the family, I'd like to get started as soon as possible."

I've watched Gerald conduct half a dozen intake interviews, so I'm reasonably sure I can take care of it. In any case, today I'd rather work in the chapel than in here.

"I can do it," I tell him. "If I run into a problem, I'll call you."

After packing the boys' lunches and driving Bugs to kindergarten, I slip into a dark skirt and white blouse, an outfit I hope conveys professionalism and competence.

By nine thirty I'm at my desk in the office. Within five minutes, I hear the scraping sound of steps on the porch. Joanne Jones's family has not wasted any time.

Through the sidelights I can see a middle-aged man and an older woman at the front door. They are arguing over whether they should walk in or ring the bell, so I spare them the debate and open the door myself.

"Hello." I give them a small smile. "I'm Jennifer Graham, the owner of Fairlawn. Can I help you?"

The man peers at me through bloodshot eyes. "I'm Charles Jones, Joanne's husband. This is—"

"Noreen," the woman says. She grips my wrist with the tenacity of a bulldog. "We've come to make arrangements for my daughter."

Because Pauline Danvers is lying casketed in the southern chapel, I step back and gesture to the smaller west chapel. "Won't you come in?"

When we're not holding a funeral in this room, we keep the sofa and two wing chairs grouped in a cozy conversation area near the double doors. Joanne's mother and husband sink onto the sofa, and Noreen grips her son-in-law's arm.

"I'm sorry," Mr. Jones says, catching my eye as I sit across from him. "We weren't expecting this. I've never had to arrange a funeral before, so I'm feeling a little lost."

I could mention that I'm not exactly a pro at this, but I don't want to say anything to dilute their confidence in Fairlawn. I may not know everything about the business, but I know people need to feel they can depend on their funeral director. I open the worn leather folder Gerald has given me and glance at the checklist. "First of all—" I set the folder on my lap—"let me assure you that I am sorry for your loss."

Noreen's eyes fill with fresh tears. "Thank you. Joanne was . . . a lovely person."

Her son-in-law, who has been staring into the empty space above the coffee table, abruptly lifts his gaze to meet mine. "She ironed my handkerchiefs. Have you ever met a woman who ironed handkerchiefs?"

I shake my head. Personally, I can't imagine taking the time to iron anything that's going to be stuffed in someone's pocket, but I'm not here to judge or inquire about anything not related to the funeral. Still, grieving people are often driven to talk of their loved ones, so I'll listen to whatever they want to share.

"Joanne was a perfectionist." Noreen pulls a tissue from her purse and dabs at the end of her nose. "That's why we called you; we thought a woman funeral director might take pains to make sure things are done with the little elegant touches of class Joanne would appreciate."

For an instant, my mind fills with the image of the body in the prep room. I have a distinct feeling that Joanne Jones would not have approved of the way she arrived at our establishment. Thank heaven these people will never see her like that.

"I can assure you that we'll do everything in our power to give your daughter a fitting farewell." I look from Noreen to the stricken husband. "If you don't mind, I have a few questions that will guide us as we seek to honor Joanne. Is it all right if we proceed?"

"Asthma," Mr. Jones says, his eyes glittering. "She's had it for years but never an attack like that."

Noreen pats his hand. "Charles, you can't blame yourself."

"But I didn't get her to the hospital in time. We didn't have her inhaler. We had the cat in the bedroom, and that could have made things worse—"

"Charles." Noreen grips his hand. "We can't always understand why things happen. But you'll drive yourself crazy if you keep second-guessing like this."

Charles nods in acquiescence.

Noreen turns to me. "Ask anything you like. We'll do our best to answer."

I take a deep breath and scan my list. "The first thing we have to decide is whether you want a funeral or memorial service and when it should be held. Unless you want to hold the service tomorrow, I strongly recommend the embalming procedure."

"We want everything," Charles says. "Joanne's life deserves to be celebrated in the best possible way. We had life insurance, so do your worst."

I hold up a steadying hand. "Despite what you may have heard, we're not here to take advantage of you in your hour of grief. Our services are reasonably priced, and I'm not going to advise anything you don't need. Do we understand each other?"

Noreen's eyes soften. "Ask your questions," she says, leaning on her son-in-law's shoulder. "We need your help."

I bow my head for a moment, reminding myself that I'm here to serve these people. Yes, this is a business; yes, sometimes the work is far from pleasant. But even when death visits unexpectedly, it is a part of life, and my job is to help people say good-bye.

I look up and smile at Charles and Noreen. "Music," I begin. "What sort of music did Joanne like?"

13

$\mathcal{I}$ lean back, grip the chair's armrest, and try not to stare into the light.

"You have marvelous teeth." Sally Jo Hawkins, my dental hygienist, nods in approval. "You don't have many cavities at all."

I want to reply that I have good genes, but I can't talk with the woman's gloved fingers in my mouth. The scent of latex tickles my nose.

"Now," she says, prodding my molars with a needlelike prong, "what did you say your problem was?"

I widen my eyes as sound escapes my throat. "Aye aww urts inn niiigh." I try to point to my jaw, but I end up slapping her dental tray and no doubt making a mess of her instruments.

Sally Jo leans back and removes the torture devices from my mouth.

Relieved, I moisten my lips. "My jaw," I tell her, grateful for the power of speech. "I've been waking up in the middle of the night in pain. I'm not sure how to describe it, but it feels like everything in my mouth hurts."

Sally Jo crosses her arms and grins at me like a vengeful tooth fairy. "I could have predicted you'd say that. You're going to keep on waking up in pain, too, unless you do something about it."

"What am I supposed to do?"

"Calm down, for one thing," she says, reaching for her dental tray.

"Something—probably stress—is causing you to grind your teeth. You have very little enamel left on your lower molars."

I gape at her. "I do not grind my teeth."

"You do; the evidence is clearly visible. You're going to need a mouth guard and crowns. Probably four of them."

"But I *don't*—"

"A lot of people don't realize they're grinding. Until they come in with pain, that is."

I consider the implications of what she's just told me. There's no denying that my life overflows with stress. I could sell it by the bottle. "Four crowns—won't that be expensive?"

"Oh yeah."

"Like . . . a couple of hundred dollars?"

She laughs. "More like a couple of thousand."

I groan. We'll have to move a top-of-the-line casket to come up with that kind of money. But who in Mt. Dora can afford to be buried in bronze?

"And we'll have to work in stages," Sally Jo continues. "First we fit you for the crowns, we give you temps while the crowns are made, and you come back in to have them applied. You're looking at two or three appointments, a couple of weeks apart."

Oh no. She may be a good saleswoman and in desperate need of a commission or something, but I haven't the time or money to invest in major dental repair. I tug at the bib around my neck. "Look. This is a really busy time for me. Can I postpone all this?"

"You want to keep waking up in pain?"

"Well—"

"You want to grind those molars down to nubs?"

"I didn't—"

"You need a mouth guard pronto, and that's not such a big deal. We can fit you and send you home with it today."

I sigh and close my eyes. "How much for that?"

"A couple hundred, I think. I'll get the girl at the desk to work it up. So can we at least stop the problem from getting worse?"

I think of Clay's urgent need for new tennis shoes and Christmas, which will arrive whether I'm ready for it or not. I'll owe another college tuition payment in January, and the minivan has developed an odd little rattle. . . .

Then again, sleep is precious, popping Motrin can't be good for me, and waking in the middle of the night is not fun. And I can put two hundred dollars on my Visa. Business may not be predictable, but it is steady.

I grip the armrests of the chair again. "I'll think about it."

"Marvelous. What about the crowns? You're gonna need them, sweetie, so you might as well get them done sooner than later."

Does this woman expect me to fund the staff's holiday party? I'm tempted to glare at her, but I know she must be right about my teeth. I have good genes and *used* to have thick enamel, so I must be grinding like a coffee mill.

What full-time mother and mortuary student wouldn't?

❧ ❧ ❧

I can scarcely find a parking place when I get home. I have forgotten about the Danvers funeral, and though Gerald assured me he was expecting a small crowd, it looks as though every Episcopalian in three counties has turned out today.

I leave the van at the edge of the road and hike through the parked cars. Pauline Danvers, Gerald told me yesterday, didn't miss a Sunday at St. Marks because she wanted a liturgical funeral. "The Episcopalians take dying seriously," Gerald explained, a smile on his face. "They have a certain gravitas the Baptists can't touch."

If I didn't have a thousand things on my mind, I might pop into the chapel to check out the gravitas, but I need to slip upstairs and hide away with my anatomy book. I spent all morning in class, and the functions of various organs and systems are churning in my brain like clothes in a washing machine. Only by sitting in silence am I going to be able to sort them out.

I'm perspiring by the time I enter the foyer and nearly run into Gerald at the foot of the stairs. He smiles, a memorial bulletin in his hand, but returns it to the stack when he realizes I'm not a funeral guest.

I pause, one hand on the stair railing. "Everyone okay in there?"

"Right as rain. The rector's well into the liturgy."

Out of respect for anyone who might step out of the chapel, I lower my voice. "Everything okay in the prep room?"

Gerald nods. "Mrs. Jones is ready to be casketed. I'll need your help for that later."

I draw a deep breath and consider the first step. "I'm heading up to study, then. Is Bugs upstairs?"

"In his room watching a DVD."

"By the way, Fairlawn wouldn't happen to have an emergency medical fund, would it?"

"Um . . . nothing other than major medical insurance."

"How about a dental plan?"

Gerald frowns. "One of the kids having problems with his teeth?"

Just then a man steps out of the chapel and gestures for Gerald's attention, sparing me the trouble of answering. While Gerald attends to our guest, I move down the hallway that leads to our office, then boot up the computer.

Five minutes later, I'm studying our accounts. Fairlawn is operating on a shoestring budget, and my family account isn't much better off. I'd consider a home equity loan, but our situation is a little murky. How would a bank handle Fairlawn, which is 50 percent home and 50 percent business? Which half gets to pay for my teeth?

I sigh and power down the computer. Before the end of the year, I have to talk to a tax attorney. Someone needs to help me devise a strategy for handling our financial affairs.

When the phone rings, I snatch it up before it can disturb the chapel service. "Fairlawn Funeral Home."

"Jen? It's McLane."

"Hi." Mindful of the Episcopalians in the next room, I keep my voice low. "Everything okay?"

"Yeah."

So she says, but her voice has an unusual tremor. "You don't sound okay. Something wrong?"

"Nothing. It's just . . ."

"What?"

"My first doctor's appointment is tomorrow, and I'm feeling a little nervous. I was wondering if—"

"I'll go." I flip the page of the desktop calendar. "I have to get Bugs to school by eight, but I'm available after that. What time is your appointment?"

"Ten thirty."

I grab a pencil. "Perfect. I'll pick you up and we'll go together."

McLane keeps talking about how much she appreciates my willingness to go with her, especially since tomorrow is the day before Thanksgiving, but I'm honored to be invited.

I am excited by the thought of welcoming a new niece or nephew into the world, and I'm glad that my boys like McLane. But every positive has a corresponding negative, and I can't forget that McLane is the result of my father's infidelity, and my mother is coming here for Thanksgiving.

Every turn of the clock brings me closer to a confrontation I'd give anything to avoid.

14

In Dr. Leibowitz's waiting room, McLane sits on the sofa while I drop into an upholstered chair. The classic decor is accented with framed pencil sketches, most of which depict raven-haired mothers cuddling adorable babies. A small fan on the floor keeps a current of air moving through the room, helping the air conditioner cool pregnant women.

A coffee table in front of the sofa offers a selection of magazines and brochures: How to Stay Happy While Pregnant, How to Eat for Two, How to Erase Forehead Wrinkles (Ask Us about Botox!). I frown at the last brochure, then remember that not all of the gynecologist's patients are pregnant.

I glance at the artwork, feel a twinge of nostalgia for my own breast-feeding days, and pick up a copy of *Good Housekeeping*. The sooner I accept that my baby days are over, the more contented I'll be.

"I had a good time at your house the other night," McLane says. She tugs on the end of her skirt and crosses her legs. "Your sons are adorable."

"Thanks." I glance at an ad for laminate flooring and wonder if it would work in the foyer, then look at McLane. "You know, that reminds me . . ."

"Yeah?"

"You've met my family, but I've never seen a picture of my brother-in-law."

She gives me an odd little smile and uncrosses her legs. "I wish I had one with me. Jeff doesn't like formal pictures, so all I have are snapshots."

"Come on. Every soldier has one of those portraits taken in front of the American flag."

"Jeff doesn't. But I can tell you what he looks like."

I close my magazine. "Okay. I have a good imagination."

McLane smiles. "He's tall, about six-two. And well built. Not skinny, not fat."

"He's a marine," I point out. "They tend to be tough and trim."

"I don't think he's ever been heavy," she says. "I doubt he ever had baby fat. He's got dark hair, brown eyes, and the best teeth I've ever seen. His smile is bright enough to make a girl squint."

I laugh, charmed by her description. "Short hair, I suppose."

"Yeah. The typical buzz cut."

"Does he look like a movie star?"

"*I* think he's handsome."

"I mean, does he resemble a particular movie star? Like Tom Cruise or Clive Owen or Lou Diamond Phillips?"

McLane blinks. "He doesn't look a thing like Tom Cruise. Who else did you say?"

"Never mind." I open my magazine again. "I'm sure my brother-in-law is as attractive as sin. And since this kid is going to be a combination of two beautiful people, he or she will be gorgeous."

"I hope so."

I look up when I hear wistfulness in her voice. I was being glib, but something I said has made her smile fade and brought a shadow to her eyes. Maybe it's time for some big-sister nosiness. She's probably missing Jeff, but talking about it might help. "What's wrong?"

She lowers her gaze. "Nothing."

I lean closer. "You can tell me anything, you know. Haven't you heard? Funeral directors are like doctors—we're trained to keep secrets."

My comment elicits a small smile, and she lifts her head. "It's my dad. He doesn't like Jeff at all."

I wasn't expecting that answer. I close my magazine and set it on the coffee table. "How can he not like the man who married his daughter?"

"That's just it. He doesn't know we're married. He kept insisting Jeff wasn't good enough for me, and he even forbade me to see him, so we had to sneak around." A tremor passes over her face, and a spasm knits her brows. "Can you believe it? At my age, I was sneaking around like a teenager, but what else could I do? To save money and keep Dad company after Mom died, I was living at home. Things might have been different if I'd had my own place . . . my own space."

McLane is staring at the opposite wall, but I know she's not looking at the picture hanging there. The focus of her wide-eyed gaze is some interior field of vision I can't imagine.

She releases a hollow laugh. "You know what? A couple of my friends told me that Jeff and I were moving too fast, and now I think they were right. But when Dad put his foot down, I became even more determined to see Jeff. When I learned he was shipping out, I told him I wanted to be married. So . . . we eloped."

I bite my lip, not certain how nosy a big sister is allowed to be. "Why? What does your father have against Jeff?"

The question snaps her out of her reverie. "Nothing. Everything. Jeff is nothing like Dad. Dad wanted me to marry a medical student or a lawyer, and Jeff's ambition is to teach elementary school." Her cheeks flame with color. "Dad thinks Jeff *has* no ambition. For him, life is all about power and prestige."

I search the area, but there are no How to Counsel Distraught Younger Sisters pamphlets on the coffee table.

"I'm sure your father isn't a total snob," I say, trying to give the man the benefit of the doubt. "If you called him with your big news, I'll bet he'd be so glad to hear—"

"Are you *kidding*?" McLane looks at me as if I've just suggested we fly to Jupiter for lunch. "Dad would not be excited about this pregnancy. He says Jeff comes from the wrong side of town and the wrong kind of people. He'll never accept this baby. Not in a million years."

She might have said more, but at that moment a nurse steps through the doorway and calls her name.

※※ ※※ ※※

Randolph stands, his heart pounding as Dexter Duggan walks into his office with a briefcase in hand. "Pardon me for interrupting your workday," the private investigator says, "but I thought you'd want to see my report as soon as possible. And seein' as how tomorrow's Thanksgiving, I wanted to catch you before you took off for someplace."

Though he has no intention of going anywhere for the holiday, Randolph manages a polite smile and gestures toward the guest chair. "Thank you for that consideration. Please have a seat."

Duggan settles in, the leather of his coat creaking as he sets the briefcase on his lap. His eyes glitter when he focuses on Randolph. "What you gave me the other day was real helpful. I found your daughter. She's safe and sound in Florida—little town called Mt. Dora."

Randolph sinks to his chair, his mind reeling. "Never heard of it."

Duggan grins. "Doesn't surprise me. The place looks like geezer heaven; it's mostly antique shops and bed-and-breakfasts all done up for the tourists. In fact, your daughter's renting an apartment in a boardinghouse run by a gaggle of old ladies."

Randolph laces his fingers. "But she's well."

"Oh, she's great. Fit as a fiddle and going by the name McLane Larson."

"So, she actually married him."

"Court records don't lie." The detective pulls a palm-size notebook from his coat pocket and consults his notes. "Jeffrey Larson and McLane Harris. Marriage certificate filed in Onslow County on September 9. The pair apparently spent a couple of weeks together; then Larson shipped out to join his company. The lieutenant is currently with the Marine Aviation Logistics Squadron in Iraq. When he flew east, your daughter headed south."

"To a town in Florida."

"Right."

"But why?"

Duggan holds up a finger. "That's where the last tip you gave me paid off. Jennifer Norris, daughter of Nolan and Joella Norris, married Thomas Graham in 1989. They divorced, but Ms. Graham inherited a piece of Mt. Dora real estate in May 2006—the Fairlawn Funeral Home, to be precise. Ms. Graham and her sons have been living there since June."

Randolph leans back in his chair, more impressed than he wants to admit. "How'd she . . . how'd you find this woman?"

"Public records. Nearly everything that gets recorded these days goes on the Internet. Public records are available to anyone who wants to pay a small fee and look 'em up."

Randolph swivels toward the window. "McLane went to find her sister."

"That's a done deal. Have a gander at this." The detective takes three black-and-white photos from his briefcase and slides them across the desk.

Randolph picks up the first and sees his daughter sitting at a booth in some sort of diner. The other woman has her back to the camera, but she wears her dark hair shoulder length, just like McLane.

The next photo shows the two women walking on a sidewalk. McLane has lifted her hands in a gesture, her habitual way of speaking. The other woman walks with one hand on her purse, the other swinging at her side. Like McLane, the second woman is of medium height and slender, but the lines in her face are sharper.

He taps the image. "That's the sister?"

"Right, that's Jennifer Graham. Apparently they've gotten pretty tight."

Randolph studies a third photograph, where the two women are sitting on a slatted bench in front of an office or shop. McLane's face is pensive, the way it usually looks before she bursts into tears, and the sister has an arm around McLane's shoulder. He bends over the picture as his nerves tighten in a full stretch. "What's wrong with my daughter?"

Duggan's face spreads into a grin. "Well, sir, that's the biggest news. I heard all about it when I stopped in at the diner—a waitress there is a fount of knowledge about all the goings-on in town. According to her, your daughter's going to make you a grandpa."

※ ※ ※

I drop McLane at the Biddle House, congratulate her on completing her tenth week of motherhood, and then take my cell phone from my purse. I had hoped to spend a little time at home since the boys are out of school today, but the Orlando airport is an hour drive in light traffic, and traffic outside Orlando is never light.

Gerald picks up on the first ring.

"Hi," I say. "Everything okay there?"

"Everything's fine," he assures me. "Mrs. Jones is in the chapel, the programs arrived, and the boys have been helping me arrange the flowers."

I still wince at the thought of Clay and Bugs arranging floral sprays in a room occupied by a casket and corpse, but the revulsion grows weaker with each Fairlawn funeral. Death is a natural part of life, so why shouldn't they become accustomed to it? After all, people used to lay their dead out in the parlor. On ice.

"I'll try to be back as soon as possible," I promise Gerald. "Mom's flight is supposed to land at two, so if it's on schedule I should be home in plenty of time for the service."

"Don't worry if you're delayed," he answers. "Lydia said Bugs could come down and help her at the shop during the funeral. So take your time and drive carefully."

I smile as I disconnect the call and toss the phone onto the passenger seat. Lydia's shop, Twice Loved Treasures, is filled with recycled gifts—puppets made from empty toilet paper rolls, aromatherapy candles poured into empty baby food jars, earring cushions that resemble hats but are really old CDs and halved Styrofoam balls. Bugs loves to explore her stock and occasionally lends a hand in the creation of some of her more artistic pieces. Last week she handed me a twenty and said it was Bugs's share of the profit from a ceramic plate he'd painted.

I drive away from the curb and head toward Orlando, turning on the radio when I reach the expressway. I flow along with the traffic, humming absently as my mind whirls with thoughts about Mother and McLane.

I have to tell Mom the truth, and the sooner the better. Half the town already knows that McLane and I are sisters, and Mother would never forgive me if Annie Watson, the waitress, mentions something before I have a chance to speak.

By the time I take the airport exit, cold panic has sprouted between my shoulders and trickled down my spine. I head toward the baggage claim lanes and watch for the security guards who will tell me to move on if I loiter too long.

Maybe, if I'm lucky, one of them will decide that I look suspicious and haul me to some underground bunker for questioning about suspected terrorist activities. While I'm being questioned, Mom will look for me, and after an hour or two, she'll be so irritated and out of sorts that she'll take the next flight back to Fairfax.

Right now, I'd rather face torture than my mother.

I check my watch again and tap the steering wheel. I need to face the truth—I look about as dangerous as a jelly bean. No one is going to arrest me. And Mom should be here in less than fifteen minutes.

How does one introduce the topic of unexpected relatives? *Mom, I know you like surprises. . . .*

Actually, I think my mother would rather be trampled in a yard sale than caught unaware. So maybe I should try the direct approach: *Mom, you know Dad was a louse, right?*

This holiday would be so much more relaxed if I'd never met McLane.

I flinch when someone taps on the passenger window; then I realize I'm looking at my mother. She's appeared from out of nowhere.

I hop out of the van and move to the back, where she meets me with a suitcase on wheels and a loaded shopping bag. I give her a hug. "Thank goodness your plane was on time. I'd hate for you to have to wait."

She frowns. "Your hair is different."

"Only a little." I reach up and tuck a clump of hair behind my ear. "The stylist thought it might be nice to feather the ends a bit."

"That just makes frizz." Mom shoves her shopping bag into the back. "Just wait till it rains. You'll see."

On that hopeful note, I heave her suitcase into the van, check to be sure she hasn't dropped anything, and slam the door. As I wait for an approaching car to pass, I peer inside the van—Mom is already in the passenger seat, ready to go see her grandsons.

I hate to spoil her trip. I really do.

Once we pull away from baggage claim, Mom chatters about the weather in Virginia, the snoring man who sat next to her on the plane, and the security agent who wouldn't let her carry a bottle of hand sanitizer on board. Despite these annoyances, she's upbeat and bright, and I can tell she's thrilled at the prospect of visiting her friends in Mt. Dora.

Something in me quivers like a bowl filled with Jell-O. I haven't been this jittery since Thomas and I watched *Jurassic Park* for the first time.

I wait until we have merged onto the turnpike to reach out and pat her shoulder. I glance at the rearview mirror to check the traffic in the left lane. "We're having a guest for Thanksgiving dinner tomorrow."

"Daniel Sladen?" She shifts in her seat and twinkles at me. "You *did* invite that handsome man, didn't you?"

"As a matter of fact—" I flip on my turn signal and ease into the lane—"I didn't. But I might, if he doesn't have plans. Probably too late now, though."

"You'd be smart not to let him slip through your fingers." Mom folds her hands atop her industrial-size purse. "I'm sure there are lots of women in town who'd love to snap him up."

"Daniel is not the guest I had in mind."

"Who, then?" She turns as far as her seat belt will allow. "If it's that old codger Eunice Daniels was trying to fix me up with—"

"It's not a man. It's a young woman."

"Lydia? Wait, she's not so young."

I roll my eyes, grateful that my neighbor isn't along for the ride.

"Actually, Lydia *is* coming. Since Brett's in California, we thought it'd be nice to invite her. She's bringing her famous squash casserole."

Why am I talking about casserole? Mom isn't making it easy, but I keep finding rabbit trails and gratefully slipping down them.

"A young woman." Mom looks out the window, then groans. "Don't tell me Clay has a girlfriend. He's too young for that sort of thing, isn't he?"

"Her name's McLane Larson," I blurt out. "She's a perfectly sweet girl, and she's become one of the family. You need to know her, so I invited her to Thanksgiving dinner."

My mother's brows descend in a frown. "I don't care if she's related to Mother Teresa. Clay is too young—"

"She's not Clay's girlfriend. Clay doesn't have a girlfriend. McLane is twenty-four and new in town. She works for Daniel, I met her at Lydia's book club, and her husband's serving in the Middle East."

Mom smiles. "I remember now. You told me about her on the phone. She's pregnant, right?"

"Yes, but I didn't tell you everything. What I didn't tell you . . . is that she's my half sister."

Mom's smile freezes, and she blinks in some sort of panicked Morse code. "She was . . . in your sorority?"

I prop my elbow on the van door and press my fingertips to my temple. "I'm sorry, but there's no easy way to say this. Twenty-five years ago, Dad had an affair with a woman in North Carolina. The woman had a baby girl. McLane is Dad's daughter."

Air rushes out of Mother in an abrupt *pfffft*. "That's impossible."

I've imagined a thousand variations of this scene, and none of them were pleasant. I consider pulling off to the side of the road, but as long as I'm driving, I won't have to look Mom in the eye.

"I'm afraid it's true. You told me Dad was always running around on you. Well, at least once he didn't get away as cleanly as he hoped to."

The corners of Mother's mouth have gone tight. "I would have known. Nolan would have told me."

"Oh, come on. Dad wasn't foolish enough to tell you everything, and you know it." My voice is hoarse with frustration. "I don't think many people knew the truth. McLane's mother gave her the entire story right before she died."

A heavy frown line twists beneath the wispy bangs on my mother's forehead. "This other woman . . . she's dead?"

I nod.

Mother's mouth curves into an expression of fierce pleasure. "And this girl—what does she want, money? She's not getting any; there's no way your father would have—"

"McLane doesn't want money. She hasn't asked for anything, really. She came to town only because—"

"She's a home wrecker like her mother?"

"She wanted to know her family. Apart from her husband in Iraq and a father who disapproves of her marriage, I'm the only family she has."

My mother, whose idea of cursing is yelling "Jiminy Cricket," abruptly releases a word I didn't even realize she knew. I glance at her, wondering if some foul-mouthed pod person has taken control of her body, and she covers her face with her hands and begins to sob.

This is what I dreaded, but what can I do?

Regret forms a painful knot within my chest as I drive and fumble in the depths of my purse. "Here." My voice breaks as I hand Mom a crumpled tissue. "Have a good cry. Let it all out before we get home. The boys will be upset if you—"

"The boys," she wails. "They've met this impostor?"

"Mom." The word is both an encouragement and a plea. I slide my hands over the steering wheel and keep my focus on the road. "McLane is not a bad person, and she's not to blame for what Dad did. He hurt you, but he hurt McLane's mother, too."

"Was it Shana?" Mom's voice brims with venom. "That blonde tootsie from the Fort Bragg Officers' Club?"

"So you knew her." I exhale in relief. Though I have no idea who McLane's mother was, at least I won't have to listen to Mom run through a long list of my father's infidelities. "Seems to me the real villain here is Dad. He told her he was divorced, and he abandoned them. The woman eventually married a psychiatrist who adopted

McLane. She didn't know about Dad—about us—until a few months ago."

"So she came down here to ruin our lives?"

"She came here in search of her family. She came looking for me." I steer around a big Buick that is constipating the center lane.

Mom blows her nose, then peers woefully at me. "I can't believe you actually like this girl."

I reach across the space between us and squeeze my mother's hand. "I was upset when I first heard the news. But I thought about it and realized that nothing happens without a reason. And McLane's done nothing wrong. She's a delightful young woman—bright and excited about being a mother. She . . . she even looks a little like me."

From the corner of my eye I see Mom's chin quiver again.

Uh-oh. I grip the steering wheel more tightly and keep the van pointed north. Mom is going to have to sort through whatever feelings she has to sort through, and nothing I can do will speed up the process. I wish I didn't have to spring the news on her this way, but better for her to hear it from me than through the Mt. Dora grapevine.

This is going to be a long drive home.

※ ※ ※

Joella steps out of the van, presses her hand to the small of her back, and studies the hulking pink Victorian at the crest of the hill. The place looks a lot better than it did when they first arrived in June, but no paint in the world is going to overcome Fairlawn's character. She will always associate this old house with death. Dead people, dead hopes, dead dreams.

Today it has buried the remaining pleasant memories of her dead husband.

At the back of the minivan, Jen is pulling out Joella's suitcase and shopping bag. "I'll take these in for you," she says, slamming the door. "We've got your room ready."

Joella draws a deep breath and follows her daughter. "If you don't mind, I'm going to sit on the porch for a while."

Jen glances over her shoulder. "You sure? We have a funeral sched-uled for later this afternoon. Things will be getting busy in about an hour."

"I'll stay until people begin to arrive." Joella nods at a rocker on the western porch. "I'll come in when I'm ready."

Jen pauses, uncertainty written all over her face. Finally she sighs and drags the suitcase and shopping bag up the stairs and into the house.

Joella shakes her head. Her daughter has lousy timing and a short memory. How would she feel if some woman drove up and parked a kid on the porch after explaining that Jen's ex was the kid's father? She'd be plenty upset, and the last thing in the world she'd want to do is invite the kid for Thanksgiving dinner.

But she's not to blame for this fiasco. Only her father is. Nolan . . . what a dog he was. Thought he could play the field, have his fun, and get away scot-free. Cancer caught up to him before his infidelity did, so now his wife and daughter will pay the price for his betrayal.

Joella ascends the wooden steps, matching the speed of her steps to the uneven beat of her heart. She crosses to the porch that overlooks the driveway and settles into a rocker. The chair creaks agreeably as she leans back, her gaze drifting toward the paneled ceiling. Jen hasn't painted the bead board yet, and the paint will be peeling before too long. . . .

Everything wears out sooner or later, doesn't it? Maybe even love and marriage. She'd tried to love Nolan, but nothing she did seemed to satisfy his wanderlust. Most of the men on the base thought him lucky to have a charming wife and an adorable baby girl, but Nolan was always more interested in chasing the closest skirt than appreciat-ing his family.

What drives men like Nolan? Are they genetically prone to infidel-ity, or is it purely a character flaw? A few weeks ago she watched a tele-vision talk show where a high-toned psychologist told the hostess that men weren't naturally monogamous. Like animals, hormones drove them to spread their seed around in order to perpetuate the species.

The shrink's drivel sounded like hogwash when she heard it, and it sounds like hogwash now. Men aren't animals. They were created in the image of God. Nolan could exhibit exemplary qualities when he chose to; he served his country with courage and loyalty.

He only was unfaithful to his family.

Joella closes her eyes as two cars turn into the driveway and roll toward the house. The funeral guests are arriving, just in time to bury the rationalization she has always clung to when faced with Nolan's philandering: *at least he didn't leave fatherless children behind.*

Perhaps it's time to abandon the past once and for all. Nolan is gone, Jennifer is grown, and her grandsons are adjusting to life in Florida. They have moved on, and they are willing to accept the stranger who sought them out because Nolan unwittingly gave her the right to do so.

Tomorrow she will go to dinner and meet this McLane person. For Jen's sake and the boys', she will be civil.

But she won't have to be happy about it.

15

Thanksgiving Day dawns bright and cool. I shower and dress in black pants and an ivory sweater set, then go downstairs to survey the west chapel for the third time.

I'm feeling nervous for more than one reason. Not only will Mother and McLane soon be facing off in this room, but last night Daniel accepted my last-minute invitation to join us. I called him, fully expecting to hear that he had other commitments, but he assured me that because his brothers all live out of state, his plans consisted of serving breakfast at a homeless shelter near Orlando and stopping at Shoney's for a burger.

I'm not sure I believe him, but I'm glad he's coming for dinner. I'm not as thrilled about having him witness what could be the combustible combination of my mother and sister.

Gerald's improvised dining room table is set up, the linens are clean, and my best dishes gleam in the sunlight streaming from the tall windows. Bugs has created construction paper place cards for our guests, so Mother will sit next to Gerald and Lydia at one end of the table, while McLane sits at the opposite end between me and Bugs. Daniel and Clay will fill in the middle.

Last night Mom and I baked pumpkin pies. I had hoped we'd be able to talk through her feelings about my news, but she stirred and poured and rolled pie crusts with about as much emotion as a terminator. Bugs kept darting into the kitchen to grab grapes from the refrigerator, but not even his grinning antics could wring a smile from my mother.

In some respects, I can't blame her. I dropped a load of bad news on her in the van, and maybe I should have told her sooner. But I didn't want to divulge that revelation on the phone, and I didn't want to tell her with the boys around. What else could I have done?

By the time the doorbell rings at eleven thirty, I'm as tense as a fiddle string and even Gerald is jumpy. He grabs a basket of dinner rolls and heads downstairs to answer the door while I hold Mother in a steely gaze. "Our guests are here. Are you going to be okay?"

She gives me a smile that would chill molten lava. "I am absolutely fine."

❄❄❄ ❄❄❄ ❄❄❄

"Our heavenly Father," Gerald prays, "how we thank you for the changes of the past year. Even through the pain of loss we have seen your hand, and so we praise you for working in our lives."

Joella opens one eye and peeks at the far end of the table. That girl sits between Jennifer and Bugs, clinging to their hands so tightly that her knuckles have gone white. What does *she* have to be nervous about?

"Despite our differences," Gerald continues, "you have brought us together and made us a family, binding us in love and affection. Keep us in your hand, Lord, and join us even more closely in the year to come. Bless the hands that have prepared this meal, and bless the fellowship around this table. In the name of our Lord Jesus. Amen."

"Amen." Joella lifts the basket of dinner rolls and passes them to Clay. "Eat up."

"Well." Gerald settles into his chair and shakes out his napkin. "Everything sure looks good. I do believe this is my favorite meal of the year."

Joella passes dishes left and right, silently filling her plate as she strains to hear the murmured conversation at the opposite end of the table. Whispering's not polite, of course, but that girl probably doesn't know any better. After all, it's not like she was raised in a decent family.

Joella picks up her fork and studies Bugs. That girl has filled his plate to overflowing, giving him a double helping of the sweet potato casserole and only a tiny dollop of the dish with green beans.

As Gerald takes a heaping spoonful of her special garlic mashed potatoes, Joella points the tines of her fork at the clump of green bean casserole on Bugs's plate. "You need to eat that, dear. It's good for you."

Bugs makes a face. "I don't like it."

"But it's good."

"He really doesn't like it," Jen interrupts, giving Joella a smile as thin as rice water. "He'll eat steamed broccoli instead."

Joella clears her throat. "But broccoli isn't beans. Beans have different vitamins and minerals—"

"They're both green, Mom." Jen shakes her head, then gives that girl a conspiratorial smile. What is that about?

Joella looks down at her plate and takes a bite of turkey. The breast meat is dry, which means Jen forgot to cook the turkey upside down. If Joella's told her once, she's told her a dozen times that poultry will never dry out if you bake the bird with its drumsticks against the *bottom* of the pan. But no, Jen wants her Thanksgiving turkey to look like the one in that famous Norman Rockwell painting. And what did Rockwell know about cooking? Nothing, that's what. Nothing at all.

Daniel Sladen, as attractive as ever, has taken a generous portion of Joella's bean casserole. So have Gerald, Lydia, Clay, and Jen, so apparently only Bugs and that girl have cultivated more discerning tastes.

Does that girl have something *against* beans and cream of mushroom soup? Her mother, the tart, probably cooked gourmet meals. That's how she snagged Nolan and later how she hooked the bigwig psychiatrist and convinced him to adopt her illegitimate kid.

Daniel beams at Jen. "My compliments to the chef. Did you make all this yourself?"

Jen smiles and passes Clay the dinner rolls. "Mom and I made the pies last night. McLane brought the sweet potato casserole, and Mom made the bean casserole and mashed potatoes. Lydia brought the steamed broccoli and the celery sticks, while I handled the turkey—the easy part."

"But it wouldn't be Thanksgiving without a turkey." Gerald winks at Jen. "Everything is delicious."

Joella frowns as Clay reaches for the marshmallow-encrusted sweet potato casserole. By her count, the boy has already eaten two helpings. "Careful, Clay," she warns. "You fill up on sweet potatoes and you're not going to have room for the good stuff."

"Sweet potatoes are good stuff," Jen says, an edge to her voice. "Let him eat what he likes."

"But all that starch—"

"It's one day a year." Jen's company smile vanishes. "Can't we enjoy one meal without worrying about the food pyramid?"

An uneasy silence seeps over the table until that girl lifts a finger and teasingly points toward Clay. "You'll want to save room," she says, her face lit by Nolan's smile. "Your grammy's made some delicious-looking pies."

Grammy? When have the boys ever called her *grammy?* Joella presses her lips together. She wasn't thinking of pie, for heaven's sake. Who thinks of pie as "good stuff"? She wants her grandsons to eat broccoli and beans and turkey, all the healthful foods growing boys need. But that girl wouldn't understand because she's never been a mother. She's probably trying to charm Clay and Bugs because she's desperate to insinuate herself into this family.

Their introduction had gone smoothly enough. By the time Joella came downstairs with the turkey, the girl had already moved into the dining room. Jen introduced Joella to McLane, and Joella greeted the girl with a nod, the turkey preventing any sort of handshake or hug—not that she'd been exactly eager for that sort of thing. While Joella got the turkey situated in the center of the table, Lydia drew McLane away and Daniel arrived. Since someone *had* to greet the lawyer, Joella did the honors.

She looks at her daughter, confident that Jen won't be able to fault her behavior this morning. She was polite, even kind, as she welcomed the outsiders to the table. Still, she couldn't help but notice that Jen seated her as far as possible from the interloper.

Joella picks up her knife and fork. What does it matter? That girl isn't family and never will be. If she wants to play around with the idea of having a sister, that's fine. The novelty will pass, and blood is thicker than infidelity.

Because no matter what Jen says, betrayal lies at the heart of the relationship between Jen and her so-called sister. And a relationship built on betrayal will never last.

❦❦ ❦❦ ❦❦

Seated at the head of his dining room table, Randolph slices into a gravy-covered turkey breast, still warm from the microwave. The dressing is thick with walnuts and celery, just the way he likes it, and the sweet potato casserole with its caramelized pecan crust is the envy of every chef in town.

Every chef, of course, but the one who prepared this Thanksgiving feast for one.

Randolph cuts another bite of poultry, then brushes it over the dollop of cranberry sauce that sits like a jewel between his whole wheat roll and the gourmet green bean casserole. The chef at Carpe Diem has outdone himself; this meal is worth every penny of the exorbitant price Randolph paid. Unfortunately, he's the only one enjoying it.

He lifts his glass and stares down the length of his table. Yesterday he nearly asked his house cleaner if she had plans for Thanksgiving. Surely she did.

All of his colleagues are presiding over tables like this one, but their guest chairs are filled with warm bodies and smiling faces. His table, on the other hand, reflects only pale memories of past Thanksgiving dinners. Surely somewhere amid the molecules of this solid surface, he can find the laughing smiles that once shone on the polished mahogany.

He takes a sip of his tea and lowers his glass. McLane should be here. This will be their first Thanksgiving without Shana, and they should be together to comfort each other. If she were here, they would take time to talk about Shana and how they missed her; they would reminisce about the time she burned the turkey or the year she spilled the carrot soup because she tripped over the dog's bone.

Today he will revisit those memories alone. McLane is gone. So is Shana. So is the dog. A man shouldn't outlive his memories.

He swallows hard, banishing the images of the past as he concentrates on the sumptuous dinner. When he has cleaned his plate, he pushes away from the table and walks into his study. The dishes can wait.

Randolph walks to his desk, picks up the copy of the detective's report, and settles into his chair. Duggan was surprisingly thorough. His expense report lists every meal he bought between Charlotte and Mt. Dora, every long distance call made, every photocopy produced for the client's file.

Randolph smirks at one restaurant receipt. The detective was generous with Randolph's money, gracing one waitress at a South Carolina truck stop with a 30 percent tip. But the money's not important. What matters is reaching McLane in time to put a halt to this lunacy and get her life back on track.

With Jeff Larson out of the country, Randolph ought to be able to persuade McLane to come home. By now she's probably homesick and in need of money. The sister might be a formidable foe, but she can't possibly exert as much influence as the father who reared McLane. In this situation, nurture will defeat nature.

He picks up the photo of the women on the bench. Though it's slightly blurred, clearly this was not a happy moment for McLane. What caused that look of pain? Did she receive bad news from Iraq? Has Larson been ignoring her since joining his soldier buddies? Or did the sister say something to disillusion whatever rosy dreams McLane has harbored about her long-lost sibling?

He studies the stranger's features. He can see a certain similarity in their bone structure—both women have oval faces, pointed chins, and arched brows beneath wide foreheads. Both wear their hair parted in the center. But McLane's hair is a lovely shade of russet, while the other woman's is dark, almost black. No one looking at them would suspect a biological link unless they were told to search for it.

Finding this woman could not be good for McLane. But what can he do? He failed at stopping her, just as he failed at stopping Shana from driving away on that awful last night.

He'd always thought of himself as a healer. He met Shana when she was distraught and depressed, pregnant by a man who abandoned her completely. He loved her then, though he had to disguise the depth of his feelings until she improved enough to stop seeing him professionally.

How hard it had been to visit her and the baby and not take her in his arms! As the years passed and their friendship grew, he rescued Shana whenever her car died, her sink leaked, and the pilot light in her furnace went out. After years of patient wooing, she finally accepted his proposal . . . and his love.

But he would never forget the five frustrating years he lived in Nolan Norris's shadow. "The General," as Shana called him, stole her heart, her pride, and her self-respect. In the face of Norris's cruelty, she could not believe herself worthy of love, even after Randolph assured her that she was indescribably precious.

Now McLane has thrust Randolph into the General's shadow again. Norris lives in the form of his daughter, and again he has come between Randolph and a woman he has sworn to protect.

But Randolph will not be defeated by a dead man. This time he will win. He will rescue McLane from her folly and restore order in his home.

A few moments ago he was content to let McLane suffer the results of her choices, but she is too much like her mother—too easily swayed and too easily tempted by carnal desires. She needs firm guidance. She needs her father.

He drops the picture and flips the pages of his desk calendar. He would like to leave as soon as possible, but he needs to see several patients on Monday. Any other urgent cases can be shoehorned into Tuesday's or Wednesday's schedules. But by Thursday, surely, he can clear his calendar for a short trip. He'll go to Mt. Dora, find his daughter, and make her see reason. He could probably stay as long as a week—his office manager can refer any urgent patients to the psychiatrist on call at the hospital.

He picks up the phone, dials his travel agent, and abruptly remembers that no one works on Thanksgiving. Sighing, he turns to power up the computer on the credenza. One way or another, he will find a flight that will get him to McLane.

※ ※ ※

I carry a stack of dirty dishes up the stairs and make a mental note: the bad thing about having a makeshift dining room in a funeral chapel is the necessity of carrying the dishes and utensils upstairs when the meal is done. But everyone, including my guests, lends a hand, and within fifteen minutes all the dirty dishes are stacked beside the sink.

Lydia has promised to show Bugs and Clay her newest batch of gerbil babies, so those three clear out and walk down to her house.

Without saying a word, Mom puts on a pair of rubber gloves and turns the tap, filling the sink with steaming water.

When McLane looks at me with a question in her eyes, I shake my head. Some women may enjoy the bonding ritual of cleaning up, but I think that's one holiday tradition we'd be wise to skip this year.

"Why don't you go downstairs and help Gerald put the table away?" I say, waving her toward the staircase. "Mom and I will have these dishes cleaned up in a jiffy."

McLane takes the hint and heads down to the chapel. Fortunately, Daniel and Gerald are still down there to keep her company. They'd be far more comfortable in the sitting area next to the kitchen, but the guys must have smelled the tension in the air. Either that, or Gerald is giving Daniel a tour of the prep room. Not exactly what I'd call after-dinner entertainment, but . . .

Thank heaven the prep room's empty.

By the time I've packaged the leftovers and stowed them in the fridge, Mom is drying dishes like a dervish. The roasting pan is soaking in sudsy water, and the saucepans have been washed.

"Well." I pick up a pair of dry dinner plates and step toward the cupboard. "That went well—don't you think?"

The dish in Mom's hand squeaks as if in pain. "I only want to know one thing."

"What's that?"

"Do you expect me to get that girl a Christmas present?"

When she narrows her eyes, I feel like I've been pinned in the sights of a rifle. "No one's going to force you to do anything, Mom."

"But is she going to be here at Christmas?"

"Her name's McLane, and I'm sure she will be. I *hope* she will be."

"Then you're expecting me to get her a gift."

I set the plates in the cupboard, then face my mother. "I have no expectations of you. But frankly, I'd rather you not get McLane anything than give her some trinket out of a sense of obligation."

Mom frowns and goes back to torturing the dishes while I grab another towel and tackle the mountain of wet silverware.

I remind myself how reluctant I was to accept McLane at first. I didn't want to think of my father as an adulterer, and I certainly didn't want to know that he'd abandoned a woman and a child. But I believe God would have us honor the sanctity of human life, so I can't say that we'd be better off if McLane's mother had had an abortion.

I drop a dry spoon into the drawer and study my mother's stony profile. I believe in her—in her sense of fairness and her commitment to doing the right thing—but I know this is hard for her. And I can't forget that Mom encouraged me to spend time with McLane out of a Christian sense of duty. When I first told her about the solitary soldier's wife who'd come to town, she'd been a lot more inclined toward sympathy and compassion.

But sometimes our pain looms larger than our pity.

I drop a handful of dry forks into the drawer and wrap several wet knives in my dish towel. Mom turns her fury on the roasting pan and scrubs the lid as if she's determined to take off the shine.

I was hoping we could spend the afternoon in the afterglow of a nice Thanksgiving reunion, but Mother has already flipped the calendar ahead five weeks.

How in the world am I going to handle Christmas with these women?

16

*B*y the time December arrives, Mom has gone back to Virginia, we have buried two more citizens of Lake County, and I am certain I am going to fail my anatomy class.

Now I understand why college is best undertaken by the young. We older students might have a better appreciation for education, but the young ones have fewer responsibilities to interfere with the learning process.

Fortunately, Bugs and Clay seem to be doing well at their schools. Aside from my nightly checkup to make sure they've done their home-work, I haven't had to spend a lot of time dealing with child-related crises. Bugs is as happy as a gopher in soft ground, and Clay has finally picked up some new friends. I haven't met them, but Clay's no longer at the age where mothers arrange playdates and sleepovers. He hangs out with his buddies after school, but he's always home in time for dinner.

Our kitchen table has been pleasantly crowded since Thanksgiving. Gerald and I sit at the ends, while Clay slips into the space between the table and the wall. Bugs and McLane squeeze two chairs beneath the table at the other side, and my spirits always lift to see them good-naturedly elbowing each other at the end of the day.

My sister and her baby have become part of the family. On the kitchen calendar we have drawn big red circles around her June due date, and Bugs keeps monitoring her belly for signs of growth. Now that she's entering her second trimester, McLane has traded her anxiety and queasiness for that pregnant glow rarely enjoyed by ordinary women. She lights up a room when she enters it, but I have exchanged my petty jealousy for protectiveness. McLane is my sister, my responsibility, and my friend.

For the last week, she's been coming to Fairlawn as soon as she's able to leave work. Though she stays out of the preparation room—because of a few understandable qualms and out of a need to avoid exposure to chemicals—she often helps Bugs with his homework and starts cooking dinner if Gerald and I are busy downstairs.

One day I came into the living room and found her playing a video game with Clay . . . and I think he let her win. Bugs openly adores her, and Clay, who's not at an age to adore anybody, doesn't seem to mind having her around. I'm relieved that they're getting on so well . . . at least I think I am.

Since it's the first weekend of December, this morning Gerald and I cull boxes of Christmas decorations from all the other containers in the attic. Several of the boxes are mine, brought from Virginia, but some came with the house. Many of the boxes are spattered with bird droppings, probably the result of pigeons, and others are covered with what looks like unmilled pepper.

"What is this stuff?" I ask Gerald as I hand him a box.

His mouth twists into a sour smile. "Roach droppings, I'd bet."

I squeal and drop the box, but Gerald catches it, sparing whatever ornaments or doodads are inside.

I can't get used to the roaches that thrive even in the finest Florida homes. They crawl up through the soil and live in the walls, creeping out at night to eat anything they can find, and I've heard they're especially fond of the glue in corrugated cardboard boxes. Gerald tells me that some houses are positively infested, but he manages to keep them under control by having an exterminator visit Fairlawn once a month.

"Still, the bug guy can't get to every nook and cranny," he says, shining a flashlight under the eaves. "That's why we find them up here."

When the last box has been carried to the second-floor hallway, I climb down the ladder and call the boys to give us a hand. "I want these taken outside," I tell them, shuddering to think about what might be living inside those cardboard walls. "We're going to empty every last box on the front porch and weed through all the decorations. We're not keeping anything we can't use or that's tacky."

Clay lifts a box. "Are we getting rid of Dad's big-bellied Santa?"

I shudder. At an office white elephant exchange three years ago, Thomas won a plastic, shirtless Santa that laughs, jiggles his belly, and raises a frosty mug when you press a button in his foot. I thought he was the ugliest Santa I'd ever seen, but Thomas wouldn't let me throw the thing out.

Today, however, Santa's journey will take him to the curb. The trashman will pick it up on Monday, if Lydia doesn't decide to recycle him first.

"This is an awful lot of work," Bugs says, huffing as he bends to pick up a small box. "How many decorations do we need?"

"I don't know." I stop folding the drop-down ladder long enough to look at Gerald. "Is there some sort of protocol for funeral home holidays? Can we string some lights, or are we limited to wreaths with black bows?"

"I can't think of a better time to celebrate the Lord's birth than at a funeral," Gerald says, picking up a box that's more spattered than most. "We usually keep the decorations subdued downstairs, but we can do whatever we want up here." He winks at Bugs. "So if you want a big tree, lots of lights, or even a blinking beacon for your room, just say the word."

Bugs's grin spreads from ear to ear. "Sweet!"

After Bugs stomps down the stairs, Gerald turns to me. "This is a lot of work, and I really need to take the hearse in for a tune-up. I hate for you to get started on this with your studies hangin' over your head."

"It's okay. I'm taking the day off, and McLane said she'd come over to help. Ours may be the only Christmas she gets to experience this year, so I want her to do as much as she wants. I may even send her and Clay out to get the Christmas tree if we finish sorting through these boxes before lunchtime."

Half an hour later, Bugs and I are sitting on the porch steps with a wad of knotted Christmas lights between us.

I lift my head when McLane's Altima turns into the drive. "Hey, kiddo—" I nudge Bugs's shoulder—"look who's here."

McLane gets out of the car and smiles when she sees my son. She comes toward us, her coppery hair blowing in the breeze, and stoops to give Bugs a hug when he meets her on the sidewalk. "Hi, big guy. You helping your mom?"

"Yeah." He releases her, then points to the mess on the porch. "Mom says the tacky stuff has to go, but I like the big-bellied Santa."

"This I've got to see."

Bugs isn't the only one to notice McLane's arrival. Skeeter, who's been roaming around the yard sniffing for squirrels, bounds over, his scarred red ball in his mouth.

McLane takes the slimy thing and tosses it across the lawn. She wipes her hand on her jeans as she walks toward me. "Hey." She sinks onto a step. "Looks like we've got quite a job ahead of us."

"It shouldn't be too bad. Honestly, I'm fighting the urge to toss all this stuff out and start over. Maybe we can establish a trend of restraint and dignity in Christmas decorations."

She snorts softly. "Where I come from, it gets worse every year. Everyone used to decorate with white lights and maybe a baby Jesus on the lawn. Then I began to see icicle lights from every peak, and they came out with those snow globe thingies. There's a house in Charlotte that has about thirty inflatable ornaments on the front lawn. When they're all lit up and blown up, the house looks like it's about to lift off."

I laugh. "People were doing the same thing in Virginia. And I'm beginning to see those inflatable snowmen here—which seems crazy, since we're about as likely to see snow as we are to see reindeer prancing through the palm trees."

McLane nods at the jumbled pile of cords on the step. "What are you doing with those?"

"I was going to test them." I tug on the first clump of green wires. "Gerald thinks half of them won't light, so if they don't, I'm throwing them out. I figured we could string one set of white lights around the porch railing. That'd be pretty yet understated—don't you think?"

"I agree." McLane reaches into the tangle, finds a plug, and begins searching for the end.

I ask her how she's feeling; she replies that she's doing great and watching her weight. Apparently the Hatters at the Biddle House keep leaving casseroles and baked goods with McLane's name taped on them.

"It's like they think a pregnant woman has to gain fifty pounds to be healthy," she says, laughing. "But Ryan's loving it. He used to bring home a burger every night. Now he raids the fridge. The Hatters keep reminding me that I'm eating for two, but the way food's been disappearing in that house, they must think I'm eating for sextuplets. I haven't had the heart to tell them I usually eat supper over here."

She yanks on the end of a string, finds the free end, then stands and walks to the covered outlet on the porch. The string lights instantly, but as I feared, nearly half the bulbs remain dark.

"Lights aren't expensive," I tell her, frustrated because I still can't find the end of my string. "Gerald might have a coronary, but I say we toss all these out and start fresh."

McLane grins as she unplugs her set. "Is Gerald frugal?"

"The man reuses aluminum foil. He washes pieces of the stuff, then folds them into little tents and sets them on the counter to dry. He also flattens the toilet paper rolls—says that we save paper if the rolls don't spin so freely."

I gather the bundle of electric lights and dump it into an empty box. "The other day he asked to use my sewing machine because he wanted to stitch up a rip in a pair of boxer shorts."

McLane is about to reply when a car comes up the drive.

I turn, afraid I'll have to stop working to conduct an intake interview, but the vehicle approaching is a yellow cab. I rake my hand through my hair and try to remember the obituaries I skimmed at the breakfast table. Did any of the deceased have survivors who might be coming from out of town?

McLane glances at me. "You expecting someone?"

I brush dust from my jeans. "We never know when someone might show up, but I can't remember anyone ever coming in a taxi. Still . . ."

I walk to one of the big porch pillars and wait for the taxi to stop. It's hard to see inside the tinted windows, but finally the door opens and a man gets out. He bends to explain something to the driver, then straightens and squares his shoulders.

I'm vaguely aware of the sound of the front door slamming as our visitor scans the house and focuses on me. I wait for the sound of footsteps, certain that either Bugs or Clay has come onto the porch, but all remains silent behind me.

I cross my arms and smile. "Hello. Can I help you?"

As the taxi idles in the driveway, the man marches toward me, his face set in a fully upright and locked position. "I'm Randolph Harris. I'm looking for my daughter."

My nerves tighten as I realize the significance of the slamming door. No one came out of the house; I heard McLane going in. She must have recognized this man almost immediately . . . but did he see her? Maybe I'm jumping to conclusions. Maybe she's not hiding from her father. If she's inside checking her makeup, she'll be out in a minute.

I stall for time. "I'm sorry, but I didn't catch your name."

"Dr. Randolph Harris," he says, halting at the bottom of the porch steps. "I'm McLane's father, and I've come to take her home."

I unfold my arms and draw a deep breath, but my mind has gone as blank as a clean sheet of paper.

※ ※ ※

When Clay hears the sound of a car in the driveway, he sprints down the stairs and tiptoes through the hallway. Gerald is waxing the hearse in the garage, so the prep room is empty and the escape route is clear.

He pauses at the warning sign on the prep room entrance and slowly opens the door. After peeking around the corner, he slips into the room and dashes for the back exit. He reaches the porch and glances toward the garage to be sure Gerald isn't watching, then realizes it doesn't matter if he is. It's not like he *has* to stay home today. Mom only said she'd appreciate his help, not that he had to give it.

And right now he'd rather be with his friends.

He takes off for the park at an easy run, enjoying the sound of the tall grass brushing against the soles of his sneakers. Toby IMed him last night, saying that the guys would be hanging out at the park this morning. More than anything, Clay wants to join them.

He thinks they like him, but he can't get over the feeling that he's on some kind of probation. They're already complaining that he's hard to reach. He doesn't have a cell phone (and his mother would flip out if he asked for one), and he is allowed on the computer only a couple of hours a day. Fortunately, those hours are at night, when Mom and Gerald are done with their work in the office. Though Mom keeps saying she doesn't like Clay being on the computer in a room alone, he's promised that he will just use it to check sports scores and do homework.

And talk to his friends, of course.

So Mom lets him use the computer at night, which is when Toby, Percy, and Tyler usually start sending instant messages. Clay likes being online with them because things are more equal in cyberspace. Tyler isn't better looking, Percy isn't brainier, and Toby isn't more daring.

Well, not usually.

The first time Toby told the others to check out a certain site, Clay learned that his mother installed some kind of block on the computer. He kept getting a *You are not allowed to view this site* message. Though he tried to bypass the controls, none of his click-arounds worked and he couldn't guess her password. What's more, he couldn't *ask* for her password without arousing her suspicion.

In the end, he typed what Tyler had typed: *sweet*. Percy followed a minute later with *unbelievable*, but Percy always uses more syllables than everyone else.

Clay cuts through the trees at the edge of the lawn, then jogs through the open gate that leads to the park. The place is mostly empty except for a young woman and her baby in the picnic shelter.

From here, the woman looks a little like Aunt McLane, but his aunt is prettier.

"Hey." Percy steps out from behind a tree and startles Clay. "Man, I didn't think anyone else was going to make it."

"I'm here." Clay shoves his hands into his jeans pockets. "So . . . what are you up to today?"

"Not much." Percy pushes at the bridge of his glasses. "I've got news for you guys, though."

"What news?"

Percy grins. "Wait till the others get here. Tyler will kill me if I tell you first."

They sit in the swings to wait. Clay wraps his arms around the heavy chains and lets his feet drag in the sand. Back and forth, his shoes dig deeper and deeper. If the other guys don't come soon, he'll have dug two trenches beneath this swing.

"Here they come."

He glances up in time to see Tyler and Toby walking through the gate. Tyler has a basketball on his hip, and Toby is shirtless. Clay can't stop a grin. It's cool for Florida, but the sun is out. If they decide to play, a game of two-on-two will work up a sweat. He'd love to play ball this afternoon, but there's no way to know what the other guys have in mind.

Percy slides out of his swing. "Hey. 'Bout time you guys got here."

Toby squints at Percy. "Yeah? Well, not everybody's in a hurry. It's Saturday."

"But I've got news. Real news."

Clay digs in his heels and stops the swing, not wanting to miss a word.

Tyler turns to Percy. "Out with it, Ex-Lax. What's up?"

"Remember what we've been trying to find? My uncle, the one in college, told me about this book he had to read. The guy who wrote it used to live around here, and he wrote *another* book that's going to help us."

Toby smirks. "Speak English, man."

"The catacombs. I went on the Internet and did a little snooping around. I found a book that might lead us straight to the place."

Tyler's brows lower. "You've been on the Internet before and never found nothing."

"That's because I didn't know what to search for. But now I know . . . and I have a lead."

Toby nudges Percy with an elbow. "So what'd you find?"

Percy takes a paper square from his back pocket and unfolds it. *"How to Survive the H-Bomb, and Why* by Pat Frank."

Tyler frowns. "And that helps . . . how?"

"It's the book." Percy rubs his nose, then folds the paper again. "This guy Pat Frank lived around here while he wrote another famous book that was sorta set in Mt. Dora. Anyway, while he lived here, he visited the catacombs. He learned all about them, and he described them in this book on the H-bomb."

"What good does that do us?" Toby asks. "And how are we gonna find some old book?"

"We go to the library, doofus," Tyler answers, jabbing his friend with an index finger. "We look it up, right?"

Percy nods, but Clay notices that he seems a little less certain now.

Toby scratches his ear. "So, we gotta wait until Monday and then we all have to ask for a *library pass?*" He grins at Tyler. "Mrs. Haversham says I'm not allowed in the library until 2010."

"Don't be stupid." Tyler spits on the ground. "You don't go around asking about bomb books at school. They'll call your parents and lock you away for sure. We'll have to go to the public library."

"That's why I told you to meet me here," Percy says. "The town library is open on Saturday."

Clay clears his throat. "Um . . . what if somebody at that library calls our parents?"

"How can they do that? They won't know our names," Toby answers. "If they ask, we'll give fake names."

"It's a free country," Percy adds. "You have the right to read about bombs. You just don't have the right to blow people up."

Clay still feels uneasy. "What if the library doesn't have that book?"

"They ought to," Percy says, sniffing. "Pat Frank was a famous local guy."

Tyler spits again. "I've never heard of him."

"Me, neither," Toby says.

Percy looks at Clay, but he shakes his head. "Sorry."

"That's okay." Percy shrugs. "Someone at the library is bound to know about Pat Frank."

"So—" Tyler holds Percy in a steady gaze—"we find this book, we read it, and it tells us where the catacombs are?"

Percy holds up a warning finger and sneezes. After the sneeze, he pushes at his glasses and grins at the others. "That's the plan."

※ ※ ※

My tension level ratchets up a notch when I hear the front door creak. I glance over my shoulder and see McLane, but the usual traces of good humor are missing from the curve of her mouth and the depths of her eyes.

"Hello, Dad," she says, no joy in her greeting.

"Hello, McLane." Dr. Harris rocks back on his heels. "How are you?"

"I'm good."

I step closer to the pillar, wishing I could somehow merge with its solidness and disappear. This conversation should be between McLane and her father; I don't need to be involved. I look back, intending to slink toward the door.

But McLane blocks my way. She shifts slightly but doesn't walk forward. "How'd you find me?"

His gaze flicks away and grazes the sky before he returns his attention to her. "I asked around," he says after clearing his throat. "And I found you just in time to bring you home for Christmas. You have no business being down here during the holidays. You ought to come home so you can be with the people who love you."

"Dad," McLane says, "I'd like you to meet Jennifer Graham, my sister."

The doctor makes a protesting sound in his throat, but he extends his hand in a stiff gesture. "Pleasure."

Not knowing what else to do, I walk down the steps and shake his hand. His fingers are cold and dry. "Welcome to Mt. Dora."

"I appreciate your taking care of my daughter," he says, his voice rigid, "but you are not responsible for her. I'm her father, and I've come to take her home."

"I'm not going home."

I waver in the charged atmosphere between them. I know McLane is not the sort to be forced into doing something she doesn't want to do, but Dr. Harris seems capable of resorting to physical action if thwarted. I study him—a solid tree trunk of a man—and wonder if he ever abused McLane. Has she concealed the real reason she ran away?

"McLane—" Dr. Harris takes a step forward—"this isn't the time or place to argue. I know you have an apartment in town. Let's go there. While you pack your things, I'll explain what we need to do next."

"I'm not going anywhere with you. I'm with people who love me, people who are going to support me no matter what." She presses her hands to her belly and smooths the oversize shirt she's wearing, revealing the soft paunch at her waist. "I'm pregnant, you see. With Jeff Larson's baby."

Something in the way she says it sends a tremor scooting up the back of my neck. Anyone else would have said *Jeff's baby* or *my husband's baby*. Why did she feel the need to be so formal?

No matter what she intended, her words have an undeniable effect. Dr. Harris exhales an explosion of air and his eyes narrow to slits. I'm afraid the quiet of late morning is about to be shattered in a million pieces.

"Please," I interrupt, my smile wobbling, "why don't we go inside? I can make a pot of coffee and you can talk. McLane, your father's come a long way, and I'm sure you don't want to send him rushing off. Dr. Harris, I bet you can understand that McLane has put down roots here. She has a job, friends, and family, so it's not going to be easy for her to move back to North Carolina on a moment's notice."

"Thank you, but I didn't fly all the way down here to drink coffee."

The doctor shifts his chilly gaze from me to his daughter; then his dark eyes soften. "Sweetheart, you need to come home. I've booked a return flight for this afternoon, two seats in first class. Come back with me and trust me to take care of things. You've been confused, but I can help you get your life back."

McLane lifts her chin and meets his gaze straight on. "I'm not going anywhere. My place is here, with my sister."

"You didn't even know this woman a few weeks ago. I'm your father, the one who raised you—"

"'Since they are no longer two but one, let no one split apart what God has joined together.'" McLane utters the sacred words in a hoarse whisper and focuses on her father. "I'm married, Daddy, so you are no longer responsible for me. Jeff is my husband. I answer to him."

"That boy isn't even here! Look at you, pregnant and alone, just like your mother! Didn't I warn you? That boy cares nothing for you; it's not in him to care. If he makes it home from Iraq, he'll leave you again, mark my words—"

Tears sparkle on McLane's lower lashes as she moves backward, one hand reaching for the doorknob. "Good-bye, Daddy."

"McLane, wait—"

She walks into the house and closes the door.

Dr. Harris and I stand in an awkward silence. A low-flying plane buzzes overhead, and somewhere in the distance I hear the thump of a basketball on asphalt.

When the man speaks again, I cannot mistake the agony in his voice. "She needs to come home."

I plant myself on the second step and try to reason with him. "She's doing well here. She has a good job, she's met some wonderful people, and we are enjoying this opportunity to know each other."

A warning cloud settles over his features. "You don't understand a thing. You don't know her like I do. And you don't know what she's married."

Before I can ask what he means, he turns and stalks toward the taxi waiting at the end of the drive.

❧❧ ❧❧ ❧❧

The W.T. Bland Public Library, Clay discovers, is a long, gray building at the back of a grassy piece of property. He'd been expecting something big and brick, but once again he's found that things are different in Florida.

They walk through the glass door and nearly run into the long table that serves as the main desk. The librarian locks her eyes on them as they stroll into the main room and head toward a table loaded with computers. Toby drifts toward a station with a sign that says Internet, but Percy tugs on his shirt and jerks his thumb toward another station labeled Card Catalog.

Clay follows, feeling the librarian's eyes burn the back of his neck like X-ray vision. This place is as quiet as a graveyard, and he gets the feeling she'd like to keep it that way.

Percy sits on a stool in front of a monitor and runs his fingers over the keyboard.

"Why isn't that a computer?" Toby asks, reaching over Percy's arm to click a key. "It looks like a computer."

"It's not, okay? I mean, it's not the kind you can use to surf the Web." Percy places his right hand on the mouse. "All the books are listed here." He clicks on a box, then types *Frank, Pat*, and hits Enter.

The screen fills with a long list of titles, most of which look exactly alike.

Tyler makes a face. "What's *Alas, Babylon*? Sounds like a TV show."

"That's the famous book I told you about." Percy scrolls down the list and finds a few other titles. "*Hold Back the Night, Forbidden Area, Mr. Adam, An Affair of State . . .*"

"Those sound cool," Toby admits. "*Forbidden Area*. Wonder what that's about."

Clay bends closer as Percy scrolls down the page. Some of the books are listed five or six times. "Why so many?" Clay asks. "Why does a library need so many copies of one book?"

"They're not all at this library, see?" Percy stops scrolling long enough to point to an entry. "This copy is in Eustis. If a book's not here, the lady can order it for us."

"Can I help you boys?"

Clay flinches as the librarian sneaks up from nowhere and drops her hand on Percy's shoulder. Clay's mouth goes dry.

But Percy doesn't even blink. "We're looking for a book by Pat Frank," he says, his voice as smooth as butter. "*How to Survive the H-Bomb, and Why.*"

The librarian's narrow face twitches. "You mean Harry Hart Frank. Pat Frank was his pseudonym."

"We don't care how they were related," Toby says. "We just need the book. For a science project."

The woman walks to another station, where she bends and taps on the keyboard. "Here." She turns the monitor so they can see the screen. "We have one copy in the system, but it's at Lake-Sumter Community College in Leesburg. I'll have to do an interlibrary loan request."

Percy pushes at his glasses. "Does that cost anything?"

The librarian smiles without showing a single tooth. "Fifty cents."

"Hey," Toby interrupts, "have you ever heard of the catacombs?"

The woman's eyes dart from Toby to Percy. "What is that—a new band?"

Tyler snorts beneath his breath, but Percy gives her a straight answer. "It's a bomb shelter. Supposed to be around here."

The librarian crosses her arms. "Sorry, but I've never heard of it. So, do you want me to put in the request for the book? Are you really going to read it?"

Clay looks at Percy, but Percy looks at Tyler, a question in his eyes.

"Yeah," Tyler says, the corner of his mouth twisting. "We'll read it."

"Fine, then." The librarian returns to her desk.

Percy slips from his stool to follow her.

"Whose name should I put on the card?" the librarian calls, breaking the rule of silence.

"Why do you need a name?" Toby asks.

The woman smiles her tight-lipped smile. "How will you know the book has come in unless I have a number to call?"

Tyler turns to Toby. "Clay Graham," he says, grinning. "Clay, give the lady your number."

※ ※ ※

When they're halfway down the sidewalk, Clay explodes in Tyler's face. "Why'd you give that woman my name? This was Percy's idea."

Tyler shrugs. "You're new in town. She won't know you, but she might have heard of us. Word gets around, you know."

"Yeah, everybody knows about the three amigos," Toby says. "The gruesome threesome—that's us."

Reminded again that he is not one of the three, Clay looks away.

But Toby isn't finished. "Tyler's been on the sheriff's bad list since he got caught egging city hall. Then he got caught pouring syrup all over the front porch at the Biddle House."

"That old lady never did like me." Tyler tucks a hank of hair behind his ear. "She was lucky I didn't burn the place down."

"Anyway," Clay says, changing the subject, "that librarian didn't know anything about the catacombs. Maybe the book is a dead end."

"She was lying," Tyler says, his voice flat. "I can tell. She had the same look my mom gets when she tells me Dad's working late."

"She could have been telling the truth," Clay insists, but no one wants to disagree with the leader.

Tyler stops by a chain-link fence, hooking his fingers through the mesh. "Don't forget—" he glances over his shoulder at Clay—"she'll call you when the book comes in. Let us know when she does."

Clay doesn't say anything else as the other three climb the fence and head for home, leaving him alone on the sidewalk.

※ ※ ※

"Would you like a drink, sir?"

Randolph blinks away the image of his stubborn daughter and looks up at the flight attendant. "Nothing for me, thank you."

She strolls on down the aisle, leaving him with his thoughts.

He has wasted an entire day. McLane landed in a soft nest, one she will not want to leave, especially in the face of his disapproval.

But sometimes a parent has to exercise tough love, especially when a child insists on pursuing an unwise and ungodly course. McLane knows how to live; she's been taught biblical principles ever since he married her mother. She knows the father is the head of the home, and she used to respect him . . .

Until Shana told McLane the truth about her background. He warned her not to unlock that door. Some secrets deserve to remain buried. Even the Scriptures advise against speaking of the sin in one's past, yet Shana did exactly that when she took McLane out and filled in the gaps of their shared history.

In all the winding length of their marriage, she never deliberately disobeyed him until that day. And then she was gone.

Like refuse from a clogged drain, images of Shana's wrecked car bubble up into his consciousness. The investigating deputy wrote it up as an accident, though the technician who checked the car found no sign of mechanical malfunction.

"She may have leaned over to fuss with the radio," the deputy pointed out. "The other day we had a major pileup because a driver sneezed. You're asking for trouble if you close your eyes even for a second when you're doing sixty."

Despite the accident report, McLane insisted her mother's death was intentional. As evidence, she cited the doctor's recent diagnosis of cervical cancer—a diagnosis Randolph didn't learn about until the day of his wife's funeral.

"Do you see this?" McLane said, rifling through Shana's desk calendar. "No other doctor's appointments. She wasn't pursuing treatment."

"She was probably praying about what to do."

McLane shook her head. "I don't think so. She was exhausted. She was too tired to fight, so she decided to check out on I-77."

Randolph wanted to argue that Shana had no reason to be tired, but the words died on his tongue. For the last several years, his wife had seemed listless and defeated. The woman who once bloomed under his protective love . . . wilted. The illness must have weakened her spirit for months before anyone realized.

But why hadn't she come to him for help? He had done everything for that woman, given her everything she needed. He adopted her daughter, moved them into his home, and provided Shana with an allowance. He took them to church and exercised his spiritual authority with loving concern. For years everything had been picture-perfect, but within the space of a few months, disobedience and rebellion shattered his household.

Shana deliberately disobeyed his command not to tell McLane of her past. She concealed her illness from him. And, if McLane was right, she had taken her own life rather than face her husband.

Then sin of disobedience spread to McLane. His precious girl began to frequent a bar, she took up with a lowlife, and she ran away. Now she was legally bound to an unsuitable man and pregnant with his child.

Randolph massages his pounding temple. What has he done to deserve this state of affairs? Nothing. Which can only mean that the problem springs from these women, from some gene or predisposition that has nothing to do with him yet affects him in every conceivable way.

Because McLane is still his daughter, and he still loves her.

If he has to take a leave of absence from his practice, he will. He will do whatever it takes to bring her home.

17

$\mathscr{M}$cLane is waiting for me on the sidewalk when I swing by Daniel's office Monday morning. I stop the van and she climbs in. "Thank you so much for doing this."

"No problem."

Actually, it *is* a bit of a problem because I had to reschedule an intake interview and abandon Gerald in the middle of an embalming, but I don't want to miss this. McLane's doctor is going to do an ultrasound this morning, which means I'll get to see my new nephew or niece.

"It's big-time stuff," McLane said when she called last night and invited me to come with her. "The doctor called it a full anatomy scan."

She sounded upbeat on the phone, but as we drive toward the highway, I can't help noticing a frown line between her brows. "Everything okay? Your father hasn't bothered you again, has he?"

McLane shakes her head. "I was afraid he'd show up at the law office, so I called his practice this morning and spoke to his receptionist. She said she expected him in at ten."

I brake for a red light. "I know he's a psychiatrist—is he any good?"

She rolls her eyes. "*He* certainly thinks so. He thinks he understands me better than anyone in the world."

"My mother's no psychiatrist, but she feels the same way about me."

"Yeah, but your mom is quiet."

I cough on suppressed laughter. "Trust me—you haven't seen any-thing. I probably shouldn't tell you this, but she wasn't quite herself when you met her at Thanksgiving. I didn't tell her about you until she landed at the airport, so she was still a little shocked at dinner."

McLane bites her lower lip and leans her elbow on the door. "Good grief, I was probably the last person on earth she wanted to see at your table."

"You may be right, but you're part of our family now." I give McLane a smile as the light turns green. "Don't worry. Mom will come around. It's just going to take some time."

We pull into the parking lot of Dr. Leibowitz's office, then go inside. While McLane signs in, I sit in my favorite chair and survey the selection of magazines. I have just picked up an interesting *Consumer Reports* when the nurse calls us into a room. I follow McLane, a little disappointed that I didn't get to read the magazine's evaluation of caskets by Costco.

This ob-gyn practice has thought of everything. The examination room has the standard table, of course, but there's also a guest chair and a curtained booth for changing. McLane won't need to change today, but I'm impressed by the thoughtful design.

The technician doesn't keep us waiting long. She comes in, intro-duces herself as Hildy, and tells McLane to make herself comfortable on the table. "Good news," Hildy says, pulling a package of film from the pocket of her pink lab coat. "You don't have to use stirrups for this exam."

McLane climbs onto the exam table and lifts the hem of her shirt. I sit in the chair, averting my gaze from her gently rounded belly, until the tech squirts the skin with jelly. I shiver, remembering how cold the goop felt during my ultrasounds.

"This will help improve the contact between the transducer and your skin, giving us a clearer picture," Hildy explains.

McLane slips one hand behind her head and smiles. "Whatever you say."

Hildy slides a rolling stool close to the table and places the curved head of the transducer against McLane's belly.

I turn to the monitor, where a grainy white image has appeared against the black screen. After a moment, I inhale a quick breath. "I can see it." I grin at McLane, who is straining to see the monitor. "Look there. Isn't that a head?"

Hildy presses a button on the machine's gray instrument panel. "We're going to make a video for posterity. I'll snap some pictures you can take to show around."

I can't tear my eyes from the screen. From the corner of my eye I see Hildy glide the transducer over McLane's belly, first one way, then another.

After taking a few pictures, Hildy stands and pushes her stool out of the way. "Back in a flash. I'm going to get another machine."

McLane pushes herself up on her elbows. "Is that normal?"

"What?"

"Using two kinds of machines."

"I don't know anything about these machines. It's been seven years since I stretched out on a table like that." I pick up one of the photographs and hand it to McLane. "Isn't that amazing?"

McLane smiles at the picture. "I'll have to figure out a way to e-mail a copy of this. Jeff would love to see it."

I lean sideways to look, too. "I think we have a scanner in the office. It's old, but I think it'll work. We can make a digital copy when you come for supper."

The door opens and Hildy returns, pushing another machine on a cart. This one is about the same size, but the instrument panel is larger and more complicated.

"Wow," I say, impressed. "Does it balance checkbooks, too?"

McLane tilts her head to see. "It looks like it could land an airplane."

Smiling, Hildy flips a few switches and places the second machine's transducer against McLane's slick stomach. "This machine takes 3-D pictures. We love it."

I hold my breath when the first image comes into focus. This ultrasound monitor is like a window into the womb. As Hildy maneuvers the transducer, I can even see folds of skin at the baby's elbow.

McLane and I both gasp when we see the baby's face. He or she is beautiful, a wonder.

While McLane and I coo and laugh at the baby, Hildy snaps several photographs and then stands. "I'll be back in a minute or two. You can use the paper towels on the counter to clean up. I just have to show these pictures to the doctor." She leaves the room, 3-D photographs and video in hand.

I rip off a length of the paper towels and hand it to McLane. "So? How did it feel to see your baby for the first time?"

Her face creases into a smile as she swipes at the layer of jelly on her skin. "It's hard to explain, but this pregnancy didn't seem real until now. I kept thinking it was because Jeff's not here, but it's hard to deny the truth when you see a baby staring you in the face." She picks up one of the grainy photographs and studies it. "I can't see much from this. Do you think Hildy could tell us whether it's a boy or a girl?"

"Are you sure you want to know?"

"Yeah, I do. I want to be able to plan things and buy clothes as I can afford them. There's no sense in buying dresses if you're having a boy, right?"

I cross my arms and smile in approval. "That's exactly how I felt. I guess Dad's practical streak was bound to come out in us. Both times I was glad I knew I was having a boy."

Hildy sticks her head into the room and gestures to us. "Ready? Now you get to sit in Dr. Leibowitz's office. She'll be in soon to give you her report on the pictures."

"Is that normal?" McLane asks, sliding off the table.

I laugh. "Are you going to ask that every time anything happens?"

McLane puts her shoes on. "I've never done this before. You have."

"Yeah, but every doctor probably has their own procedure, and I don't know this woman. Plus, I had my babies a long time ago. Things change, you know."

McLane and I walk to the office at the end of the hall. Two plush chairs stand before a file-covered desk, and we sit and wait.

I glance around the office. I'm not likely to need an obstetrician in Mt. Dora, but since every woman needs regular gynecological checkups, I might as well come here. Dr. Leibowitz's office is pleasant enough—the sea green wallpaper is flooded with natural light from the windows. The wide bookcase behind her desk is loaded with best sellers as well as medical journals. An eye-level shelf of framed mother-and-baby snapshots keeps the atmosphere from becoming too academic.

"What do you think about this doctor?" I whisper so no one in the hallway can overhear.

McLane leans forward and peers at the snapshots. "I like her a lot. She's nice and really seems to know what she's doing."

"How'd you find her? Did one of the ladies at the Biddle House give you a recommendation?"

McLane laughs. "Not hardly. I found her in the yellow pages."

Our conversation halts when a short woman in a white coat breezes through the doorway. "McLane," she says, offering her hand to her patient, "good to see you again."

McLane shakes the doctor's hand, then gestures to me. "This is my sister, Jennifer Graham."

The woman offers me her hand, too. "Brooke Leibowitz."

I return her greeting and sink back into my chair as the doctor walks behind her desk and opens the folder in her hand. She sits, sets her reading glasses on the end of her nose, and studies something inside the folder. When she draws a deep breath before looking at McLane, my inner alarm bell begins to clang.

※ ※ ※

Gerald listens intently, but it's hard to make out the words. "It's . . . it's Buddy," the man on the phone says, his voice rough. "He's gone."

Gerald groans inwardly. He had almost forgotten about his promise to Russell Solan. When several days passed and the old man didn't call, Gerald assumed the Solans had decided to have the old dog put to sleep and cremated.

But now Russell is calling with sad news and undoubtedly waiting for Gerald to make good on his promise to help.

Gerald clears his throat. "I'm so sorry to hear that. When did he pass?"

"This morning," Russell answers, more composed now. "He was barely able to thump his tail when I got up to bring in the paper, but when I came in, he was waiting by the back door, ready to go out. I tell you, that dog would do anything to keep from soiling the carpet. He was real particular about that; he had pride."

"I'm sure he did." Gerald glances at the body on the prep table. Peterson "Pinky" Perry is only half-juiced, and he can't leave until the process is complete. Jen may be out for another hour, but it's a sure bet the Solans won't want to step over a nearly three-hundred-pound carcass for too long. "Mr. Solan, I've given your situation some thought, and I've come up with what I think is a workable plan. I hope you agree."

Russell sniffs. "Let's hear it."

"Well—" Gerald draws a deep breath—"I'm sure you understand that there are laws about who—and what—can be interred in a cemetery. We can't bury a dog as big as Buddy with people; some folks would take exception to the idea of their loved ones resting kitty-corner to a canine."

"But people like that have no sense a'tall."

"Not everyone is a dog lover. So here's what I propose. I'll pick up Buddy this afternoon, as long as you're available to help me load him. It's been a long time since I lifted anything as big as your dog without help."

"Two sixty-five," Russell says, his voice mournful. "He was losin' weight at the end."

"That's to be expected, I suppose. After I get Buddy, I'll drive him over to the crematorium in Apopka. They'll cremate him and put the cremains in an urn. I'll return those to you. If you want to be buried with Buddy one day, we can set the urn inside your casket."

"Nobody'll mind that? Having his ashes in the box with me?"

"I don't think so. Frankly, I doubt anybody will know. Not many folks peek too closely inside a casket."

Russell falls silent a moment; then he exhales into the phone. "You don't have an oven up at your place?"

"No, sir, we don't."

"And you're sure you can't bury him in Pine Forest, where Trudy and I have our plots?"

"Yes, sir, I'm sure."

"Well . . . all right, then. But I want a service."

Gerald lowers his head into his hand. "We've never done a funeral service for a pet. I'm not sure folks would understand—they might think the idea a tad blasphemous."

"Nothing blasphemous about honoring a faithful creation of God, is there? I'm not asking for a choir, just some flowers, a minister, and an hour in your chapel. Whatever it costs, Trudy and I will pay."

"It's not a question of money. It's a matter of propriety. Protocol. And I'm not sure we're going to be able to find a pastor willing to preach at a dog funeral."

"Then I'll preach." The voice that must have been as strong as iron in younger days suddenly wavers. "I'll do whatever I must to get through it, but I'll not say good-bye to Buddy without a proper service."

Gerald sighs. The old man will not be dissuaded now; he's still in the throes of grief. Perhaps he'll be more amenable to reason later this afternoon. "I'm away from my desk right now, but why don't we discuss it when I come out there for the pickup?"

Russell grunts. "All righty, then. I'll see you later today. In the meantime, I'll write the notice for the paper."

※ ※ ※

"McLane—" Dr. Leibowitz's eyes are level under drawn brows—"the sonogram has given me reason to be gravely concerned about your fetus."

When McLane gasps, the doctor glances at me, probably wondering if I'll be able to support my sister if she faints or grows hysterical.

"It's too early to know for certain," the doctor continues, watching McLane, "but the sonographic measurements are not what they should be. We found what we call fetal ventriculomegaly, and the next step would logically be a fetal MRI. I would like to set up that procedure within the next few days. The sooner we know what we're facing, the better off we'll be."

I can almost hear McLane's thought: *Is that normal?*

No, sweetie, it's not.

McLane lifts a trembling hand. "Wait. Back up, please. What did you find? I can't even say it."

The doctor removes her reading glasses. "Let me explain. During prenatal development, the brain starts out as a tube. As it grows, the inner tube becomes a series of interconnected cavities known as ventricles. Within the ventricles, cerebral spinal fluid, or CSF, flows through the brain and around the spinal cord. If the flow is blocked for any reason, CSF accumulates within the brain and places pressure on the ventricles. They begin to dilate, which causes the cerebral mantle to thin and stretch. We call this condition hydrocephalus."

That's a word I recognize, and at the sound of it my stomach drops, the empty place filling with dread.

McLane must be familiar with the word, too, because a muscle quivers at her jaw. "Why is this happening? I've been so careful. I haven't had any alcohol, not even wine with dinner, and I don't smoke. I've been eating right and—"

"You can't blame yourself," Dr. Leibowitz interrupts. "Fetal ventriculomegaly occurs in approximately one out of every one thousand births. In half of those cases, no other abnormalities exist."

I groan. "You mean . . . there could be something else?"

Dr. Leibowitz looks at me. "Sometimes we also see spina bifida, heart defects, or chromosomal abnormalities like Down syndrome."

McLane swallows hard, her eyes bright with repressed tears.

"The normal fetal brain," the doctor continues, "has ventricles less than ten millimeters wide. When the ventricles measure between ten and fifteen millimeters, the baby is diagnosed with mild ventriculomegaly. If the ventricles are more than fifteen millimeters wide, the enlargement is considered severe."

McLane presses her hand to her mouth, too choked up to speak.

I ask the question she can't: "How wide are her baby's?"

The doctor glances at the photographs in McLane's chart. "I can't be certain until we read the results from a fetal MRI. But I'd guess that we're looking at a mild case . . . but borderline."

"Borderline . . . meaning there may be nothing wrong?"

"Meaning the condition may be severe." The grim line of the doctor's mouth softens. "I'm sorry," she says, her eyes brimming with concern. "I know this is distressing news, but we are going to do the best we can for you. We're going to do the MRI, and I'd recommend amniocentesis as well. With the results from those tests in hand, we can decide how to proceed."

"To fix the problem," McLane says.

"If—" the doctor arches a brow—"the problem can be fixed. Treatment will depend on the type of hydrocephalus, fetal age, and parental inclination."

McLane peers at the doctor through tear-clogged lashes. "My inclination?"

Dr. Leibowitz rests her arms on her desk, her palms covering the photographs of my little nephew or niece. "Fetuses who develop ventricular enlargement and cortical thinning before twenty-eight weeks may have irreparable damage by thirty-two weeks. Since the fetus's survival is doubtful, some families decide it's best to end the pregnancy early."

McLane's hands flatten against her stomach. "My husband is a marine in Iraq," she says, her voice quavering. "This baby is all I have of him. I can't lose it."

"No one is going to force you to do anything you don't want to do. Now—" the doctor shifts her gaze from McLane to me—"do either of you have questions?"

I have dozens, but I don't think this woman has the time or the knowledge to explain why this is happening to us. McLane looks at me, probably hoping for an encouraging word, but I'm as stunned as she is.

I came to give her moral support, but I thought I'd be cooing over photos and promising that the pain of labor is nothing compared to the joy of motherhood.

I have no idea what to say to her now.

❧❧ ❧❧ ❧❧

I make an impulsive decision on the drive home. "I'm not taking you back to work," I tell McLane, who is shaking like a woman with a fever. "I'm taking you to Fairlawn. You can have the guest room for as long as you like."

McLane stares out the window. "I-I couldn't impose."

"Nonsense. When you receive a blow like this, you need to be with family. So you're coming home with me."

"Why?" The word slips from her like a ghostly whisper. "Why is this happening? Is it because of something I did? Is God punishing me?"

"Don't even think that." I turn my head away from the road long enough to give her a warning look. "The God I serve wouldn't punish a baby for his mother's mistake. And *what* mistake? You can't think that way. I won't let you."

She is crying in earnest now, tears rolling down her face while her nose runs. She opens her mouth to speak, but I can tell that any effort to talk will only turn into a sob.

"Don't." I reach over and quickly squeeze her shoulder. "I don't know why God does everything he does, but I know he promises to make all things work for good for those who love him. It's going to be fine. Your baby's going to be fine, and so are you. We'll pray, all of us, and we'll ask the people at church to pray, too. With all those prayers begging God for a miracle, I have to believe God is going to give us one."

She nods, but she doesn't stop crying.

When I turn into the driveway, I'm grateful to see that the parking area is empty. McLane slips out of the van and moves toward the sidewalk, walking as if she's afraid to jostle the child within. I run after her, then take her arm and guide her inside. Anyone watching would assume that her every bone and muscle ached.

I lead her upstairs and put her in the guest room. Without speaking, she curls up on the bed and wraps both arms around a pillow.

When I'm sure she's settled, I close the door and go downstairs.

I find Gerald in the prep room, massaging embalming fluid into Pinky Perry's limbs. His eyes fill with tears when I give him the sad news.

"I've asked her to stay with us awhile," I finish. "I don't know what we can do, but I couldn't leave her at work in that condition. She's in shock."

Gerald takes off his glasses and wipes his eyes with a handkerchief. "I don't know what to do either, but I can pray. If God cares for the wee sparrows in the field, he certainly cares about tiny babies waiting to be born."

*W*hile Clay and Bugs eat their breakfast cereal, I pack their lunches and try to pretend this is an ordinary Tuesday morning. My mindless chatter isn't working, though, because the boys are unusually quiet.

They have to know something is wrong. McLane was here when they came home from school yesterday, but she didn't come out of the guest room to eat supper. When she finally did step out, she said very little to anyone before she announced that she had to go home.

"I don't have anything here," she said, looking vacant-eyed at us as we sat in front of the television. "My makeup, my prenatal vitamins, my clothes—everything's at the apartment."

I stood to walk her to the door. "Come whenever you want to. If you want to spend the night, it's okay. Anytime."

Yes, the boys have to know something's up.

I'm about to walk into the living room to turn on *Good Morning America* when Clay stops me. "Is it Uncle Jeff?" A tide of fear washes through his eyes. "Is he dead?"

I halt in my tracks, grateful that I can dispel at least one set of worries. "No, honey. Jeff is fine."

"Then what's wrong?" Bugs turns sideways to ask the question and stares at his swinging legs as he waits for me to answer.

I've been dreading this, but I need to be honest. "McLane's doctor is pretty sure there's something wrong with her baby," I say, shifting my gaze from Bugs to Clay. "She's upset, of course, but she's going to have some tests. Then they'll figure out what to do."

Clay stirs his cereal, not meeting my eyes. "Is the baby gonna die?"

"Oh no. No one's said that."

Bugs grips the back of his chair. "Will Aunt McLane be sad all the time now?"

I stoop to his level. "She's going to be sad for a while, I think. But we're going to pray for her and the baby, so we can trust that everything will be okay." I go back to my sandwich making at the counter, hoping my explanation will suffice.

But Bugs's next question catches me off guard. "Does Jesus always make babies better?"

I pick up the mayonnaise jar and search for wisdom. "Not always. Sometimes Jesus wants babies to go to heaven and be with him."

Behind me, Clay's chair scrapes against the linoleum. "So how come we're against abortion? Doesn't that send babies to heaven?"

This question requires my full attention. I lower my knife and the mayonnaise and face my sons. "What if it was your birthday and I worked really hard to make you the perfect gift. How do you think I'd feel if you said you didn't want my present? if you threw it back at me without even unwrapping it?"

Bugs's eyes go as round as marbles. "You'd be mad."

"Well, mostly I'd be hurt. Sure, I could take the gift back, but I made it for you. I had a good reason for wanting you to have it." I lean against the counter and fold my arms as I study Clay. "Do you see what I'm saying? God has his own reasons for sending babies. Yes, if they die they go to heaven, but he doesn't want us to shove his gift back in his face. He wants us to unwrap the package and realize what a miracle babies are. He wants us to love them."

I think Clay understands, but who can tell what a thirteen-year-old boy is thinking? He stands and rushes out of the kitchen but comes back to grab his lunch bag.

"There's no sandwich in that bag," I call after him.

"'S all right. I don't care." Clay shrugs his way into his backpack, then stomps down the stairs without saying good-bye.

"Don't worry, Mom," Bugs says as the front door slams. "I'm never gonna get that cool."

※ ※ ※

Gerald turns onto his side, moaning as the sound of voices slips beneath his bedroom door. He's slept late this morning, undoubtedly the result of an overtaxed body and overstressed emotions.

He sits up and lowers his feet to the floor, taking a moment to let the world shift into sharper focus. He listens as Jen explains McLane's situation to the boys, and some of the sadness lifts from his own shoulders.

Jen is right. God knows what he's doing. If they exercise a little faith and spend a few hours on their knees, everything will be fine.

It has to be.

He pushes himself into a standing position, groaning as a muscle in his back bites at his midsection. He shouldn't have tried to lift that dog yesterday; he should have known that he and Russell Solan couldn't carry 260 pounds of deadweight. Russell kept insisting they could do it, but Russell's arms were no longer in their prime. Trudy came out to help, but she'd have been more useful if she'd stepped back and held the door open. Somehow, by half dragging and half lifting, they got Buddy into a body bag and the bag into the back of the call car. But Gerald would pay the price today.

Where did he put his Doan's pills?

He's moving toward his bathroom medicine cabinet when the phone rings. He waits, hoping Jen will answer it, then hears the singing of the old pipes in the walls. She's running water, probably brushing her teeth. She'll need him to grab the phone.

He suppresses another groan and reaches for the receiver. "Fairlawn."

"Gerald Huffman?" The voice is familiar, but he can't quite place it.

"Speaking."

"This is Trudy Solan."

Has the old man asked his wife to do his pleading for him? He might have had her call at a more civilized hour. Gerald gingerly lowers himself onto the bed. "I tried to tell your husband yesterday; we simply can't hold a funeral for a dog. As much as I'd like to honor your wishes, it wouldn't set a good precedent for our mortuary. We could say a prayer or something when I deliver the cremains, but that's all I can promise—"

"I'm not calling about the dog." Trudy sounds odd and detached. Not at all like the woman who thanked him so warmly yesterday.

"Then . . . is there some other way I can help you?"

"You can come get Russell. He was stone-cold dead when I woke up this morning."

❦ ❦ ❦

I'm in the office, checking on details for Pinky Perry's funeral tomorrow, when Gerald tells me he has to make a pickup. I flip a page in the desk calendar. "So we're looking at another funeral . . . Friday?"

"That's what I'll recommend," he says, pulling on his sweater. "Trudy Solan will be in this afternoon to set things up. I told her you'd be in class all morning."

I look at him, convinced I've misunderstood. "Mrs. Solan?"

"Some people are so stubborn." Gerald shakes his head. "Russell Solan wanted a funeral for that dog, so it looks like he's gonna get one. They'll be buried together by the weekend."

I'm too startled to speak. The old man with the dog passed away?

Gerald notices my stupefied expression. "That's how I felt when I heard. Stunned and sorry that I didn't take a little more time to make the man happy. I'll be honoring his wishes now, but it's too late to make him happy."

I'm remembering how I rushed Mr. Solan whenever he called or came by. A dying dog didn't matter much to me, but it mattered a lot to Russell Solan. I still have a lot to learn about this business, and most of what I have to learn isn't taught in school.

I want to tell Gerald how sorry I am, but we've no time to discuss

170

the matter. Through the wall I can hear Bugs tramping down the stairs and the quick click of Skeeter's toenails. I've got to take Bugs to school, and then I have to get to class.

Even Gerald looks surprised when the doorbell rings. I experience an instant of pure panic, imagining a cop at the door with the news that Clay was hit by a car as he rode his bike to school.

But it's McLane who stands in the foyer, and she's carrying an overnight bag. "Do you mind?" she says, catching my eye as Bugs throws his arms around her.

I shake my head and point up the stairs.

She smiles at Bugs, tousles his hair, and carries her bag up the steps while Skeeter trails her.

Gerald looks at me. "Is she staying for a while?"

"Looks like it."

Operating on a hunch that McLane's been too distracted to think of such things, I go back into the office and dial Daniel's law firm. After inquiring about Mrs. Potter's grandchildren in Kentucky, I tell her that McLane will be out for at least another day or two. I hear concern in the secretary's reply, but she doesn't pry.

I have no sooner hung up than Edna Nance calls from the Biddle House. She's been worried about McLane, and she has a message from the doctor. "The nurse called yesterday afternoon, but McLane's been in and out so quickly. . . ."

"Don't worry, Edna. McLane is staying with us for a few days. May I have the message?"

"That's just it. The nurse wouldn't tell me a thing; she said McLane had to call the office herself."

"I'll have her call the doctor. Thank you."

"Are you . . . are you sure everything's all right?"

"Everything's going to be fine. Thanks for calling."

Bugs is pacing on the front porch, anxious to be away, so I tell him to go ahead and get in the van. I grab my purse, notebook, and anatomy textbook from the foyer table, then jog up the stairs. I rap on the guest room door and tell McLane about the doctor's message, but the only answer is a muffled reply.

I head down the stairs again, glancing at my watch as I go. Barely 7:45, and already my day is a blur of activity. Life had better slow down, or I'll never make it to Christmas.

❀ ❀ ❀

Trudy Solan doesn't look like the sort of woman who would dote on a bear-size dog. After hearing about Russell and Buddy, the king of canines, I expected a large woman with mannish hands and the demeanor of a lion tamer.

Instead I meet a small woman with a tight white perm through which I can see a pink and vulnerable scalp. This woman should be carrying a sequined pet carrier with a poodle or a Yorkie peering through the mesh.

"Mrs. Solan?"

My guest turns and offers a timid smile. She's been standing on the front porch, one of the dozens of folks who are reluctant to walk in, even during business hours.

"Call me Trudy, please," she says, locking her hands at her waistline. "You must be Jennifer. Gerald speaks very highly of you."

"Please come in. I am so sorry for your loss."

She nods and follows me into the chapel, where I've pulled a couple of chairs close to the sofa. She sits on the couch and waits while I sink into one of the chairs.

"I was so surprised to hear of Mr. Solan's passing," I begin. "Gerald was just telling me about the time he and your husband had loading Buddy into the call car."

"That dog did him in," she says, pressing her lips together. The thin line of pink lipstick emphasizes the pallor of her face. "The doctor said it was too much work. Russell's heart just gave out. But I think it was more than that. He loved that dog. Always said he couldn't live without Buddy. Now, I guess he won't have to."

Her blue eyes brim with threatening tears, so I slide the box of tissues toward her.

"No need," she says, waving the tissues away. "At our age, Russell

172

and I felt that every day was an unexpected blessing. We promised we wouldn't sorrow when the other passed on."

"All right, then." I open the folder I've pulled from the file. "Gerald mentioned that you and your husband made some preneed arrangements."

"Bought the plots, bought the boxes," she says. "Russell didn't think we needed to do much more than that."

"You bought . . . boxes?"

Trudy rolls her eyes. "A couple of years ago Russell got to reading about how caskets and such are marked up to such ridiculous prices. He didn't want anybody taking advantage, so he went onto the Internet and bought two oak coffins." The beginnings of a smile tip the corners of her mouth. "I know that sounds odd, but the boxes are really lovely and well made. I've never seen anything I liked so well, and I've been to lots of funerals."

In a paroxysm of panic, I remember that this funeral is scheduled for Friday. "You've already bought coffins? Do I need to have your husband's shipped here?"

Trudy chuckles. "Don't you worry; they're at the house. We've been using mine as a coffee table, and I use Russell's to store linens. Of course, now that he needs it, I suppose I'm going to have to find another place for the sheets." A worry line appears between her brows. "I could move all the linens into the bottom of the china closet . . . or move the dishes into the coffin and let you bury Russell in the buffet."

I blink. Is she serious?

She looks up and smiles. "I'm kidding. Russell was dead set on using that coffin, seein' as he got such a good deal on it."

I straighten in my chair, relieved but still a bit uncertain. We learned about independent suppliers in my Introduction to Funeral Services class, but my teacher assured us that few people are even aware of such businesses.

Trudy leans forward to pat my arm. "Please don't feel that I believe *you* would take advantage. I've heard you're a nice young woman. We only wanted to save some money by cutting out the middle man. Russell was always keen on cutting out the middle man, though sometimes I had trouble figuring out who the middle man *was*, exactly, and why Russell was so set on cutting him out. . . ."

I glance away and cough in an effort to cover the laughter that threatens to bubble up from my throat. "I have no objection to you furnishing your husband's coffin. Federal law says you can buy a resting vessel from anyone you please."

"That's good. Now . . . is there something else we need to discuss? I'm assuming we should talk about music and such. And paperwork— is there a lot of paperwork? The doctor's already signed the death certificate."

I refer to my planning notebook. "This page—" I take out a pre-printed form—"lists all the services we offer and the cost for each. You can select whatever options you like."

I pass the form to Mrs. Solan, who holds it up and begins to read.

"You'll see that we do everything from applying for the Social Security death benefit to arranging for cremation, if desired. As you know, we don't cremate here, but if you are absolutely set on it, we can transport a client to a crematorium and have the urn delivered afterward."

Trudy recoils from my suggestion. "Why would I want to burn up my beautiful oak box?" She frowns and studies the price list again. "Of course, mine does have a coffee ring on it. And the dog chewed the corner of Russell's."

"I'm sure the boxes are still quite lovely." I jump in before she can detail every nick in each coffin. McLane is upstairs with the boys, and I haven't had time to sit down and talk to any of them. I have school-work to study and a dinner to prepare, and Pinky Perry's funeral is tomorrow morning. I still need to talk to the organist about music. "As you can see, you can select from many packages—the first covers everything most people consider standard in a funeral, but we'd deduct the cost of the coffin and the cemetery plot. We will prepare and file all the necessary authorizations, permits, and notices."

"You'll write the obituary?"

"Yes, ma'am. I'll need to ask a few questions about your husband's accomplishments, but it won't take long."

"Just be sure to mention the dog's appearance on *Letterman*. That was the high point of his life."

"Really? *Letterman* was the highlight of your husband's life?"

"Not Russell's, Buddy's."

"But this is your husband's obit."

"Listen." A dim flush races across Trudy's pale face. "I know it's crazy, but Russell wanted to be buried with that dog—wanted it bad enough that I think he just stopped livin' so it'd work out. So I'm gonna go along with what he wanted. I want you to treat this like a joint funeral, Russell's and Buddy's."

"But—"

"I know," she says, lifting the list again. "It's unheard of. But it's what Russell wanted." She points to an item on the page. "What's this about?"

"Where are you reading?"

"Embalming." She looks at me with implacable determination on her face. "I don't want Russell to look like he's been pickled."

I smile. "I can assure you that your husband will look quite natural by the time the embalming is finished. We have a cosmetologist on staff."

She sniffs. "As long as he doesn't look *dead*."

Because I'm not sure there's any way to make her husband look *alive*, I point out another option. "You don't have to select embalming. Anyone who chooses cremation, immediate burial, or green burial doesn't have to be embalmed. If more than twenty-four hours pass between death and the viewing and funeral, however, we strongly encourage embalming."

Mrs. Solan crinkles her nose. "I had an uncle who died at home. They laid him out on dry ice, put him in the parlor, and turned him every few hours. He lasted a day and a half before the air got so bad they had to bury him."

"Um . . . we don't do dry ice."

"Glad to hear it. Now—" she sets the price list on the coffee table and takes a folded paper from her purse—"let's talk about the music. Russell made a list of songs he wanted to play in honor of Buddy."

I heave a silent sigh and fold my hands, ready to hear her out.

19

The next morning I take Bugs to school and come back to the house to shower and dress. Gerald heads to the cemetery to make sure the crew has prepared the grave site for Pinky Perry's ten o'clock service; then he has promised to return to the house and arrange the flowers for the funeral. Ordinarily I'd take care of that detail, but I intend to go with McLane and stay with her until the MRI is finished.

I find my sister sitting at the kitchen table, awake, dressed, and determined to do whatever has to be done. I point to the coffeepot as I walk by. "Want some? It's decaf."

She shakes her head. "I've already had juice. Folic acid, you know . . . it's supposed to be good for the baby."

The closest hospital with an MRI machine is the Florida Hospital Waterman in Tavares, a neighboring city. Though the facility is only a little over five miles from Fairlawn, McLane doesn't know her way around that area, so I've promised to come along. I've also printed out a sheet of directions in case I get lost.

While she brushes her teeth, I go down to the west chapel, which Gerald has prepared for the Perry funeral. He has set up about twenty chairs, but because we didn't have time to get a notice in the paper, I'll be surprised if anyone outside the immediate family shows up. Pinky Perry left Mt. Dora thirty years ago and died in a New Jersey nursing home. Because he had a preneed contract with Fairlawn, his body has been flown here.

I step into the foyer and check my watch. McLane is taking longer than I expected, and a florist's van is already moving over the driveway. He pulls parallel to the house, then shifts into reverse and cuts hard, backing up to the front porch. I turn at the sound of McLane's steps on the stairs.

"Sorry," she says, slipping her cell phone into her purse. "But Jeff finally got a chance to call. I had to tell him everything."

"Of course you did." I tilt my head to look into her damp eyes. "Are you okay? Can you do this today?"

"I have to." Somehow she has found strength she didn't have two days ago. "Let's go."

We are walking across the porch as the deliveryman opens the double doors at the back of his van. "Got a casket spray for you," he calls. "And a couple of pots of lilies on stands."

"Will you leave them in the west chapel? I have to go out this morning."

"That I can do."

I am halfway down the steps when Gerald's car rattles up the driveway, leaving a low wake of gray dust. The vehicle spits up a last handful of dirt and shudders to a halt. Gerald gets out and rushes toward us.

I glance at McLane. "What in the . . . ?"

"Idiots," Gerald mutters, his nostrils flaring. "They don't even have a backhoe down there yet."

I snatch a wincing breath. "Backhoe?"

"And the vault—they haven't placed the vault. It's still sitting on the grass, as pretty as you please. The crew messed up on this one. I've gotta call them and get an emergency backhoe operator down there pronto. If we're lucky, they'll get the vault in before the hearse comes down the road, but if I don't get somebody moving, I'll be down there digging myself."

Like a witness to a fatal accident, I stand rooted to the step and watch a spray of lilies sail by. My plans are crumbling around my feet, and there's not a thing I can do about it. "Here." I hand the sheet of directions to McLane. "I can't go with you."

"What? Why?"

"Gerald needs help. But the hospital's not hard to find, and you can ask for imaging at the information desk."

"Oh." McLane takes the directions and gives me a wavering smile. "I was thinking maybe I should go alone, anyway. I don't want you to waste your morning in another waiting room."

"But I wanted to be with you."

"You'll be here when I get back, right?"

I nod.

"That's what matters. I'll see you in a little while."

I draw a deep breath and force a smile as McLane strides away. The scent of lilies trails on the air, and from within the house, I hear Gerald bawling directions to the neglectful cemetery crew.

They're going to be sorry they picked up the phone.

❦ ❦ ❦

McLane and my father are waltzing. Though I'm smiling amid a crowd of onlookers, I can't deny the dart of jealousy that pierces my heart with every breath I take.

My father is wearing his dress uniform, and McLane has never looked so lovely. Her red hair is arranged in a jumble of curls studded with white flowers, and tiny tendrils frame her oval face. She is laughing in my father's arms, and my smile fades when I remember that I haven't danced with my father since the night I married Thomas.

Not fair! It's not right that she should have him when he's off-limits to me. A velvet rope prevents me from entering the dance floor, and an ocean of blue tile stands between us.

I glance at the clock as it begins to strike twelve. I must hurry because something terrible will happen at midnight. I push through the crowd, rush past faces I've never seen.

Daniel Sladen takes my arm, leading me to a pumpkin coach that waits on a gardenia-lined avenue. "It's all right." He extends a gloved hand. "Everyone knows you bought her ticket to the ball."

I accept his help, step into the coach, and squint at the darkness, trying to figure out what is making that odd little sound.

As my eyes adjust to the dim light, I recognize the walls of my bedroom. I am awake. A night-light gleams from the hallway, and the boys are safely asleep in their rooms. Pinky Perry is buried, Russell Solan is in the prep room, and McLane has gone back to the Biddle House. Unless Gerald or one of the boys is moving around, I'm the only one awake at this hour.

The house is still, the only sound the steady *critch, critch* of the clock on my nightstand. I glance at it and see glowing hands positioned at twelve and three. Why am I wide awake at 3 a.m.?

A dull pain answers—my jaw. It has announced its displeasure with a deep, throbbing ache that goes all the way to the bone.

Great. I sit up and push hair out of my eyes, then toss off the covers and pad into the bathroom. The medicine chest offers the same collection of pain relievers, so I shake a Motrin into my palm and turn for the kitchen.

A cold drink would feel good; something with ice might numb the pain. Water . . . or diet soda. Now that I'm awake, I may as well ingest a little caffeine and use this time to study.

Another night-light glows from an outlet above the kitchen counter, and it's all I need to find a glass and fill it with ice from the fridge door. I cringe as the grinding dispenser disturbs the silence, but I'm fairly sure Gerald could sleep through a nuclear bomb as long as the phone didn't ring during the explosion.

I take out a diet cola from the pantry, pop the lid, and pour dark fizz into my glass. I'm stifling a yawn and waiting for the bubbles to settle when a childish voice nearly makes me jump out of my skin.

"Did you put Skeeter in the pie?" Bugs stands in the curved kitchen archway, his hair glowing like an auburn halo. He's clutching his teddy bear and looking past me—no, *through* me.

I bend to peer into his eyes. "Did I what?"

"Did you put Skeeter in the pie?"

I can't stop a smile. Bugs used to sleepwalk almost every night, but he hasn't done it in a long time. The noise of the ice maker must have roused him in the middle of a dream. "Skeeter's probably in your bed, kiddo. Come on. Let's go see."

I grab my glass, then take Bugs's hand and lead him to his room. Skeeter is asleep at the foot of the bed, but he lifts his head and pricks his ears toward us before settling back to sleep.

After helping Bugs into bed and covering him with the quilt, I sit on the edge of the mattress and sip my soda. Bugs and I haven't spent much time together since I started school. His bedtime used to be my favorite part of the day, but lately all I've done is kiss his forehead and ask him if he's brushed his teeth. I haven't prayed with him in a long time.

"Mom?"

I turn, not sure if he's awake, asleep, or somewhere in between. "Yes, honey?"

"Is Clay going to be okay?"

"Clay's doing fine. Were you dreaming about him?"

Bugs doesn't answer but shifts closer and rests his hand on my arm as his breathing deepens.

I may not be the most attentive mother these days, but I'm smart enough to recognize a heaven-sent opportunity when I see one. I rest my hand on my precious son's head and ask God to watch over and protect this sleeping boy.

When I've finished, I go back to bed. As soon as my head hits the pillow, the fragrance of gardenias washes over me, as if I've left remnants of my dream on the pillowcase.

I don't need a therapist to understand why I dreamed of Dad and McLane. As happy as I am to know my sister, some part of my heart resents her. I'm glad my boys adore her, but something in me shrivels each time Bugs runs to her instead of me. Even Gerald loves her and, bless my heart, something in me is even unhappy about that.

I know I shouldn't be jealous. I'm not a perfect person; the Lord and my mother know that for certain. All I can do is try to be better.

※ ※ ※

After seeing Clay out the door and dropping Bugs at school, I head to the Coffee House for a quick breakfast with McLane. She's going back to work today, trying to return to some semblance of normal life, but I know she's still terribly unsettled about the baby. She learned nothing after the MRI yesterday. The technicians simply said they would send the results to her doctor, who would call her with news.

I turn onto Dora Drawdy Way and park in front of the restaurant. McLane's Altima is already here and so is the morning coffee crowd.

I hop out of the van and spot my sister sitting at one of the small tables on the sidewalk. She's sipping from a tall cardboard cup and seems to be studying the Christmas decorations on the light poles.

"Hey," I call, stuffing my keys into my purse as I join her. "Sorry I'm late."

"You're not late. I couldn't sleep, so I got an early start." McLane nods toward a second cup on the table. "I got you a tall coffee with skim milk. That's the way I drink it. I hope it's what you like."

"That's perfect." I take the seat across from her and reach for two packets of artificial sweetener. "How are you feeling this morning?"

"A little better," she says, lowering her cup. "But I was awake all night. Thinking."

I rip the top off the pink packets. "And?"

"I keep wondering if it's fair to bring a severely handicapped child into the world. The kid would have so any problems and face so many obstacles."

I freeze in midmovement, my hand suspended above the coffee cup. Of all the things I expected her to say . . . I never thought I'd hear talk about ending the pregnancy. I blink, then focus on her. "You're not seriously considering an abortion."

Her eyes keep flicking away, as though she's afraid to look at me. "Well, maybe it's the best thing. I went online last night and found this site filled with letters from women whose first-trimester fetuses were diagnosed as hydrocephalic. They all talked about what a heart-breaking choice it was, but they agreed it wasn't fair to bring a damaged child into the world. By stopping the pregnancy, they eased the baby's suffering."

I sit in stunned disbelief. Ten minutes ago, I looked forward to helping McLane through a challenge. A major challenge, certainly, but nothing prayer and faith couldn't handle. By supporting her, I was going to show my boys, my friends, and my community what God could do.

But now . . . I'm not sure I even *know* the woman across from me. Is she really so ignorant? Has she been brainwashed by those who would have her believe that a baby is only a mass of cells and tissues? Where are her Christian convictions?

Until this moment, I have been able to imagine that we are two of a kind, separated only by a twist of fate. After hearing her last comments, however, I find it difficult to believe we have anything at all in common.

"McLane." I drop the sweetener and press my hands to the table. "Do you believe in God?"

It's a reasonable question, but she recoils as though I've stabbed her with it. "I've gone to church practically my entire life."

"Then you have to be familiar with the Ten Commandments. Remember the sixth one? 'Thou shalt not murder'?"

"There are exceptions," she says, a flash of irritation in her eyes. "Capital punishment and self-defense, for instance."

"Those aren't murder. Yet what you're suggesting—"

"Don't. Say. It." Her face twists with frustration, and in that instant I realize how inflexible I sound. I'm giving her the unvarnished truth, but she probably feels like I'm clubbing her over the head.

Maybe I am. But at times like this I can't help but remember that she grew up as the privileged daughter of a wealthy psychiatrist while I endured the gypsy life of an army brat. I am the legitimate daughter, yet she had far more material advantages and went to better schools. So how can she be so obtuse?

I take a moment to remind myself that she's vulnerable, upset, and confused. And young.

"Sweetheart—" I summon a smile and reach for her hand—"I'm

sorry. I'm not trying to judge. I only want to make sure you have all the facts before you make a decision you may regret the rest of your life."

She turns away, her tears barely dammed.

"Think about your mother," I say. "She was pregnant, alone, and abandoned." I'm unable to escape the realization that my father was to blame for that situation, but I press on. "Your mother could have had an abortion, but she chose to give you life."

"That was different," McLane says, her voice husky. "I was perfectly healthy."

"McLane." I whisper her name, wrapping it in the tenderness I would use with one of my boys. "How far along are you?"

"Thirteen weeks." She says this in a hoarse whisper, as though the words are too dreadful to speak in a normal voice.

I stare at her and struggle to find the right words. I want to help her, and I want to be everything a sister should be, but maybe I'm not cut out for this. I've had no training in sisterhood, no experience. And my nature has always been seriously deficient in warm fuzzies. "We have less than three weeks until Christmas. Promise me you'll wait to make a decision until after the holiday. I know it'll be harder if you wait, but there's so much going on at this time of year. You need time to think."

Her eyes fill up and overflow until the tears drop, full and round, on her pale cheeks.

I squeeze her fingers until she looks at me. "I want you to be sure about your decision. You're carrying a unique gift from God. You are this baby's only hope. Don't throw it away so quickly."

Even though I've offered a temporary compromise, my words have thrown up a barrier between us. She pulls her fingers from my grasp and bends to pick up her purse. "I've got to get to work."

I offer what I hope is an apologetic smile. "Thanks for the coffee."

She doesn't even glance in my direction. "Forget it," she says, walking away.

20

ook," Lydia says, panting as we climb the one true hill in Mt. Dora, "if you were to ask me if I am opposed to abortion, I'd say of course. Abortion is wrong for women who are careless with their birth control or who find it inconvenient to raise a kid. But there have to be exceptions. Like when the life of the mother is at stake or in the case of rape."

I shake my head in the rhythm of our power walk. "I disagree. A child of rape is an innocent child, and he can't be blamed for the circumstances of his conception. Once you start saying that certain humans have no right to exist, what's to stop other people from deciding that we aren't entitled to life?"

"Oh, come on." Her lips pucker with exasperation. "Nobody's talking about eugenics today. We have laws to protect the living."

"And we had laws to protect the unborn until 1973. Slavery was legal until the Emancipation Proclamation. If man-made laws are our final standard, why do we keep changing them?"

Lydia increases her pace, her arms pumping faster. "Quality of life should be the standard. See how we're enjoying this walk? If this hypothetical baby could never walk or talk, how will it enjoy life?"

"So you'd euthanize people who are dependent on wheelchairs? or those who can't speak? Maybe you think deaf people should be euthanized. Or maybe anybody over seventy."

"That's not what I meant."

"Why isn't it? If you follow your premise to its logical conclusion, anyone who falls below an arbitrary definition of 'quality life' is unfit to live."

We stop at the railroad track, our usual resting place, and I bend forward to catch my breath. We've been lax in our promise to walk together every other morning, and I can tell. This Friday morning has barely begun, and already I'm exhausted.

"It's a good thing," Lydia says, breathing heavily through her nose, "that we're friends. Or I might have to turn and walk home alone."

"You wouldn't do that," I answer, grinning at her through my sweaty bangs. "Because it's my turn to buy the smoothies."

Lydia rolls her eyes at me, then props her hands on her hips and paces in a circle. "Sometimes you have to love someone enough to let them go. I don't see why you're so worked up about this. You believe babies go to heaven, right? Why not send the baby to a place where it'll be perfect, happy, and whole?"

I stand upright and push the loose hanks of hair out of my eyes. "Because God has a purpose for that baby *here*."

An old pickup rattles by, so we turn our heads away to avoid the gray cloud of exhaust. When it has passed, Lydia draws a deep breath. "Be honest with me. Are you really talking about a hypothetical baby? Or are you talking about McLane's?"

I look down the long railroad tracks that stretch far beyond my field of vision. As much as I want to answer, maybe I should hold my tongue until McLane has decided what she wants to do.

"Whatever." Lydia adjusts her headband for the second half of our power mile. "But if you really believe what you've just said, how are you going to explain that baby's purpose if it dies?"

She sets off again, leaving me too startled to answer.

※ ※ ※

At eleven o'clock, Gerald steps inside the double doors of the packed chapel and nods to Jen. She, in turn, gives the organist a discreet wave.

Ruby Masters holds the last chord of "How Great Thou Art," then lifts her hands from the keyboard and dips her chin toward Ryan Evans, who is sitting beside the organ with a boom box. At Ruby's cue, he presses the button on the tape player. A hiss emerges from the speakers, followed by a scratchy recording of Patti Page singing "How Much Is That Doggy in the Window?"

Gerald's mouth curves into something not quite a smile. Trudy Solan has chosen the music for this service, honoring her husband's final request.

Russell Solan lies in his prepurchased oak casket, the masticated corner repaired with wood putty and oak stain. No one in the crowd can see that Russell reposes at a slight angle, his legs having been shifted to the left in order to make room for the two-quart urn holding Buddy's cremains.

What the mourners *can* see is unconventional enough. A professional portrait of Russell and his dog stands on an easel to the right of the casket. On a table to the left, Jennifer has arranged two vases of red roses, Buddy's favorite blanket, and a basket of gnawed rubber bones. Another framed picture sits on the table, featuring a photo of a smiling mastiff and an unsmiling David Letterman.

Trudy smiled when she brought the blanket, the bones, and the picture. "That was a happy day," she said, placing the frame in Gerald's hand. "Letterman liked Buddy just fine until he got a little slime on his pant leg. That's a hazard with the big dogs. They tend to be a bit drooly. Russell never minded, though. When you love someone, you learn to overlook the little inconveniences."

Gerald has done his best to honor the Solans' wishes, though he has not advertised the fact that Russell's casket contains an urn, one of Trudy's old quilts, and a worn leather leash. No one coming into the chapel has asked where—or if—Buddy has been buried, and for that Gerald is grateful.

He blows out his cheeks as the song ends and the minister approaches the lectern. Trudy asked for a simple service, something brief to honor her husband and his best friend.

"Good morning." The minister acknowledges the crowd with a

smile, then grips the lectern with both hands. "I don't know if you've come here to honor the man, the dog, or both, but I think it's fitting that Russell and Buddy, who were so close in life, are being remembered together.

"I once read that the duty of the dog—and this I say with all due respect—is the same as the duty of Christianity: to teach mankind that the universe is ruled by love. We all know how Russell adored his wife and his Buddy. We can take comfort in knowing that God loves us even more deeply."

The minister lifts his Bible and begins to read: "'What we suffer now is nothing compared to the glory he will reveal to us later. For all creation is waiting eagerly for that future day when God will reveal who his children really are. Against its will, all creation was subjected to God's curse. But with eager hope, the creation looks forward to the day when it will join God's children in glorious freedom from death and decay.'"

He bows his head. "O Lord, what a variety of things you have created! In wisdom you have made men and all the animals. We thank you for giving us an earth full of your creatures. Help us to be benign stewards of your creation and loving masters to the creatures who serve us. Now comfort our hearts as we entrust Russell's body to the earth and his soul to you." The minister steps aside as the pallbearers move forward.

From his hideaway by the organ, Ryan presses the button on his tape player. As Elvis sings "Hound Dog," Russell Solan and Buddy depart for their resting place, nestled together in one of Trudy's quilts and a comfortable oak box.

21

*R*andolph removes his raincoat, hangs it on the hall tree by his private door, and steps into the sanctuary of his office. A thin fringe of gray daylight borders the blind on the window. He lifts it and looks into the wet parking lot beyond.

No one parks in the back lot except doctors and their receptionists. Most of the spaces are already filled, as most of his colleagues are eager to begin another week.

His week, however, will be short. He will see patients today and until noon tomorrow; then he will begin a long-overdue vacation.

He sighs and crosses to the desk that stands before a wall crowded with diplomas and certificates, attesting to his accomplishments in psychiatry and community service. He buzzes his receptionist to tell her he has arrived. "Who's first on the schedule?"

"Howard Reed, for eight o'clock."

"Fine."

"Did you want coffee, Dr. Harris?"

"No, thank you. Just give me ten minutes before sending in Mr. Reed." Randolph drops into his chair and glances at the stack of patient charts waiting in his file drawer. Howard Reed's file is first, as it should be. His receptionist is extraordinarily efficient. Why, then, does he feel so irritated?

He rubs his forehead. He slept very little last night, and yesterday's church service brought him little comfort. Few people spoke to him, and those who did made pleasant inquiries about McLane—inquiries he was forced to answer with false smiles and even falser assurances. She was well, he was well, and they were both doing as well as could be expected.

No one at church knows about Jeff Larson. No one will ever know.

He lifts his head, the misery of the previous day still haunting him. McLane will come home, of course. It is only a matter of time. Either he will bring her home or she will come home on her own; regardless, she will need him to rescue her from a dire situation. Like her mother before her, after her lover casts her off, McLane will depend on him to step in and rectify a mortal mistake.

Randolph opens a desk drawer and pulls out the thick phone book. He flips through the pages and runs his finger down a column—there. Three entries in Charlotte alone, and they can always go outside the city. Finding an adoption agency won't be difficult. Placing the child might be a challenge, but he will leave that to the professionals. He uses a slip of notepaper as a bookmark and returns the heavy volume to his drawer.

When the time comes, he will be prepared. Surely, with Christmas around the corner and all hearts yearning for home, McLane will listen to reason when they meet again.

❧ ❧ ❧

After suffering through an entire weekend with an aching jaw, I stop at the dentist's office on Monday morning.

The receptionist grins and hands me a brochure as I approach the check-in desk. "We knew you'd be back."

"What's this?"

"A brochure about the NTI. Sally Jo says this device will solve all your grinding problems. It's a night guard."

I'm not thrilled to be back at the dentist's office, but I can't deny my problem has been getting worse. With everything going on in my life—the business, my schoolwork, McLane's pregnancy, and my family—it's a wonder I haven't worn my teeth down to stumps.

I set the brochure on the desk. "I've seen magazine ads. Plus, I wore braces as a kid. Believe me—I know what it's like to endure a mouthful of metal and plastic."

"The NTI is not a mouthful," the receptionist insists. "The device is no bigger than the end of your thumb. It slides over your two front teeth, and as long as it's in place, you can't bite down. You'll feel better in no time."

I open the brochure and see an actual-size picture of a plastic gadget that reminds me of one of those plastic supports that slip into pre-drilled holes and hold up my bookshelves. "That's it?"

"Cool, huh? It's a hard plastic, so you can't bite through it. We just have to squirt a bit of resin in there so it'll fit snugly against your teeth. We wouldn't want you swallowing the NTI in the middle of the night."

I shake my head and wonder if anyone has yet choked to death on a plastic tooth guard. I turn the publication sideways, trying to find a better perspective. "It's really that small?"

"Trust me—you won't even know you have it on."

A few minutes later I am escorted to Sally Jo, who fits me with my own NTI-tss device, the official name of this tiny dental thingamajig. She's right about one thing—it is comfortable. But I think I've discovered one reason they call it an NTI-*tss*. When it's clipped to my two front teeth, my lips don't fully close and I can't talk without lisping.

The hygienist checks the fit, then beams at me. "Does it feel comfortable?"

"Ith fine."

"Marvelous. Let me pop off the NTI, and I'll get you ready to go."

I exhale a deep breath as Sally Jo pries the device from my front teeth and carries it away for gift wrap. I drop my head to the back of the chair and close my eyes. I probably look stupid with the thing on, and the boys will crack up if they hear me lisping. But what does it matter? I have no husband, so who cares what I look like at night?

As Elvis croons about his blue Christmas on the intercom, I hand the receptionist my charge card, whisper a fond farewell to another two hundred dollars, and accept my NTI-tss.

Sally Jo hands me the device—which comes with its own glow-in-the-dark carrying case—and thanks me for coming in.

I justify the expense by telling myself that this is a Christmas gift. Maybe the only one I'll receive this year.

But for two hundred dollars, this thing should have come with a secret agent decoder ring and a box of Cracker Jack.

※ ※ ※

I didn't intend to go downtown, but after leaving the dentist's office, my van heads toward Baker Street, home of Lawson, Bridges, and Sladen. I haven't seen McLane since our unhappy breakfast last Thursday, but I have checked up on her. I called her apartment Friday and Saturday (no answer either time), and I caught Ryan at church to ask how she was doing. He said she was fine, but she'd been sleeping a lot.

I thanked him and quietly prayed that she wouldn't go off and have an abortion without first talking to me. I don't think she would.

At least I *hope* she wouldn't.

But how well do I really know her? More than once I've made assumptions about her based on my own tastes and inclinations. Some of my assumptions have been right, but others have been way off the mark. I would never have guessed, for instance, that she drinks her coffee without sugar. Everyone in our family has a sweet tooth; even Dad had to fight the battle of the bulge.

I brake at a stop sign and tell myself that my fears are groundless. McLane's still waiting to hear from her doctor about the MRI results. She won't do anything until she knows more about the baby's condition.

I park in front of the building that houses the law office, then glance at my watch. Eleven thirty isn't too early for lunch, is it? I probably should have called ahead.

I check my lipstick in the rearview mirror, get out of the van, and stroll into the office. McLane has her own desk now; together she and Mrs. Potter guard the waiting area like the crouching stone lions often found at the entrances of Buddhist temples.

I greet Mrs. Potter with a smile while walking to McLane's desk. She's on the phone, apparently talking to a client, so I wait until she hangs up.

"Long time no see." I smile and drop my purse on her desk. "Are you free for lunch?"

She tilts her brow. "You know . . . I don't think I am. I have to type up a deposition."

Behind me, Mrs. Potter clears her throat. If that signal is intended for McLane, she seems not to notice it.

"Are you sure? I was hoping we could talk."

"I don't think there's anything to talk about . . . ," she says, her voice trailing away. She swivels her chair and places her hands on the keyboard. "Besides, I have to stay here so Mrs. Potter can go to lunch—"

"Don't worry about me," Mrs. Potter interrupts. "We can always let the machine answer the phones."

"Thanks, but I need to get to work." When McLane gives me a bland smile, I realize we are having a major disagreement. We're not screaming at each other, but she's treating me with the polite disdain usually reserved for door-to-door salesmen.

"Well, then." I lift my purse from her desk. "You have my number if you want to talk."

"I do."

I would have turned and sailed away in a dramatic show of indifference, but Daniel opens the door of his office. "Jen," he says, his voice ringing with pleasure, "just the woman I wanted to see. You free for lunch?"

What can I do? I nod.

Instantly his hand is at the center of my back, propelling me toward the door. "Let's go to the Lakeside Inn. Their dining room is wonderful. Have you eaten there yet?"

Not until we are outside and on our way to his car do I realize that his steady chatter has prevented me from returning McLane's snub. I don't know how much he heard at the door to his office, but obviously he heard enough to know that my sister and I are having problems.

You gotta love a man who picks up on the undercurrents.

✖✖ ✖✖ ✖✖

The Beauclaire Dining Room at the Lakeside Inn is far classier than what I'm accustomed to at lunch. I settle the linen napkin on my lap and unfold the oversize menu, wondering if they have something as simple as a grilled chicken salad.

"So—" Daniel sets his menu aside—"how are you and McLane doing?"

I close my menu, too. "Has she told you anything about why she missed those days last week?"

"I assumed she wasn't feeling well."

"It's more than that."

"Let me guess." A knowing look darkens his eyes. "She's worried about her pregnancy."

"Did she say something?"

"I have three sisters-in-law, so I know that pregnancy can be rough. But she's doing okay, right?"

"She was fine . . . until she had a sonogram." I glance around and lower my voice. "I don't know if I should say anything. After all, you're her boss."

"But I'm your friend. And I'm not about to use anything you tell me against her."

Briefly, I tell him what little we know of the baby's condition. "McLane is seriously considering an abortion, and that possibility horrifies me. I know it's not my life or my baby, but she's my sister and I feel responsible for her."

Daniel folds one arm on the table and reaches for his water glass. "Maybe . . ."

"Go ahead," I urge when he hesitates. "You can be honest with me."

"All right, then. Maybe she thinks you care more about the baby than about her. If this child is born with severe medical problems, she'll be the one who spends her life taking care of it."

I sputter in disbelief. "I never said—why, I would help her. I'd do anything to help her. Besides, what normal mother doesn't want to take care of her baby?"

"I'm just saying," Daniel continues, "that sometimes we who are pro-life sound callous when it comes to the lives of the already born. I may be wrong, but I think McLane may need to know that you're committed to her no matter what she does."

"She's my sister. How can I not be committed to her?"

He lifts a brow and gently swirls his water glass. "Would you be as committed to continuing your relationship if she decides to have the abortion?"

The question rocks me with its honesty. If McLane has an abortion, I'd feel defeated. I'd feel betrayed. I'd feel cheated. But I can't say these things aloud, not even to Daniel. "I'd hate it." That much I can admit.

Daniel nods. "Ever get the feeling you've taken on more than you can handle?" He smiles just long enough to ease the sting of his words. "I've been watching you. In fact, the entire town's been watching you. It can't be easy, having a sister drop into your life out of thin air— especially a sister with major problems."

I lean back in my chair, grateful for an opportunity to confess the truth. "I want to be her sister. But I've never had a sibling, so I'm new at this. I thought I could advise her. . . ."

"Let me tell you something," Daniel says, his mouth lifting with the beginnings of a smile. "As the oldest of four sons, I can assure you that younger siblings are not your genetic twins. They have minds of their own, and they're determined to use them. You can give advice until you're blue in the face, but there's no guarantee they'll listen."

I frown at the saltshaker, disturbed by the possibility that McLane might abort her baby no matter what I say or do.

"The thing is," Daniel says, his voice softening, "love speaks louder than words. Give advice, but if you really want to reach McLane, love her. No matter what she does. No matter how she messes up. No matter if she breaks your heart."

I draw a deep breath and rest my chin in my hand. Daniel would probably think I'm a horrible person if he knew how conflicted I sometimes feel. I want to love McLane—I know I ought to love her— but do I have to love her if she chooses to do the wrong thing for her baby?

I lift my gaze to meet his. "That'd be so hard. If she aborts that baby, I'll know it, God will know it, and unless I lie, my *boys* will know it. How can I support her if she goes through with something that contradicts everything I believe?"

"You don't have to support her decision," Daniel answers. "You only have to love her."

✻✻✻ ✻✻✻ ✻✻✻

McLane is sitting on the green park bench outside the office when Daniel and I pull up. At first I assume she's waiting for him, but she looks at me as I get out of the car and walk toward the sidewalk.

A breeze ruffles her hair as she squints through the bright afternoon sun. "Can we talk a minute?"

"Jen," Daniel says, waving, "thanks for lunch."

I thank him and sit on the bench next to McLane. For a long moment we say nothing as awareness thickens between us—we've been acting like children.

"I'm sorry, McLane."

She looks at me, her eyes soft with pain. "I'm sorry for acting like such a snot. I meant to stay away, but I can't. I got a call from the doctor this morning, and I went to her office."

"Alone?"

She lowers her head. "I was still upset with you. So I went by myself and listened to the test results and the diagnosis. It's . . . it's not good."

Disappointment strikes like a fist in the stomach. I swallow to choke back the grief that rises in my throat; then I rest my elbow on the back of the bench and turn to better study her face. "Tell me everything."

McLane folds her hands below her belly and stares at the ground. "They call it aqueductal stenosis. No chromosomal problems, no infections, but there's nothing they can do but keep an eye on things. They want to do periodic ultrasounds to see how the baby's growing. If her head keeps getting bigger, they predict a poor outcome."

I blink. "*Her* head?"

McLane nods. "It's a girl."

"Wow." Despite the poor prognosis, my spirits rise. Instead of praying for a nameless baby, I can now pray specifically for my niece. Little Audrey or Arianna or . . . "Have you decided on a name?"

McLane gives me a denying glance. "How can I name her? The doctor said that if I decide to terminate the pregnancy, it'd be better to do it now than to wait."

"No, no, you have to wait." Despite my best intentions, once again I become emphatic and dogmatic. "You can't do this now. You have to take some time to think about it. Doctors aren't infallible, you know, and sometimes tests are misleading. You need to get a second opinion; you need to give our prayers time to work."

She closes her eyes and turns her head in search of the sun. Her twenty-four-year-old face looks middle-aged and careworn. These last few days have exhausted her . . . and I've been thinking they were hard on *me*.

"McLane." I soften my voice. "I've done some searching on the Internet, and I've found stories of women who got the same diagnosis but gave birth to healthy babies. They prayed and God answered, so I'm going to pray for you and your baby. My boys and Gerald and Lydia and my church are going to pray. We're all going to ask God to work a miracle for you and Jeff. All you have to do is watch and wait."

I don't know if she believes me or if she even believes in prayer. But the flutter of a smile crosses her face, and before she gets up to go back to work, she gives my hand a gentle squeeze.

⚔ ⚔ ⚔

I come through the front door and rush up the stairs, determined to reach the kitchen table before the mail I've piled atop a package of Aron Alpha instant adhesive spills onto the floor. I nearly trip over a pair of sneakers, probably Bugs's, but I finally reach the kitchen. As I open my arms, a dozen assorted catalogs, a couple of bills, and a notice from the Book-of-the-Month Club slide onto the table.

Bugs thumps the box of Aron Alpha adhesive with his finger. "What's that?"

"You've heard of Krazy Glue?"

"I think so."

"Pretty much the same thing." I tuck the bills into the napkin holder and pick up the Book-of-the-Month Club envelope. I sent away for an information packet shortly after my evening with Lydia's reading group, but I haven't had the time or energy to read anything but textbooks. Lydia keeps inviting me to come back, but there's no way I'm going to find time to read for pleasure before I finish school. I toss the envelope into the trash. "Good day, Son?"

"Great," Bugs says as he unrolls a flattened fruit snack from a sheet of plastic.

"Good." I blow him a kiss and pick up the box of adhesive, then head downstairs. Gerald is in the prep room, working on Mrs. Gloria Stratten. "How's it going?" I ask, glad to see that he seems to have the situation under control.

Gerald nods as he massages arterial fluid into the tissues of the woman's lower arm. "Everything's fine, but my hands are feeling a little stiff. Would you like to take over from this point?"

"I'll be right there," I promise. "I just want to check something on the computer first." I duck into the office long enough to pull up my calendar on the monitor. I have to register for the spring semester before Christmas, and I'd love to be able to get all my classroom courses on a single day of the week.

After I type a reminder into my calendar, my gaze falls on a pink memo pad near the phone. The top message has been written in Gerald's blocky printing: *Ms. Prose called from the library. Clay's book has come in.*

I gape at the note in pleasant surprise. I met Ms. Prose right after we moved to Mt. Dora, but I didn't know Clay even knew where the public library was. Well, sometimes kids make you scream; sometimes they make you proud.

I slip the note into my pocket and go into the prep room to help Gerald massage Mrs. Stratten.

Not until we're in the kitchen munching on pizza do I remember the memo in my pocket. "Clay—" I pull out the message—"I almost forgot. Your library book came in."

For some reason, his cheeks flush to the color of the pizza sauce. "Oh. Thanks."

I hand the note to him, then reach for a second slice of the pepperoni pie. "You working on a research project or something?"

"Something." Clay takes a huge bite of crust, effectively halting his half of the conversation.

"I didn't know you ever went to the public library," I continue, grateful that my eldest son has renewed his interest in books. "It's a nice place, isn't it?"

Gerald draws his brows into an affronted frown. "Whassa matter with the school library? Last year the town council voted to give the middle school extra funding. We even held a book drive and a raffle. Why didn't the school have the book you need?"

Clay stops chewing and swallows hard. "It's an old book," he says, his voice breaking in midsentence.

"It's an old school," I point out. "I have to admit, I was surprised at how old the building is. So many things around Orlando are new, but here . . ."

"Mt. Dora is a historic city," Gerald says, lifting his chin. "And that school building has a proud history. At one point it housed the Milner-Rosenwald Academy, a fine institution that could boast of a state championship girls' basketball team. In 1970, though, everything got changed around. The academy disappeared, and the building became Mt. Dora Middle School."

"Why did everything change?" I ask.

"Integration." Gerald smiles at Clay, who looks confused. "That's when the law said black and white children had to go to school together."

Bugs's forehead crinkles. "They had to walk together on the sidewalk?"

Gerald laughs. "Not quite. Until integration, black kids and white kids went to separate schools. Milner-Rosenwald was the black school, and East Town is where most black people lived. I don't know where the white kids went because I wasn't living here then."

I pull a dangling string of cheese from the edge of my plate. "I can't imagine living under segregation."

"You're young," Gerald says. "I'm old enough to remember the days of separate restrooms, water fountains, and swimming pools. I remember when a black man couldn't sit at a lunch counter and when black ladies had to ride standing up at the back of the bus."

Bugs's eyes have gone as round as saucers. "Why? Because they didn't have indignation?"

"Because people were ignorant," I tell him. "And the word is *integration*. But don't worry about it. Just eat your pizza."

Clay drops his crust to his plate. "I'm done, okay? I have homework."

I catch Gerald's eye and know what he's thinking. Clay is either hiding something or he's coming down with some kind of bug because the boy never eats less than four slices of pizza and he *never* rushes off to do homework.

"You may be excused."

The words are barely out of my mouth before Clay bolts from the table.

Looking at Gerald, I add, "And I certainly hope he's not sick or in trouble."

22

$\mathcal{A}$fter our power walk on Wednesday morning, Lydia and I stop at the Coffee House for two tall lattes with skim milk and artificial sweetener—two packets each. We haven't talked much about McLane—obviously Lydia realizes it's a touchy subject. Instead, she fills me in about the Stratten family so I can prepare for the upcoming funeral.

She's giving me details on Gloria Stratten's infamous nose job when I stiffen in my chair.

Lydia glances around. "What?"

"Over there." I twist my head. "Don't turn suddenly, but if you look toward the street . . . See that man in the brown short-sleeved sweater?"

Lydia puts her hand to the back of her neck and indulges in a dramatic and extended stretch. "Oh yeah," she finally says, reeling her arms back in. "Who is he?"

"Randolph Harris." I lean forward to better keep an eye on him. "Dr. Randolph Harris."

"We have a new doctor and nobody told me?"

"I don't think he's here to practice medicine. He's McLane's father."

"Ohhhhhh." Lydia turns again. "He's definitely from out of town. Tourists should never wear short sleeves when their forearms are as pale as lilies." She drops her voyeur pose and faces me. "Have you talked to McLane lately?"

"She came for dinner last night. We're okay again."

"Did she mention her father?"

"She never talks about him."

"You don't think she invited him down here, do you? Maybe she asked him to come for Christmas."

I sip my coffee and consider the possibility. McLane doesn't tell me everything, but I can't think of any reason why she wouldn't tell me about inviting her father for the holiday. She needs all the support she can get right now, but I don't see her turning to him, especially if he still hates her husband.

"Unless he's changed his mind about Jeff, I can't see her giving him the time of day. If they're still butting heads, the only reason Randolph Harris would come to Mt. Dora is to confront McLane again. And in her present state of mind . . ." I exhale through my teeth. "Well, that confrontation won't be pleasant."

Lydia and I watch as Dr. Harris takes a newspaper from a machine, folds it under his arm, and gets into a white Saturn sedan.

I stand and grab my coffee. "Come on."

"Okay, but where are we going?"

"Wherever *he* goes. We're going to follow that pale-armed man."

❊ ❊ ❊

Clay's heart thumps like a hammer against his rib cage as he pedals behind the other boys. He's breathless by the time they pull up to the library and drop their rides beneath a huge oak.

Tyler tosses hair out of his eyes. "We're goin' in."

Clay cuts in front of Percy and walks behind Tyler. He IMed the other guys last night, telling them he had the 411 and they should meet by the bike racks after school. He made Percy wait until Toby and Tyler arrived. He grinned when Tyler asked what the big deal was. "Guess," he said.

Percy guessed right away, but Clay didn't care. For the first time, he'd known something before the others.

Now Clay pushes his damp hair off his forehead and leads the way into the library. Tyler and Toby hang back while Clay walks to the desk and tells the librarian he's come for his book.

The woman looks him up and down. "Your name?"

"Clay Graham."

"Uh-huh." The librarian turns and runs her hand along a row of books on a shelf, then removes one with a green rubber band around it. Someone has written Clay's name on a pink slip of paper under the rubber band. She glances at the pink slip and sets the book on the desk. "That the one you wanted?"

Clay reads the title: *How to Survive the H-Bomb, and Why.* "Is this the one by Pat Frank?"

"That's his name on the cover, isn't it?"

"Yeah."

"Well, then." The woman leans her elbows on the desk and smiles. "All I need is your library card."

Clay's stomach drops. "Um . . . what if I don't have one?"

"Maybe you should get one." She takes out a form and pushes it toward Clay. "Fill this out, get a parent or guardian to sign it, and you'll have your card. Then you can check out the book."

He blinks. His mom would probably turn cartwheels if he asked her to sign this paper, but she'd ask questions, even more than she asked the other night. He turns to the others. "Can any of you check out books in this place?"

He might as well have asked if they could drive him to the mall. Tyler gives him an are-you-serious? look, while Toby gapes at the librarian.

"I'm sorry," the woman says, resting her hand on the book. "I can't let you take this out unless you have a library card."

Clay steps back as his stomach tightens. Are they to come so close and end up with nothing?

"Hang on a sec." Percy steps up to the desk and looks the lady square in the eye. "You said we couldn't take the book out. Can we read it here?"

She gives him a disbelieving smile. "You want to read this entire book. Here. Now."

Percy shrugs. "We're sorta doing research, and we don't need the whole book. We just need to look up a few things."

She frowns at Clay. "You boys aren't building an H-bomb, are you?"

He forces a laugh. "Like, no."

The woman glances at Percy, then at Toby, then at Tyler. Her lips compress into a thin line as she studies Percy again. He stands there, looking like the brain he is, and something about him wins her over. "I suppose I could let you use it." She nudges the book toward Percy and lifts an eyebrow at Clay. "You boys be careful with that, okay?"

"No prob." Percy takes the book, and Clay follows him and the others as they move to a table. Tyler and Percy drop into chairs on opposite sides of the table, but Clay and Toby stand behind Percy and peer over his shoulder.

Percy opens the book and turns the yellowed pages. Even from where he stands, Clay can smell the dusty scent of old paper.

Percy pauses at a mostly blank page. "'For Anina, Pat Jr., Perry, and all other children,'" he reads. He grins at Clay. "Whaddya know? This book is for us."

"Dude, get on with it," Tyler grumps. "We don't have time to read the whole stinkin' thing."

"Yeah, yeah." Percy turns to the table of contents. "'Shelter,'" he says, tapping the paper. "Sounds right, huh?"

"Just look," Toby urges.

After Percy flips a few pages, he begins to run his finger down the printed lines.

Clay watches, awed. "Are you really reading that fast?"

"Shh," Toby says. "Let the brainiac do his thing."

"It's not a matter of reading," Percy says, sniffing as he turns another page, "but of looking for key words. For instance, I'm looking for *Mt. Dora*, *catacombs*, or *bomb shelter*, maybe even *underground*. Any of those words could apply."

He stops when he comes to a new chapter. "Whoa, listen: 'In Sylvan Shores . . . there has been constructed the most elaborate group shelter, privately financed, of which I have knowledge.'" He lifts his head as his eyes widen. "'Some of the people hereabouts disrespectfully refer to it as 'the Catacombs,' or 'that underground country club,' but it is a serious enterprise . . . designed to exorcise the specter of total war with the assurance of total survival.'"

Tyler straightens in his chair. "So it *is* real."

"Told ya," Percy says.

Toby tugs on his arm. "What else does it say? Don't read it. Just tell us."

Percy draws a deep breath and reads silently, flipping one page, then another. "Bulldozers," he says, "excavation . . . in the middle of what had been a neat orange grove. Sylvan Shores . . . with six months' supply of foods, grains, seeds, plows, and tools. Bunk beds, luxuries, tobacco, chocolate bars, brandy, and books."

"Brandy?" Tyler's jaw drops. "And cigarettes?"

"Do you think all that stuff is still down there?" Toby asks.

Percy keeps reading. "The shelter has its own diesel generator, with a four-thousand-gallon reserve of fuel oil, plus a generator that runs on gasoline. It has a well . . . and a decontamination room. A clinic, complete with body bags. And listen to this."

He draws the book closer as the other boys crowd in. "'Naturally, the Sylvan Shores shelter will operate under stringent rules. Only subscribers and their immediate families will be admitted. Even visiting friends and close relatives will be barred. And the twenty-five families have arms to defend the shelter against those who try to force their way in and plenty of ammunition.'"

Toby grins at the others. "I knew they had guns!"

"That's tight," Tyler says. "But how do we find the place?"

Percy skims again. "It says they covered the shelter with dirt and planted the land with citrus trees. And . . . well, that's all it says."

"Citrus trees?" Toby rolls his eyes. "There's only about a million orange trees around here."

"Wait a minute." Clay hopes what he's about to say isn't lame. "You mentioned Sylvan Shores twice. What is that, anyway?"

"It's a subdivision," Tyler says. "With lots of houses."

Percy picks up the book again. "'In Sylvan Shores, a central Florida exurb of spacious lakeside homes and small citrus groves.'"

"What's an exurb?" Clay asks. When not even Percy can answer, he jerks his thumb toward the reference desk. "Let me find a dictionary. Dudes, that could be a clue."

He leaves the others buzzing over the book while he talks to the librarian. She points him to a thick dictionary on a stand at the center of the room, and it takes him two or three minutes to find the word he wants: *exurb: a prosperous residential area outside a city and beyond the suburbs.*

"This Sylvan Shores place," he says, joining his friends. "Is it pretty far out? Away from downtown, I mean?"

Tyler nods.

"Then that's where the catacombs are buried." Clay looks at Percy. "And unless people built on top of the entrance, we can still get inside."

"Nobody's built on top of anything," Percy answers, pulling a wadded tissue from his pocket. "My mom read about the catacombs in the paper a couple of years ago. She said you can still get in."

"If a newspaper reporter got into the place," Clay says, "so can we."

※ ※ ※

I step out of the van, smooth my slacks, and pull my purse onto my shoulder. The Lakeside Inn sprawls before me, looking just as it did this morning when Lydia and I followed McLane's father to this historic hotel.

Lydia would die if she could see me now. She's gutsy, but she would never confront a virtual stranger and demand to know why he'd come to town. Then again, she has never worked on Capitol Hill. There I learned to ingratiate myself into the most intimidating conversations.

I march toward the building's entrance and tell myself this is no different from facing one of my former boss's hostile constituents. I'm not coming to pry or make demands; I'm only looking out for McLane's best interests.

Whatever those may be.

I enter through the grand old hotel's double doors and glance

around the beautifully decorated lobby. A wide sitting area opens
before me, bordered by the reservations desk at the back of the room.
The designers have created several conversation areas in the enormous
space by situating sofas and chairs in intimate groupings. The entrance
to the Beauclaire Dining Room, where Daniel and I had lunch two
days ago, lies on the far side of the lobby. I hope McLane's father will
join me there for a cup of coffee.

I move toward the house phone, but the rustle of a newspaper
diverts my attention. Behind an extravagant arrangement of holly and
ivy, a man is sitting on a nearby sofa. The newspaper obscures his face,
but he's wearing a short-sleeved sweater and his forearms are as pale as
milk. Randolph Harris, as I live and breathe.

I walk over to the sofa and clear my throat.

The newspaper lowers, and his gaze meets mine over the top of the
page. For a moment confusion flits through his eyes; then his brow
quirks and his mouth tightens. He's remembered who I am.

"Dr. Harris." I extend my hand. "How nice to see you again. May
I ask what brings you to Mt. Dora?"

He drops the paper and looks around, probably suspecting some
kind of trap. When he sees that we're alone, he stands and returns
my greeting. His handshake is unenthusiastic, but his voice is warm
enough. "Mrs. Graham, isn't it?"

"Please call me Jennifer. We're practically related."

Abruptly, he releases my hand. "I must remember to send a letter
to your visitors' bureau and compliment them on their efficiency. I've
been in town less than eight hours, and already one of the city's leading ladies has stopped by to question my intentions."

Touché. I return his insincere smile. "I am here only because I'm
concerned about my sister."

"Mrs. Graham, may I remind you—"

"Does McLane know you're in town?"

I read the answer in his eyes. "I didn't think so. So why did you
come? I know you're McLane's father, but she's dealing with some
issues right now. I'm not sure this is a good time for you to put addi-
tional pressure on her."

His face flushes, and for an instant I'm sure he's about to shout at me. Then he closes his eyes, opens his mouth, and gestures to the upholstered chair situated at the corner of the sofa. "Will you have a seat?"

I hesitate, not sure what he has in mind, but he seems calm enough. In any case, I'd rather have a civil conversation in the middle of the Lakeside lobby than a heated debate anywhere else.

I sink into the proffered chair. He sits, too, and neatly folds his newspaper. We stare at the mammoth Christmas tree dominating the lobby.

Finally he draws a deep breath. "Mrs. Graham—Jennifer—I didn't come here to confront you. I came because—" a slow smile crosses his face—"if the mountain won't come to Muhammad, perhaps Muhammad should go to the mountain. I love my daughter, Christmas is coming, and I know McLane will need support through this difficult pregnancy. Why shouldn't I try to make amends before the holidays?"

I sink back, as surprised by his words as by his attitude. Maybe time has softened the man's heart; maybe he's now willing to accept McLane's marriage.

And McLane must have spoken to him. How else would he know about her difficult pregnancy? The bitter gall of jealousy burns the back of my throat, but I shake off the feeling. So what if she talked to him? I will not force her to choose between us. If Randolph Harris is ready to accept McLane's new family, he has become an ally. And in the battle to save McLane's pregnancy, I can use all the allies I can get.

"If that's really why you've come," I say, measuring my words, "I'm glad to hear it. McLane's been under a lot of stress."

"So you said." His eyes crinkle with concern. "Has something happened to that boy she married?"

"No, Jeff's fine. It's—" I stop, the words on the tip of my tongue. The news really should be delivered to a father by his daughter. I fold my hands. "I should let McLane tell you the latest developments."

"I look forward to seeing her—*if* she'll see me. So far, she hasn't returned my calls."

"Well . . ." I smile as the strains of "I'll Be Home for Christmas" drift through the lobby. "I was planning on having McLane join my family for dinner Saturday afternoon. Would you like to come?"

"You'd invite me . . . knowing that McLane might call out the National Guard to prevent me from entering the house?"

I can't stop a grin. "It's my house, so I'm allowed to invite whomever I want. So please say you'll come. I thought I'd experiment with some new holiday recipes."

When he smiles without malice, Randolph Harris can be almost handsome. "Jennifer Graham," he says, "I'd be delighted."

❧❧❧ ❧❧❧ ❧❧❧

"Anything else, sir?" The waiter pauses at Randolph's table, the payment folio in his hand.

"I'll take the check. Thanks."

"Very good, sir." The man sets the folio at Randolph's right hand and discreetly retreats.

Randolph signs the check, jots down his room number, and adds a generous gratuity. After closing the folio and setting it on the edge of the table, he picks up his iced tea glass to savor the final moments of a pleasant meal.

Two more evenings alone, then he will dine with McLane and that Graham woman's family. For his daughter's sake he will endure the petty annoyance of having to meet and charm a roomful of strangers. By the time the meal ends, McLane ought to realize that he is not her enemy. He has come a long way and made sacrifices to be with her. He has done it all out of love.

He sips his tea, then swirls the liquid to pick up the sugar at the bottom of his glass.

Mt. Dora really is a lovely town, and this a perfectly fine hotel. He has told his colleagues he is taking a vacation, and he can almost persuade himself to relax. He has packed three novels on the *New York Times* best-seller list, books he would never read at home. When he and McLane have reconciled and solidified their plans, perhaps he will finally be able to open one of the books and read.

Across the room, a woman giggles and hides her blush behind the large menu. Randolph watches, sipping his tea, as her male companion leans across the table to whisper something only she can hear. Her blush deepens, and Randolph feels heat at the back of his collar as the woman's date extends his hand until his fingers brush the cocoa-colored skin of her upper arm.

Randolph's gaze clouds as his blood soars with unbidden memories. His mother adored his father, but his father had been far too fond of the young women who attended his college classes. Apparently several of them had been attracted to the professor, and he returned their interest on more than one occasion.

Randolph had been an oblivious teenager until the afternoon when he stopped by the college to run an errand for his mother. His father's office door was closed, but Randolph knew he wasn't in class. So he walked in . . . and found his father in flagrante delicto with another woman. A black woman.

The memory returns with such force that Randolph drops his glass, spilling his tea. The liquid saturates the linen. He pushes away from the table, his face as hot and burning as it had been all those years ago.

The waiter springs to help. "So sorry, sir. Let me handle that."

Randolph stands and waves his hand over the mess. "My fault. Let me help."

"No need, sir. We'll take care of it."

He draws a deep breath. Everyone in the place is staring, even the couple across the room. "I'll be going, then."

"Have a good night, sir."

"Yes. Thank you." He walks out to the lobby and gulps great mouthfuls of air. A fire crackles in the fireplace, overheating the room. Two couples are sitting on the sofa and chairs where he and Jennifer Graham spoke earlier. Another couple is playing checkers in a corner.

Driven by the smoldering anger that frustrated him as a teenager, Randolph strides toward the stairs. Why didn't his mother believe him? He had sworn to rescue her from that sham of a marriage, but she refused to see the truth. The anger she should have directed at that faithless man and his lover had been aimed at her son instead.

At the stairs he lifts his gaze to the landing. He will go to his room and read or, if he's unable to concentrate, perhaps watch television. He will open a window and let the chill of a Florida December cool his fevered memories.

And this time he will succeed in his plans.

23

At 10:12 on Friday morning, December 15, I slip into a college classroom and take an empty desk. I recognize only a few of the faces around me. Most of the community college students in this room look like children. These underclassmen are getting basic classes out of the way before moving on to more expensive liberal arts colleges. In three or four years some of them will be nurses; those who go on to medical school will endure many more semesters of study before they become doctors. They will care for sick patients as best they can. When they have exhausted all their resources, I will tend to those patients at Fairlawn.

I am musing on this continuous chain of care when our professor enters the classroom with an armload of thin booklets. "Today's final examination," he says, without so much as a *how are you today*, "is neither a multiple choice nor a true-false exam. It is a simple test of your knowledge. The more you have learned, the better you will fare."

He moves down the rows, dropping a booklet onto each desktop. "In a moment I am going to display three charts—one featuring the principal systemic arteries, one featuring the major organs of the thoracic region, and one featuring the deep fascia of the human hand. You are to label and describe as many elements of each diagram as possible. You have ninety minutes to complete your work."

I stare at the simple booklet as it slaps the surface of my desk. I use a fingertip to lift the cover, but there are no further instructions on the pages within. Nothing but blank paper.

I glance around the room. Every student sits in stunned silence. The girl across from me, a nursing major, catches my eye and swallows hard.

Multiple choice would have been easier. A true-false test would have given us a 50 percent chance of passing. But this?

The professor, his hands empty now, walks to the front of the room and lifts the cover on the first of three flip charts. An outline of a human body fills the page, with bright red lines flowing throughout the torso, head, and limbs. Numbers point to various arteries. Apparently we are to write the numbers and each corresponding artery's name in our blank books.

I close my eyes and wonder if my aging brain has managed to retain anything. A jumble of words fills my mind, accompanied by photographs that look nothing like the cartoonish figure on the professor's chart.

I say a quick prayer for grace, remind the Lord that he brought me to this moment, and open the cover of my blank book. I squint at the first chart, where the number *1* points to the cartoon figure's hand.

I pick up my pen and write: *1. The superficial palmar arch.*

I move on to number two.

❧ ❧ ❧

Clay pedals his bike, his legs burning and his palms slick with sweat. He and his friends have been riding through Sylvan Shores ever since school let out, and all they've seen so far are houses, SUVs, basketball hoops, and mailboxes. To make matters worse, most of the homes back up to orange groves, but there are way too many to investigate.

Tyler stops at an intersection. Clay brakes, too, sliding to a stop beside Percy.

"I gotta go," Tyler says, his eyes narrowing as he studies the horizon. "My brother's coming home for Christmas break, and Mom says I need to be there when he gets in."

Toby sighs. "I guess we've hit a dead end."

"But we haven't," Percy insists. "By learning that the catacombs are somewhere in this area, we've eliminated a lot of territory. We just have to keep looking."

"But where?" Tyler scowls. "I mean, there are about three thousand orange trees around here. Which one are we supposed to dig up?"

Percy shakes his head. "I don't think we have to dig. I'll go online tonight and see if I can find some other clues."

Toby turns to Clay. "You down with that?"

"I guess so."

Tyler grips the handlebars of his bike. "Cool. We'll check in later tonight and meet again tomorrow. We'll have all kinds of time during Christmas break to search, so we'll find the catacombs. Until we do, remember—don't breathe a word to anybody."

24

*O*rdinary women serve Christmas dinner on Christmas Eve or Christmas Day, but ordinary women don't have to contend with sensitive sisters, estranged fathers, and resentful mothers.

Because there's no way on earth I can get all my loved ones around one table for a lovely holiday meal, I decide to serve a series of Christmas dinners. The first will be this afternoon, with McLane and her father as the guests of honor.

I only hope McLane doesn't mind that I've invited the man she's traveled several hundred miles to escape.

I crawl out of bed early Saturday morning and wrestle with the turkey in the kitchen sink. In previous years I spent up to fifteen minutes struggling with the restraining wire or partially frozen drumsticks, but this bird is pliable and cooperative.

I pull the bag of innards from the body and find myself admiring the beauty of the hollow cavity. It would be easy to embalm a turkey, providing I could find a large enough artery to send formaldehyde through the muscles. On the other hand, it might be possible to pump a nice marinade through the bird with the Porti-Boy, but I don't want to take a chance on our turkey tasting like embalming fluid. . . .

When our entree is finally dressed and in the oven, I mix up a couple of pecan pies, a sweet potato casserole, and dinner rolls. I know

I promised Dr. Harris special holiday recipes, but I didn't have time to search for unique dishes *and* study for my anatomy final.

By ten o'clock all my dishes are either baking in the oven or waiting their turn. I direct my attention to the house, which looks far less Christmassy than the festive funeral home of my intentions. I'm embarrassed to admit that we haven't even put up a Christmas tree.

I hoped to enlist Clay and Bugs to help me decorate, but Clay scoots out the door before I can catch him. Bugs isn't as quick, so he agrees to make place cards with the names of our guests while Gerald brings in the sheet of plywood that serves as our dining room table.

I dash through the house with a can of cinnamon-scented air freshener, spritzing every pillow, curtain, and potted plant. Gerald has hung a simple pine wreath on the front door, so I snatch a length of red silk ribbon from my scrap bag, tie it in a jaunty bow, and attach it to the wreath with a twist tie from a box of garbage bags. By now I'm pretty sure McLane has figured out that I'm not Martha Stewart.

With the plywood panel in place on the casket table, I pull out my best linen tablecloth and spread it over the surface, then groan when I see a grease stain in the center—probably from the Thanksgiving turkey. I don't have time to wash it, so I run into the display room, pull a purple satin pall from one of the caskets, and position it like a runner down the center of the table.

Gerald lifts a brow when he spies my improvisation.

"What? It's a festive color."

"Yeah, but what if we need it?"

I give him a reproving look. "When's the last time someone asked for a purple pall?"

By eleven thirty I'm wearing my favorite holiday sweater, a green cashmere turtleneck that Thomas gave me the year before the divorce. I have a pair of ruby earrings to provide just a spark of red, and my dark pants are forgiving of stains and the inevitable holiday meal belly bulge.

McLane arrives early, greeting me, Bugs, and Gerald with an embrace. She follows me upstairs and hands me a bag of chocolate-covered cranberries. "It's not much of a hostess gift," she says, spreading her hands, "but I love those things."

"Me, too." I reach for the candy dish. "You can go ahead and set them out. They won't last long, but we'll enjoy them."

She opens the cellophane bag as the doorbell rings. "Don't worry. I know where to get more."

I hesitate as I hear heavy steps and the creak of the front door. Gerald greets our guest, who responds with an indistinct masculine murmur.

McLane pours the chocolates into the crystal dish and gives me a teasing glance. "You expecting someone else? Maybe Daniel Sladen?"

"Not this time." I give her a wobbly smile and pick up the turkey platter. "Come on downstairs, and bring the candy."

I start down the steps, moving carefully so as not to lose the turkey. Gerald, I notice, has escorted our guest into the chapel, out of sight.

"You know," I tell McLane, tossing the words over my shoulder, "holidays aren't quite right if we're not with family. My mom's coming next week, but today we wanted to honor you. So we invited someone special."

"Oh yeah? Like Ryan?"

"Not today."

I reach the bottom of the stairs and move into the chapel, where Randolph Harris waits beside our Christmas table. I know McLane's right behind me, so I'm not surprised when she turns the corner and her footsteps halt.

I *am* surprised when she cries out and runs past me, straight into her father's arms.

❊❊❊ ❊❊❊ ❊❊❊

The librarian doesn't look happy when Clay and his friends walk in, so he wonders what they could have done to upset her. They returned the stupid H-bomb book, didn't they?

Percy heads straight for the computers, drops into a chair, and begins hammering the keyboard. Clay sits in the chair next to him and watches as Percy brings up the Google search engine.

"I found this last night." Percy types in *Sylvan Shores* and *catacombs*. "Watch and be amazed." He hits the Enter key and grins as the screen fills with a long list of items. Percy leans forward and clicks a link.

"What is that?" Tyler asks.

"Houses for sale," Percy says, "in Sylvan Shores."

Toby snorts. "We don't want to buy a house."

"That's not the point, Sherlock. Watch and wait." Percy clicks another link and another until Clay and the others find themselves staring at a black-and-white photograph that looks like it's been taken from an airplane.

"Satellite reconnaissance," Percy says. "Watch this." When he clicks a box on the page, roads appear over the photo. "Northland Road, Eudora Road, Morningside Drive." He tilts his head to read the vertical street names. "Sound familiar?"

Clay feels a slow smile creep across his face. "We rode down those roads yesterday."

"Two points for the newbie." Percy crosses his arms. "And we know they haven't built anything over the catacombs, right? So all we have to do is look for open spaces in orange groves. Seeing it like this, from the air, we'll be able to pinpoint possible locations in a flash."

Clay studies the photo and realizes that Percy is right. From the ground, it's impossible to tell what lies behind fences in people's backyards. But here, in a single picture, they can see every building and every tree and every open space. "That's still a lot of ground to cover. If only we could get someone to tell us where the thing is."

Percy rubs his nose. "Or give us a clue. I know we tried with the candy store guy—"

"There are people who still know about the catacombs," Tyler interrupts. "Maybe they're planning on hiding out down there. People may not be worried about the Russians anymore, but they're plenty worried about terrorists."

"But man, they'd have to be geezers." Toby leans against the back of a nearby chair. "If they were thirty or forty back when they built the place, they'd be seventy or eighty now. So they'd be—"

"Dead," Tyler says, smirking. "Or in the old folks' home."

Percy taps his chin. "We have to approach the problem with logic. Somebody in town knows where the catacombs are and probably had a stake in them. So . . . who knows about everybody in town?"

Toby snaps his fingers. "Annie Watson at the diner. My mom says she's the town gossip."

"She's too young," Tyler says. "We need to talk to somebody *ancient*."

Clay lifts his head. "My mom is friends with those ladies at the Biddle House. Maybe one of them would know."

"Yeah, but your mom can't ask about the catacombs. That'd give it away." A grin crawls to Tyler's mouth and curves like a snake. "But *you* could go over there, dude. Go looking for your mom or something and talk to the grannies. I'll bet one of them could tell you exactly what we want to hear."

Clay nods as something inside him churns. His mom would kill him if she knew what he was doing, and he's never been real crazy about old ladies. But if the guys need him to do this . . . "I could talk to them, if I get a chance to go over there. It's not like I go to the Biddle House every day."

"You could go now." Toby glances at the clock. "It's only noon, so you could ride over—"

"Noon?" Clay rockets out of his chair. "I've gotta go home. My mom's having a dinner and I'm late."

"Tomorrow, then," Tyler calls. "Tomorrow you'll talk to the old ladies, right?"

Clay waves over his shoulder as he heads for the door. "Whatever."

❈ ❈ ❈

If not for Clay's late arrival and the glower I felt obliged to give him when he sat down, my preholiday dinner would have been perfect. The turkey was moist and delicious, the rolls didn't burn, and the pecan pies didn't taste like they came from a fast-food restaurant.

Randolph Harris sat next to McLane and remained on his best behavior. Gerald sat by my side and kept sending me smiles, his way of congratulating me, I think, for being a peacemaker. At the end of the table, Bugs didn't burp aloud even once and remembered to say "please" before every request.

I'll deal with Clay later.

Right now I'm going to sit and bask in the glow of good food, good friends, and good fellowship. Clay and Bugs have gone upstairs, and Gerald has poured fresh cups of steaming coffee. McLane is sipping her coffee with one hand draped protectively over the life just beginning to burgeon into her lap. For a little while at least, she has managed to put aside her worries about the baby.

A merry Christmas, indeed.

"Delicious," Dr. Harris says, setting his napkin on the table. "I don't know how you get the turkey to stay so moist. My wife never quite managed the trick."

"Mom had our Thanksgiving dinner catered," McLane says as she smiles at her father. "At least, for the last few years she did. I think she gave up on turkeys."

I sip my coffee and smile. "I'd love to take the credit, but it's a trick of my mother's. You just cover the bird in foil and bake it upside down."

"Really?" McLane twinkles at me from across the table. "Next year, I'll have to remember that. Jeff will think I've become a master chef."

At the mention of her absent husband's name, an almost tangible tension settles over the table. Dr. Harris, who has been leaning back with an arm propped on McLane's chair, stiffens noticeably.

I reach for Gerald's hand and squeeze, a silent SOS.

"Do you have to speak of *him*?" Dr. Harris says, an edge to his voice. "We were having a perfectly lovely time."

Color drains from McLane's face, leaving two round roses, one on each cheek. "Tell me, Dad—why did you come here?"

"I came because I love you. I want to see you. And it's Christmas."

"You love me?" Her voice ripples with anguish. "If you love me, you'll accept me and Jeff."

He lifts his arm from the back of her chair and straightens, his eyes going the color of thunderclouds. "I cannot accept," he says, his voice low and intense, "what is wrong in the eyes of God."

"Jeff and I are not wrong. He is my husband."

"For now. But you could rectify your mistake—"

"I'm carrying his child."

"But you don't have to keep it. You can stay here and have the baby, then find a place for it and come home. No one will know. You can start over, go back to school, pick up the life you were meant to have—"

"Dr. Harris." The words come from my lips, but I'm barely aware of having spoken. I only know that this man is not the ally I thought he was. I'm lost in this conversation, but clearly McLane is no longer being comforted by his presence. I stand and press my fingertips to the edge of the linen-covered table. "I think you should go now. You're upsetting my sister."

He lifts one eyebrow at me, masculine shorthand suggesting that I stay out of the conversation, but I will not be intimidated in my own house.

"Please," Gerald says. "You are no longer welcome here."

Dr. Harris eyes Gerald as though he's wondering if the older man has the strength to forcibly eject him; then he pushes away from the table. "You—" his eyes bore into mine—"led me to believe she was having regrets."

"And you," I answer, "led me to believe you loved her. Love doesn't make these kinds of demands."

He looks at me, his face hardening in an effigy of contempt. "You don't know what you're dealing with here."

Before I can respond, he yanks his coat from the back of the chair and stalks out of our house.

Like shell-shocked victims on whom a vicious tornado descended from a cloudless sky, we sit in silence. McLane stares at her dessert plate while Gerald plants both elbows on the table and rests his head on his folded hands.

I slump in my chair and try to sort through my thoughts. Randolph Harris obviously cares for his daughter, for why else would he come to Florida in the hope of reconciling with her? And though McLane is angry with her father, she does care for him. I watched her run into his arms; I heard them laughing together at dinner. Obviously they used to be close . . . until Jeff Larson came between them.

A horde of unruly and unwelcome thoughts jostles and shoves at the threshold of my mind. Is Dr. Harris *jealous* of Jeff Larson?

I'm done with second-guessing. If I'm to be of any real help to McLane, she needs to tell me everything.

"McLane—" my voice sounds broken in my own ears—"why does your father dislike Jeff so much?"

She presses her hands over her face and breathes deeply. "I told you. He says Jeff isn't good enough for me."

I shake my head. "That can't be the only reason. Your dad said you and Jeff were wrong in the eyes of God. I don't know what that means where you come from, but around here there's not much God can't forgive. So what is it? You can tell me."

McLane picks up her fork and begins to trace the pattern woven into the tablecloth. "Why did you tell him I was having regrets?"

"I didn't. I told him you were under a lot of stress, but he seemed to already know that. He said something about coming to help you through a difficult pregnancy, so I assumed you'd talked to him."

She shakes her head. "I haven't talked to him at all before today."

"Then it's time you started talking—first, to me. You have to help me understand. Your father resents Jeff. Why?"

Her expression changes as some thought hardens her eyes and tightens the corner of her mouth. "Because of the way things are and the way they've always been. In my father's circle, things always look nice and smooth on the surface, but underneath, some things never change."

I turn to Gerald, whose brows have furrowed in a frown. "Are you understanding this?"

"I think," he says, "I'm beginning to."

McLane smiles without humor. "Mt. Dora isn't so different from North Carolina. I know things are changing, but they aren't changing fast enough. Jeff and I knew we'd have a hard time, but he said it wouldn't matter. If things got rough, we could move away, find someplace new to live."

What sort of past is this young man trying to outrun? I lean forward, growing more alarmed by the moment. "What did Jeff do?"

"He didn't *do* anything." She drops her fork and looks at me with a strangely level gaze. "It's what he *is* that drives my father insane."

"What is he?" My mind fills with several possible answers, any one of which might trouble a man like Randolph Harris: *liar, lazy bum, thief, atheist, Communist, psychopath, serial killer . . .*

McLane looks at me and blinks hard. "He's black."

I experience a blank moment as my mental picture of dark-haired, brown-eyed, Italian-looking Jeff Larson shatters into bits. I struggle to come up with a substitute image of my brother-in-law, but the pieces won't fit together.

Beside me, I hear Gerald exhale through his teeth. At least I'm not the only one astounded by this news.

"My dad's church," McLane says, her voice flat, "has a sign on the outer door: No Women in Slacks, No Blacks. And they mean it."

"Jeff . . . is black." My gaze automatically lowers to my sister's mid-section. "So your baby—"

"Is ours," she says, a flash of defensiveness in her eyes. "Don't you dare put a label on her."

I swallow hard as my mind fills with unpleasant words: *half-breed, mixed race, colored.* They're old words, leftovers from segregation, and I wouldn't use any of them in conversation. But I *thought* them.

I swallow hard and meet McLane's gaze. "I wish you'd told me sooner. I would have understood."

"Would you?" She releases a hollow laugh. "Have you looked around this place? It's one of the whitest towns I've ever lived in. And you—your friends are white, your church is white, even the people you bury are white. I wanted to trust you, but I wasn't sure you'd understand."

I straighten in my chair and look at Gerald, hoping he'll jump to my defense. "I am not prejudiced, but we can't force anyone to call our funeral home. Our church is open to people of all races; we certainly wouldn't turn anyone out."

"But what have you done to bring people of color *in*?" She stares at me with weary eyes, and suddenly she looks much older than her twenty-four years. "It's really true what they say—Sunday morning is the most segregated hour in America."

For that, I have no answer. And I'm too exhausted for debate.

"Thank you for dinner," McLane says, pushing up from the table, "but I'm really tired. I'm going home to take a nap."

Desperate to make amends, I stand with her. "You could rest upstairs. The guest room is yours anytime you want it."

"Thanks, but I want to go home." She gives Gerald a smile, then pulls her purse onto her shoulder. "Give the boys a kiss for me, okay?"

I wriggle my fingers in a small wave as she walks away, more of a stranger to me now than on the night we met.

*O*n Monday morning, the first official day of Christmas break, Clay finds his friends waiting at the park.

Last night they met on the computer, IMing each other about the catacombs and ideas of where they might be.

Percy tried to find more information on the Internet but came up empty. He finally signed off. *CU tomorrow. U haf 2 C the old ladies.*

Now Clay hopes the brainiac has come up with a better plan than visiting the Biddle House, but Percy says nothing as he mounts his bike and pedals away from the park.

Nothing to do but follow. Clay stays with the others until they stop at the end of Charles Avenue.

"We'll wait here," Tyler says, resting his arms on his handlebars as he looks at Clay. "You go in and talk to the grannies. Come back as soon as you've got the info."

Clay bites his lip. "What if they don't know anything?"

"They know," Percy says. "Their husbands were the town leaders when the catacombs were being built. They probably have rooms reserved down there."

"You can get 'em to tell ya." Toby's face twists in a smirk. "Turn on the charm. Pretend you're talking to your grandma. You can do it."

Right. Clay blows out a breath and pedals down to the Biddle House, then drops his bike in the grass. Strolling up the sidewalk, he glances at the list of names above the doorbell and hopes his aunt McLane isn't home. He rings the bell.

A moment later the door is opened by Mrs. Baker, a woman he recognizes as one of his grandmom's Red Hatter friends. She smiles at him and blinks as if trying to remember where she's seen him before.

"I'm Clay." He forces a smile. "I'm McLane's nephew."

The woman peers at him again. "Clyde?"

"Clay Graham. Joella Norris's grandson."

"Oh yes! Come in, young man. I don't believe McLane is here, but I suppose she might come home for lunch. Would you like to have milk and cookies? It's not often we get boys of your age around here, but we have plenty of snacks in the kitchen."

When the woman turns her back, he follows her into the house and down the hall to the kitchen. Another woman is knitting at the table, and he tries to look polite as Mrs. Baker introduces him. "Frankie, do you remember this young man? He's Joella's grandson."

The woman lowers her knitting needles and studies him through her glasses. "The funeral home boy—sure, I remember him. How are you, son?"

"I'm fine, ma'am."

"And your mama? and Gerald?"

"They're all good."

"That's so nice." She looks down and begins to click her needles together. "Good to have a family living at Fairlawn again."

Mrs. Baker practically pushes Clay into an empty chair. "You just take a load off and rest your feet. Now what kind of cookie would you like, oatmeal raisin or snickerdoodle?"

He likes both, but there's no way he's going back to the other guys with snickerdoodle breath. "Oatmeal, please."

"Coming right up. Let me warm those cookies in the microwave. Frankie, why don't you get the boy a glass of milk?"

The knitting lady gets up and goes to the fridge while Clay sinks in his seat. He shouldn't be having milk and cookies under false pretenses. He hasn't done anything wrong yet, but a voice in his head keeps whispering that this isn't right. His mom would be upset if she knew, and

God might allow a bite of cookie to stick in his throat and choke the life right out of him. He glances at the knitting woman and wonders if she knows how to do the Heimlich maneuver. Probably not.

But he can't go back to the guys with nothing. They're expecting him to get the full story; they're counting on him to get the job done. If he comes back with nothing but a milk mustache, they'll never forget it. But they'll forget *him*. Oh yeah, they wouldn't think twice about that.

"Mrs. Baker," he asks, "have you lived here long?"

She hesitates, a plate of cookies in her hand. "In the Biddle House? Land sakes, child, I don't live here. I live with my daughter, but I come here to give her and her husband a little space."

"I meant in Mt. Dora. Have you lived in Mt. Dora long?"

"Just all my life. Frankie, too. We're local girls, born and bred."

Miss Frankie sets a glass of milk on the table, and Clay can tell it isn't the skinny milk his mother buys. He takes a sip and closes his eyes—delicious. This may not be such a rough job, after all.

"I was wondering," he says, watching as Mrs. Baker lowers a plate of cookies to the table, "about the bomb."

Mrs. Baker presses a hand to her chest and steps back, her eyes wide. "What bomb?"

"The H-bomb," he says, taking a cookie. "You know, during the Cold War. I heard everyone was worried about the Cubans and the Russians and about bombs falling from the sky. The way I hear it, some people around here got together and built a bomb shelter."

Mrs. Baker sits in the chair next to him and reaches for a cookie. "That's right. They did." She winks at Clay. "Built quite a complex, as I recall."

He takes a big bite, then swallows. "Was the complex near Sylvan Shores?"

Despite Mrs. Baker's wrinkles, a dimple tugs at her cheek when she smiles. "You little rascal. How'd you hear about that?"

He shrugs. "It's not a secret. Some of my friends and I read about it in a book. We know about the rooms, the clinic, the generator, everything."

"I guess the cat's out of the bag, then." Mrs. Baker turns to her friend. "Whatever happened to the catacombs?"

"Still there, I reckon. Do you remember Bessie Hall? Her family had a room in the shelter, but they've all died or moved away. One of her grandchildren still owns the grove, I think."

Clay takes another bite of cookie and tries to hide his excitement. So they were right to search for a grove. He smiles at Mrs. Baker. "It's all pretty amazing. But if the bombs started falling, how were you supposed to find the place? I mean, if you panicked and went running around in the middle of the night . . ."

"The shed," Miss Frankie says, her knitting needles clicking like clockwork. "The entrance was covered by a utility shed, the kind folks use to keep their tractors and lawn mowers out of the rain. But there was nothing in that shed but a red door."

"A *steel* door," Mrs. Baker adds. "A two-thousand-pound blast-proof door designed to seal everybody in for a long time." She shivers. "One night, after everything was finished, we had a drill. All the parents gathered their children, and everyone went down to spend the night in our rooms. The men ran the generators, and the women prepared dinner from the canned goods and supplies we'd stored in the pantry. We slept on our cots and even took showers. Everything felt so serious and real that the next morning I remember feeling surprised to discover that the world hadn't disappeared while we were down there."

Clay pops the last bite of cookie into his mouth and drains the glass of milk in one long swallow.

Mrs. Baker chuckles. "I do love to see a growing boy with a hearty appetite."

"His mother will scold you if you spoil his lunch," Miss Frankie says.

"Then this'll have to be our secret." Mrs. Baker leans over and pats Clay's arm. "You won't tell your mama about this, will you?"

"No, ma'am," Clay says, unable to believe his good luck. "Thanks for the cookies and milk, but I've gotta go."

"We'll tell McLane you stopped by," Miss Frankie calls as he stands and pushes his chair under the table.

"That's okay," he answers. "I'm sure I'll see her at home."

✳✳ ✳✳ ✳✳

I push my cart through the grocery store and realize that McLane has a point. Everyone around me is Caucasian. Not everyone in town, of course, but everyone in this part of town is as white as Wonder bread—the girl at the checkout, the man behind the meat counter, and the guy stocking the dairy shelves, as are all the shoppers in my range of vision.

I never noticed before. In a country where television shows, movies, and commercials are populated by actors of European, African, and Asian descent, I've somehow assumed that my world is thoroughly integrated.

I've been wrong.

I didn't want to be wrong. After McLane left on Saturday, I pulled out a stack of information the chamber of commerce sent after we moved to Mt. Dora. According to the latest demographic study, 77.3 percent of Mt. Dora's population is white, 19.2 percent is black, and 6.7 percent is Hispanic.

Where are the nonwhite citizens of our town? My kids go to school with all kinds of children, but McLane was right about me not mixing with people of color at work or at church. But I don't know what to do about it.

I pick up the items on my shopping list and check out, but I don't head immediately to the car. Desperate to see if this all-white aspect exists only in my imagination, I push the cart out of the way and sit on the bench outside the store. The weather's breezy and cool, so my frozen foods and milk will be fine while I take a few minutes to check out my world. I cross my legs and hum along with a Christmas carol as I survey the parking lot.

I startle when Lydia drops onto the bench next to me. "Hey there."

"Oh." I press my hand to my chest. "I wasn't expecting you."

"I didn't expect to see you, either." She takes a roll of Life Savers from her purse and offers me one. "You waiting for someone, or is this your idea of Christmas vacation?"

I laugh and wave the candy away. "I was just . . . enjoying a quiet moment. It feels great to be finished with school for the semester."

"That's right." She pops a cherry Life Saver into her mouth, then drops the roll in her purse. "How'd you do on your final?"

I exhale in a *pffft* sound. "I finished. I wrote an answer for every named part, but right now only the professor knows if I wrote the right answers. I'll find out if I passed when I get my grades in the mail."

"What a thing to have hanging over your head at Christmas."

"I'm trying not to think about it."

We sit in relaxed silence, watching other customers come and go. "Who's minding your shop?" I ask, suddenly remembering that Lydia usually doesn't go out during business hours.

She laughs her throaty chuckle. "I guess Gerald didn't tell you."

"Tell me what?"

"I told Bugs I'd pay him fifty cents to mind the store long enough for me to run over here and pick up my blood pressure medication. Of course, I didn't know I'd run into you. I'll probably owe him a dollar by the time I get back."

"You can be sure he'll want to collect." I laugh, but the sound dies in my throat when a couple gets out of a car in the parking lot. The man is black, the woman white. I've never seen either of them before, probably because their license plate is registered in Brevard County.

The first African-American I've seen this morning doesn't live here.

Lydia is telling me about Bugs and something cute he said the other day, but I'm only half-listening. I'm watching the approaching couple and noticing the easy way they interact with one another. He pulls a grocery cart from a grassy median and guides it toward her; she drops her purse into the child seat and playfully swats his hand away.

They're walking toward the grocery store when a patrol car rolls to a stop in the fire lane. A deputy gets out of the passenger's side and swaggers toward the couple, his billy club swinging with each step.

"Uh-oh." Lydia has focused on the cop. "What do you think this is about?"

I glance to the left and right, but I don't see anything unusual. Nothing has changed outside, and no one inside is shouting for help. Unless someone has pushed a silent alarm.

The other deputy parks the patrol car and gets out while his partner nears the sidewalk where we are sitting. He steps onto the curb and calls to the out-of-town couple, "Excuse me?"

Lydia and I have fallen silent, our attention completely diverted.

The man and woman turn toward the cop. The man's face, which had been creased in a smile, goes as blank as stone. The woman looks irritated.

"Excuse me," the cop says again, moving closer. He places his hand on his belt, his thumb hooked over the edge. He nods to the woman, then jerks his chin toward her companion. "Is he bothering you, ma'am?"

The irritation on her face deepens into a scowl. "Why don't you mind your own business?"

"Honey, don't." The man drops his hand to the woman's arm, an action that seems to alarm the deputy even further.

"Ma'am," the deputy says, "I asked a simple question. Is this man bothering you?"

Thunder rumbles in the distance as the woman glares into the deputy's face. "And I told you to mind your own business!"

"Storm's coming." Lydia stands and tugs on my arm. "Grab your cart and let's go."

I stand and follow her into the parking lot, but as voices rise in confrontation behind me, I feel the undeniable sting of guilt.

If that had been McLane and Jeff, would I have hurried away or stopped to help?

*   *   *

Clay picks up his bike and studies the end of the road where Tyler, Percy, and Toby are supposed to be waiting.

They're gone.

He clenches his fist, then realizes that the sky has darkened. Thunder growls, and a fat raindrop splats on the back of his hand, followed by another that smacks his cheek. The other guys probably took off as soon as the clouds began to form.

He turns his bike toward Fairlawn, lowers his head against the rain, and pedals as hard as he can.

He's not surprised his friends didn't wait. Tyler probably didn't think Clay would score any news, and Toby thinks whatever Tyler thinks. Percy might have waited around, at least until it began to rain.

None of it matters because he'll show them all. They didn't think he'd come through, but he's stumbled on the best information yet—news from two little old ladies who not only know where the catacombs are but have actually spent the night inside.

Now Clay knows exactly what to look for.

26

$\mathcal{I}$ never knew Levina Gifford, but she has the smoothest skin I've ever felt on a dead woman. According to the chart attached to the body bag, our latest client died in her bed at the age of eighty-eight. She was unmarried, childless, and had been living in a nursing home. A handwritten note adds that Ruby Masters, a family friend, will assist in planning the funeral.

Gerald picked up Ms. Gifford last night while the boys and I were baking Christmas cookies. Baking is one of our annual traditions, but Bugs seemed to be the only person having fun in the kitchen. I smiled as I rolled out the dough, but I kept thinking about McLane and that couple at the grocery store. Clay stayed at the table only because I asked him to, and he didn't want to decorate the freshly baked results. He didn't even want to eat them.

Adolescence has a way of draining the joy from family adventures. Either that, or the persistent rain has turned my outlook gloomy.

"Don't forget the elbow."

Gerald's reminder brings me back to the task at hand. Rigor mortis has stiffened Ms. Gifford's body, so we have to bend and flex her limbs, working through the rigor until we can position the body in a more natural state. Gerald has already bathed our client; now we are preparing her for the embalming.

I lift Ms. Gifford's left arm and press gently on the elbow joint. The body resists, then surrenders to the steady pressure of my right hand. Gerald stands at the head of the table, massaging the muscle stiffness out of the forehead, cheeks, and eyelids.

If there's one thing I've learned since I entered this business, it's that people don't want to peer into the casket and see death. They want their dearly departed loved one to appear as though he or she is sleeping.

"Gerald—" I reach for the can of shaving cream, knowing what comes next—"are we preventing people from accepting death by making it so . . . attractive?"

He blinks behind his glasses. "You'd rather they see oozing bodies and sunken eyelids?"

"Of course not. But you do such a good job that no one really looks dead when you're finished. Isn't that misleading? I mean, isn't it possible that some child might see a body and think we're burying people who are only asleep?"

Gerald snorts through his surgical mask. "I'm good, but I'm not that good." He takes the shaving cream from me, squirts a handful into his gloved palm, and lathers Ms. Gifford's face. "Besides, what's the harm in making people look like they're dozing? Death *is* a kind of sleep. After all, we will all wake when the Lord returns."

"I know." I sink to my stool as Gerald strokes a double-edge razor over Ms. Gifford's face. This is probably the first time the woman's cheek has ever felt the touch of a razor blade, but the powdered makeup will look better if the underlying skin is perfectly smooth.

While Gerald finishes the shaving, I massage the joints of the woman's fingers until they bend easily. Then I cup her hand around a clump of cotton and position her hands so they meet at her waist.

Ms. Gifford's arms are gray because she died in bed and blood pooled at the back of her limbs and torso. Embalming fluids will flush the blood away and tint her skin with whatever dye Gerald mixes with the formaldehyde.

When Gerald rinses his razor, I look at Ms. Gifford's hair. The short strands are almost yellow and surprisingly wiry. They stand out from her head like a halo.

From out of nowhere, a thought skitters across my brain: why *don't* we have any African-American clients? I'm about to ask for Gerald's opinion, but I'm interrupted by the telephone.

I sigh when I read the caller ID. It's my mother, probably wanting to know if she still has to buy a Christmas gift for "that girl." "Hello?"

"Hi, sweetie. Did I catch you at a bad time?"

If she only knew. I snap off a rubber glove and lean against the counter. "I can talk a few minutes, but I'm helping Gerald."

"Oh. I'll be quick then. Are we still on for tomorrow? You'll pick me up at baggage claim?"

Rats, I'd nearly forgotten. I glance at the calendar, where Gerald has penciled in Ms. Gifford's service at 3 p.m. "What time do you get in?"

"Ten thirty."

"I'll be there. But we'll have to hurry back because we have a funeral at three."

"That's no problem, dear. I'll just pop over to the Biddle House while you're working."

I look at Gerald and smile in relief.

His eyes crinkle as he begins to loosen Ms. Gifford's rigor-clenched jaw.

"Anything new going on at Fairlawn?"

I'm tempted to reply that everything's fine, but Mom will soon see how not fine everything is. "Well . . . we've had a few problems. Bugs and Clay are doing great, but McLane's baby has hydrocephalus."

"Water on the brain?"

"That's what some people call it. The doctor keeps hinting that she ought to abort."

Mom murmurs in sympathy. "That's a tragedy."

"But that's not all. I also learned why McLane's father is so against her husband—it's because he's African-American."

Stunned silence rolls over the line; then Mom clicks her tongue. "Bet you didn't see that one coming."

"I didn't."

Mother exhales a deep sigh. "I don't know what to say, hon, except that maybe the doctor has a point. A baby with all that working against it—health issues *and* social issues—well, surely God would understand if a woman couldn't go through with that pregnancy."

I can't believe what I'm hearing. "Mom—"

"Think about it—that baby won't belong in the white world or the black world. Is that fair to the child?"

I stare at Ms. Gifford's bare legs, pale skin shining under the lights, dark skin touching the table. Why is that skin so smooth? "I thought we all lived in the same world."

"Legally, but be realistic. Those people keep to their own just like we do—"

"I gotta go. See you tomorrow." I hang up the phone and return to the table.

Gerald has wired Ms. Gifford's jaw shut and is using a large syringe to squirt mastic into the cheek area.

"Did you know her?" I ask, watching as the woman's face rounds to a more lifelike contour.

"Levina Gifford?" Gerald shakes his head as he switches nozzles on the mastic applicator. "I didn't know her. But I knew *of* her."

I give him a bewildered smile. "This woman had a reputation?"

He tests the cap on his finger and runs a narrow ribbon of mastic onto the woman's upper and lower gums to plump her lips. "Not the kind of reputation you're imagining. Levina was housebound; no one ever saw her out in the sun. I heard she was allergic to UV rays or something like that. But we knew about her because she sent letters to every church in town."

"Whatever for?"

Gerald lowers the syringe and pushes Levina's lips over the mastic and into a gentle curve. When they are perfect, he seals them with a thin line of Aron Alpha instant adhesive. "This all happened before I came to Mt. Dora, but the gist of it was that she wanted to do something useful for the town. Since she couldn't get out and didn't want to bother anybody, she asked that we mail her our prayer requests so she could stay in her house and pray for people."

He runs his hand over the wide forehead and smooths our client's pale hair. "I used to walk by Levina's place and think of her sitting behind the drapes, praying for people and their lists. I never wrote to her, but lots of people did. They'd go to her house after dark, when she could sit outside on the porch. Volunteers had to read the prayer requests to her. Apparently her eyes were weak even in her younger years."

Gerald steps back and smiles at his handiwork. "We'll want to remind Ryan to use the red lipstick. They say she always wore red."

❧ ❧ ❧

After dinner, Clay waits until his mom is busy loading the dishwasher and Gerald is reading to Bugs. When he's sure no one will interrupt, Clay tiptoes to the office, where the computer whirs quietly. His mother doesn't care if he uses the machine, but he always feels a little creepy when he comes downstairs at night. Especially when the wind is howling and lightning cracks the skies apart.

He opens his instant messaging program, logs on, and types in a message.

As always, Percy is the first to respond.

```
PW: hey.
Deadhead: sup?
PW: n2m. u?
Deadhead: got the 411.
PW: sweet.
```

A warbling sound tells him that Toby has logged on, too.

```
MasterBlaster: sup, dudes?
PW: clay needs 2 meet.
MasterBlaster: 2morrow?
PW: parkside.
Deadhead: cool. b early. u tell ty?
MasterBlaster: MOS. CUL.
```

Clay clicks out of the program when he hears the groan of the staircase. At least Toby and Percy got his message, and Toby will let Tyler know they're meeting at the park. If Toby's mom hadn't been reading over his shoulder, Clay might have been able to give them some of the details. . . .

Then again, why not make them wait? It'd serve them right for going off and leaving him alone at the Biddy House.

He looks up as Gerald lumbers into the office and flips on the lights. "Oh! Sorry, Clay. I didn't know you were in here." The old man moves to the filing cabinet and shuffles through the folders. "You going to be long on the computer?"

"Nope, I'm done." Clay stands and leaves the machine, glad that he's finally one step ahead of his friends.

❊ ❊ ❊

After cleaning up the kitchen, I look in on the boys, then head downstairs to check on our client.

Gerald and I finished the arterial embalming late this morning and moved on to the process of injecting the body cavity with embalming fluid. This stage gives most people the willies, but it's a necessary step in a thorough embalming.

With Gerald's help, I've become a lot more efficient with the trocar, the long, narrow tool we use to pierce and drain the internal organs. The process took about an hour, but now Ms. Gifford is as well preserved on the inside as she is on the outside.

Inside the prep room, I lift the sheet over our client and examine the body. If we failed to eliminate all pockets of bacteria, I might see signs of swelling, but Ms. Gifford looks just as she should. Her skin, which had been naturally pale from a lack of exposure to the sun, is tinged pink from the embalming fluid.

I lower the sheet and smooth the fabric beneath Levina's chin. Tomorrow someone might remark that she looks rosier in her casket than she ever did in life, but that's okay. She'll look better than this in heaven.

So . . . tomorrow I only have to pick up my mother, take care of my kids, oversee a funeral, and counsel my sister, *if* she decides to come by or call. I haven't heard from McLane since my disastrous holiday dinner, and I'm beginning to worry.

I glance over my shoulder when the door opens.

"How's she settlin'?" Gerald asks, coming toward me with a rocking limp, a sure sign that he's tired.

"She's good." I check the calendar on the wall. "Is Ryan coming in the morning?"

"He'll be here early, before his shop opens. And we're in luck—he said he used to do Ms. Gifford's hair at the home."

"Really." I lean against the counter and cross my arms. "Gerald . . ."

"Yeah?"

Words pour out of me in a confused jumble. "I'm worried about McLane. She promised me she wouldn't do anything until after Christmas, but I won't be able to stop her if she decides to terminate her pregnancy. And look at what she's facing—her father will never accept that child, her husband is thousands of miles away, and even my mother says God will understand if McLane aborts this baby."

I rake my hand through my hair and glare at the rain-streaked window. "I want to support her; I promised I would. But how can I support her if she makes that decision? I don't know what to do. I can't tie her to a chair for nine months."

Gerald says nothing as a thunderclap explodes outside the house. I flinch, but he waits, patient and unmovable, until the baritone rumble fades away.

"Do you love this girl?" he asks.

I stare at him. Gerald is a man of few words, but the few he uses pack a punch. "I'm trying to, but it's not easy. The other day I got the credit card bill for a gift I gave her—a christening gown for the baby. When I saw that charge, I wanted to march over to the Biddle House and ask her to return my present. I can't bear the thought of sacrificing for something she might never use or appreciate."

"Then give her some space. She knows how you feel. And she loves that baby, too." Something that looks like a faint flicker of guilt moves in the depths of his brown eyes. "If the topic comes up, though, let her know that regret is a terrible burden to bear."

❊❊ ❊❊ ❊❊

Ruby Masters, the woman apparently in charge of planning Levina Gifford's funeral, is the organist at our church and one of Mother's Hatter friends. Ruby has played for many a Fairlawn funeral, so she's not at all anxious about Levina's service.

She's so relaxed, in fact, that she waits until 7:30 p.m. to pop in and give us final instructions. Her arrival is anything but convenient because Gerald and the boys pull up right behind her, with our Christmas tree protruding from the back window of the call car.

I stand on the front porch and direct traffic, guiding Ruby toward the west chapel while I point Gerald, Clay, and Bugs toward the south. I wistfully watch the boys struggle with the scraggly tree before picking up my notebook and following Ruby into the chapel.

"I want you to know that Ms. Gifford's funeral expenses have been prepaid," I tell her. "However, we would like to hear what kind of memorial service she would have wanted—"

"Bless your heart," Ruby says, flapping a hand at me. "I've spoken to the family and they agree that we don't need to spend a lot of time fussing over Levina's funeral. She was ready to be with the Lord, and few people really knew her since she moved to the nursing home. That's why I figured I could just drop by and give you two words: *no fuss.*"

I sit in a chair across from Ruby and set my notebook on my lap. "I'd still like to get some background information for the program. What was your relationship to Ms. Gifford? Were you related?"

Ruby blanches. "Good heavens, no. Her mother used to clean for my grandmother. Because no school would take her in those days, Levina had to come to the house, so my family got used to havin' her underfoot. She was grown and living alone by the time I came along, and she kept to herself. Don't really blame her. She didn't fit with her people or ours."

I frown, more confused than ever. "Why couldn't she go to school?"

"Why, because of her skin condition. She couldn't go outside."

"But surely there were special programs, even back then. Any good public school should have made allowances."

Ruby's forehead knits in puzzlement. "Didn't you *see* her?"

"Of course."

"Then what don't you understand? The answer's as clear as the nose on your face."

I study my guest. Ruby must be speaking in some kind of code known only to longtime Mt. Dorans, because I have no idea what she's talking about . . . and I'm pretty sure my nose has nothing to do with it.

Ruby rolls her eyes, then leans forward and clasps her hands. "Most schools might have made allowances, but Levina couldn't go to just any school. She was colored."

"She was *what?*"

"Not on the outside, maybe, but on the inside. Levina was—" Ruby leans closer—"an albino."

Surprise siphons the blood from my head. I stare at Ruby and am startled to discover that her explanation makes sense. I don't know much about albinism, but Gerald said Levina had weak eyes and was allergic to the sun. But how can someone be colored on the inside?

I'm about to ask when Ruby snaps her fingers. "I just remembered something. Levina loved that old spiritual about shoes."

"Come again?"

"'I Need Shoes' . . . no, 'I Got Shoes.' That was the name of it. Slaves didn't have shoes, you know, so they sang about having shoes in heaven. Levina loved that song to pieces."

Like a wooden puppet, I nod and make a note of the title.

"If you can have somebody sing that song, I'll play, and we'll give Levina a send-off she would have enjoyed."

I lower my pen. "You think I can find a singer at this late hour?"

Ruby gives me the smile she would give a small child. "Don't you watch *American Idol?* Shake any tree out there and somebody's bound to fall out and start singing."

I give her a weak smile and promise to do my best.

After Ruby leaves, I go into the office and wonder why I made such a rash promise. The Mt. Dora phone book doesn't have a listing for funeral singers, wedding singers, or rock bands. And despite Ruby's contention that singers dangle from every tree in town, I can't think of a single acquaintance who wouldn't make people wince on karaoke night. I can't sing, Gerald can't sing, and I've *heard* Lydia sing.

In a flash of inspiration, I remember Carol Conrad, who often sings solos with our church choir. I dial her number and hold my breath, only to exhale in a disappointed gasp when she answers the phone. Croaking. She has laryngitis.

So I'm stuck.

I'm still pondering the problem when McLane drops by to help us decorate the Christmas tree. While we're sorting through cracked ornaments and tangled garlands in the south chapel, I summon up all my hope. "McLane, do you sing?"

She laughs. "You've got half my genes—what do you think?"

"Sorry I asked." I look up to see Clay trying to pry two wooden ornaments apart. Why didn't I think of him sooner? His music teachers have always told me he sings like an angel. Of course, he might feel better about his talent if he didn't sing like a *soprano*. . . .

When he stands with two hand-painted ornaments safely separated, I crook my finger and motion him toward me.

His eyes narrow. "What?"

"How would you like to earn twenty bucks?"

He frowns at the ornaments. "You got more of these hidden in the attic?"

"Nothing so frustrating. All you have to do is sing at a funeral tomorrow. The song's easy and you only have to do a verse and a chorus. You could learn it in ten minutes."

He grimaces. "Aw, Mom."

"It's twenty bucks—probably the easiest money you'll ever make. And I think the crowd will be small."

Clay swallows hard, then glares at Bugs. "If I do this, he has to promise not to tell anybody."

Bugs grins while McLane pulls him onto her lap. "Tell him you'll keep quiet for ten bucks."

"Wait." Dazzled by the brilliance of a sudden inspiration, I grin at my sons. "You boys can sing together and I'll pay each of you. Deal?"

Bugs and Clay look at each other and nod in unison.

"Good." I lift the dangling ornaments from Clay's fingers. "The funeral's at three, so be sure to stick around so you can practice with Miss Ruby. She'll probably show up around two thirty."

"Sweet, Mom." Bugs is clearly delighted by the thought of earning some money.

But Clay remains silent. I hang the ornaments on the tree and turn to find him staring into space. "Clay? Did you hear me?"

His shoulders sag as he sighs. "Two thirty. Got it."

27

As his mother and Bugs get ready to pick up Grandma at the airport, Clay zips his jacket, then walks his bike out of the garage and sets off for the park. Rain fell during the night, leaving puddles on the street and a clean feeling in the air.

He finds Tyler, Toby, and Percy waiting at the basketball court. Tyler leans against a pole, looking bored, but Percy and Toby are jumpy with nerves.

Clay slides off his bike and drops it at the edge of the asphalt.

"So?" Percy says, striding toward him. "What'd you find out?"

"A lot." Clay unzips his jacket, which already feels too warm. "I talked to two ladies who've actually spent the night inside the catacombs."

Toby drops his jaw. "For real?"

"No, dude, I'm making it all up."

Percy laughs. "So what'd they say? Where is the place?"

"Sylvan Shores, like the book said." Clay shrugs out of his jacket and drops it on his bike. "The entrance is hidden in a grove, but you can't miss the door if you know what to look for. They couldn't have people walk right by the secret entry when the bombs started to drop."

Tyler pulls himself off the pole and struts toward the others. "So, what are we supposed to look for?"

Clay feels his smile fade in the face of Tyler's sneer. "I'm not sure

I should say. What if I tell you and you guys run off and leave me like you did yesterday?"

"We wouldn't do that," Percy says, turning to glare at Tyler. "Right?"

Clay crosses his arms. "I think maybe you would. I think I could tell you everything and we could start riding over there, but then it'll get cloudy or start to rain and you'll head for home. Then you'll go back without me and have the catacombs all to yourself." He stares at Tyler until the taller boy cracks a smile.

"Okay, so don't tell us," Tyler says. "We'll ride over there and you can keep your little secret. But when we get to Sylvan Shores, you've gotta talk. We're not going to spend the whole day walking around orange groves for nothin'."

"I'll talk when we get there." Clay seals his promise with a nod. "I'll tell you so much your head will explode."

❧ ❧ ❧

I smile, wave, and count my blessings when Mother appears on the curb precisely at eleven. Her flight must have landed on time, she found her bags without difficulty, and all is right with the world . . . for once.

If only we can keep from snapping at each other on the ride home.

She pulls the passenger door open and eyes me with a narrow gaze. "You're not about to tell me your father was a bigamist, are you?"

I gesture to the backseat. "Bugs, look who's here. Grandma made it."

Mom's face dissolves into a soft smile as she releases the handle of her suitcase and reaches for Bugs, who drops his video game to greet her.

We need to talk about McLane and I know we *will*, but I don't want to talk about her yet. That's why I bribed Bugs to come along. Mom won't discuss Grandpa's infidelity with young ears in the car.

I walk around to her side of the van, smiling as she hugs Bugs and asks him about Christmas. I set her suitcase in the backseat and rest in the knowledge that she'll be on her best behavior on the trip back to Mt. Dora and McDonald's, because I promised Bugs an ice cream cone.

I'm shameless, I know. Only a calculating, conniving, cowardly woman would hide behind a cherub-cheeked six-year-old.

But in the battle of wits with my mother, I'll employ any weapon within reach.

❧ ❧ ❧

Clay tips his head back and smiles at the sun, relishing the warmth on his face. It feels good to ride at the head of the pack; it feels great to be leading this adventure. Tyler isn't thrilled about letting Clay hang on to his secret, but what choice does he have? This is Clay's day and Clay's victory.

He leads the others up Park Place and laughs when a long-legged crane flaps into flight to get out of the way. While the world around them concentrates on Christmas, he and his friends will solve the last mystery of Mt. Dora.

When they find the catacombs and walk out with the story, people will be amazed that a few kids could discover what dedicated reporters have been unable to find on their own. Maybe they can bring up a few bottles of whiskey or boxes of yellowing bandages, souvenirs that might sell for a fortune on eBay. Tyler wants to cash in on guns and cigarettes, but he's always looking for trouble. Percy, on the other hand, will appreciate the value of a fifty-year-old book or a Geiger counter.

Maybe they'll make the national news. CNN might even send reporters, and Clay will be as cautious with them as he's been with his friends. He won't tell the location until they promise to pay for the story. Then they'll have to sign papers saying they'll never reveal the secret entrance to another soul.

Maybe the reporters will pay a thousand bucks for the story . . . maybe more than a thousand. He'll use his share of the money to buy new video games and a new mountain bike or skateboard. Mom can't complain if he buys stuff with his own money.

The old folks in town will have a fit, of course. They've kept the place a secret for so long they probably feel like the catacombs belong to them alone. But the bomb shelter belongs to the town and everyone in it. Anybody who builds a secret shelter designed to keep everyone else out—well, selfish people like that deserve to lose their exclusive little hideaway.

Clay brakes at the intersection of Park Place and Morningside Drive, waving the others forward when the way is clear. They cut over to Gertrude Place and startle two old ladies walking beside the road; then they coast to a stop on Sylvan Point Drive.

Behind Clay, Tyler and the others are breathing hard.

"Where are we?" Toby glances around. "The road ahead is a dead end."

"This is Sylvan Shores." Clay turns and pulls a folded sheet of paper from the inside pocket of his jacket.

The boys crowd closer. "The map," Percy says, his eyes widening. "You went back to the site with the satellite photos."

Clay points to one of several rectangular city blocks. "The ladies told me," he says, reluctant now to share his secret, "that the entrance is disguised by a utility shed. The shed's in an orange grove, and by now it's probably pretty beat up. But you'll recognize the spot right away, because the entrance to the catacombs is a red steel door."

"A red door?" Percy's eyes are shining like lanterns. "Is the red door *on* the shed or *inside* the shed?"

Clay's confidence deflates. "I-I don't know. I think it's inside." For a moment he's afraid they're going to call him stupid for not checking.

But Tyler only takes the paper and studies it. "These little things here are houses, right?" he says, squinting at the page. "And what are these things that look like lines?"

"Those are orange trees," Clay says. "You're seeing the rows from the air."

Tyler squints at the page again and hands it back to Clay. "I get it."

Clay squats at the edge of the road and spreads the paper on the asphalt. "I marked several things that could be sheds in the photo." He points to circles he drew last night. "The shed we want should be in the middle of an orange grove, so we need to check out these three locations. They're our most likely prospects." He touches each circle, then looks up to see if Percy agrees.

"Sounds like a logical plan," Percy says, grinning. "Good work, Sherlock."

Clay stands and folds the paper. "What are we waitin' for? Let's ride."

⚜ ⚜ ⚜

By one o'clock, Mom is safely tucked into the guest room, Bugs has had his lunch, and I've helped Gerald with the casketing of Levina Gifford. Ruby, who cleared out Levina's belongings at the nursing home, dropped off a red dress of double knit, a shapeless outfit that must be thirty years old. I hate the thing, but Gerald says we don't have time to search for something more stylish. Because there is no viewing, Levina's going from casket to funeral to burial site in record time.

"Besides," he says, his mouth quirking, "how do you know this wasn't her favorite dress? If you don't ever leave the house, I don't suppose you care much about what other people are wearing."

While Gerald checks the job Ryan did on Levina's makeup, I slit the red dress up the back so we can work it onto the now-stiff body. Ruby also brought underwear, stockings, and a pair of shoes, but the shoes won't fit on the inflexible feet. I make a mental note to place them at the end of the casket.

When we have finished dressing our client, Gerald steps into the hallway, where a lovely mahogany casket waits on a gurney. He pushes the gurney into the prep room, aligns it with the table, and moves to Miss Levina's head while I stand at her feet.

Working with the ease of partners, he nods and we lift together. We settle our client into her resting vessel; then Gerald adjusts the pillow beneath her head.

I smile at Miss Levina Gifford, whose surviving relatives will see her as a peacefully sleeping prayer warrior. That is the memory they will carry the rest of their lives, and Gerald and I are pleased to provide it.

As I tug off my rubber gloves, though, I glance at the clock and frown. The flowers will arrive at any minute and the guests will soon follow.

Where are my singing sons?

※ ※ ※

Clay wipes sweat out of his eyes and stares at the crumpled paper. They've already checked out two likely sheds on his map, but they haven't found a red door. The first shed held a lawn tractor, a set of folding chairs, and an empty dog crate. The second held a rottweiler that wasn't happy to see them. Fortunately, the dog's chain ran out before the boys' luck did.

"There could be a shed up here." Percy taps a clump of trees behind a house on Morningside Drive. "There's a grove behind the house, just like the book said."

"What about here?" Clay points to a group of trees much closer to their present location.

"No orange grove," Percy says.

Clay turns the map. "There's a grove right across the street. For all we know, the street wasn't there when the catacombs were built."

"These streets have been here at least forty years," Percy says. "Sorry."

Clay studies the paper, his brow wrinkling in thought.

Percy moves closer and points to the house on Morningside. "Why not this one?"

Both boys jump when a car stops and someone honks its horn.

"Clay Graham!"

Clay feels the back of his neck heat when he recognizes Gerald's voice. He turns. Gerald didn't yell at him from just any car. The old man is driving the beat-up station wagon he uses to pick up bodies. Could this moment possibly get any more embarrassing?

"You need to climb in," Gerald says, hanging one arm out the window. "You promised to sing at Miss Levina's funeral, remember?"

Clay closes his eyes. Oh yeah. Leave it to Gerald to make a bad situation worse.

Behind him, Tyler is snickering. "You gotta run off and *sing*?"

"At a funeral?" Toby presses his hand to his chest and warbles like some kind of opera star.

"Shut up, doofus," Clay says. He gives Percy the map and picks up his bike. "You guys better not find the catacombs without me!" He wheels his bike toward the car and doesn't look back until he's in the station wagon and headed home.

❧ ❧ ❧

Clay sits in the foyer with his elbow propped on his knee and his chin in his hand, dying to get out of the house. Every gray head in Mt. Dora must be inside the chapel, and at least two dozen old ladies have stopped to tell him and Bugs how handsome they look in their suits. Bugs loves it, but Clay does nothing but smirk until his mother moves to block people's view of him on the steps. Fine.

Mom promised the service would start soon, but it's already after three. These people move like glaciers. The dead lady will be growing moss if they don't shove this service into gear.

He still can't believe Gerald drove out to get him. If it hadn't been for Ruby Masters, one of the old ladies he saw power puffing around Lake Gertrude, Gerald wouldn't have found him in time for this stupid funeral. Bugs could have sung a solo. It might not have been good, but people wouldn't care as long as Bugs was cute.

He groans and closes his eyes as Mrs. Baker and Miss Frankie totter over the front porch, the smaller woman clinging to her friend's arm. He slides over the step and tries to hide behind the newel, but he's exposed when his mother moves forward to welcome them.

"Why, look!" Miss Frankie beams at Clay as she accepts a program from his mom. "It's the oatmeal cookie boy."

Mom blinks. "I beg your pardon?"

"Your handsome boy." Miss Frankie winks at Clay, deepening his mortification. "You're lookin' mighty spiffy this afternoon."

"Good to see you," Mrs. Baker echoes, her hand wavering as she leans on Miss Frankie's arm. "Stop by the Biddle House again sometime. We've plenty of milk and cookies."

253

When the ladies have moved into the chapel, his mother turns. "You went to the Biddle House?"

Clay shrugs. "I was looking for McLane."

"Whatever for?"

"I . . . uh . . . wanted to see if she was coming over here for dinner. I didn't want to ride home in the rain."

Mom puts on that I-don't-believe-you look, but just then Gerald steps out of the chapel and taps her shoulder. "Ruby's ready. Time for the song."

Mom gestures for Bugs and Clay. Bugs is practically peacocking in eagerness, but Clay only rolls his eyes as Mom brushes the shoulders of his jacket. "Just go in there and sing your heart out. You'll do a beautiful job."

He gives his mother a pained smile, then follows Bugs to the front of the room and tries not to look at the sea of faces. At least there are no kids his age here—everyone is old, at least thirty.

Clay stares at the back wall as the music begins and he and Bugs sing: "'I got shoes, you got shoes, all of God's children got shoes. . . .'"

❊❊ ❊❊ ❊❊

"Do you know," Preacher Wright says, "why funeral home folks call these wooden boxes *caskets* instead of *coffins*?"

I assume the question is meant to be rhetorical, but the crowd—the first gathering of black and white mourners I've seen since coming to Mt. Dora—calls out answers.

"No, sir."

"Tell us, Preacher."

"Because by definition a casket is a container or receptacle for treasured things." He pauses to look at Levina in her mahogany box. "Levina was a treasured part of our community. Only in eternity will we learn the full effect of her prayers. Her eyes may have been weak and her skin too frail for the sun, but her prayers were strong."

"Amen, brother."

"They were!"

"That's what I'm sayin'."

The minister, invited here by Levina's niece, nods solemnly at the gathering. "Our sister's body will not remain weak. At the sound of the trumpet, God will resurrect all of us who believe. Our bodies, feeble though they are now, will be raised in perfection."

"Glory!"

"I'm ready now, Lord!"

"Hear the word!"

I could get used to an interactive service.

I move from the back wall to the foyer as Preacher Wright offers a closing prayer. The sound of footsteps on the front porch distracts me, so I open the door to see who the latecomer is.

McLane stands on the porch, a foil-covered plate in her hand. She gives me a shaky smile. "I saw all the cars. Is this a bad time?"

I draw her into the house and whisper, "We're finishing up a service in the chapel, but the boys will be out in a minute. They'll be thrilled to see you."

She looks at me and hesitates. "I made cookies," she says, lifting the plate.

"The boys will love them."

"Actually, they're for your mother. Sort of a peace offering."

I'm too touched to speak. I'd been planning on keeping Mom and McLane apart as much as possible, but McLane must have realized how I've been dreading this aspect of the holidays. Christmas will be so much easier if they can get along. I reach out and squeeze her arm. "That's really sweet of you. Go on up and make yourself at home."

As McLane climbs the stairs, I walk back to the chapel doors and wait for the pallbearers to escort Miss Levina Gifford to her temporary resting place. Gerald was worried about being able to find people who really knew Levina, but though these friends and relatives may not have spent much time with her, they remember her prayers. And they've come to honor her.

Ruby said Levina didn't belong to the black or the white community.

I'm beginning to think she belonged to both.

***

Clay thumps up the staircase, runs into his room, and yanks so hard on his tie that he hurts his neck. The knot resists for a minute before it surrenders. He throws off his jacket and steps out of his pants, then throws his suit onto his bed.

He ought to leave his pants on the floor. He ought to stomp on them and show Mom exactly what he thinks about being hauled away from his friends in a corpse car, but right now he has more important things to do.

He has to find Tyler, Toby, and Percy before they turn on him. It'd be just like them to find the catacombs, make themselves at home, and hide for the rest of Christmas break. Oh, they'd come out long enough to open their presents and keep their parents from worrying, but they'd hoard the secret like prize money, not even giving Clay a peek.

After he did the really hard work!

He changes into his jeans and grabs a T-shirt, then stuffs his feet into sneakers.

"Clay?"

He grimaces when his grandmother calls from the living room.

"Honey, come see what your friend McLane has brought."

He steps into the hallway and sees Grandma and Aunt McLane sitting on the sofa. Grandma is holding a plate of cookies and wearing a funny little smile.

"Hey, Grandma. Hey, Aunt McLane." He stops long enough to check out the cookies, but they're the fancy little chocolate kind that women like. Mom and Bugs can eat 'em.

"Clay," Grandma says as he heads for the stairs, "aren't you going to tell us where you're going?"

No, he isn't. That's the point of having a secret hideout.

***

The crowd files through the doorway, walking in a funereal hush as they follow the pallbearers escorting Levina's casket to the hearse. The

256

mourners fan out along the porch until Gerald positions the casket and closes the door; then they move down the steps and head toward their cars.

Without looking, I know what will happen next. Family members will follow Gerald to the graveside, and those who came out of politeness or curiosity will drive home.

I walk back into the chapel, expecting to find it empty, but two guests remain. One is a young woman in pants and a tunic top; the other is an older woman in a black suit and a veiled hat. I recognize the older woman immediately—she's Levina's niece.

"Ms. Masters left this in Levina's room," the young woman says. She's holding a cardboard box with *Bounty paper towels* emblazoned on the side. "When Miss Levina couldn't sleep, she'd ask us to read these to her. So we read them over and over. Since they meant a lot to her, I just couldn't throw them out."

Levina's niece accepts the box and murmurs a polite thank-you.

The younger woman ducks modestly and retreats on crepe-soled shoes.

Levina's niece turns and looks at me and shakes her head. "I don't know what to do with this," she says, her lips trembling in an uncertain smile.

I hurry forward. "Is it . . . ?"

"It's more letters." She lowers one hand into the box and pulls out a clutch of handwritten envelopes, folded pieces of stationery, and note cards. "About the time Auntie went into the nursing home, we wrote to the local ministers and told them to ask people to stop sending her letters. We thought it'd be too much for her, but apparently she couldn't let go . . . even though these have to be years out of date."

I look into the box, where the faded prayer requests of dozens of Mt. Dorans lie in a heap. I'm sure the letters are personal, entrusted from one heart to another. I meet the woman's gaze. "I don't know what to tell you, but I don't think it'd be right to toss them out with the trash."

"Then could we . . . ?" Her wide eyes fill with hope. "I don't know the protocol of such things. But I think Auntie would like it if we could bury them with her."

For a split second I'm afraid she wants us to put all this paper in the casket—an idea that doesn't appeal because the hearse is already loaded and ready to go to the cemetery. But perhaps we have another option.

"In some cultures," I tell her, thinking aloud, "it's traditional for family members to toss a handful of earth into the open grave. Why not have your family toss in a few of these letters?"

Levina's niece gives me a grateful smile. "I'm Claire Douyon," she says, extending her hand, "and it's nice to meet you, Mrs. Graham."

※ ※ ※

With his bike like a winged instrument beneath him, Clay flies over Park Place and Morningside Drive. He can't see his friends from the road, so he rides to the last location they were going to investigate.

He steers to the curb and slows, searching for some sign of Percy, Tyler, or Toby. The last house he circled on his map sits close to the street, and a pool takes up most of the backyard. A shed lies beyond the pool, however, and behind the shed are several rows of citrus trees. The trees in this grove are smaller and thinner than others they've seen.

Clay drops his bike at the curb, then hunches forward and runs past the house and into the backyard. No one is moving, so he sprints around the pool and crosses the open space in front of the shed. He relaxes once he enters the orange grove, but these scraggly trees don't provide much cover. Besides, if anyone was looking out the window, they'd have seen him by now.

He bends forward, his hands on his knees, and scoots beneath the low-hanging branches of an orange tree. He wants to scout out the shed, but in his quest for a camouflaged position he accidentally stumbles into a spiderweb. He backs away, spitting and flailing, until he's sure the spider's not clinging to his shirt, his arms, or his hair.

On his second approach, he stands *beside* a tree and stares at the back of the utility shed. Is this the opening to the catacombs? No way to know unless he checks.

He glances toward the windows in the house, but nothing disturbs those shadows. He bites his lip and tries to think—should he sneak over and peek inside the shed, or should he stand up and stroll over there as if he's just taking a shortcut through the lawn?

Where is Percy the brain? He'd be handy to have around right now.

Finally Clay straightens and makes a decision. He's never been very good at sneaking, and whoever lives here is more likely to be alarmed by a sneaking kid than a nosy one.

He slips a hand into his pocket, starts to whistle "I Got Shoes"— the only song in his brain—and walks to the shed. The sliding door is open a couple of inches, so Clay sticks two fingers into the gap and pushes to the right. The rusty door doesn't budge.

Clay pushes again, casual-like, but the door still resists. He gives the door a two-handed tug. It slides with a metallic screech and reveals . . . nothing. Nothing interesting, anyway. Only a bucket of chlorine tablets, an old front door with peeling paint, and some aqua blue pool equipment.

He closes the door and hopes the screech doesn't alarm anyone who might be nearby. Then he walks back into the grove and darts behind a tree, peering at the windows of the house. Still no movement. Whoever lives there must be out for the afternoon.

Clay turns and considers the grove. On his map, the rows of trees stretch for quite a distance. Who knows what else might be out here?

He jogs through the orderly lines, careful to avoid the fruit that has fallen and now lies rotting on the sand. He runs between two trees and furiously backpedals because a spider as big as his fist is dangling on a web that sways between two branches like an invisible suspension bridge.

Finally he reaches the last row of orange trees. Behind it looms an apartment complex, a fortress of painted cinder blocks topped by a gray shingle roof. The wide windows stare down at him, accusing him of—what? He's not the one who abandoned his friends.

He walks to a dirt road that cuts through the grove and begins the long hike back to Morningside Drive. A half-eaten grapefruit lies in one of the ruts, its edge cleanly scissored away by fruit rats. Clay kicks the fruit and grimaces when the odor of rotting citrus fills his nostrils.

Then he stops. Ahead, just to the left of the rutted road, he spies three bikes hidden beneath an orange tree: Tyler's, Percy's, and Toby's. But where did they go?

He spins, searching for another shed, but he can't see anything except the trees. Besides, his growling stomach reminds him that it's nearly dinnertime. Above him, the sun is sliding down the sky, though it hasn't quite reached the rooflines of the apartment buildings in the distance.

Clay pushes at the damp hair on his forehead and tries to concentrate. He could sit down and wait for his friends to come out of the grove, but that might take a while. He could be sitting out here with the spiders and rats for an hour, maybe longer.

Or . . . maybe they've already spotted him and are waiting for *him* to leave. Either Tyler or Toby might suggest such a thing because they sure didn't like it when he had the upper hand. They might be hiding behind a tree right now, smothering their laughter while they watch him stomp around in frustration.

So he won't stomp. He won't wait. He'll let them have their fun, and tonight he'll IM them and ask if they found the catacombs. He'll be cool and act like he really doesn't care what they found.

If he pulls it off, they'll confess everything and let him in on the secret. If they don't, he'll threaten to go to the house on Morningside Drive and tell those people that something strange is going on in their backyard.

Feeling better now that he's made a plan, Clay strolls toward his bike as if the only thing he cares about is his dinner.

❊❊ ❊❊ ❊❊

I watch as Gerald pulls away and a dozen cars follow, their headlights on and their pace slow. Claire Douyon and her husband ride immediately behind the hearse while a Lake County deputy, his lights flashing, officially leads the procession.

Mt. Dora is so small and the cemetery so close that we don't often get police escorts for funeral processions. The fact that the sheriff has sent someone for Levina says a lot about her reputation with the local people.

When the last car has disappeared from the end of the street, I go inside the house. The fragrance of lilies still wafts from the chapel, but I'll distribute the remaining flowers later. Right now I need to think about feeding my family and talking to McLane. Though she said she stopped by to bring cookies for my mother, the fact that she's still here tells me she has really come to talk.

I find most of my family in the gathering area at the top of the stairs. Bugs is tucked under McLane's arm, watching cartoons with the volume turned down. Mom is sitting on the love seat, her eyes glued to a book. The plate of cookies waits on the coffee table, mostly uneaten. No one has to tell me they haven't been speaking. I feel the crackle in the air when I step into the room.

McLane catches my eye. "You got a minute?"

I nod. "Come on into the kitchen."

My kitchen isn't the most private place in the house, but I need to start dinner. If we keep our voices low . . .

"Funeral's over, Bugsy," I announce, dropping my hand to the top of his head. "You can turn up the TV now."

McLane takes a seat at the table while I set my heavy skillet on the stove and fill it with six cups of hot water. I look through the doorway and see that Mom hasn't budged; she's still attempting to read. I haven't seen her actually turn a page, but at least she's giving us some space.

"Nice funeral?" McLane asks after a few minutes.

"Very nice." I glance over my shoulder and lift a brow. "Did you notice that this one was integrated?"

The corner of her mouth droops. "Okay. Only 99 percent of your funerals are all white."

"I have to admit—" I lean back against the counter—"what you said the other day has made me think. You were right. I really do live in a mostly white world."

"You *did*. Now you have a multiracial family."

I snatch a quick breath. "I never thought of that."

"Your water's boiling," she says, pointing to the stove.

Still adjusting to a change in perspective, I dump two cans of tuna, two packages of noodles, and two packets of Tuna Helper sauce mix in the skillet. I stir the stuff together, turn the heat to simmer, and cover the skillet with a lid. Then I take the chair kitty-corner from my sister. "Okay, talk to me. I know you didn't come over here to watch Road Runner cartoons with Bugs."

Her eyes grow moist as her hand moves over the table and brushes my elbow. "What I need to know," she says, her voice breaking, "is if you can give me a ride to and from the clinic in Orlando. They say I'll be groggy . . . after."

I bring my hand to my mouth, afraid to verbalize what I'm thinking. In the back of my mind, I was hoping she'd come to ask for help or advice. Now I see that this is an announcement, not a consultation.

I draw a shuddering breath, then turn my face so she won't see my disappointment. What should I do? My heart breaks for her, I sympathize with her, and I want to support her. But how can I stand back and hold her hand while she destroys the life God sent her for safekeeping?

"So you've decided to get the abortion."

She bites her lip, making the same face I make at least a dozen times a day. "You have to know that I've given this a great deal of thought."

"I know you have. But you have to understand where I'm coming from—this is wrong."

"Wrong for *you*, maybe."

"No, wrong for *everyone* because it's the taking of innocent human life. I love you and I want to help, but I can no more drive you to an abortion clinic than I could drive the getaway car if you wanted to rob a bank."

Tears fill my eyes, a wellspring of frustration and grief. McLane has every legal right to do what she's decided to do, and nothing I can say will stop her. I would throw myself in front of the door to prevent her from leaving this house, but I can't hold her prisoner.

And the law is on her side. I could enlist the sheriff to help me stop her from killing a neighbor or a dog, but I can't legally do anything to stop her from dismembering her baby.

She swallows hard, as if trying to dislodge something in her throat. "I thought that's what you'd say. Don't worry. I can find someone else to drive me."

"McLane, I—"

"It's okay." When she looks up, her eyes are pools of entreaty. "Just tell me you won't hate me when this is all over."

I cover her hand with mine. "We'll always be sisters. But you know how you needed time to make a decision? I'll need some time to grieve. You can come here while you recover, and I'll put you to bed and make you a cup of tea. But don't expect me to be happy or even relieved. I want to support you, but that'd be asking too much."

She drops her lashes, probably to hide her hurt, but how else can I respond? If I throw my arms around her and say I'll love her no matter what she decides, am I not making it easy for her to do something horrific? I *do* love her, but I can't support her if she chooses to do something that violates every sacred belief I hold. Love is not blind acceptance . . . is it?

Jesus accepted and loved sinners, but he also told them to "sin no more." I correct my children because I love them. God corrects me when I step out of line.

So how do I deal with McLane? It'd be easy to support her and say nothing; some people might even applaud me and call that unconditional love. Refusing her is hard, and though she wants our relationship to remain the same, sometimes a tiny obstacle can become a wall between two people.

From some dark territory of my heart, an idea sprouts like a weed: maybe McLane will be so upset with me that she'll never want to speak to me again. Maybe she'll go back to North Carolina. Maybe she'll go to Jeff's aunt. If she leaves Mt. Dora, my life will be so much simpler. I could wash my hands of the entire situation and concentrate on Fairlawn and my children. Aren't they my first priority?

If only ignoring the problem would make it go away.

If only I could abort this relationship as easily as she wants to abort her child.

But I can't.

263

I squeeze her shoulder. "Do you like tuna? I'm making a double batch."

McLane shakes her head. "Ryan's making spaghetti at the Biddle House. I promised he wouldn't have to eat alone."

"You could call him and ask him to come here. We'll make room for another place at the table."

"I need to get home." She stands, and before I can repeat the invitation, she's on her way down the stairs.

❊❊ ❊❊ ❊❊

Clay tries to IM his buddies after dinner, but they don't answer. So . . . they're still ignoring him. They probably have him blocked because they don't want to share their big secret. Or maybe they've really armed themselves with snacks and flashlights and gone back to the catacombs.

He imagines them exploring one of the secret rooms, maybe smoking cigarettes, sampling brandy, and bragging about how they cut him out of the action. They'll have all Christmas break to avoid him and enjoy their hideout.

Well, they can have the old place. And the gruesome threesome can stay a threesome for all he cares.

Before they came along, he didn't have to go to the library, he rarely got into trouble, and he didn't run into spiders and rats in smelly old orange groves.

He will not let them diss him ever again.

Clay turns off the computer and goes upstairs.

❊❊ ❊❊ ❊❊

I'm having a love/hate affair with the plastic dental appliance that spends its nights parked on my front teeth. Though the guard has eased my jaw pain and probably prolonged the lives of my molars, I feel like a beaver when I'm wearing it.

I snap it into place, toss my dirty clothes in the hamper, and pull the ponytail holder from my hair. As my last ritual of the night, I look at the assortment of cosmetics jars on my vanity, close my eyes, and lift one at random.

Ah—the pectin-enriched Retina Magic Fade Spot and Wrinkle Remover. I have no idea if this stuff works, but I'll use it until the jar is empty. Those of us who are thirty-nine have to do something to hold the line. One of these nights, I'm going down to the prep room to see if formaldehyde works on wrinkles.

I dab the magic stuff on my face and hesitate when I hear heavy steps on the stairs. I look down the hallway, then watch as Clay turns at the landing and heads toward his bedroom, his head bowed and his shoulders slumped.

And I thought adolescent girls were moody.

I toss my towel toward the vanity and pad down the hall in sock-covered feet. "Clay?" I rap on his door. "You okay?"

He doesn't answer, so I give him a minute before opening the door and peeking in. He's under the covers, pretending to be asleep. I am Mom. I know better.

I step into the night shadows, picking up his jeans and T-shirt as I go. I fling these onto his desk chair and sit on the edge of his bed.

Finally, he gives up the ruse. "Mom?"

"Yeth?"

A quick glimmer of teeth shines in the gloom. "You sound so funny when you have that thing in your mouth."

"Juth wait, buddy boy. If you have to get bratheth, you'll know what thith feelth like." I reach up and smooth the damp hair from his brow. "Are you doin' okay?"

He doesn't speak, but I feel a subterranean quiver through the mattress as he nods.

"Okay, then. I love you."

He rolls over and faces the wall.

I sigh and stand, but before I close the door, I hear a barely audible answer: "Love you, Mom."

Nice to know somebody does.

28

Clay is halfway through his bowl of Lucky Charms when a phrase from the television snags his attention. He drops his spoon and stands, straining to see past Bugs. Grandma is sitting in the living room with a cup of coffee.

And pictures of Tyler, Percy, and Toby are on TV.

"If you have seen these boys," a woman says, "please call the Lake County Sheriff's Department. That number is—"

Grandma clicks the remote, and the channel changes to that blonde woman who's always cooking or cutting flowers.

Clay feels his stomach flip, and for an instant he's convinced he's going to barf cereal all over the kitchen. He falls back into his chair and stares at a green clover floating on the milk.

This isn't right. Tyler, Percy, and Toby might have hidden out for a few hours, but there's no way they would have stayed in the catacombs overnight . . . is there?

He closes his eyes as words from other television reports crowd at the back of his brain. Other kids have been kidnapped, taken away from their families. Some have disappeared for years, and others have been found dead. Could someone have snatched his friends?

He grabs the edge of the table as his stomach lurches and the room seems to tilt. Everything in his world has changed, but no one else seems to notice. Bugs is trying to read the back of the cereal box,

Mom is looking at the newspaper, and Grandma has settled back to watch the blonde lady make rose radishes.

"Fun, cup, m-mix," Bugs announces. "I can read this box, Clay."

He looks at his little brother as the sour taste of fear fills his mouth. "So what?"

"Clay." His mother drops the paper and frowns. "That's no way to encourage your brother."

He's not in the mood to encourage anybody, but he can't explain that to Mom. He can't explain anything without getting himself into tons of trouble. He loosens his hold on the table and wipes his damp palms on his jeans. He can't panic; he has to think things through. Percy, Tyler, and Toby are okay. There's no way they could have been kidnapped. Kidnappers don't take three kids at once. They take one kid who's been left all alone somewhere.

They're not kidnapped. They're hiding out.

He takes his cereal bowl and spoon to the sink, then goes to the living room and sits on the edge of the sofa. He leans forward, his elbows on his knees, until the blonde lady smiles and says something about being right back. "Grandma? Can I change the channel for a minute?"

She sighs and hands him the remote. "I didn't know they ran sports scores this early in the morning."

Clay clicks to channel nine, the station that carries nothing but local news. A man and a puffy-haired woman are sitting behind a big desk, their faces serious. The woman says something about missing kids, and the screen fills with pictures of Clay's three friends.

He stares at the photos, which he's never seen before. Tyler looks totally bored and a little dangerous, Toby looks like he's trying to be cool, and Percy is smiling. They've put Percy's picture in the center, and Clay wonders why. Did they mean to order them white-black-white, or did they just want the smiling kid in the middle?

"Clay?"

He flinches at the sound of his name. "Yeah?"

His grandma looks at him, concern in her eyes. "Do you know those boys?"

Uncertain of how much he should say, he nods. "They're in my class."

"That's terrible." She turns toward the kitchen. "Jen? Did you know that three of Clay's classmates have gone missing?"

Mom's chair scrapes across the kitchen floor, and Clay hears the thump of her footsteps. "My goodness." Her hand goes to her throat as she listens to the reporters. "Clay, do you know these boys?"

He nods again.

"Do you know anything about where they might be?"

They're drunk, probably. Maybe snoring away in the catacombs. But if he tells, they'll hate him forever. They don't deserve his loyalty, but you don't cross Tyler Henton without consequences. "Could be anyplace, I guess."

※ ※ ※

I'm worried about my son. Mom and I had planned to drive to Orlando to do some last-minute Christmas shopping, but I don't want to leave Clay home alone. Gerald will be here, but if he has to go out on a call, Clay will be left with Bugs . . . and with the television, which keeps flashing photos of the three missing boys.

If something has happened to those kids, Clay will never forget it. Even though we live in a mortuary, we haven't done many children's funerals, and Clay has never had a friend die. It's sobering enough to realize that elderly people die of advanced age and parents can die in car crashes. How do you prepare your child for the reality of evil?

That's what we fear, of course. Anyone who reads a newspaper or watches television has heard about pedophiles and psychopaths who steal children and use them in despicable ways. I can't imagine anyone like that wandering the quiet streets of Mt. Dora, but no one ever expects a pleasant stranger's smile to dissolve into a menacing leer.

My mother understands all this without my having to explain, so we stay home and do our best to distract the boys. Mom turns off the television and puts a holiday CD on the stereo. I bake a pitiful-looking Yule log and tape this year's Christmas cards to the woodwork around the kitchen doorway. Gerald takes Bugs to the garage to work on "Christmas projects," whatever that means, and Clay sits in his bedroom with the door closed.

Several times I stop what I'm doing and go stand outside Clay's door. I hover in the hallway and wonder if I should knock, but I'm 90 percent sure I'll find Clay sleeping or playing one of his video games.

After all, he'd tell me if something was bothering him. I'm sure of it.

29

Though since yesterday his grandmother has kept the TV off, Clay powers it on in time for the Friday noon news. The puffy-haired reporter is still behind the news desk, and she's still talking about the three missing boys.

Clay sinks to the floor as the scene shifts to an orange grove. "Shortly after sunrise this morning," a man says, "searchers found this group of bicycles in a citrus grove off Morningside Drive in Mt. Dora. Family members related to the missing eighth graders have identified the bikes as belonging to middle school students Tyler Henton, Toby Talbott, and Percy Walker."

The camera cuts to a black woman, whose chin quivers as she stares into the camera. "Percy, please come home," she says, leaning on a tall man who keeps his arm around her shoulder. "If you have my son, please let him go. Please. Let Percy go so he can be home with us at Christmas."

At the thought of Christmas morning, an eel of fear wriggles in Clay's gut. None of the gruesome threesome seemed to care much about the meaning of the holiday, but they had talked about what they wanted for Christmas presents. Percy was hoping for a new gaming computer, Toby wanted a karaoke machine, and Tyler was hoping to sneak several cigars out of his older brother's secret stash.

The squirming eel wriggles lower in Clay's guts. The threesome might have spent one night in the catacombs for kicks, but Clay doesn't think they'd want to stay in that place for two days. Not with Christmas coming.

He clicks off the TV and listens to the hum of the house around him. Some guy on Mom's CD player keeps yowling about being home for Christmas, a thought that makes Clay feel like throwing up.

But what is he supposed to do? He's not even sure the guys are still in the catacombs. What if Tyler tried to sell the guns or the booze and they ran into some really rough characters? They could be tied up in the back of some dude's pickup, heading to California or Mexico or Canada. Or they could be holed up in the catacombs, laughing and smoking and drinking.

They could be hurt . . . or sick. And even though it'd be their own fault for wandering off without telling anyone where they were going, Clay *knows* where they were going. And he ought to tell someone.

He stands and moves to the staircase, then grabs the banister and starts down, hesitating on each step. He can tell his mom, but should he begin with the catacombs or talk about how they wanted an adventure? Mom would understand about the adventure because she knows there's not much to do around here. She might cut him some slack.

He lands on the bottom step as a vehicle rattles over the gravel outside. A white car pulls up to the house and stops, raising a cloud of dust. A Ford Crown Victoria with the Lake County seal painted on the side.

Clay halts, his scalp freezing to his skull, as his mom comes out of the office and walks through the foyer without glancing back. She crosses her bare arms and shivers as the deputy gets out of the patrol car.

"Afternoon, Mrs. Graham," the man says, his smile fixed and wide beneath his sunglasses. "I wonder if your oldest boy is at home."

Clay doesn't wait. He leaps off the step and turns down the hallway, then sprints through the empty prep room and onto the back porch. His bike lies near the ramp, so he picks it up and pushes it through the underbrush, choosing to struggle over the grass instead of taking the road.

He'd be too easy to spot out in the open.

※ ※ ※

Randolph stands as McLane enters the restaurant, her cheeks rosy and full. He waves to catch her attention, then sits down again at the linen-covered table.

Once the waiter has pulled out her chair and given her a menu, he drops his napkin into his lap. "You're looking lovely, McLane."

Her answering smile holds only a ghost of its former warmth. "Haven't you heard? Pregnant women are supposed to blossom. We're supposed to enjoy the best hair, best skin, and best appetite of our lives." Her smile fades. "Unfortunately, I'm not going to be pregnant much longer."

He tenses, the muscles of his forearm hardening beneath his sleeve. "Should I guess what you mean or are you going to explain?"

She looks at him with a weight of sadness on her face. "My baby is sick. Hydrocephalic. The only reason I've come here today is because . . . well, I need a ride to and from the women's health clinic. It's in Orlando."

Beneath the table, Randolph clenches one hand in a triumphant fist. He dares not reveal his feelings, though, especially when McLane's eyes are as lifeless and damp as they are now. He arranges his face into an expression of sympathy. "Of course, honey. And I'm so sorry."

McLane picks up the menu. "I don't think you mean that, but I appreciate the token support. I'll let you know when I've made the appointment."

"Sweetheart." He pauses, hoping the endearment will soften her heart. "I know how painful this must be, and I'm sorry you've had to go through it alone. If you'd been at home—"

"I wasn't, so don't belabor the point. And I haven't been alone. My sister's been with me."

He lifts both hands in an I-surrender pose, then rubs his chin. "They say the almond-crusted grouper is excellent."

Her gaze remains on the menu. "I hate grouper."

"The chicken breast, then. I had it yesterday; it's very good."

She closes the menu and drops it on the table. "Why did you

invite me to lunch? I don't think you wanted to discuss fish and poultry."

"Can't a father spend time with his daughter? Just because you're working while I'm on vacation doesn't mean we can't—"

"Cut to the chase. That's what you like to do, isn't it? You're here because you want me to come home. You want me to divorce Jeff, and you're probably thrilled that our baby isn't healthy—"

"That's not fair."

"What's not fair, *Daddy*—" McLane looks around and lowers her voice when other diners turn to stare—"is that you refuse to accept my marriage. At this point I can't help my baby, but I can support my husband. I'm staying married, and when Jeff gets back from Iraq, I'm going to have half a dozen light brown babies with kinky hair."

"McLane!" Without intending to, Randolph slams his hand on the table, rocking a candle and rattling silverware. Again, heads turn, but he doesn't care. Anger fills his mouth, the acid burn of long-suppressed resentment. "You shouldn't be so glib about mocking the laws of God. Holy people were never supposed to mingle with the cursed seed of Canaan—"

"That curse has nothing to do with the color of a person's skin," McLane hisses back. "And the Canaanites were destroyed when the Israelites entered the Holy Land. They never even lived in Africa."

"The races were intended to remain separate. God's people are not to intermarry with other races."

"Nations. The Israelites were not to intermarry with heathen *nations*, but God's reasons were spiritual, not racial." McLane's eyes are blazing. "Jeff serves the same God I do. Furthermore, Rahab, Ruth, and Moses' wife were all from other races, yet God blessed them when they married into the nation of Israel."

"You are twisting the Word of God."

"I can't do this." McLane tosses her napkin onto her empty plate and yanks her purse from the back of the chair. "I thought maybe you'd softened. I was hoping you could accept us, that you'd come all this way to tell me you'd had a change of heart."

"How can I change my position when the Word of God stands forever?"

"The Word of God may be eternal, but those who misinterpret it are not. At least I *hope* they're not."

Randolph draws a long, quivering breath, barely mastering the anger that quakes him. "What will it take for you to realize that your problems are God's chastisement for your sins?"

"And when will he chastise you for *yours?*"

The flash of fury stuns him like a white-hot bolt of lightning through the chest. "If you leave now," he says, his voice metallic and brittle, "you are no daughter of mine."

She stands, white-knuckled hands clutching the strap of her purse. Her complexion has paled, but two deep patches hover over her cheekbones, as though he has slapped her on both cheeks.

For a moment her face seems to open, so he can peer inside and watch his words take effect. He sees bewilderment, a quick flicker of fear, and aching regret.

Then something comes down behind her eyes. McLane nods, the iron in her gaze piercing his soul. "Have a nice life, Dr. Harris."

※ ※ ※

Clay pedals furiously over downtown streets, glancing at signs and searching for cars until he spots Aunt McLane's Altima. He coasts to the sidewalk, drops his bike next to a park bench, and double-checks the painted sign over the brick building: The Law Offices of Lawson, Bridges, and Sladen.

This has to be the place.

He opens the door and steps inside. The air smells of coffee and paper, and somewhere that same guy is singing "I'll Be Home for Christmas." Two desks sit just past the doorway, but they're empty, and for a minute he's afraid the office is closed.

Then he hears laughter from somewhere in the back of the building. The sound gives him the confidence to move forward, and he sighs in relief when Aunt McLane walks into a hallway with a glass of red punch in her hand.

She gives him a weak smile, but her eyes fill with confusion. "Have you come to join our Christmas party?"

He folds his arms and lifts his chin, trying to look calm and mature. "I need a lawyer."

Her smile deepens. "You need a law—" Her voice cuts out like somebody flipped a switch. She sets her cup on a desk, then comes closer and bends to study his face. "Are you okay?"

Clay tries to smile the way his dad did in tough situations, but he can feel his mouth bobbling out of control. "I can't talk to anyone but my lawyer."

She tilts her head. "Lawyers cost a lot of money. Wouldn't you rather tell me what's on your mind? Did you have a fight with your mom?"

He pulls out the money he was saving for Christmas presents and drops it on the desk. "That's thirty-one dollars and sixty-five cents. Is that enough to talk to a lawyer?"

Maybe the sound of rattling coins brought him out because Daniel Sladen suddenly appears in the hallway behind McLane. The lawyer glances at Clay, at the money on the desk, and at McLane. "Everything okay out here?"

Aunt McLane shakes her head. "Clay says he needs to talk to a lawyer. And as you see, he's willing to pay."

Clay speaks before his courage completely dries up. "If I pay you, you can't tell any of my secrets, right?"

Mr. Sladen looks at McLane again, then nods. "That's called attorney-client privilege. And, yes, that's the gist of it."

Clay scoops his money together and reaches for a nickel that has rolled under a stack of envelopes. "I need to hire you, Mr. Sladen. And I need to talk to you now. It's important."

The lawyer points to an open doorway. "That's my office. Go on inside and I'll be right there."

Clay takes two steps down the hallway, then turns. "You're not calling my mother, are you?"

"Should I?"

"No. Don't call the sheriff, either."

Mr. Sladen shrugs and folds his hands behind his back. "I won't call anyone. Let's you and I have a talk."

Clay walks into the lawyer's big office and sits in a fancy leather seat.

Mr. Sladen takes the chair behind the desk and gives Clay a bewildered smile. "How can I help you, son?"

To his great shame, Clay bursts into tears.

❈ ❈ ❈

"Gerald—" I enter the prep room, where Gerald has been bathing a new arrival—"have you seen Clay? Mom promised to take him out to do his Christmas shopping, and she wants to go before it gets dark."

Gerald sets down the shower nozzle and picks up a towel. "I haven't seen him since this afternoon."

I glance at the man on the table. "Do I know this one?"

Gerald gives me a humorless grin. "Floyd Fontenetta. He's the electrician you hired to rewire this place."

I halt, my hand frozen in midair. "Did he . . . ?"

"Heart attack," Gerald says. "We always teased Floyd about electrocuting himself, but the Lord had other plans."

I hand Gerald his can of shaving cream. "When you saw Clay, did he say where he was going?"

Gerald squirts a generous dollop of shaving cream into his palm and begins to lather Floyd's face and neck. "He tore out of here on his bike. Sorry that I can't be of more help."

The mention of the bicycle bothers me. Before he found new friends, Clay often spent his days off lazing around the house or shooting hoops at the park, which is only a short walk away. He only rides his bike if he's planning to meet his friends; that's why he didn't leave the house yesterday. As long as those boys are missing, I can't see Clay going far, yet if he took his bike . . . Where was he planning to go?

"I told the deputy Clay was probably at the park," I say, thinking

277

aloud. "He drove off in that direction, so I assumed he found Clay there."

"Did he want to ask Clay about those boys?"

I nod. "People around town have seen the four of them together, so he was hoping Clay could tell him something. If a stranger has been following them—"

Gerald gives me a sharp look. "Now, don't be worrying yourself over such things. I know these are troubled times, but you can't allow yourself to get so fretful that you don't let your boys out of the house."

I force a smile and turn away, but Gerald's sense of social awareness petered out in about 1960. I'm sure he hears about the awful things happening in the world, but he steadfastly refuses to believe anything truly dreadful could happen in Mt. Dora.

I, on the other hand, am far too familiar with what can happen to innocents who stumble into the wrong place at the wrong time. We were living in Washington, D.C., at the time of the Beltway sniper shootings. For three weeks in October 2002, I was afraid to pump gas, get groceries, or drop Clay off at school. I know what terror feels like. And I'm beginning to feel it again.

In the foyer, I pause when I hear the sound of an approaching car. I glance through the sidelights and recognize Daniel's black BMW. I'm always glad to see a friend, but right now, I think I'd rather see the sheriff with my son. I step onto the porch and rub my arms in the chilly air.

Daniel looks up at me, gives me an uncharacteristically quick smile, and hesitates at the front of his car.

My pulse quickens. What is this about?

I stare as the passenger door opens. Clay climbs out, but he keeps his head down as he and Daniel approach the sidewalk.

My uneasiness deepens.

When they are finally standing on the porch, Daniel places his hand at the back of Clay's neck. "Why don't you go inside while I talk to your mom?"

Clay murmurs something that sounds like agreement, then slips past me and races into the house.

I look at Daniel and hope he can answer my questions. "What are you doing here? With Clay?"

"Your son has retained me."

"What? Why does he—?"

"Have a seat," he interrupts, gesturing to the rocking chairs on the porch. "Clay wants me to tell you a story."

Not knowing what else to do, I obey my son's lawyer.

※ ※ ※

At six o'clock, we gather in the living room to watch the news. Clay sits beside me while Bugs cuddles with Mom at the other end of the sofa. Gerald has commandeered the love seat, and Daniel has pulled a kitchen chair into the circle. I don't know what we are about to hear, but I'm hoping for the best.

An on-location WFTV reporter launches right into the top story. "Three Mt. Dora boys, missing for two days, have been found," she says, squinting in the bright lights. "Though the story brings relief to two families, the discovery results in tragedy for another. Details in a moment."

I look at Mother, not sure Bugs should remain in the room. Mom meets my gaze and nods, her way of saying we should stay put. This story is going to be the talk of the town for weeks to come, so Bugs might as well hear the truth while we're around to answer his questions.

Clay shudders beneath my arm. Though he's thirteen and prone to resist displays of affection, he's welcoming them tonight.

I wrap both arms around him and hold him tight.

After a quick commercial, the news anchors announce the headline again, then cut to the on-site reporter. She relates the history of the catacombs—a history I had never heard until Daniel filled me in this afternoon—then she steps back and points to a nondescript building.

"The utility shed behind me conceals the opening to the fabled bomb shelter," the reporter continues, "the underground shelter three Mt. Dora youths were determined to find. Find it they did, on

Wednesday afternoon, but they failed to realize that the steel door they pried open was designed to hold refugees inside for several months."

"I found that shed," Clay says, his face pale. "But I didn't see the steel door. It musta been hidden behind something."

The camera turns to a man in a fireman's uniform. Sweat glistens on his forehead as he gestures to the shed. "In there, hidden behind a pile of equipment, is a two-thousand-pound blast-proof steel door. Unless a safety lever is engaged, it's set at such an angle that people inside can't lift it open. I'm told the survivors were supposed to finish a partially dug tunnel in order to exit. The designers of the structure figured they'd have several months before radiation cleared the area."

Clay shivers when the reporter begins to talk again. "The sheriff's department informs us that another eighth grader, a friend of the three missing youths, told deputies that the group had been searching for the underground shelter they called the 'catacombs' for some time. Because he went to the authorities, sheriff's department personnel were able to find the hidden shelter, open the door, and rescue the boys."

The blonde at the anchor desk shifts her expression from mild interest to grave concern. "We understand that two of the boys were unharmed—what happened to the third child?"

"That's the tragedy of this story," the reporter says, her face set in grim lines. "Two of the boys are in good condition at the hospital. Though they are slightly dehydrated, they will recover with no lasting effects. The third boy, however, suffered from severe respiratory allergies. When the property changed hands a few years ago, the new owners shut down the ventilation systems and dehumidifiers. Down those concrete steps, I'm told, mold and mildew have covered almost every surface. It's no place for a person with breathing difficulties, as one grieving family has tragically discovered."

"So . . ." Clay trembles in my arms. "Percy died because he couldn't breathe?"

I hold him tighter. "That's what it sounds like, honey. He might have had asthma that kicked in when he breathed all that mold."

"So I killed him?"

"No." The abruptness of Daniel's answer startles me. He leans forward and looks directly into my frightened son's eyes. "You didn't tell those boys to go in that place, so you didn't have anything to do with Percy Walker's death. In fact, you probably saved the other two boys. In some ways, Clay, you're a real hero."

Clay is shivering so hard that his teeth chatter. "I-I don't feel like a hero."

"That's okay," Daniel answers, his gaze moving to mine. "True heroes never do."

※ ※ ※

Clay sits on the edge of the tub and hugs the toilet bowl. The odors of toilet cleaner and the dinner he just threw up mingle in his nostrils.

He squinches his eyes tight and fumbles for the handle, then flushes the toilet and staggers to the sink. He splashes his face with cold water and rinses his mouth to get rid of the sour taste on his tongue.

Finally he looks in the mirror. His bangs are wet, his eyes are glassy, and his skin is pink, like it always is after a hard run. Mom might look at him and guess that he's just lost his supper, but then again, Mom might not look at him at all. Ever since the news went off, Mom and Grandma have been sitting in the living room and talking in low voices.

He puts his hand on the doorknob and presses his ear to the wood. Mr. Sladen is still out there; his voice booms over the women's as he says good night. Gerald is still there, too, but he's talking to Bugs, telling him a fishing story.

Clay wishes he could trade places with Bugs. He'd give anything to sit cross-legged on the floor and pretend he didn't know what was going on outside.

He wishes he'd never heard of the catacombs.

He wishes he had allergies instead of Percy.

He wishes he'd never been born.

※※ ※※ ※※

Gerald drops Clay and me at the hospital's front entrance while he takes the station wagon around to the morgue. The call came over the Fairlawn business line a few minutes after the news ended. I wasn't sure Clay would want to make this trip, but when he saw Gerald put on his cardigan, Clay said he wanted to go, too. Mom volunteered to remain at the house with Bugs, freeing me to go with my son.

Inside the lobby, we walk to the desk and ask about Tyler Henton and Toby Talbott.

"They're together," the receptionist says after consulting her computer. "Both of them are staying overnight for observation. Room 202."

Clay and I find the elevator and take it up to the second floor. There's no need to ask for directions at the nurses' station because one room is overflowing with people and noise. I suppose the relief that these two, at least, are safe and sound has overridden the hospital standard of peace and quiet.

Clay hangs back at the sight of so many strangers, so I grip his shoulder. "You still want to see them?"

"Yeah."

"Let's go, then."

I nod at a pair of older teenagers standing in the hallway, then wait near the door as Clay pushes into the crowd around the boys' beds.

"Clay!" The boy in the first bed, a kid with shaggy brown hair and a scrape on his cheek, grins at my son. "Man, are we glad to see you."

Clay takes a half step forward. "For real?"

"Yeah." The boy glances at a man and a woman hovering at the head of his bed. "This is Clay. He's the one we were counting on."

"Excuse me, please." A young woman in black pants and a white blouse jostles me to the wall as she shoulders her way into the room. From the huge bag on her shoulder, she pulls a microrecorder and a notepad. "Hello, boys," she says, her voice bright. "I'm from the *Daily Commercial*. Do you mind if I ask you a few questions?"

Both boys turn to adults for permission—the first boy looks to the man and woman at this side; the second, a dark-haired, thin kid, turns to a tiny woman who wears her graying hair in a tight bun.

"I'll need these consent forms signed," the reporter says, sliding papers from a folio. She hands one to the first couple. "And you are?"

"Toby's parents," the man says, taking the form. The reporter strides to the other bed and gives another form to the quiet woman. "You must be Mrs. Henton."

Tyler's mother takes the page and nods. Her son chews on a fingernail and doesn't speak.

The reporter looks at Clay. "You have to be Clay Graham. Is your mom here?"

I step forward, irritated that she's been able to identify everyone but me. "I'm Clay's mother."

"Then this is for you." She hands me a sheet of paper and launches into her interview, focusing first on Toby. "So how did you boys find the catacombs? And what happened once you got in?"

Toby and Tyler look at each other; then Toby begins to jabber. "Percy and Clay did most of the work, and—"

He clams up when his father squeezes his shoulder and extends the unsigned consent form. "I think we should let our lawyer speak to the press," he says, his voice firm.

The reporter's lips curve in a smile, but her eyes narrow with annoyance. "No one is accusing these boys of a crime."

When Mr. Talbott shakes his head, I understand his reluctance to let Toby speak. No one is accusing the boys yet, but anything could happen in the days ahead. The owners of the property could claim they were trespassing, and Percy's parents could sue the property owners, the city, the county, or the people who originally designed the bomb shelter.

I've spent enough time with Daniel to know that people don't always need legitimate reasons to file a lawsuit. In our society, people can sue for almost anything. They may not win, but they can make other people miserable for a long time.

For the first time in a long time, I miss Thomas. Lawsuits rarely rattled him.

"You can read the police report," Mr. Talbott tells the reporter. "The boys got in, they couldn't get out, and Percy was overcome by respiratory distress. Toby and Tyler tried to get help, but they couldn't open the door."

Toby shrinks back in the pillows and stares at his hands, his face going pale beneath his tan. Whatever these children endured in that subterranean death trap, I'm glad they're not being forced to relive it.

"Mr. Talbott," the reporter says, "I'm not here to accuse or incriminate—"

"You can say it was scary." Every head swivels toward the boy in the second bed when he speaks. "You can say we were scared spitless, but we did our best to help Percy. For a while we thought we would die, too, but we knew Clay would bring help once he figured out where we were. We were counting on him . . . and he came through."

Tyler Henton's dark eyes—which seem older than thirteen or fourteen—lock on my son, and I see something pass between them. I'm not sure what it is, but Clay lifts his head, and his shoulders seem to broaden before my eyes.

The reporter turns. "Clay—"

"—is leaving." I drop the unsigned consent form onto Toby Talbott's bed, then squeeze Clay's shoulder. "Come on. Gerald will be waiting."

Before she can ask another question, we worm our way out of the hospital room and head toward the elevator. After we pass the receptionist, I can see the call car waiting under the sheltered entrance and Gerald's drawn face behind the wheel.

I keep my hand on Clay's shoulder as we join Gerald in the front seat. Together, the three of us escort Percy Walker to Fairlawn.

30

I rise and shower early on Saturday morning, so I'm dressed when someone knocks at seven thirty. "Hello?" someone calls after the front door opens. "Jen, are you up?"

I step out of the kitchen and see McLane on the stairs. She's heard the news, and she's rushed to be with us, her family. I greet her at the landing and hold her in a long embrace.

Beneath the long shirt she's wearing, I can feel the soft bulge of her belly, so she's still pregnant. I don't know if she's waiting for a convenient day off from work or if she still hopes for my approval, but I'm glad she hasn't scheduled an abortion.

I also don't know if she's been reading baby books, but I've glanced at a couple with her due date in mind. McLane is fifteen weeks along, so my niece is about the size of a softball and weighs nearly two ounces. Our little girl may already be sucking her thumb.

I want to share this with McLane, but I don't want her to think I'm unfairly pressuring her. If only I had a way to assure her that prayer works, so everything will be all right. . . .

But how can I make that assurance with someone else's young son downstairs in the prep room?

I release McLane and rub her shoulder. "Want some juice?"

"No thanks. Is Clay awake? I thought I might stop in and say hi."

"Take a peek in his room. If he's still asleep . . ."

"I won't wake him."

I watch as she tiptoes down the hall and pauses at Clay's door. I'm glad those two have made a connection. Between the demands of school, work, and community, I'm afraid my family has suffered.

I'm on my way back to the kitchen when I hear another knock on the front door. The door opens again but less confidently this time. A man's voice says, "Hello?"

I hurry down the stairs. An African-American couple stands in the foyer, the man and the woman wearing the shell-shocked expressions of the suddenly bereaved. The woman is carrying a brown paper bag, neatly folded at the top.

Percy's parents.

My mouth goes dry as I approach them with outstretched arms. "Mr. and Mrs. Walker?"

The man takes my hand. "I'm Nathan Walker, and this is Amma, my wife."

I squeeze Amma's hand. "I'm so pleased to meet you . . . and so sorry for your loss. But I was honored when I heard you are trusting us with your son's burial. Percy meant a lot to my Clay."

Mrs. Walker dips her chin in a small nod. "Percy talked a lot about him. Sometimes he said he didn't know about Tyler and that other boy, but he liked Clay. Said he didn't need to worry when Clay was around." Like a rising fountain, her eyes fill with water and spill over. "I wish Clay had been with them when those foolish boys went into that musty old tomb. Then we'd be planning a Christmas celebration instead of a funeral."

I press my hands together and lower my gaze, not knowing what to say. We could spend all morning torturing ourselves with what-ifs, but conjectures won't help, not now.

I stayed awake for a couple of hours last night, convinced that if Clay had been there, he would have followed the others without a second thought. What would have happened then? We might never have found any of them, and all four would have died in circumstances too horrible to imagine.

"Please." I gesture to the smaller chapel. "Let's sit down and talk about the service, shall we?" I step aside to let Mr. and Mrs. Walker precede me, and as I glance back, I see McLane on the stairs, her eyes filled with compassion and sorrow.

❦ ❦ ❦

I carry the brown paper bag into the prep room, set it on an empty table, and burst into noisy, gulping sobs.

Gerald glances up, then goes back to massaging Percy's limbs, working the embalming fluid through every vein.

When I have finished crying, he makes soft clucking noises behind his mask. "The first child is always hard. With older people, you tell yourself they had their chance to live, love, and laugh. But when it's a kid and you have to face those grieving parents . . ."

I reach for tissues from the box on the counter. Gerald doesn't know, of course, that my tears aren't only for Percy. He's telling me how hard it is to bury a thirteen-year-old, but I can't stop thinking about the four-inch girl swimming around upstairs. If McLane goes through with her plans, my precious niece will not only be deprived of a chance to live, she won't even have a decent burial. No one will treat her shattered remains with dignity or tenderly lay them in a receptacle for precious treasures. They will most likely be considered medical waste and tossed out with the trash.

"Percy's funeral," I whisper when I can finally speak, "will be on Christmas. I can't think of a more awful day, but Mrs. Walker said the family would be together anyway, so they might as well . . ." Emotion rises in my throat and chokes off my words.

But Gerald understands. "Any special requests from the family?"

"Just this." I open the paper bag and pull out a pair of soccer shoes, socks, shorts, and a jersey. "They want him buried in his soccer uniform. Mr. Walker said soccer was the only thing Percy did without Toby and Tyler. I get the feeling he would have liked to see Percy play soccer year-round, anything to keep him away from those other boys."

Gerald clucks again. "The service?"

"Two o'clock, and the minister from their church will speak.

287

They'll bring a youth choir, too, so we don't have to plan any music . . . except for the viewing. They didn't specifically mention the viewing. I'm thinking it'd be nice to have something quiet playing in the background."

"Maybe a soundtrack?"

"Something like that." I walk to where Floyd Fontenetta waits in his casket. The man looks just as he did when I met him only a few months ago. "Nice work on Floyd," I call over my shoulder. "Did you paint on the color or use the airbrush?"

"Paint," Gerald says. "Only had to do the backs of the hands, neck, and face. If he'd been wearing short sleeves, I woulda used the machine."

"And he's all ready to go?"

"Funeral's tomorrow at the Baptist church. His wife handled all the arrangements, so you don't have to worry about a thing."

Given the time of year, I'm grateful to have one less funeral at Fairlawn. My mind still resists the combination of Christmas trees and funeral sprays.

Finally my steps bring me to the table where Gerald is working. I gather up my courage and study Percy Walker, who reminds me of a darker, rounder version of my son. His body is smooth and unmarked, and the embalming fluid has restored his color. Gerald has been hard at work because Percy no longer looks dead. He looks as if he has just dozed off.

I squeeze my mentor's arm. "You must have been up late last night."

He grunts. "No later than usual."

"You do good work, Gerald Huffman. Thank you."

❧ ❧ ❧

Because we will be working on Christmas Eve and Christmas Day, Mother and I decide to have our holiday dinner tonight. She gets on the phone to invite Daniel and Lydia and then reports that Lydia will be unable to come because she's hosting a Sneaky Santa gift exchange for the Kiwanis Club.

I point to my list. "What about the others?"

"Too busy," Mom says, beelining to the refrigerator. "I've got to start chopping the celery for the stuffing."

So I sit down to call McLane, who's delighted to accept our invitation. I hesitate before ringing the Lakeside Inn to invite Randolph Harris. When the operator tells me he's not in, I leave a message. He may not come, but it'd be a shame to leave him sitting alone in a hotel room when he could be enjoying the questionable comfort of a Christmassy funeral parlor.

In a moment of inspired madness, I pick up the phone book and dial the number for Claire Douyon, niece of the late Levina Gifford. To my surprise, she and her husband accept.

Out come the makeshift tabletop and my holiday linens and china. Once again Bugs makes place cards, and I try to seat our family members in the least volatile positions. I place Mom, Gerald, and Clay at the far end of the table, while Daniel and Bugs will keep me company at the opposite end. McLane and her father will sit, Lord willing, on one side of the table, while the Douyons sit on the other.

While we're setting the table, I wonder aloud if Dr. Harris will sit down to eat with African-Americans. Mom says eating with people of another race is a far cry from marrying them, but I'm not so sure.

As the clock strikes six and Daniel arrives, I greet him with a friendly embrace and a whispered warning: "I can't promise peace on earth, but we do have tissues and bandages."

By six fifteen, every chair around the table is filled except for McLane's and her father's. I try not to worry and even manage a smile when Mother says, "The girl is likely to be late to her own funeral."

The comment is tactless, especially considering that the Douyons have recently buried a family member, but they don't respond. I look at Daniel, who has to be tracking with my train of thought: could McLane have taken her day off to have the abortion?

But my sister breezes through the door just as I'm about to ask Gerald to say grace. She drops a pair of shopping bags in the foyer, spouting apologies like a geyser. "I'm so sorry. Please forgive me. I got held up in the gift wrap department—the woman ahead of me didn't like the only foil design they had left. I thought they were going to have to call security before she'd accept poinsettia paper." She slips into a chair and smiles at the Douyons, who watch her with blank expressions. Then she notices the empty chair to her right. "Are we expecting someone else?"

"Possibly," I say, hurrying to fill the silence. "But we're not waiting."

After making the introductions, I am about to turn to Gerald when Lamont Douyon, who looks like a little wet bird next to his stately wife, lifts his hand to catch my attention. "Would you mind if I thanked the Lord for this meal?"

I smile at him in pleased surprise. "I'd be delighted."

The gray-haired man stands and lifts his open hands toward heaven.

From the corner of my eye, I catch Bugs gaping at him, so I give my son a stern look and pointedly bring my hands together.

"Our most gracious Father and God," Lamont prays, his voice simmering with barely checked emotion, "we come to you acknowledging that you are Lord yesterday, today, and tomorrow. We would not understand how we can overflow with joy one day and stagger beneath a weight of sorrow the next had you not sent your Son to walk among us. But you did, and for that we are most grateful. We are thankful for many gifts, but most of all we thank you for the gift of eternal life through Jesus our Savior. Without that, we'd have no hope of ever seeing our loved ones again. So please, Lord, bless the kind hearts around this table. Fill us up with love for you and one another. And remind us that you are enough. You are all we need. Amen."

When Lamont sits down, I wonder if he knows of the grief in our hearts. Then I look into his eyes and see the pain flickering there.

"Nathan and Amma Walker," he says, his voice husky, "are our neighbors. We knew their boy. And we are grateful for your kindness to that family."

So . . . pain binds us together, even on a night of celebration.

I nod my thanks to Lamont and start the cranberry sauce around the table.

After we've discussed the weather, the town parade, and the frenzied

shopping crowds, the topic turns to race relations. I suppose I introduce the subject when I remark on the different speaking style favored
by most black ministers. "Though the preaching at Levina's funeral
wasn't what I was used to," I say, waving a forkful of turkey over my
plate, "I enjoyed it tremendously."

Claire smiles at me from across the table. "I'm glad, because that
same minister is going to preach at Percy's service. I spoke to Amma
about it this morning, and she said it's all been arranged."

I catch McLane's eye across the table, silently sending her a message. This dinner and Percy's service certainly ought to convince her
that I'm sufficiently integrated. "My father," I continue, emboldened
by my apparent success, "was a general in the army. Of course he
worked with people from all races. He and Mom raised me to be
color-blind, to treat people as individuals, not as members of any
certain race."

"That's right," Mother echoes. "If more folks were color-blind, we'd
have a lot less trouble in this country. People need to stop being so
sensitive and picky about things."

I'm slicing a section of turkey breast when I realize that silence is
sifting over my dinner table like a snowfall. Bugs and Clay are quiet—
not too unusual in a roomful of adults—but even Gerald and McLane
are holding their tongues.

I look up. Daniel is watching me with an intense but guarded
expression while McLane's mouth has gone tight and grim. The
Douyons have become markedly somber, but Mother is focused on
her food, apparently unaware of the change in the atmosphere.

Lamont braces his elbows on the table and clasps his hands. His
face empties of expression as he faces me. "If you remove the color
from a red rose, what remains?"

Sensing a trap behind the words, I glance at Daniel and Gerald, but
neither man rises to my aid. "Well . . . I suppose you'd have a white
rose."

Lamont waggles his finger at me. "Not exactly, because white is a
color, isn't it? So what would you have left?"

This time I look to Mother for help. She has stopped eating, so obviously she's wised up to the change in mood, but now she looks like a frightened rabbit.

I sigh and catch McLane's eye. "If you remove all the color, you'd be left with an invisible flower."

Lamont gives me the indulgent smile a teacher gives a bright pupil. "So if you refuse to see my color, what are you seeing?"

I glance around the table again, feeling pinned down, but everyone has abandoned me. Gerald is smiling behind his napkin and Daniel has developed an unusual interest in the china. McLane wears a smug smile, proof that she enjoys watching me squirm. "I'm saying . . . you're invisible."

Lamont nods. "I mean no disrespect, but if you don't see my color, you don't see me."

Mother harrumphs from her corner. "I see you just fine. And I say political correctness is running amok in this country, simply amok."

I'm new at this, but even I know that Mother has waved the verbal equivalent of a red flag in front of Claire Douyon. She has shifted in her seat; in a minute she'll be lighting into Mom with the force of a hurricane.

"Mom—" I gulp and jump in to save her—"how would you feel if men stopped giving you their seats on the bus?"

She looks at me as if my logic has sprung a leak. "I haven't ridden a bus in thirty years."

"Forget that, then. But think about being a woman. You can vote, you can own property, and you can take any job you can handle—all because someone before you paved the way for women's rights. Now even though you can do practically anything a man can do, how would you feel if people on the street didn't acknowledge your femininity or if they treated you like every man who walks by?"

She lowers her chin, resisting, but gradually her face takes on an inward look. A frown appears between her brows when she realizes what a truly genderless society might look like. "You mean," she finally says, looking at the Douyons, "the bag boys might not offer to carry my groceries to the car?"

Lamont buries his smile in his eggnog while Mrs. Douyon beams.

"Exactly!" I lift my cup in Mother's honor, certain that on some level, at least, our group has reached an understanding.

"To embracing our commonality," Daniel says, making a toast. "And celebrating our differences."

Around the table, we clink our holiday glasses.

_B_ecause this year's Christmas Day will focus on a funeral, I'm grateful that Christmas Eve falls on a Sunday. We get up and go to church, and for a few precious moments the spirit of nativity wraps around me. With Bugs on my left and Clay on my right, I'm almost able to forget about impending memorials and the soccer-suited boy in our prep room.

McLane doesn't join us. When Clay asks if she's coming to church, I make a vague remark about the possibility of her not feeling well.

I stare at the flickering candles around the altar and wonder if things will ever be good between us again. We haven't really talked in the four days since she told me she wanted an abortion. Will we ever have another heart-to-heart?

The congregation sings all my favorite Christmas hymns: "O Little Town of Bethlehem," "Good King Wenceslas," and "Joy to the World!" Carol Conrad, recovered from her laryngitis, leads the choir in "O Holy Night." Then Carol's daughter, one of six or seven stair-step Conrads, stands to play "Silent Night" on her violin. The sharp sound of the strings cuts clean through me.

Our pastor preaches on keeping the spirit of Christmas in our hearts all year round. In my lifetime I've heard at least a dozen variations of that sermon, but the Lord must have known I needed a reminder.

When we arrive back at the house, Mom rushes to the kitchen to make sandwiches from our leftover holiday feast. I change from a dress to jeans and pull on a sweater. It's fiftysomething degrees outside, far from cold, but one of the cooler days we'll experience this season. I might as well wear my sweaters while I can.

I'm pulling my hair into a ponytail when I hear a car approaching. A glance out the window reveals a white Saturn sedan, the rental Randolph Harris has been driving.

Afraid he's bringing news from McLane, I sprint down the steps and reach the front door before he has a chance to ring the bell.

He blinks at the sight of me, then gives me a tight smile. "I thought my daughter might be here. She didn't answer the door at her apartment."

I cross my arms and lean against the doorframe. "I expect to see her this afternoon."

"Would you give this to her?" He gestures to the floor, and for the first time I see that he's brought a huge gift basket wrapped with cellophane and ribbons.

I toe the door open wider. "Why don't you come in? You can make yourself at home and give it to her—"

"No, I'm flying out this afternoon; I'm on my way to the airport. I need to get back to my practice."

Randolph Harris has never been predictable, but this announcement is the most surprising of all. I pull myself off the doorframe and uncross my arms. "Why do you have to rush off? It's Christmas."

"McLane and I have had a falling-out. I'm afraid the breach is irreparable." His eyes, which I've always considered implacable, darken with undeniable pain. "I love that girl—honestly I do—but she insists on violating the values I've spent a lifetime teaching her. I can't force her to change. Apparently I can't convince her to do anything."

I stare at him, amazed to hear my own thoughts spill from his lips. Even more astonishing is the seam of vulnerability underlying his words. My face must be idiotic with surprise. "Dr. Harris—" I catch his sleeve—"I've been struggling with McLane, too."

I smile when he lifts a brow. "Regardless of what you may think, I don't see you as the enemy. I've found my own values tested by McLane's situation, and I've struggled to figure out how God wants me to respond to her choices—choices I can't support."

His wide mouth twists. "And have you found a solution?"

"Nothing definitive. Only love."

He stiffens. "Are you inferring that I don't love my daughter?"

"I don't think that at all. But I've been watching, and every time you two begin to make progress, you issue some sort of demand. You imply you'll love her *if* she comes home or *if* she divorces Jeff. I'm no psychiatrist, but it seems to me that love shouldn't have so many strings attached."

Dr. Harris glances down, smiles to himself, and then looks at me. "Do you want her to have this baby?"

"Don't you?"

He turns toward the lawn and shrugs. "This child is a mistake. Maybe the hydrocephalus is God's way of working things out for the best."

I step back, feeling as if hot hands have gripped my heart and are slowly twisting the hope from it. I had thought that in matters concerning the baby, at least, Randolph Harris and I might be allies. I clench my jaw to stifle the sob in my throat. "I will never believe that. I simply can't accept that God would—"

"I have strong beliefs, too," he says, interrupting with savage intensity. "I don't believe God intended the races to mix in marriage. So if you want me to respect your principles, please respect mine."

"Would you sacrifice your daughter for *principles*?"

"Would you sacrifice your sister?" He pins me with a long look, his pupils glowing fiercely. "When McLane comes over here after having that abortion, remind yourself of everything you've told me about unconditional love."

Speechless, I retreat and watch as he broadens his shoulders and walks away, resettling his convictions around him like an impenetrable mantle.

※※ ※※ ※※

After a lunch of turkey sandwiches, warmed-over sweet potatoes, and pumpkin pie, Gerald, Clay, and I load Floyd Fontenetta into the hearse. Clay and I stand back and wave as Gerald pulls out to take the casket to the Baptist church, where Floyd's family will be gathering for the funeral.

As we walk back to the house, neither Clay nor I mention Percy, though he is heavy on both our minds.

"Kinda sad, isn't it, to have a funeral at Christmas?" Clay asks as we walk up the ramp that leads into the prep room.

I rest my arm on his shoulder. "No sadder than at any other time of year, I suppose."

"Yeah, but doesn't it sort of ruin Christmas forever? I mean, that man's family won't ever think of Christmas trees or colored lights without remembering his funeral."

I stop and turn to face Clay before we enter the prep room, where Percy lies beneath a sheet. "I can think of at least one reason why Christmas might be a great time for a funeral."

Clay looks at me with guilt-filled eyes.

"If I lost someone during the holidays," I continue, "every time I began to feel sad, I'd think of that baby in a manger. Because Jesus came and died for us, everyone who trusts in him will go to heaven. Without the Christmas baby, we'd have no hope of seeing our loved ones again. But Jesus came . . . and we have hope. And eternal life."

I'm not sure how comforting I've been, but Clay gives me a distracted nod. I open the prep room door to reenter the house, but Clay hops off the porch and races around to the front porch.

I can't say I blame him. At thirteen, I wouldn't have wanted to walk past my dead friend, either.

The afternoon passes quietly. I apply a few cosmetic touches to Percy's face, then stand back when Ryan drops by to check my work.

"You're getting good." He cocks a brow in my direction. "You're not planning to take my job, are you?"

"Never," I promise, picking up the envelope containing his holiday bonus. "And here's this—it's not much, but Gerald and I wanted to do something extra for you." I give him a hug. "Don't forget to stop by the kitchen. Mom's been baking fruitcakes, and she'll want you to take one."

Ryan rolls his eyes. "I don't mean to seem ungrateful, but if there's one thing the biddies know how to bake, it's fruitcake. I'm afraid I'm going to be selling them as doorstops at the Spring Fling."

"Speaking of the Biddle House . . ." I lock my hands behind my back and lean against the wall. "Did you see McLane this morning? I was hoping she'd join us at church."

He shakes his head. "It's been so quiet I thought she was staying here for the holidays."

"Mom's in our guest room." I force a smile. "McLane will probably pop in later. Have a merry Christmas, Ryan."

❧ ❧ ❧

Drawn like moths to a lamp, friends and family appear at the house after sunset. McLane shows up, sprinkles a few packages under the tree, and stretches out on the sofa to watch TV. Clay sits on the floor in front of her, and she spends the next half hour trying to guess how many freckles are on the back of his neck.

Lydia comes by, bringing jars of honey, a platter of soft sugar cookies, and a box of homemade dog biscuits for Skeeter. Ryan breezes in with coupons for free haircuts at his salon, and Ruby Masters, our organist on call, arrives with a basket of Avon products.

"You'll have to share," she announces as Lydia, Mother, McLane, and I paw through the packages. "And remember that some of these formulations are age-appropriate."

I glance at Mom. "I think she's hinting that McLane should leave the antiwrinkle potions to you and me."

"Me," Mom says, pulling out a jar of some miracle-working mixture. "You have at least ten years before you have to start worrying about your face."

The phone rings at seven thirty, and I give Gerald a worried look as he moves to answer it. Our Christmas Eve couldn't get any more low-key, and I'd hate to spoil it further by running out to pick up a body.

"No need to worry," Gerald announces when he comes back. "That was Daniel, just checking to see if we were home. He's on his way over."

Mother gives me a triumphant look, which I steadfastly ignore. I'm not in the market for romance, a boyfriend, or an escort. But I will always appreciate a friend.

By eight, McLane has moved into the kitchen to mix up a pot of wassail, and the Douyons have come by to deliver a portrait of Percy Walker. I meet them downstairs and help them set it on an easel that will stand by the casket at tomorrow's funeral.

I embrace Claire and her husband before they leave. "Merry Christmas," I say, the words seeming out of place in this chapel.

Claire squeezes my hand. "Thank the Lord for it," she says. "Else I don't know how we'd get through any of this."

I wait on the front porch as the Douyons pull away and remain in the shadows when I see another pair of headlights approaching. They belong to Daniel's BMW, and I'm startled when he steps out of the car in a tuxedo.

"I should have warned you that this is a casual affair," I call, uncomfortably aware of my jeans and baggy sweater.

His smile spreads as he jogs up the steps. "Sorry," he says, handing me a bouquet of roses. "I've just come from a candlelight service. I didn't change because I'm late enough as it is."

I frown at the fine pleats in his shirt. "A black-tie church service? Around here?"

He laughs. "I'm in the orchestra."

"And you play . . . ?"

"The violin. Sorry. I thought everybody knew."

For an instant, I'm afraid my knees will buckle. Aside from the human voice, I believe the violin to be the world's most perfect instrument. I've always held an undying admiration for skilled violinists. But this is not something I can share with Daniel, especially since my mother has practically painted a target over his heart and placed a bow in my hand.

"I'm glad you came." I give him a hug. "And don't worry about out-classing the rest of us. This place could use a touch of elegance."

We go inside and climb the stairs, where we find Bugs, Clay, Gerald, McLane, and Mom gathered in the sitting area. Gerald is reading the second chapter of Luke, and Bugs is in my mother's arms, hanging on every word.

Clay is listening, too, from his place in the wing chair, and I see thought working behind his eyes.

I join Daniel in leaning against the wall while we listen to the beloved and familiar words:

"'The Savior—yes, the Messiah, the Lord—has been born today in Bethlehem, the city of David! And you will recognize him by this sign: You will find a baby wrapped snugly in strips of cloth, lying in a manger.'

"'Suddenly, the angel was joined by a vast host of others—the armies of heaven—praising God and saying, "Glory to God in highest heaven, and peace on earth to those with whom God is pleased."'"

❊❊ ❊❊ ❊❊

By ten, the boys have gone to bed, Gerald has retired to his room, and McLane is ready to go home. Before leaving, she pulls Daniel into the hallway and gives him an envelope, probably something from work.

From her place on the love seat, my mother notices and arches a brow. "Christmas Eve," she whispers, her voice brimming with signifi-cance. "A time when emotions rise to the surface and men tend to feel sentimental."

I roll my eyes. "Forget it."

"He's a very handsome man. And he owns a tux."

"Well, I'm sure he owns tennis shoes, too. And shorts and under-wear and maybe even a couple of pairs of pajamas."

She harrumphs and turns up the volume on the television as McLane waves at us. "Good night," she says. "I'll be by tomorrow."

"The funeral's at two," I remind her. "And—oh!" I leap off the couch and head toward the staircase. "There's a gift for you downstairs."

McLane follows me into the south chapel and stares in disbelief when I pull the cellophane-wrapped basket from beneath the Christmas tree. "This is for you."

Her mouth curves with tenderness as she takes the gift. "That thoughtful man. This is from Gerald, right?"

"From your father. He brought it by on his way out of town."

The animation leaves her face as she puts the basket on an end table. "There's been some mistake. I have no father, not anymore."

"McLane—"

"Give it to someone else. I'm sure it's nice; Randolph Harris is never chintzy when it comes to presents." She turns and strides toward the foyer.

I look at Mother, who has followed us downstairs, but she has pulled the basket closer and is peering through the plastic wrap.

"Mom! Put that down!"

"What?" She gives me a look of offended innocence. "I was just peeking."

I sigh and hurry after McLane, but her car is already pulling away. I am standing at the front door, feeling tired in soul and spirit, when a hand covers mine.

The hand belongs to Daniel. "Want to sit on the porch?"

"Yes. I do."

The calm of the outdoors soothes my soul even better than a Christmas carol. Daniel sits beside me, looking deliciously dapper, and after a few moments of cricket chorus and creaking rockers, the night fills with the soft drizzle of rain.

"That reminds me," he says, taking a white envelope from his jacket. "McLane asked me to give this to you. She said she took it from your mailbox because she wanted to save it for a surprise. Though I suspect her action may have violated a couple of federal laws, I trust you'll forgive her . . . since it's Christmas." He hands me a long envelope with my school's logo emblazoned in the upper left corner.

"My grades?"

"I expect so."

I laugh. "What kind of present will this be if I failed my classes?"

"She didn't say she wanted it to be a *present*. She said she wanted it to be a *surprise*, so I hope it's a good one."

I slip my thumbnail under the flap and rip the envelope open. Last semester I took three courses: Introduction to Funeral Services, Introduction to Infectious Diseases, and Anatomy.

I got an A in each class. A note at the bottom of the page says I earned a 98 on the anatomy final.

"Brachiocephalic," I murmur, "has nothing to do with dinosaurs." I look at Daniel and try to smile. "I passed."

"I had no doubt. And I'll take your word for the dinosaur thing."

I want to answer with something charming and glib, but instead I burst into tears. Daniel stops rocking; I can feel the pressure of his gaze on the back of my hand as I cover my face and weep.

For a long moment the clouds and I cry together. We have no need for words, no urge to explain. Christ has come, and the world rejoices, but death remains, along with sickness and struggle and hardness of heart.

Finally, I stop sobbing. I wipe the water from my cheeks and look up to find Daniel watching me, his face alive with troubled question. "Are you all right?"

I almost laugh. How many men have uttered those words out of politeness, and how many women have lied and answered yes?

"I don't know," I answer truthfully. "Sorry about the crying jag. It's just . . . sometimes I don't know what I'm doing here. I don't know why God thinks I can handle this mortuary, and I don't know why he's brought me to such a sad place."

Daniel searches my eyes, then takes my hand. "I don't know why, either," he says, leaning on the armrest of his chair, "but I'll help you look for the answers."

We fall silent and resume our rocking as the soft sound of rain wraps around us.

Randolph presses his spine against the hard wood of the pew and struggles to focus on the nativity scene someone has placed on the altar. He should be filled with the wonder of the Lord's birth, but all he can think about is his wayward daughter's indifference.

The choir is noticeably thin this morning; every year the crowd at this Christmas service is smaller than in years past. Have people forgotten their spiritual moorings? Or are they yielding to the plaintive cries of children who would rather stay home and play with toys than acknowledge the infant king?

He returns his gaze to the altar as the choir begins another chorus of "Joy to the World!" The nativity set, which is even larger than the one he has at home, features a long-haired Mary, whose blue eyes gaze at the Christ child with a proper mixture of awe and respect. Even the blond Joseph kneels in reverence, as he surely did when the holy child entered the world.

He frowns when he realizes that Mary, Joseph, and the baby are blue eyed and blond. Not terribly realistic, this set, though surely the artist is to be commended for his keen sense of color. All the lovely shades have been well blended.

Still, a blond Jesus when everyone knows the holy parents were Jewish . . .

He shakes his head and averts his gaze. McLane would not like this nativity set at all.

❧ ❧ ❧

Clay fidgets with his collar as he stands in the foyer, a stack of memorial programs in his hand. Mom asked him to pass them out and he said he would, but now he's wishing he were inside the chapel like everyone else.

He didn't think many people would show up for a Christmas funeral, but several kids from school have come, along with most of Percy's teachers. The chapel is filled with people from the Walkers' church, too, including a preacher who wears a long black coat and shaves his head. The church choir arrived in white robes with gold collars. They're standing at the front of the chapel now, gathered around Percy's casket like sad angels.

The Mt. Dora regulars have arrived, including Ryan and most of the Hatters. The old folks must love funerals, because they come out in packs, leaning on each other's arms and craning their necks to see who's missing.

When the choir starts singing and Clay feels his throat begin to tighten, he's suddenly glad he's out in the foyer. He watches through the doorway, fascinated by the swaying choir; then he hears the snap and crackle of another car on the gravel driveway.

Two vehicles are coming down the drive. He picks up the stack of programs and assumes his position, swallowing when he recognizes the people coming up the sidewalk: Toby and his parents, Tyler and his mother.

For an instant he wants to turn and run up the stairs, but he'd look like a fool. Mr. Sladen keeps saying he did nothing wrong and a lot of people consider him a hero.

Trouble is, he doesn't feel at all heroic.

Clay gives Toby a program without speaking. Toby dips his chin in a small nod and moves into the chapel as his mother prods his back. Tyler walks by with his hands in his pockets, not even looking at Clay, but his mother takes a program and gives Clay a sad smile.

After scanning the parking lot to be sure no one else is coming, Clay sets the papers on the foyer table and leans against the door. The preacher is speaking now, his voice rising and falling like a song, and people in the audience are taking his words and tossing them right back. Though the man is talking about heaven and Jesus and rejoicing, Clay can still hear sniffling and the occasional sob.

Can people be happy and sad at the same time?

The minister preaches for a long while, working the crowd until even the white people are talking back; then the choir sings a happier song. Not a stupid chorus about shoes but a tune about going to see the king "soon and very soon."

They keep singing as Gerald helps six men wheel Percy's casket out of the chapel. Clay moves out of the way and climbs to the second step of the staircase, a good place to watch them slide it into the back of the hearse.

Soon and very soon, we are going to see the King. . . .

Mr. and Mrs. Walker walk out, both of them dressed up. Mrs. Walker clutches a tissue in one hand and clings to her husband's arm with the other. Mr. Walker keeps patting her hand and tilting his head as if he wants to peek into heaven and ask God what Percy's doing up there. Several other couples follow the Walkers, probably relatives, because all of them are crying.

Next comes Toby and his parents. Toby's mom is sobbing and holding Toby's hand as if she will never let it go.

Hallelujah! Hallelujah! We're going to see the King. . . .

Mom and Aunt McLane step out next, and Aunt McLane smiles at Clay before moving onto the porch. Behind them, the rest of the crowd streams out of the chapel and scatters into the parking lot. After getting into their cars, they turn on their lights and follow the hearse as it heads toward the cemetery.

Clay realizes he forgot to ask his mother if black people can get buried in the same section as white people. Maybe they can now, but he's pretty sure they weren't allowed to before. Aunt McLane told him that only twenty years ago, the Ku Klux Klan tried to participate in Mt. Dora's Christmas parade.

He knows about the KKK—his history teacher said they hated everybody who wasn't white, including the Jews. Some of them even claimed to be Christians, which makes no sense because everybody knows Jesus was Jewish. He hopes none of those people are living in Mt. Dora now.

Clay waits until the long black car has pulled away before peering into the chapel. The choir is still up front, quietly humming. Some of them look like they're praying.

Because three people are still inside the room. Tyler Henton's mother is sitting in a chair, her head bowed. Daniel Sladen is standing in the center aisle, while Tyler is hugging the lawyer and crying like crazy.

❈ ❈ ❈

McLane comes back to the house with us after the funeral, and I'm glad she wants to spend the rest of the day with family.

The boys, Gerald, and I have already opened our presents, but we gather around the Christmas tree with McLane for one more gift exchange. She bought Clay a video game, Bugs a book on dinosaurs, and Gerald a nice red cardigan.

To me, she gives a hand-stitched pillow that says, "Life made us sisters. Love made us friends." I'm so choked up I can't thank her properly.

The boys and Gerald give her their gifts (perfume, perfume, and more perfume), and she laughs as she opens the third bottle. "Do you guys think I stink?"

"You don't," Clay assures her, "but we don't know what else girls like."

I slide my gift toward her and silently thank the Lord that she's here to accept it. It's a scrapbook of photographs of our father, culled from old albums, yearbooks, and newspapers.

"Mom even contributed a few photos," I whisper, mindful that my mother is taking a nap in the guest room. "Maybe it'll help fill in a few of the gaps."

"Thanks, Jen." A tear slips down her cheek, and she scrubs it away with her fist. "Good grief, I've cried more in the last week than I have in my whole life."

"No more tears," I say, struggling to get up from the floor. "Now we go into the kitchen and concentrate on the leftovers."

In a corner of the living room, McLane spies the bright cellophane of her father's gift. "Is that thing still here?"

I shrug. "I wouldn't let Mom take it."

"Then let's divvy it up."

While I attack a stack of dirty dishes in the kitchen sink, McLane sets her father's gift basket on the table and unwraps it, revealing a collection of sausages, cheese, jellies, jams, and fruit butters. Then she releases a sarcastic, bitter laugh.

Gerald gives her a curious look. "Don't you like to eat?"

"Sure I do," McLane says. "But look at this—is this what you give your daughter or your business client? I mean, there's nothing in here he couldn't give to anybody he'd just met on the street."

Gerald lifts a brow, acknowledging her observation. A half smile twists the corner of his mouth. "So . . . what'd you give *him* for Christmas?"

McLane's grin fades into emptiness. "Nothing." She sinks into a chair at the table. "I didn't tell you, but we had a fight. He says I'm no longer his daughter."

"But he brought you a gift," Gerald says. "So he couldn't have meant it."

"Oh, he meant it," McLane says. "This—" she fingers the crinkly wrapping—"is probably a parting gift."

Gerald sighs and lifts a jar of apple butter from the basket. "At least we'll be eating good the next few days."

McLane clears her throat. "Jen? Can we talk?"

Grateful that she still *wants* to talk, I take my hands out of the soapy sink and reach for a dish towel. "Sure. Want to go to the office?"

"You don't have to go anywhere," Gerald says. "I promised Bugs I'd walk him down to Lydia's. He wants to take her the picture frame we made in the garage." He stands and leaves the kitchen, calling for Bugs.

I do a mental check—Clay is in his room, Mom is napping in the guest room, and Skeeter will go with Bugs and Gerald. My family is completely accounted for, and no one is likely to interrupt us . . . for a few minutes at least.

I step toward the cupboard. "Want something to drink? Iced tea? We have some wassail left over from last night. . . ."

"I just need to talk to you."

Something in her voice—a note of vulnerability—tugs at my heart and draws me to the table. I sit and face her, waiting to hear what's on her mind.

She studies her hands, rubs the simple gold band on her ring finger, and begins to cry.

I bite my lip and repress a groan. I'm afraid I can guess the pain that is causing those tears, and I'm amazed she's been able to remain silent for so long. She couldn't have gotten the abortion today, so could she have gone to the clinic yesterday? Probably not on a Sunday. That leaves Saturday . . . and she *was* late to our holiday dinner. If she couldn't find anyone to drive her, she could have called a taxi.

In that moment, when I am certain I know what she's done, the advice I gave Randolph Harris strikes me like a blow: *love shouldn't have so many strings attached.*

My heart breaks to think I've lost my precious niece, but I can't lose McLane, too. I have to love her through the confusion and guilt that's bound to follow.

"McLane, sweetie." I stroke her face, her tears burning my fingers like hot wax. "I'm so sorry."

She lifts her gaze and looks at me, her lips trembling. "I didn't do it. I can't. When I sat in the funeral . . . saw those parents . . . and that boy. When I watched you comfort them, I knew I couldn't do it."

I clutch at her hands. "You're still pregnant?"

She nods, but fresh tears well in her eyes. "And I'm scared to death. This baby isn't normal. She has serious problems. I . . . I don't know how to handle this. Jeff's not here and neither is my dad. . . ."

"I don't know how to face this, either," I confess, smiling through my own tears. "But God is good and he is faithful. He's going to help us through this; I know he will. He might even work a miracle."

"You think so?"

"I hope so." I reach for the box on the counter and pluck out several tissues, then divide them between us. I blow my nose and wipe my eyes.

McLane is calmer now, clear-eyed and beautiful, though her eyes have the glassy look I've come to associate with the recently bereaved.

"I don't get it." I wipe my nose one more time, then cross my arms on the table. "How could a funeral change your mind?"

She draws a deep breath. "It really began before the funeral. I saw that boy's parents on television and heard them begging for his return. Their love was so obvious, and I knew they'd do everything—anything—to get their son back."

I nod, remembering the Walkers' heartfelt pleas.

"That's when I knew that an abortion would be the easy way out. I could say I was doing it to prevent the baby's suffering, but that wasn't the real truth. I wanted the abortion because *I* was scared. Because I didn't want to suffer. And when I watched the Walkers, I realized that if I ended the pregnancy, for the rest of my life I'd know I didn't do everything I could for my child. No matter what happens, I want to be able to say that to Jeff and to God. At the end of my life, when I meet my little girl in heaven, I want to be able to say that to her."

"You will," I promise, "and I'm going to help you through this. You can move in here with us; the boys and I will support you in whatever you need. We'll pray for you and the baby. Speak the word, and we'll be there."

She balls her hands into fists, fighting back more tears. "I know you will," she whispers, her voice hoarse. "I knew you'd help me even if I made the other choice."

I look at her and realize that she's giving me more credit than I deserve. I've been agonizing in a maelstrom of indecision, but for now, at least, our way is clear.

"I'm your sister," I remind her. "And I think that's what sisters do."

*A*fter the holidays, McLane returns to her doctor and announces that she's decided to carry her baby to term. Dr. Leibowitz does not try to change her mind, but she says she will refer McLane to a specialist who might be able to pursue some type of prenatal treatment.

Why didn't she offer that suggestion before McLane made her decision? I wonder.

For the first time since the ominous ultrasound, McLane begins to talk about her baby. Her conversation is guarded—I know I won't hear her worrying about college or even preschool—but she often sits with her hand on her belly and wonders aloud if little Mia Nicole is swimming, sleeping, or sucking her thumb.

The name, she says, is a combination of what she and Jeff wanted. Jeff wanted Mia and she favored Nicole, so they put the two names together. I am delighted. Now that our little girl has a name, it's easier to think of her as a real person.

Even Clay and Bugs are fascinated. We pray for the baby every morning and night, asking God to keep McLane and Mia safe. When he's not praying, Clay tries to remain aloof from all the baby talk, but when we gather in the living room, Bugs sprawls on the couch and props his chin in his hands, apparently the best position for staring at McLane's burgeoning belly.

The next few months are going to be interesting. Because Lydia's fertile gerbils are not nearly as fascinating as my sister, Bugs and I are going to have to talk about where babies come from.

Ryan and the Hatters are sad when they hear that McLane will be leaving the Biddle House, but I think Mom is secretly pleased to know that McLane is moving into our guest room. She may not want to admit it, but McLane's sweet spirit and our prayers for the baby have won her over. When I drive Mother to the airport in early January, she gives me a fierce hug and makes me promise to take care of Clay, Bugs, Gerald . . . and that girl.

I promise to do my best.

By the end of January, McLane has entered her twenty-first week (the baby, I announce at breakfast, is now the size of a large banana), and I am once again occupied with college courses. I am taking four classes this term: Funeral Home Management, Thanatology, Funeral Service Computer Application, and Restorative Art. The first two consist mostly of textbook reading and online exams, and the latter two are four-hour practicums scheduled for Saturdays.

I'm grateful that this semester I won't have to spend every Tuesday morning in a classroom. With my more relaxed schedule, I'll be able to shoulder more of the business burden and be available to help McLane. Now that we're definitely having a baby, I intend to spend a great deal of time helping her study hydrocephalus and its treatment. I'm also going to pray my socks off.

Every night before going to sleep, I whisper my loved ones' names to the Lord and ask him to bless them.

Then I beg for a miracle to help the smallest of them all.

※ ※ ※

One night McLane and I take advantage of the brief time between dinner and sunset to walk in the park near the lake. McLane needs the exercise, and I enjoy the opportunity to go outside and stretch my legs.

Now that her secrets are out in the open, McLane talks a lot about Jeff. She e-mails him every night and receives a reply almost every day.

He's doing well, she says, and he fully supports her decision to have the baby.

"'Sweetheart, you know I trust you completely,'" McLane says, reading from his e-mail, "'and if you feel good about going ahead, I'll stand behind you all the way. I only wish I could be there to hold your hand during this journey.' By the way," she adds, grinning, "he says he can't wait to meet you."

I don't know if that's a compliment because I'm not sure what McLane's told him about me. Depending on when and what she's written, Jeff may think of me as a hard-hearted, lily-white divorcée who's fixated on caskets and corpses.

"It must have been hard for you and Jeff," I say, stepping over a broken pine branch. "Dating, I mean. Did everyone in the area disapprove the way your father did?"

She breathes deeply and moves carefully around the fallen limb. "We didn't date all that long, but yeah, you could say that we didn't meet with much approval. Ingrained opinions die hard, especially in the South. I don't think people meant to be cruel. In fact, if you were to ask most of our friends if they were prejudiced, they'd say they weren't. But Jeff and I could never go out without people staring. Sometimes we'd overhear comments—everything from people calling me white trash to calling him . . ." She crosses her arms as a blush rises from her collar. "Never mind what they called him. It's a word I don't like to use."

I walk beside her in silence, then squint at her in embarrassment. "I have to admit, I was shocked when you told me the truth. I had pictured Jeff a thousand ways, but I never pictured him black."

She gives me a rueful smile. "I don't think his family ever pictured me white. His aunt and cousins haven't exactly been thrilled by our marriage, either." She squeezes my hand. "But thanks for being honest."

34

On Friday, January 26, McLane turns on *Good Morning America* so
we can listen to the news while we eat breakfast. News of the war in
Iraq has special meaning for us now, and all of us, even the boys, halt
in midmovement when we hear a newsman report that a Black Hawk
helicopter has gone down outside Baghdad. Everyone aboard is either
dead or missing.

McLane's spoon clatters to the tabletop.

"Mom?" Bugs calls, a thread of fear quavering his voice. "Look at
Aunt McLane!"

I rush to her side and draw her close as we continue to listen. The
reporter gives no other news—nothing, that is, to give us hope.

"It's going to be okay," I promise, rubbing McLane's back. "If
something's wrong, they'll call us, right? or send someone to the
house?"

She nods, but her eyes have filled with tears and the hand that
clings to my sleeve is trembling.

※ ※ ※

I whip into the carpool lane at Round Lake Elementary and check my
watch. I'm late and Bugs is probably worried. This time I don't even
have an embalming as an excuse.

I edge forward and duck to wave at him. His frown turns into a smile, and I see him tug on his teacher's hand and point to the van. She nods and brings him toward me.

"Hey, kiddo." I whip up a smile and flash it as though I didn't have a care in the world. "Did you have a great day?"

He says nothing as his teacher belts him into the backseat, but after the door slams, he leans toward me. "Is Jeff okay?"

I put away my fake smile. "We don't know. But we're praying for him." I shove the van in gear and pull out, eager to get home in case someone from the marines calls or stops by.

But Bugs isn't finished with his questions. "What if Jeff is dead?"

"Bugsy, you shouldn't worry about such things."

"Who will take care of the baby if he dies? Babies need a daddy, don't they?"

I glance at my son in the rearview mirror. His face has drawn into a look of deep concentration; this isn't the first time he's pondered this question.

At the red light on Highway 441, the realization hits me. Bugs is concerned about little Mia Nicole, but he's also frightened for himself. We lost Thomas only six months ago, and my boys are still adjusting to the idea of a fatherless future. . . .

Right now, Bugs's world is spilling over with fatherless children.

I ease onto the shoulder of the road, put the van in park, and unsnap my seat belt so I can turn and face him. "Bugs—" I underline my voice with quiet emphasis—"you don't have to worry about little Mia. God says he is a father to the fatherless, and he places the lonely in families. Don't you see how he brought McLane to us? She's part of our family now, and Mia will be part of our family, too. God is going to take care of all of us."

A glow fills his face, as if he contains a candle that's just been lit. "God will be our daddy?"

"That's right." I reach out and pat his leg. "He will take care of us, and we will take care of each other."

✺ ✺ ✺

I am unpacking a shipment of embalming fluid, casket liners, and stippling brushes when the phone rings. I jot down the number of bottles and pick up the phone. "Fairlawn Funeral Home."

"Jen? He . . . he was on that chopper." McLane's voice is in tatters, like my nerves.

I clutch at the edge of the counter as the room shifts and my stomach fills with a frightening hollowness. "Is he . . . ?"

"He's listed as MIA. They can't find his body."

"This is good," I assure her, blinking as I wait for the prep room to right itself. "He probably got lost in all the confusion."

"Or they can't recognize him. That chopper burned."

I press my lips together, not knowing what else to say.

✺ ✺ ✺

After work, McLane goes straight to her room. I give her a few moments alone, and then I knock on her door.

"Come in."

I step inside the doorway and see her lying on the bed. "I don't want to bother you, but I was wondering if you had an extra picture of Jeff."

She pushes herself up on one elbow. "Why?"

"A prayer reminder," I say. "I thought we'd put it on the refrigerator. I know I'll remember to pray every time I see it."

A grateful smile flickers over her face; then she rolls toward the nightstand and lifts a small framed photo. "Here," she says, sliding out the cardboard backing, "I tucked an extra copy behind this one."

The photo is a candid picture of a young black man with kind eyes and clear-cut features. He's attractive, but if I saw him on the street in his single days, I'd find it difficult to think of him as an eligible bachelor.

Like most people I know, I've never thought of myself as prejudiced. But I've also never thought of African-American men as possible relatives. Even when my family lived on the military base, a thoroughly integrated setting, I recognized that some institutions were still divided along lines of "us" and "them."

McLane and Jeff are erasing those lines for me . . . and someday, I hope to look Jeff in the eye and tell him so.

I smile at the picture in my hand. "He's handsome."

"Of course he is. I have great taste."

I back out of the room, ready to give her privacy.

But she stops me. "Jen?"

"Hmm?"

"Any calls . . . anything for me?"

I shake my head, not sure if she's expecting to hear from her father or from the military. "Did you check your e-mail?"

"There was nothing from Jeff."

"Well, we haven't heard from the Marine Corps, either. And that's good, right?"

"I don't know." She falls back to the bed and presses her palm to her forehead. "I don't know anything anymore."

"Don't worry." I give her what I hope is an assuring smile. "The God I serve always answers the prayers of his people."

"Thanatology," the professor says, "is the scientific study of death and practices associated with it, particularly the study of dealing with the terminally ill and their associated families."

My instructor, who comes to me via videotaped recording and the Internet, is about as exciting as a ten-year-old almanac. His voice sounds like two pieces of sandpaper rubbing together, and his gestures consist of awkwardly swinging an arm toward a flip chart and occasionally scratching his neck.

I'm sitting in the office, battling worry and weariness and trying not to count my teacher's neck scratches and arm swings. Behind the professor's dry-as-dust commentary, I remind myself, lies a crucial reality: all people die, and those who work in mortuary service must know how to deal with the dead and their survivors in a compassionate way.

As the man drones on, I think of Mr. and Mrs. Walker, who are undoubtedly missing their precious son. Percy's absence has left a gaping hole in their lives, and they will probably spend several years adjusting to the empty place.

Even Levina Gifford, who left no immediate family, has been missed in our community. Claire Douyon, who dropped by the other day with a pair of crocheted booties for McLane, reported that the nursing home continues to receive prayer requests, all marked with Levina's name.

"I don't know why people keep sending them," Claire said, shrugging. "I'm sure everybody in town knows she's passed on."

"Maybe," Gerald answered, "they like to think of her talking to God about them in heaven. God can hear our prayers anywhere, can't he?"

The grooves beside Claire's mouth deepened into a full smile. "Can't argue with you there."

"Jen?"

I glance up as footsteps pound the stairs. The voice is McLane's, and I have to warn her about taking those stairs too quickly. She could slip and fall.

She swings around the corner, her eyes alight. "Jeff called. He's okay." Tears sparkle in her lashes. "He was on that chopper, but he and a couple of the other guys got out and got away. They had to hide for a few hours, but they finally made it to safety. He's fine. He's not hurt."

"Thank the Lord." I stand and give her a hug, then send an appreciative smile winging toward heaven. McLane may not yet realize it, but she's just witnessed a powerful demonstration of how God answers prayer.

35

On the last day of January, I am again sitting beside McLane as she has a sonogram in the gynecologist's office. This time my sister is twenty-one weeks pregnant and the ultrasound technician is not smiling.

"The doctor will meet with you in her office," the tech says, snapping off power to the machine. "I'll escort you when you're ready."

McLane pushes herself into a sitting position and looks at me, her wide eyes filled with fear.

"I'm here." I grip her hand. "We're going to get through this together."

A few minutes later, we're sitting in the doctor's office. Dr. Leibowitz comes in, a chart in her hand, and begins to explain her interpretations of the sonogram without even taking the time to greet us.

"The good news," she says, giving us a quick smile that seems a mere social necessity, "is that your fetus is developing appropriately in most areas. The bad news—" she sinks into her chair—"is that the ventricles have expanded considerably, so the hydrocephalus is worse. Brain damage is likely, though we won't know the extent of the damage until after delivery."

She lowers the chart and folds her hands. "I'm going to recommend that you set up a meeting with a pediatric neurosurgeon as soon as possible. I'm also going to advise you to find a neurosurgeon who has privileges at the Winnie Palmer Hospital for Women and Babies. It's in Orlando, but that's the closest hospital with a Level III NICU."

McLane's mouth forms a perfect O. "NICU?"

"Neonatal intensive care unit." Dr. Leibowitz shifts her gaze from McLane to me. "She is not going to be able to carry this child forty weeks—the head is too big. And since there's no way we'd want to put an enlarged brain through the trauma of a vaginal delivery, she can count on having a C-section. We'll want to take the baby as soon as tests reveal that the baby's lungs are mature. "

I think of the calendar hanging above the kitchen sink. "And when will that be?"

"Most likely around thirty-six weeks. A premature infant with insufficient lung development is in no condition to cope with shunting. And shunting will be necessary to drain excess fluid from the brain."

"So . . . you can drain the fluid," I say, wanting to be sure I understand. "Do you ever shunt while the baby is still in the womb?"

Dr. Leibowitz's mouth curves in an expression that can barely be called a smile. "You've been on the Internet. There's a lot of chatter about prenatal shunting, but no hospital in this country is still doing the procedure. Fluid flows both ways, and if you insert a shunt while the baby is in the womb, there's always a possibility that amniotic fluid will pass through the shunt and leak into the brain, making the hydrocephalus even more severe."

"But you *can* drain the fluid after birth." I know I'm repeating myself, but the procedure sounds so simple I can't understand why we were led to believe this condition was a matter of life and death. "Our little girl may be perfectly fine."

Dr. Leibowitz crosses her arms and sighs. "No one is going to be able to give you a definite prognosis at this point. Once the shunt is inserted and pressure on the brain is relieved, the brain tissue will expand. It may expand to normal size. It may remain compressed. The child's condition will depend upon the state of the brain after the excess fluid has been allowed to drain."

I smile at McLane as hope flows like a river between us. "Her brain may be normal," I whisper.

"*Near* normal," the doctor says. "And let me stress that shunting does not remove the problem. It only treats it. The shunt will have to be checked throughout the child's life. Some children are prone to infection and have difficulty with a shunt; others do not. At this point, there's no way to predict the outcome."

She stands. "Have you any other questions? If not, I'd urge you to consult with a perinatologist at Winnie Palmer Hospital right away. They deal with high risk pregnancies, and they'll want to know you are coming."

She smiles, her eyes filled with pity, but her words have given me far more encouragement than I expected. All we have to do is pray that the shunting goes well and Mia's brain expands.

Compared to raising Lazarus or feeding the five thousand, that doesn't seem like much of a miracle at all.

$\mathcal{T}$ime passes as it always does, dulling our pain and renewing our hope. McLane visits doctors in Orlando and follows their instructions to the letter. She also puffs up like a pincushion, a condition not unusual for women carrying hydrocephalic babies, and bears the inevitable teasing with a surprising and sweet grace.

Though Daniel sees McLane nearly every day, he often calls to ask me how she's faring. I'm amused by the old-fashioned sense of propriety that won't allow him to ask a pregnant woman about her condition, yet I'm touched that he's able to set his embarrassment aside long enough to ask me.

With every passing day, I'm more grateful for Daniel and the partners of his law firm. Not only have they given McLane a job that keeps her busy and prevents her from obsessing over the future, but their generous health insurance, along with Jeff's, will cover whatever expenses she incurs at the hospital. After hearing Dr. Leibowitz talk about intensive care, shunting, and cesarean sections, I know Mia Nicole's treatment won't come cheap.

At Fairlawn, all of us fuss over McLane like mother hens. We snap pictures of her ballooning belly and e-mail them to Jeff. He responds with photos of himself and his buddies in the Marine Aviation Logistics Squadron. Bugs and Clay are delighted to hear from a real, live soldier and thrilled to know this brave man is their uncle. My boys, I notice with quiet relief, don't seem to care what color Jeff's skin is.

I've been watching Clay closely these last few weeks. I expected a certain amount of withdrawal after Percy's death, but I've been surprised that he's still avoiding Toby Talbott and Tyler Henton. These days Clay comes home right after school and does his homework on the kitchen table. Then he usually pops into the office and asks if he can use the computer to e-mail Jeff.

I'm happy to allow him, especially when he lets me read some of Jeff's replies. I don't know what I expected of my brother-in-law, but judging from his letters, Jeff Larson is bright and funny and loves kids as much as McLane says he does.

I can see why she adores him, and these days I pray for him with special urgency. He needs to come home soon and meet his daughter.

We don't hear anything from Randolph Harris during the months of January or February, but I haven't given up on him. McLane's birthday is March 6, so as winter shifts into spring, I keep an eye on the mailbox and listen for the UPS man, certain that Dr. Harris will send a gift or at least a card.

We celebrate McLane's birth with a cake, candles, punch, and lots of pink balloons. Ryan, Daniel, Mara Potter, and several Hatters drop by, but nothing—and no one—arrives from North Carolina.

I'm sure McLane notices, but she doesn't mention her father. Instead she rests her hands on her rounded belly and tells the festive gathering that Mia Nicole is dancing the merengue on the walls of her bladder.

I smile, knowing from my research that Mia now weighs two pounds. I've heard her heartbeat during doctor visits, a squishy pulse that thrums with determination.

McLane has gained twenty-two pounds and now lumbers around the house with one hand pressed to the small of her back. She complains of sore ribs and apologizes for whining.

I nod in sympathy and tell her not to worry. That pain will pass soon enough.

On a Saturday in mid-March, I shift in an uncomfortable chair and stare at the screen in the Orlando Hyatt Regency ballroom. One of my courses requires that I sit through a four-hour seminar on the practice of restorative art.

Ordinarily the topic would be fascinating, but I'm not sure this seminar is entirely educational. At the front of the room, a booth displays various wares of the embalmer's trade: smocks, face shields, trocar buttons, eye caps, and a handheld gizmo that reminds me of the automatic paint sprayer Thomas and I bought two years ago to freshen our house.

We have each been given a goody bag with samples of several mortuary products—plugs and caps, buttons and brushes, and several jars of what looks like pancake makeup. The bag jingles each time I pick it up.

The presenter flashes an image of Lanobase 18 Synergistic Dual Humectant and Tissue Texturizing Formula. "This little jar," he says, rolling his wrist toward the screen with the ease of a professional spokesmodel, "will solve all your problems if you are dealing with a dehydrated body that has been refrigerated for too long. Far better than most arterial embalming fluids, it will restore the blush of life to the client in your care. Let me offer proof."

I cross my legs and squirm as the next slide displays the "before" photo of a badly mangled head and shoulders. I've never seen anything like this in the prep room at Fairlawn, and I hope I never do.

"Gunshot victim," the presenter says, his voice as matter-of-fact as if he were describing the weather in Alaska. "When a body is as discombobulated as this one, the first thing you do is mark the known areas—bits you can readily recognize. Teeth. Nose cartilage. Ears. Once you mark the knowns, you can work with the unknowns."

The next slide shows a man with two closed eyes, a nose, and a mouth. The peach-colored skin has been smoothed and shaped. He's not exactly movie star material, but his family will be able to have an open casket.

"Of course, most of the face was built of embalmer's putty," our instructor explains, "but the Lanobase solution has worked wonders with the skin texture."

From inside my purse, my cell phone chooses that moment to chime. I shrink in my seat as dozens of heads swivel in my direction. It seems these people are bored by the slide show, desperate for something to divert their attention.

I dive for my bag and whisper "excuse me" in a repetitive loop. With my purse on my shoulder and that noisy sample bag in the other hand, I hurry toward the back door, fishing for the phone as I go. My pulse quickens when I read the caller ID. Gerald is calling, and he knows I'm attending a seminar.

He wouldn't call unless he had an emergency.

"Gerald?"

"Jen," he says, his voice breathless. "It's McLane. She's havin' labor pains."

"No way." For some inexplicable reason, I glance at my watch. "It's too soon."

"I know. I know. So what do I do?"

"Take her to the local hospital. If she's dilating, have them take her by ambulance to the hospital in Orlando. I'll leave for home now, but call me the minute you know something."

He hangs up without saying good-bye, and I feel my heart rise to my throat as I rush to the parking lot. Gerald will teach me everything I need to know about restorative art; right now, it's more important that I be with my sister.

Twenty minutes later, I'm sitting on an eight-lane stretch of Orlando highway when my cell phone rings again. I snatch it up. "Hello?"

"Hey." This time it's McLane.

"What are you doing on the phone?" I screech. "You're supposed to be at the hospital."

"Two words," she says. "Braxton Hicks."

I exhale in relief as my lane finally gets a green light. "False labor?"

"Apparently. They examined me and sent me home."

"Well, thank goodness. It's too soon."

"I know." She hesitates. "Where are you?"

"Sitting behind a red Lexus. Are you headed back to the house?"

"Yeah. Gerald's driving me. I was thinking about picking up something for dinner."

"Don't worry about food. I'll swing by a Wendy's on the way back. Go home and put your feet up. That's all you need to do today."

She sighs, but I hear a smile in her voice when she says good-bye.

37

"Thanatopsis" by William Cullen Bryant strikes a chord before I am able to place it. Then a memory swims up through the years: Mrs. Williams, my high school English teacher, required us to memorize this last stanza.

The poem might have been my first introduction to the formal study of death. In any case, my professor has included it in the materials we are to study for our thanatology midterm.

I prop the book on my lap and whisper the words, careful not to disturb my sleeping family:

> *So live, that when thy summons comes to join*
> *The innumerable caravan which moves*
> *To that mysterious realm, where each shall take*
> *His chamber in the silent halls of death,*
> *Thou go not, like the quarry-slave at night,*
> *Scourged to his dungeon, but sustained and soothed*
> *By an unfaltering trust, approach thy grave*
> *Like one who wraps the drapery of his couch*
> *About him, and lies down to pleasant dreams.*

I smile at the memory of Mrs. Williams. She passed away several years ago, but this poem and its attendant memories will always be a part of me.

I wonder why she thought it important that we study a poem about death at sixteen and seventeen. In high school she had us read these lines aloud, and we couldn't pass her class until we could recite this last stanza from memory.

My head falls to the back of the chair as my heavy eyelids submit to the power of gravity. It's past midnight, and I've enjoyed more than two hours of peace. I'm already in my pajama bottoms, T-shirt, and tooth guard, so I ought to crawl into bed. I could close my eyes and call it a day, but I don't often have blocks of uninterrupted quiet time.

I startle when I feel a hand on my arm. Did the phone ring? Does Gerald need me to help him with a pickup?

I blink my bedroom into focus, expecting to see Gerald or one of the kids, but McLane stands by my chair. One hand is pressed to the small of her back, and the other grips my arm so fiercely I'm bound to have a bruise tomorrow.

"Jen." Her voice is low and urgent.

Adrenaline pumps through my veins when I see a wet spot on the front of her nightgown. "Did you drop a glath of water?"

Please, Lord, let her have spilled something.

"My water broke." She presses her lips together as her eyes flood with tears. "The baby's coming, and I don't know what to do."

"Don't worry. Juth head toward the van." I yank the dental appliance from my front teeth, toss it onto the nightstand, and grab my purse. I panic for a moment, unable to remember where I kicked off my shoes, then spy my house slippers by the bed. They'll have to do.

McLane has only made it to the top of the staircase, so I help her down the steps, lead her outside, and open the door of the van. A thousand thoughts rush through my head—I need to tell Gerald what's happening, I need to call the doctor, and I need to e-mail Jeff. I need to do a dozen things, but more than anything I need to get my sister to a hospital with a neonatal intensive care unit.

A sudden thought halts me—I can't take the van. The odd little rattle I noticed a few months ago is a loose thingamajig, and Gerald has the part in the garage.

"Your car," I tell McLane, pulling her away from the door. "We have to take your car."

Her eyes widen with panic. "No gas. I'm on empty."

"Then . . ." I press my hand to my hairline and struggle to think. The call car is in the garage, but Gerald's workbench is blocking it. The thing is covered with tools I don't have time to move, so that leaves only the hearse.

"Come on." I grab McLane's hand and guide her toward the side of the house.

"Jen." Her voice fills with agony as her free hand presses against her back.

"Almost there. Come on now."

The contraction or whatever passes, because McLane is alert and lucid when I drop her hand and lift the garage door. Inside, like a shiny black chariot, sits our 2001 Cadillac funeral coach, Gerald's pride and joy.

McLane stops groaning and stares at me. "You don't mean it."

"You got a better idea?"

She exhales through her teeth, then waddles to the passenger door.

I scan the shelf holding Gerald's collection of screw-filled jars and find the one with the hearse keys. I spin, the keys in my hand, and the vinyl sole of my slipper encounters a spot of grease. My foot slides out from under me and down I go to the concrete floor.

"Jen?" McLane's voice is muffled by the car.

"I'm still here." I push myself off the floor and ignore the throbbing sensation in my left cheek. A moment later I'm behind the wheel. Before turning the key, however, I glance at McLane. "Are you having contractions?"

She braces her hands against the dashboard and whimpers. "I don't know," she says when the moment has passed. "Something's going on, but I thought it was Braxton Hicks. . . ."

"Just relax." I put the key in the ignition and give her a determined smile. "I'm driving you to Orlando, where you and the baby will be looked after by experts. Buckle your seat belt, though, because I'm driving as fast as this car will let me."

Fear radiates from McLane like a halo around the moon, but she draws the seat belt across her chest, snaps it, and pushes the lower section below her belly.

I turn the key and whisper a prayer.

❧❧ ❧❧ ❧❧

At 2 a.m., I'm on the phone, waking people across the country. Gerald, of course, rises like a jack-in-the-box and promises to watch the boys and pray. Lydia asks if we need anything, and I suggest that she bring some of McLane's clothes and personal items to the hospital later this morning. Mother, pulled from a deep sleep in Virginia, is groggy when she picks up, but she snaps to alertness when I tell her where I am.

"What do you mean, you're at the hospital? It's too soon."

"I know. But McLane went into labor, and they're going to do an emergency C-section."

"I'll be praying, sweetheart."

I call Randolph Harris's North Carolina home and get an answering service. I leave a message with my cell number.

In the waiting area, I pace and thump my phone against my palm, not knowing how to contact Jeff. Should I even try? At this point I have no news that would comfort him, and I don't want him to worry. On the other hand, McLane and Mia are his wife and daughter. Surely he has a right to know they are in need of his prayers.

I dash to a nurses' station and lean over the counter. A nurse sits at a desk, scrolling through a computer screen. She doesn't glance my way until I say, "Excuse me? Is there any way I could send an e-mail from the hospital? It's really important."

Her dark brows slant in a frown. "We don't have computers for public use."

"Please. My brother-in-law is a marine in Iraq, my sister is having a baby, and it's way too early. E-mail is the only way I know how to reach him."

She gives me a doubtful look; then her brows relax. "Sometimes the doctors have laptops in the cafeteria. You might find someone with a wireless card."

"Thanks."

Twenty minutes later, I have persuaded a young resident into handing over his laptop long enough for me to type an e-mail to Jeffrey Larson, U.S. Marine Corps.

✉

Jeff—

McLane's in labor. She and Mia need your prayers.

Jen

I thank the resident, offer to buy him a cup of coffee, and feel like kissing his feet when he grins at me.

"No problem," he says, the light of understanding in his eyes. "If you need to send another e-mail, stop by radiology and ask for the good-looking guy."

"I will."

"By the way—" his dark eyes dance above his mustache—"I like your slippers."

🎀 🎀 🎀

Movement flutters all around me, but I am thinking only of McLane, whose eyes cling to my face as though I am a life preserver in a stormy sea. She is sitting on a gurney, her legs straight out, her shoulders hunched over her belly as a green-gowned anesthetist gives her a spinal.

"There," the nurse says, lifting her hand and revealing a syringe big enough to alarm an elephant. "In a minute or two you won't feel anything lower than your rib cage."

"Jen?"

"I'm right here, sweetie." I move closer. "I'm not leaving unless they throw me out."

"And we're not about to do that," another woman answers, her eyes smiling behind her surgical mask. I recognize her as the labor and delivery nurse who took charge of McLane when I brought her through the doors.

I tug on the sleeves of my sterile gown and look around. This room has filled with people. A team from the neonatal ICU waits near the double doors, and the surgical team surrounds the operating table.

I step back, wishing I'd thought to bring a camera or something to occupy my hands, as a nurse inserts a catheter and positions surgical drapes over McLane's abdomen. One of the screens is set up by McLane's face, blocking her view of her belly.

A lightning bolt of worry flashes in my sister's eyes. "Is everything okay?"

"It's fine, hon," the smiling nurse says. "That's standard procedure. Everything's just fine."

But it's not. I can see concern in the grim line of the doctor's face as she holds her sterile hands aloft and reads something on a chart.

The doctor nods at a nurse and then leans over the drape. "Good morning, McLane," she says, a polite smile crinkling her eyes. "Are you ready to have a baby?"

This woman may be a brilliant surgeon, but that was a stupid question. McLane's eyes fill with tears. "It's too early."

"Your little girl has already kicked the door open," the doctor says, glancing at something below the drape. "So we're going to help her along. For safety's sake we have to restrain your movements. Nothing to worry about."

As a nurse fastens Velcro straps around McLane's arms, my sister closes her eyes. Is she praying?

The surgical team gathers around the table, and one nurse positions me at McLane's head. "This is your spot," she says, her voice firm. "You talk to mama while we take care of things down here."

"Will do." My voice comes out hoarse, forced through a tight throat, but McLane doesn't seem to notice.

"This isn't exactly how I planned it," she says, giving me a jittery smile. "For one thing, we were supposed to be doing this in June."

"June, schmoon." I pull a stray hank of hair away from her mouth. "June's too hot."

"I'm going to give you a little pinch," the surgeon says, "and you tell me if you feel it."

I glance over the drape as the doctor nips McLane's taut belly with a hemostat. McLane doesn't even flinch.

"That's good." The doctor turns to her nurse. "Scalpel."

"McLane," I whisper, bending closer, "are you sure you can't feel anything?"

She nods. "Just you. I can feel you standing there."

I close my ears to the surgical team's chatter and try to focus on my sister, but it's impossible to ignore the odor of burning flesh and the crackle of the cautery gun.

"All right," the doctor says. "Let's get this little girl out."

"Mia," McLane whispers. "Her name is Mia."

I stroke McLane's hair and watch from the corner of my eye as the doctor and a technician use gloved hands to draw back the outer layers of the abdomen. The bag of water has already broken, so they move quickly. Another woman—the midwife, I think—leans across McLane's belly and applies pressure to help push the baby out.

I see a head—a small, perfectly shaped head—appear between the surgeon's hands. A nurse suctions the mouth and nose. Then the doctor lifts a gray baby into the cool, clean air of the operating room.

I shiver, recognizing the lifeless shade I've seen on so many corpses.

"Clamp," the doctor says, and almost instantly a nurse clamps the umbilical cord twice—one near the baby, one near the mother—and another nurse cuts the cord. A different technician places a tiny hemostat next to the baby's belly, and my blood-smeared niece is whisked away by the neonatal ICU team.

"How is she?" McLane lifts her head and struggles to watch as the ICU team works in the opposite corner. "How is she, Jen? Can you see her?"

I stroke McLane's hair again and bend to whisper in her ear. "She's alive. She's tiny. And she's beautiful."

I remain bent over my sister while someone on the neonatal team says the one-minute Apgar score is two.

It's been a while since I had a baby, but I know that's not good. They'll evaluate Mia again in a couple of minutes, and her score ought to improve.

Meanwhile, the doctor and her team continue working on McLane. They remove the placenta and stitch up the uterus. A moment later I stifle a bark of laughter when I see a technician seal the outer layers of skin with Dermabond—the same sort of glue we sometimes use at Fairlawn to keep lips and eyelids from gaping in the casket.

"Jen," McLane says, her voice insistent, "is everything okay with the baby?"

I glance over my shoulder.

"Apgar score is four," a nurse calls.

I squeeze McLane's hand. "She's better now," I say, summoning a smile. "She's so tiny."

"Three pounds," a technician says, coming over to us. "Fifteen inches long. We have her on a respirator."

"Tell me the truth," McLane says, her eyes meeting mine. "Does she look . . . freakish?"

I give her a sincere smile. "She's lovely. You'll see."

One of the nurses moves to the head of the table. "Ready to go to recovery?"

"Can I see my baby there?"

"In a little while," the nurse says. She looks at me as she repeats the promise. "You'll see her in a little while."

38

"Hello?"

Clay peers out of the kitchen as Lydia comes up the staircase, taking the steps two at a time.

"Morning, boys. How are you? Finding everything you need?" She stands in the kitchen doorway, her hands on her hips, and surveys the breakfast table.

Bugs, who is gulping down a banana, stops chewing long enough to wave at her.

Clay pulls his second slice of bread from the toaster. "We're good."

"I can see that you are." Lydia is speaking in that extrashiny voice adults use when something is wrong. His grandma talked the same way right after his mom and dad decided to get a divorce.

Gerald comes out of his room and nods at Lydia, taking over. "Morning."

"Jennifer called," she says, speaking slowly and extracarefully. "I'm supposed to pack a bag for McLane. Apparently the girls left in a hurry last night."

"It's okay. The kids know everything." Gerald pulls his last suspender onto his shoulder, then gestures toward the hall. "Want me to show you where Jen keeps the suitcases?"

After the grown-ups leave the kitchen, Clay returns to his chair at the table. Bugs is craning his neck, watching Lydia, but Clay doesn't bother. The adults are going to take care of things without his help. All he's supposed to do today is go to school, come home, and stay out of trouble.

He notices the uneaten pastry on Bugs's napkin. "You'd better eat that," he says, reaching for his knife. "A banana's not going to fill you up until lunch."

"I'm not hungry." Bugs drops the last half of the banana onto the table, then looks at Clay. "Did you hear Mom leave last night?"

"I was asleep."

"Did you hear Aunt McLane screaming? Women on TV always scream when they have a baby."

Clay makes a face. "What have you been watching? And, no, I didn't hear screaming. There was no screaming."

Bugs presses his lips together and sits on his hands. "Gerald says Mia is born, but she's really tiny. What happens if she dies? Will everyone be sad?"

Clay ignores him and concentrates on spreading jelly onto every centimeter of his toast. Bugs ought to know the answer to that question; he's seen enough dead people to know everyone is sad when someone dies.

He picks up the first piece of toast and eats. When he finishes the last crust, he finds that Bugs is staring at him with deadly concentration. "Will Aunt McLane go away if the baby dies? Will Jeff stop being our uncle?"

"Good grief, don't you know anything? Aunts and uncles are like freckles. They stick around forever."

"Not if they die."

"They're not gonna die."

"But sometimes people—"

"Nobody's dying today, okay?" Clay glares at Bugs, then points to the uneaten pastry. "Finish your breakfast and brush your teeth. Gerald's going to take you to school and you don't want to be late."

Bugs picks up the pastry, but his eyes remain wide and thoughtful. "I don't want to lose Uncle Jeff. I don't want to lose anybody."

Clay leaves his second piece of toast on the table while he gets up and drops his knife into the sink. He doesn't want to lose anybody, either, but what he wants doesn't matter.

Sometimes bad things happen, even to nice people. The sooner Bugs learns this, the better off he'll be.

"Look—" Clay stops by his brother's chair—"people die all the time and somebody's always sad. I was sad when Percy died. But you know what? Tyler Henton's been different ever since. He doesn't get into trouble, and he doesn't act nearly so cool."

"So . . . it was *good* Percy died?"

"His parents would never think so," Clay says, "and I'd rather have Percy for a friend than Tyler. But things happen, and then other things happen, things you'd never expect. Things are always changin', so you'd better get used to the idea."

�✖ ✖ખ✖ ✖ખ✖

"Jen?"

The voice seems to come from far away, but it's enough to summon me to wakefulness. I open my eyes and squint at a flood of sunlight pouring from a window, then uncoil my arms and legs.

I've fallen asleep, again, in a chair—an uncomfortable vinyl and chrome chair—but thoughts of my stiffness fade when I look across the room and see McLane. She's propped up on pillows and her complexion is pale, but I'm reasonably sure she looks a lot better than I do.

"Hey." I push myself up and gimp my way toward her, my muscles complaining with every step. "How are you feeling?"

"Okay . . . and I want to see the baby. Will they bring her in, do you think?"

I draw a deep breath as my thoughts turn to the isolation ward at the end of the hall. Mia is sleeping in an incubator, monitored by dozens of wires and the watchful eyes of a team of expert nurses. Hard to believe such a tiny baby could be attached to so many machines.

I pinch the bridge of my nose and close my eyes. "I think it'd be easier to take you to Mia than to bring Mia to you. She was a lot more portable when she was in your belly."

I was hoping to win a smile, but McLane's eyes darken with worry. "Is she okay?"

"She's good; last time I checked she was on a respirator and doing fine. As soon as you can walk, I'll take you down there."

McLane grips the rails at the side of the bed. "Help me with these, will you?"

"Whoa." I press the button for the nurse. "I'm not sure you're supposed to be walking yet."

"Then get me a wheelchair, because I'm going to see my daughter."

❈❈ ❈❈ ❈❈

I wheel McLane closer to the incubator, mindful of the eagle-eyed nurse watching from her station. "That's Mia."

McLane brings her hand to her mouth as her eyes glisten with tears. I can't blame her—the sight of such a little baby is enough to fill even the weariest heart with wonder and awe.

Mia lies in an incubator, tubes taped to her nose and arm, sensors attached to her chest. The smallest diaper I've ever seen engulfs the lower part of her body. My open palm, held just above Mia's bed, is large enough to completely obliterate my view of her body.

How something so fragile can live and breathe is a mystery to me. The doctors are feeding her intravenously, and a ventilator assists her breathing.

Her head, the subject of so much discussion and concern, is larger than that of the other preemies, but its size is not something I would notice at first glance. I am too taken with the miracle of her dark brows and the thick eyelashes above her button nose.

I stand aside as McLane leans forward and runs her fingertips over her daughter's downy head. I focus on those dimpled feet, which lift and kick at McLane's touch. The right foot is no bigger than my thumb, but this child has the potential to grow every bit as big and strong as my children.

Please, Lord, let this child live.

"She *is* beautiful," McLane whispers.

344

"Told you so."

"I thought you were just being an aunt."

"I am. But I'm also being honest."

We watch the sleeping baby for a long while. Finally McLane looks up at me. "Is she really mine?"

"All yours."

"And Jeff's."

"Sure . . . of course." I am slower to respond this time, because I'm not sure Jeff will ever see Mia. I haven't heard from him since I sent a second e-mail, so I don't know if he knows that his daughter has been born.

McLane's chin quivers as she presses her lips together. "It feels wrong, you know."

"What?"

"To think of her as a rental—something you check out, enjoy, and have to turn in again."

Her words aren't registering in my tired brain. "Want to run that by me again?"

"If we lose her, I mean. I'll be handing her right back to God."

I turn and kneel by McLane's wheelchair. "Listen—" I search her face—"don't assume the worst. You gave this baby a chance, and we've been praying for her. We're going to keep praying, and I know God has a purpose for Mia. Trust him."

Tears run down her cheeks, glittering like silver in the warm nursery lights. "I wish I could trust him like you do."

"You can." I catch her hand and hold it tight. "You can begin by trusting him with Mia."

❧ ❧ ❧

I am helping McLane back into bed when Daniel sticks his head into the room. "Hello! Is this a good time to congratulate the new mother?" He's carrying two bouquets, one of which he sets on McLane's bed, and the other he presents to me. "I figured the birth coach deserves flowers, too."

I press my face into the tissue-wrapped roses and breathe deeply. "Mmm. I didn't do much, but I appreciate the gift."

"Don't listen to her," McLane says, gingerly drawing the sheet over her legs. "I couldn't have done it without her, especially considering that Mia caught us unprepared."

"So I hear." Daniel smiles at me, and for an instant I see something that could be admiration in his eyes. "The story around town is that Paul Revere could take lessons from the Fairlawn undertaker. The baker at Krispy Kreme says he saw sparks flying as that hearse sped along the highway."

I wave the joke away. "It's a good thing Mia decided to come in the middle of the night. If she'd waited until rush hour, my frantic drive wouldn't have been nearly as effective."

Daniel sinks to the end of the hospital bed. "I don't know about that. I'm beginning to think you can pull off just about anything you set your mind to."

I smile at him, hoping he can hear the words I can't bring myself to speak. If I had the power to pull off anything, I'd find a way to guarantee the survival of that tiny baby down the hall. I'd promise McLane that everything will be all right, and I'd extend my reach across the miles and bring Jeff home to be with his family.

But I can't do everything I want to do. I have no power at all, only faith that the God I serve works all things for my eternal good.

Even when that good is hard to see.

*J*oella wraps her sweater more closely around her and presses her fingertips to the window. The glass is cold and streaming with rivulets of rain.

Behind her, the television blares its programming into a living room that has remained clean for three days. Her ice maker has stopped dumping cubes because no one is emptying the bin, and her freezer is packed with boxes of Lean Cuisine.

Her life is orderly, calm, and pleasant. And as boring as a chemistry lecture.

She picks up the snapshot on the desk. It was taken at Fairlawn over the holidays, a goofy shot of her grandchildren trying to help Jen clear the table. She took the photo herself, intending to focus on the boys, but McLane is a blur in the background, as is Gerald. And there, in the lower right corner, is Jen's arm. Just her arm, but with it this photo represents all the people who are now living at Fairlawn.

Outside, the March wind howls and rain bounces off the roof of a car inching down her street. Spring has been slow in coming to Virginia this year; the dogwoods have not yet begun to bloom. Joella's tulips reared their lovely pink heads last weekend, but she didn't enjoy them as much as usual. Perhaps it's because they showed up before the hyacinths . . . or perhaps it's because her heart is in Mt. Dora.

With that crazy quilt of a family.

She drops the picture and reaches for the yellow pages. Nolan has been in his grave more than six years. She ought to let his sins rest with him. McLane is no more to blame for Nolan's infidelity than Jennifer is to be faulted for Thomas's. Both men were wolves in lambs' wear. No doubt about it.

Now McLane is in the hospital and Jen will want to be with her, so Gerald will be tending to the business *and* the boys, far too much responsibility for an old man. Fairlawn needs her, and she's never been the type to let an unspoken call for help go unanswered.

Joella flips to the listings for travel agents, then taps an ad. If these people are any good, they can get her on a flight today or tomorrow.

⚬⚬ ⚬⚬ ⚬⚬

Friday morning I go home to change, shower, and check in with Gerald. He assures me the boys are fine.

"McLane is doing well," I report. "She'll be sore for a while, and she's not allowed to drive for at least two weeks. They had her up walking yesterday, and they think she can come home tomorrow."

"And Mia?"

I draw a deep breath. "Three pounds, Gerald. They've had a lot of success saving babies that small, but they're also dealing with the hydrocephalus. They need to put in a shunt, but they can't do anything until her lungs mature and she puts on some weight."

Gerald harrumphs, then coughs into his hand—an effort, I suspect, necessary to clear a lump in this throat. "Has our new mother gotten a second opinion?"

I give him a sympathetic smile. "I can't find any fault with the doctors in this hospital. Just this morning we talked to the director of neonatology, the chief perinatologist, and a pediatric neurologist."

"Don't be impressed by all those syllables, missy. I want to know if they care about our baby."

"Yes." I soften my voice. "They care."

My peace shifts to alarm an hour later when I walk into McLane's hospital room and find her in tears. She's sitting on the bed in a pretty robe I've never seen.

Not sure where to begin, I perch on the arm of the guest chair. "The robe," I finally say. "It's nice."

"Lydia." McLane swipes tears from her cheeks. "She brought it. She brought all kinds of things."

"And . . . she made you cry?"

"No." Her face draws in on itself; then she buries her face in her hands and sobs.

I'm bewildered until I walk over to her. That's when I see a breast pump and a sheet of printed instructions, probably left by the nurse. Then I understand. McLane must be aching to hold her precious little one, but she can't. She'll not be able to nurse her daughter in the way she expected, if at all. I'm not sure what the latest doctor has told her, but I know it'll be weeks before Mia can leave the security of her incubator.

Because McLane cannot embrace her baby, I move closer and offer my arms instead.

$\mathcal{L}$ike guilty schoolgirls, McLane and I are sitting side by side on her hospital bed and giggling at Saturday morning cartoons.

"Ohhh," McLane says, holding her stomach, "please don't make me laugh."

I offer her another handful of the cheese crackers I sneaked into the room. "Want some more?"

"Good grief, no. Nurse Ratched will smell the cheese on my breath and fuss at me."

"What are you girls doing in here?"

I flinch, half-afraid a stern nurse really is descending on us; then I recognize the form in the doorway. "Mom?"

"In the flesh." She breezes into the room and plants a kiss on my cheek, then leans over to gently embrace McLane. "Did you think anything could keep me from my grandbaby?"

Stunned speechless, I catch McLane's eye and lift a brow.

Mom steps back and glances around the room. For a moment I'm afraid she's going to start rearranging furniture, but she nods and gives us an approving smile. "You've got the place looking real homey. That's nice."

I have to admit she's right. Alongside the flowers from Daniel, Lydia has brought tokens from everyone at Fairlawn—crayoned dinosaur pictures from Bugs, a portable DVD player and a copy of

Nacho Libre from Clay, a box of chocolates from Gerald. Lydia herself contributed a stork planter overflowing with golden pothos, a nearly indestructible houseplant.

"You look good," Mom says, eyeing McLane with a critical squint. "Now—take me to that baby."

Wordlessly, I slip off the bed and offer my hand to McLane. Together, we'll escort Mom to the nursery.

※ ※ ※

The hospital discharges McLane late Saturday morning, but she's not ready to go home. Since she will no longer have a bed in the maternity ward, she camps out in the waiting area outside the NICU and hopes to snatch a few hours' sleep at Fairlawn later.

After cooing at the baby through the NICU window, Mom heads for Mt. Dora, where she plans to take charge of the house and the boys. Ordinarily, I'd resist her domineering attitude, but today I'm grateful. Gerald and Lydia have been lifesavers, but I can't ask them to assume my responsibilities for more than a day or two. That'd be asking too much.

McLane and I spend a couple of hours flipping through old magazines until we're allowed to don masks and gowns and spend a few precious moments in intensive care. The nurses here are strict about visitors—parents, grandparents, and two people approved by the parents may enter anytime during visiting hours. But visitors are discouraged when the babies are sleeping because preemies grow faster and put on weight more easily when they sleep.

"To a preemie, even routine hospital noise is stressful," a nurse tells us, keeping her voice low. "Slamming cabinet doors, running water, telephones, and monitor alarms can overwhelm a preemie's delicate system. That's why we try to limit visitors when we can. When the babies are awake, we play lullabies and encourage moms to sing to their infants. After all, they already know and love her voice."

McLane shoots her a skeptical glance. "What if the mom can't sing?"

The nurse smiles. "Doesn't matter. Just do what you can."

I tap my fingers against my lips as McLane attempts to sing "Truly Madly Deeply" to her little daughter. Fortunately, the melody only requires about a six-note range.

As we shed our gowns and masks in the hallway, I tease her about her choice of lullaby. "A song by Savage Garden?" I pretend to be horrified. "Don't you know 'Rock-a-Bye Baby'?"

I can tell she's feeling better when she scowls. "'Truly Madly Deeply' was my favorite song in high school. It was the one song I could sing without screeching."

I would have teased her again, but I'm distracted by the ding of the elevator. "That might be Gerald. He promised to drop by this afternoon."

I look at McLane, but she is staring down the hallway, her hand at her throat. I step forward, afraid she's overexerted herself, but she waves me away and flies toward the elevator, moving more swiftly than I would have thought possible for a woman who's just had major surgery.

I turn. Gerald is walking toward us, his red cardigan a bright spot in a sea of beige, but McLane isn't running to him. She is running to a tall soldier who catches her and locks her in an embrace.

When Gerald reaches me, I jerk my thumb toward the man in uniform. "I assume that's my brother-in-law."

An easy smile plays at the corners of Gerald's mouth. "I was going to call, but he wanted to surprise her. I picked him up at the airport about an hour ago."

I tug on the hem of my shirt, hoping to yank out a few wrinkles, and run my hand through my hair.

"You look fine," Gerald says, grinning. "Besides, I don't think that soldier's going to be looking too closely at us for a while."

I lean against the wall and smile as McLane buries her face against Jeff's throat and quietly goes to pieces. "Maybe—" I tug on Gerald's sleeve—"we should go down to the cafeteria and give these two some time alone."

Gerald offers me his arm. "I always knew you had good sense."

※※ ※※ ※※

The next few days are a blur of lullabies, drives to and from the hospital, and time spent in the chapel.

My family and I keep praying for Mia, and word spreads throughout our community. Our church sends the news over the prayer chain, and I'm comforted to know that dozens of people, even strangers, are lifting our baby to the Lord and asking him to strengthen and heal her.

Claire Douyon asks Preacher Wright to stop by the NICU, so he drops in every few days to pray with us. I'm impressed with his kindness because I know the Orlando hospital has to be out of his way.

One afternoon I peek through the window and see him lifting the baby with both hands, wires and tubes dangling in all directions. When I ask McLane what he was doing, she says he was praying a prayer of dedication. "I asked him if she should be baptized, and he said his church reserved baptism for older children and adults. Then he offered to dedicate her to the Lord, so Jeff and I agreed."

When we're not praying, McLane, Jeff, and I spend our days pacing outside the NICU or we gown up and go inside to talk and sing to our precious Mia. McLane seems stronger now that Jeff is here, and I'm grateful for this opportunity, however unfortunate the reason, to spend time with him. He is everything McLane says he is—loyal, intelligent, and caring.

Often I catch him sitting in a rocker beside Mia's incubator, his eyes drinking in the sight of her as if he can never get enough.

Every day one of Mia's doctors stops to give us an update. She must gain weight and breathe on her own, the doctors tell us again and again, before they can even think about placing the shunt.

We become friendly with other parents who are keeping anxious vigils; the nurses learn our first names. When Bugs sends a crayoned picture he drew for his cousin, the head nurse tapes it on the NICU window "for all the babies to see."

It's a picture of Fairlawn, in all its pink and gray glory. Outside, a crew of stick figures smiles and lifts skinny arms in a wave. *Hury home, Mia,* Bugs scrawled at the bottom. *Now yr the littlest.*

We pray and hold our breath as Mia struggles to gain weight. An ounce gained one day, a half ounce lost the next. At home we keep a graph on the refrigerator and chart her progress. When she reaches eight pounds, Gerald promises, we'll have a pizza party and invite all the Biddle biddies.

Mom jokes that she'll happily donate a few pounds to the baby. "Just lead me to the liposuction machine."

I am anxious, because I can't deny that Mia's life is fragile, but I am also confident that God will hear and answer our prayers. McLane may have gone to church all her life, but something—her father's bigotry, her mother's death, or some situation I'm unaware of—has cooled her love for the Lord.

God wants to draw McLane closer, I know; so if healing Mia is the way to do it, that's what he'll do.

41

$\mathscr{G}$erald presses the 2 on the elevator control panel and jingles the change in his pocket as the door closes. He's come on a somber mission, one that might not be well received.

According to Jen, the doctor's latest report was not good. Mia has stopped gaining weight, and she's developed a fever. Despite all the medical precautions, some sort of infection has attacked her tiny body.

He steps out onto the second floor and makes his way to the waiting area. There he sees Jen curled on the couch, her eyes glued to the television set, her face utterly blank.

He sits in the chair across from her. "Jen?"

She blinks. "Gerald! Sorry. I must have been in a daze."

"That's okay; you're tired." He glances around. "Where are McLane and Jeff?"

"I sent them to get something to eat. They'll be back soon."

Gerald settles into his chair. For the moment, he's relieved Jeff and McLane are away. They're trying to keep their hopes up, as they should. But Gerald has been in situations like this before.

Jen straightens and gives him a sleepy smile. "Thanks for coming. Everything okay at home?"

He forces a laugh. "Your mother's running a tight ship, and the boys are fine. Lydia wants to know if she can bring Bugs a couple of gerbils. She says she has a cage and everything."

Jen snorts. "Only if they're the same gender."

"I'll make a note of it."

Jen yawns, then taps her fingers across her mouth. "Excuse me. How's the McKenzie preparation coming?"

"All done. Ian's been casketed and the funeral's tomorrow. Should come off without a hitch."

"Good. Sorry about not being much help these days."

"You're needed here."

"My classes—I'm going to have a load of makeup work."

"You can handle it. You always seem to do fine."

Gerald rubs his palms over his thighs, wiping away traces of perspiration. He draws a deep breath and looks at the coffee table, littered with empty paper cups and ragged magazines. All is quiet but for the television and the ticking fluorescent lights overhead.

He scratches his chin and finally takes a card from his shirt pocket. "I learned about these folks a few years back," he says, not looking at Jen. "They're good people and they do good work. If the situation here gets to the point where it looks hopeless, you call them. Don't wait until it's too late."

Jen accepts the card and studies it. "'Jonathan Vaughn, professional photographer.'" A line appears between her brows. "What's 'Now I Lay Me Down to Sleep'?"

Gerald uncrosses his ankles and wipes his damp hands again. "Promise me you'll look 'em up on the Internet," he says, rising. "Then you'll understand." He bends and kisses the top of Jennifer's head, then turns toward the elevator.

※ ※ ※

On Wednesday afternoon, a doctor walks out of the NICU to tell us that Mia has displayed signs of bleeding on the brain.

As McLane and Jeff rush to their baby's side, I watch from the wide window. Mia's little limbs, which had been tense with life, are now limp in her mother's arms.

I turn away as the doctor speaks to Jeff and McLane. I can't bear the sight of their raw anguish, and there's something I promised Gerald I would do.

I slide the photographer's business card from my wallet and move down the hall in search of quiet. I phone Jonathan Vaughn and briefly explain the situation. He promises to meet me at the NICU in an hour.

I thank him, disconnect the call, and creep to the nearest restroom. Barricading myself inside a stall, I bury my face in my hands and weep.

🟥 🟥 🟥

At 3:13 on a sunny afternoon in Orlando, the cafeteria special is a grilled chicken salad, "Baby Mine" is playing on the NICU CD player, and Mia Nicole Larson dies.

Jeff comes out to tell me. He and McLane have been inside the NICU with Jonathan Vaughn for about twenty minutes; I urge Jeff to go back and stay longer. I'll make the necessary calls, I hear myself say in a detached voice. I'm a professional at this sort of thing.

I phone Fairlawn and close my eyes when Gerald answers. I give him the news and ask him to tell Mom, Lydia, and the boys. Then he'll need to come here for a pickup.

I click my phone off and drop it in my purse. Without glancing at the NICU, I head toward the elevator and the first-floor chapel.

When I arrive, the small room is deserted, as it has been the other times I've visited. For days I've been coming here and dropping to my knees to offer quiet, confident prayers for my niece's life.

I am no longer in a quiet mood.

I stride to the front of the room and place both hands on the wooden table that serves as an altar.

"How could you?" I speak the words loudly and distinctly, as if the Almighty is hard of hearing. "Do you know what you're doing? We prayed so often and so hard. We had so much riding on those prayers—not only Mia's life, but McLane's and Jeff's faith."

I lift my gaze to the empty space above the pulpit, an area lit by a single overhead light. "I was going to give you all the glory. My boys were looking to you because I promised you'd answer their prayers. Lydia was waiting to see you act; so many people were faithfully claiming your promises for healing. Why didn't you answer us?"

The heavens do not rumble in reply, nor does lightning strike me for impertinence. Out in the hallway, some hospital employee pushes a roaring vacuum cleaner, oblivious to my crisis.

My jagged questions hang in the silence as I wait. I will not leave without an answer. I must have *something* to give my sister and my sons.

I sit in a pew. I'm still sitting when the door squeaks behind me. I assume some other tortured soul has come in to pray or rail at God, so I'm startled when a hand grips my shoulder and a man sits beside me.

Gerald.

"You okay?" he asks.

"What do you think?"

He takes one look at my dry eyes and draws the obvious conclusion. "The problem is not in him, you know—" he glances toward the altar—"but in us. We can't see things from an eternal perspective."

"I know that." I throw the words like stones. "But what would it hurt to save this baby? If she wasn't meant to live, then surely she was a mistake."

"God doesn't make mistakes. If he cares about the sparrows that fall, we must trust that he has his eye on these little ones. He has his reasons, Jen. And you must trust them."

I recoil at his words. If he had blamed the devil or sickness or the depredations of this world, I would understand. I could accept an explanation that involved imperfection, mankind's fallen state, or even my own lack of faith. What I cannot accept is that God might have allowed this death, that he might have worked to save Mia's life from abortion only to take it now. How does that make sense?

Gerald slips an arm around me. "Do you remember how excited you were when you first met McLane? You found a sister, a young woman who was so much like you."

An age has passed since that day, but I nod. "I remember."

"But as you got to know her better, you discovered that she's not exactly like you. You have different tastes, different skills, different beliefs. I saw your face after some of your outings with her—you came home frustrated and maybe a little sad because you couldn't understand her."

I shrug. "No two people are exactly alike."

"Yet you wanted her to be like you. You wanted her to have your values and your views. Am I right?"

I frown, not sure why he's rehashing our history. My days of frustration with McLane are over; now she needs my support and consolation. . . .

And she needs an answer from God.

I shift to face him. "I love McLane. She's different—so what? I've learned to accept that we're not always going to agree."

He stops me with an uplifted finger. "Think about it. Think about you and McLane . . . and you and God. How many times have you wanted to bring him around to your way of thinking? How many times have you felt frustrated with what you couldn't understand? The situations are not as different as you might suppose."

"He's God. I'm only a person."

"Right. And if you love him, you'll accept him. Along with his right to do as he pleases." The wooden pew creaks as Gerald stands. "I'm going to pick up Mia and take her home. Do you want to ride along?"

I shake my head and look toward the altar. "Thanks. But I don't think I'm ready to go . . . quite yet."

42

*R*andolph stares at the note on his desk.

Mia Larson, your granddaughter, died April 4, age thirteen days.
The funeral will be held Friday, 10 a.m., Fairlawn Funeral Home.

Jennifer Graham left the message and her number with his receptionist and hasn't called again.

He leans back in his chair as a dozen different emotions collide.
He ought to go to the funeral, just in case McLane realizes how foolish she's been. Strong personalities often reach a point of change after
they've endured a crisis, and McLane has undoubtedly been shaken
by this experience. Ill-suited couples often separate after the death of a
child, so this may be all that's required to help McLane see the error of
her thinking.

He shifts his gaze to the window as the thought of his daughter's
grief slices his heart with a pain more intense than anything he has
experienced in months. He remembers the happiness of the early days
of his marriage and once again sees McLane at five, tipping the brim
of Shana's bridal hat as she gives him a dimpled smile. He had been
the center of her world in those days—the provider and father, the
man who lifted them from poverty and gave them security.

He does not know why the memory should rise in his mind nor
why it results in an ache that persists long after the vision fades.

A casket, I once heard a wise man say, is a receptacle for holding treasures. A baby's casket, then, must be the most precious receptacle of all.

Mia Nicole Larson, wearing the vintage christening gown I bought for her months ago, lies in a small oak box at the front of the Fairlawn chapel. So many flowers surround her that I'm tempted to bring in a fan to dissipate the heavy fragrance of lilies and roses.

The casket, as precious as it is, is not the focus of the mourners' attention. Our Mia has gone to be with Jesus, but we will never forget her.

Gerald has made sure of that.

Mounted on easels at the front of the chapel are large studio portraits of our beloved baby and her parents. Jonathan Vaughn, a volunteer with an organization of professional photographers, understands that parents who lose infants grieve in a unique way. After Mia took her last breath, Jonathan waited while the nurses removed the tubes, tape, and sensors; then he snapped several photos of McLane and Jeff cuddling their little one.

My favorite photo is a shot of Mia's dainty hand resting on McLane's and Jeff's intertwined fingers. To me, the picture speaks of infinite trust . . . a quality I have been sorely lacking of late.

Gerald's words did not fall on deaf ears. I didn't accede easily, but in the chapel I realized that I had been entirely too blithe about my assumptions concerning God's will. How many times did I assure our friends and family that God wouldn't take this baby because I didn't want him to? I told myself God's reputation hung in the balance as if he needed me to defend him.

I have learned that it is one thing to trust God when he answers yes. It is another matter to trust him when he answers in a way we don't expect.

When Mia died, I learned that even my best efforts couldn't save a baby, bring McLane closer to God, or reconcile an estranged father and daughter.

All I can do is love them.

I stand at the back of the chapel with Gerald and survey our arriving guests. Nathan and Amma Walker have come, along with Lamont and Claire Douyon. Ryan Evans, Daniel Sladen, and Mara Potter are sitting in the second row, surrounded by a group of Hatters. Mom, Bugs, and Clay are sitting with Lydia and Preacher Wright, McLane's choice to lead the service.

Though McLane has lived in Mt. Dora for only a few months, nearly everyone in town has prayed for little Mia. All our regular funeral attendees have filled the chapel: old-timers and newcomers, residents from downtown and East Town.

I search for Randolph Harris's close-cropped head and find nothing. So . . . he didn't come. He'll be the poorer for it.

Just before the foyer clock strikes the hour, McLane and Jeff come downstairs, both of them clear-eyed and resolute. Hand in hand, they walk to the front of the chapel and sit beside Bugs and Clay. Their faces do not turn toward the casket but toward those tender photographs.

Preacher Wright came to the house yesterday. While Gerald and I tended Mia's body in the prep room, the preacher, Jeff, and McLane talked in the chapel. By the time Gerald and I finished our work, Preacher Wright had finished his. I'm not sure what they talked about, but Jeff and McLane emerged from the chapel with red-rimmed eyes and hopeful smiles.

Thank God for godly men and women who have the courage to step up and extend honest comfort in the face of death.

Now Preacher Wright stands and lifts his Bible. "We have come here today not only to mourn with this young couple but to praise the God of all mysteries. The psalmist wrote, 'You have taught children and infants to tell of your strength.' How can tiny babies praise God? By reflecting his image . . . and compelling us to place our faith in the heavenly Father. When a precious baby dies, we must trust the character of God, who is love and truth and holiness. We rely on him not only to care for the tender soul we commit to him but to sustain those of us who are grieving the postponement of so many smiles, so much love. But we will not grieve forever. We who know Jesus send our treasures, even our loved ones, on to heaven."

I lower my head as he continues to speak. I thought I had shed the last of my tears, but water flows from my eyes like a leaky faucet.

When the preacher reaches the point where friends typically come forward to speak about the deceased, my brave sister stands and faces the gathering.

"I want to thank you," she says, her eyes glittering with tears, "for your love, compassion, and concern. Jeff and I haven't always been accepted, but here we've felt love and support." She reaches for Jeff's hand, which wraps tightly around hers. "When I first learned that Mia had a problem—" she pauses, covering her face as she struggles for self-control—"I wanted to know why God was doing this to us. After all, we loved each other, we were married, and Jeff was doing his part for the country. Were we being punished?"

The question echoes in the silence of the chapel, which has gone so quiet I can hear the steady tick of the foyer clock.

"I decided to keep the baby," McLane continues, "and Jen and her family prayed for us. Even after Mia was born, I was sure God would let her live. So I prayed, too, for hours. Jeff and I prayed beside Mia's bassinet. Even the nurses prayed with us."

She halts, choking on her words again, and turns to look at the photographs around the casket table. "You see these pictures? As we were holding the baby and the photos were being snapped, I realized something: Mia had brought me back to Jesus. Like an umbrella you only pull out of the closet when it's raining, I had set him aside, but Mia's needs sent me running back to him. Prayer bound me to him."

I pull a tissue from my pocket as McLane points to a picture of herself in profile. Her hands are open, and the baby rests on her uplifted palms.

"That is my favorite shot," she says, "because that's the moment I gave Mia back to the Lord. That's when I surrendered . . . and began to feel peace."

She looks at Jeff, who keeps his hand in hers as he stands, every inch a solider in his uniform. He smiles at his wife, then draws her arm through his as he nods at the gathering. "Thank you for praying for my family. I don't know how to convey my gratitude . . . but to say thank you for everything."

As Jeff and McLane sit down, I see several of the Hatters—white women whose husbands built the catacombs to keep undesirables out—reaching for tissues and lace-trimmed hankies.

If a nuclear bomb were dropped today, I believe those folks would open their arms to anyone who needed shelter.

※ ※ ※

Randolph stands in the shade of a live oak outside the white fence around Pine Forest Cemetery. Beyond the gate, at a distance of several yards, a small group of people watches as his granddaughter's body is lowered into the earth.

A wind rises, undoubtedly riding the edge of an approaching spring shower, and flurries of fallen leaves swirl past him with the sound of small, skittering feet.

The feet of a pajama-clad toddler, perhaps . . . a little girl who will not be climbing on his knee or greeting him with delighted cries.

He shoves his hands in his coat pockets and lifts his chin. He cannot soften in the wave of so-called political correctness that has swept the country. Some things are wrong and always will be, but few people are willing to speak up for biblical separation. He knows the other doctors in his practice whisper that he's racist, but they are deluding themselves. They claim to be open and accepting, but they'd sing a different tune if one of their daughters brought home a black husband.

Coming here has confirmed his worst fears. McLane has lost all sense of proper separation, for not only is she standing with her arm around a black man, but a black preacher is leading the service. Several blacks have joined those around the grave, probably drawn by the prospect of a spectacle.

He retreats behind the tree as the group disperses. He had hoped to find McLane broken and ready to return home, but apparently that Graham woman has stood in the way of true repentance. The marines have released that boy, too, and his arrival can't have done any good.

Randolph peers around the broad tree trunk, but if he heads to his car now, he'll be seen . . . and perhaps recognized. So he waits, his eyes on the horizon, as the wind increases and leaves continue to blow.

Several cars pull away as rain begins to fall in soft spatters that strike his face and dampen his lashes. He steps forward, ready to dash toward his vehicle, and nearly runs into Jennifer Graham.

Her lips part in surprise; then her face shifts into neutral. "Dr. Harris. Will you come to the house? McLane and Jeff would welcome you, I know."

"I-I don't think so. I have done all I came to do."

"Have you?" A faint smile spooks over her lips and her eyes soften. "If it's any consolation . . . I'll admit it took me a while to get used to the idea of interracial marriage. But Jeff is truly a remarkable young man. I think you'd like him."

He feels the corner of his mouth lift in a wry smile—an expression that rises from sheer disbelief. No wonder McLane hasn't broken. This woman is relentless.

"'From one man,'" he quotes, "'he created all the nations throughout the whole earth. He decided beforehand when they should rise and fall, and he determined their boundaries.' We are to remain separate."

She smiles, but with a distracted look, as though she is listening to a voice he can't hear. "From one man," she repeats, "he created

many nations and *one* race—the human race. 'There is no longer
Jew or Gentile, slave or free, male and female. For you are all one in
Christ Jesus.'" Her smile deepens as she looks at him. "I have to thank
you. Until I met you, I never really understood how important that
verse is."

"It's raining," he says, gesturing toward the dark sky above, "and
I have to get to the airport."

"Are you sure?"

"Quite." He nods in farewell and strides toward the car, aware that
her eyes are burning holes in his back. So, this is what defeat feels like.
He can accept it. Life, after all, is a series of battles, and this will not
be his last.

But as he sits in the car and listens to the thrum of rain on the roof,
he wonders if this battle's loss was too high a price.

44

In an act of unexpected generosity, the United States Marine Corps lends us Jeff for three full weeks. I'm delighted to have him with us, for his coming not only supported Mia and McLane, but he has fulfilled my sons' longings for a totally cool uncle.

As an only child, I often dreamed of having a brother or a sister. Now, through a miracle of God's sovereignty, I have been granted both.

In this, my year of mortuary school, I have learned so many things. Along with my lessons on anatomy and funeral home management, I have learned that my mother is capable of forgiving hurts a lesser woman would carry to the grave.

I have learned that Daniel looks great in a tux and plays the violin. And you can't say that about every man on the street.

I have learned that prayer changes us . . . and faith conquers fear.

Randolph Harris taught me that racism is alive and well beneath the mantle of social correctness that blankets most of our nation. Only after looking at prejudice in its full and hideous flower could I spy its tendrils in my own heart. Six months ago I was content to live a "separate but equal" life. Now I know I must do my best to love, encourage, and befriend anyone who crosses my path because we are all members of my Father's beloved human race.

And through McLane I have learned that I can't force people to be or do anything. What I can do is speak the truth . . . and love.

Because Fairlawn is bulging at the seams, Mom packs her things for the trip back to Virginia. Clay, I suspect, will be thrilled to move out of Bugs's room, but all of us will miss Mother. While we grappled with illness, grief, and exhaustion, she kept us fed, clothed, and comfortable.

Before she leaves for the airport, Jeff, Clay, and Bugs present her with a Civilian's Distinguished Service Award, a certificate designed by Bugs and signed by all three admiring young men. Mom blushes and promises to display it in her living room.

In mid-April, McLane and Jeff learn that the marines have decided to keep him stateside. Instead of going back to Iraq, he is being transferred to the New River Air Station in Jacksonville, North Carolina. McLane will be able to go with him.

I am disappointed, of course, at the thought of losing someone who has become such an important part of our family. But McLane's place is with her husband, and she and Jeff will always be only an e-mail away.

Because she is still recovering from surgery, I help McLane pack. I stack clothes in suitcases and toss shoes into boxes. I slide the large portraits of Mia into special crates, along with Bugs's dinosaur pictures.

"What about this?" I point to the golden pothos vine in the stork planter.

McLane winces. "Will Lydia be hurt if she comes over here and sees it? I'm afraid I'll kill it in the move."

"It's more likely to take over the base," I say, setting the planter aside. "But don't worry. Lydia won't mind if you leave it here." I hesitate as I pull a pair of hand-crocheted booties from a drawer.

"Claire Douyon made those," McLane says, her eyes misting. "I'll save them."

"For the future." I set the lacy booties on my open palm. "If God wills, there'll be another baby."

We fall silent, the empty space between us vibrating with memories of Mia.

Sometimes I think God used Mia Nicole Larson to accomplish more in her short lifetime than some people do in scores of years. She taught my sons about the miracle of pregnancy and childbirth. She taught McLane the meaning of unselfishness. She taught me how to thank God for unanswered prayers . . . because when God says no, I have to trust that his ways are perfect.

"You know," I say when our moment of silence has passed, "when you're living in Jacksonville, your father won't be far away."

"You mean the father who cast me off?"

"The father who came to Mia's funeral and couldn't face you. I don't know what that means, exactly, but I'm sure it's psychologically significant. You should call him someday and ask him to explain it."

With those delicate booties on my palm, I draw a deep breath and blow. The breeze catches the lace and sends the tiny footwear tumbling onto the bed, landing amid my sister's shirts and shorts and lingerie.

McLane scoops them up and stands them, like a pair of soldier's boots, on the bureau. "Who knows," she says, smiling at me in the mirror, "maybe I will."

About the Author

Christy Award winner Angela Hunt writes books for readers who have learned to expect the unexpected. With over three million copies of her books sold worldwide, she is the best-selling author of *The Tale of Three Trees*, *The Note*, *Magdalene*, and more than 100 other titles.

She and her youth pastor husband make their home in Florida with mastiffs. One of their dogs was featured on *Live with Regis and Kelly* as the second-largest canine in America.

Readers may visit her Web site at www.angelahuntbooks.com.

Discussion Questions

1. Have you read the first book featuring Jennifer Graham, *Doesn't She Look Natural?* How has she changed since her early days at Fairlawn?

2. What are some of the major themes of this novel? Did any of the themes particularly resonate with you?

3. How important is Mt. Dora as a setting in this story? Does it seem like the sort of town you might enjoy visiting?

4. Does Jen's description of the embalming process make the death industry less mysterious for you? Did you learn anything that might prove useful when and if you need to deal with a mortuary?

5. Do you think Jen made the right decision when McLane asked her for a ride to the abortion clinic? What would you have done? Why?

6. Jennifer says McLane and Jeff are "erasing the lines" between black and white as well as the prejudices of her past. How did the following section of Paul's letter to the church at Galatia "erase the lines" of his day: "There is no

longer Jew or Gentile, slave or free, male and female. For you are all one in Christ Jesus" (Galatians 3:28)?

7. Read the last stanza of "Thanatopsis" by William Cullen Bryant (chapter thirty-seven). Why do you think Jen's English teacher had students memorize those lines? Do you find its message comforting?

8. Could you identify with any of the characters in this story? Which character is most like you? Which do you most admire?

9. Consider the character of Randolph Harris. Do you think he really loved McLane? Do you think he really loved God? Why did he refuse to join the mourners at the graveside? Will he ever change? Why or why not?

10. Have you stopped to consider that Paul (who prayed for deliverance from his "thorn in my flesh") and Jesus (who prayed that the "cup of suffering" would pass from him) experienced unanswered prayers? (See 2 Corinthians 12:7-9 and Matthew 26:39.) How were they able to accept these situations without becoming bitter or depressed?

11. Have you looked at the sample photographs found at www.nowilaymedowntosleep.org? How do you think these keepsakes would comfort a young couple who has lost an infant?

12. McLane and Jeff do not suffer from prejudice, but others in the story do. Jen says she found traces of racism in her own heart. What can we do to eradicate racist attitudes we may have somehow picked up?

Hot Chicken Salad

. . . one of Fairlawn's most comforting funeral foods

Ingredients:

    2 cups cooked boneless chicken breast, cubed

    1 cup mayonnaise

    1 (10.75 ounce) can cream of mushroom soup

    1 (4.5 ounce) can mushrooms, drained

    ½ cup slivered almonds

    ½ cup chopped celery

    1 cup grated sharp Cheddar cheese

    1 cup crushed butter crackers or potato chips

Preheat oven to 350 degrees. In a small skillet, sauté the mushrooms in oil. Then mix together the chicken, mayonnaise, soup, sautéed mushrooms, almonds, celery, and cheese.

Place mixture in a 13 x 9 inch casserole dish that has been sprayed with nonstick vegetable oil. Top with the crushed crackers or potato chips.

Bake for 30 minutes or until bubbly.

References

No novelist writes alone, and I owe a debt of gratitude to the following people and sources:

Now I Lay Me Down to Sleep, an organization of professional photographers dedicated to preserving precious moments between infants and their parents. Remembrance photography is a wonderful way for moms and dads to have a lasting memento of children who die too early. Learn more about their work at www.nowilaymedowntosleep.org.

Bryant, William Cullen. "Thanatopsis."

Frank, Pat. 1962. *How to Survive the H Bomb, and Why*. New York: J.B. Lippincott Company. The sections referred to in this book are actual quotes from Mr. Frank's book, pp. 25–28.

Harris, Mark. 2007. *Grave Matters: A Journey Through the Modern Funeral Industry*. New York: Scribner.

Hastings, Celia. 2005. *The Undertaker's Wife*. Grand Haven, MI: Faithwalk.

Sacks, Terence J. 1997. *Opportunities in Funeral Services Careers*. Chicago: NTC Contemporary Publishing Group.

Stair, Nancy L. 2002. *Choosing a Career in Mortuary Science and the Funeral Industry*. New York: The Rosen Publishing Group, Inc.

A special thanks to Randy Alcorn, whose book *Heaven* (Tyndale House, 2004) turned my thoughts toward things eternal; Nancy Rue for supplying me with the right lingo at the right moment; Karen Watson and Becky Nesbitt for a brainstorming session; Gaynel Senka for her operating room expertise; and my excellent editors Becky

Nesbitt and Lorie Popp. Thanks, too, to my novelist pals who spent an afternoon giving me feedback about an issue I offered for discussion.

One final note: Mt. Dora is a real city in Lake County, Florida. If you have an opportunity to visit that lovely town, you will discover that many of the buildings, landmarks, and streets described in this novel actually exist, *including the catacombs.* Unlike Clay and his friends, however, I have no idea where the bomb shelter is, nor have I ever been inside.

The location remains a carefully guarded secret.

Other Novels by
Angela Hunt

Contemporary:

Doesn't She Look Natural?

She Always Wore Red

Uncharted

The Elevator

The Novelist

A Time to Mend

Unspoken

The Truth Teller

The Awakening

The Debt

The Canopy

The Pearl

The Justice

The Note

The Immortal

Historical:

The Nativity Story

Magdalene

The Shadow Women

The Silver Sword

The Golden Cross

The Velvet Shadow

The Emerald Isle

Dreamers

Brothers

Journey

For a complete listing, visit www.angelahuntbooks.com

CP0158

"... a smashing success of a story packed with strong characters, a unique plot, and proved story-telling abilities. I didn't want to put the book down."

– At Home with Christian Fiction

Watch for the third book in the Fairlawn series, *She's in a Better Place*, coming fall 2008!

CP0222

The controversial woman with a past only one man could forgive.

A true love story that changed the face of history.

For more information visit:

www.tyndalefiction.com

www.angelahuntbooks.com

it's never too late to begin a new life

CP0132

The Nativity Story—A novelization of the major motion picture. Best-selling author Angela Hunt presents a heartwarming adaptation of *The Nativity Story*. Hunt brings the story of Christ's birth to life with remarkable attention to detail and a painstaking commitment to historical accuracy.

Also available in Spanish.

have you visited
tyndalefiction.com
lately?

Only there can you find:

- ❖ books hot off the press
- ❖ first chapter excerpts
- ❖ inside scoops on your favorite authors
- ❖ author interviews
- ❖ contests
- ❖ fun facts
- ❖ and much more!

*Sign up for your **free** newsletter!*

Visit us today at: tyndalefiction.com

Tyndale fiction does more than entertain.

- ❖ *It touches the heart.*
- ❖ *It stirs the soul.*
- ❖ *It changes lives.*

That's why Tyndale is so committed to being first in fiction!

TYNDALE FICTION

CP0021